Praise for C.J. Carmichael

"Carmichael's story is a poignant one that will capture readers from start to finish."

—*RT Book Reviews* on *Remember Me, Cowboy*

"Carmichael's dialogue sparkles... [The] relationships are so genuine, the feelings are practically painful to read."

—*RT Book Reviews* on *Perfect Partners?*, Top Pick, 4.5 stars

"Carmichael provides a fascinating story and irresistible characters with real, heartwarming emotions... compelling."

—*RT Book Reviews* on *Receptionist Under Cover*

Praise for Gail Barrett

"A fresh, intriguing plot, building suspense and strong sexual tension...make this a stellar read."

—*RT Book Reviews* on *Fatal Exposure*

"A tale of nonstop excitement, passion, broken hearts mending and a heroine who has to discover the brave, determined woman she really is."

—*RT Book Reviews* on *Meltdown*, Top Pick, 4.5 stars

"Intriguing and suspenseful with a complex and well-crafted plot, this story will hook readers in from the first page. Add to that heroic characters and a tender love story, and Barrett delivers one exciting read."

—*RT Book Reviews* on *Seduced by His Target*

HOME ON THE RANCH:

HER MONTANA RANCHER

——————— ✄ ———————

C.J. CARMICHAEL

GAIL BARRETT

Previously published as *Remember Me, Cowboy*
and *Cowboy Under Siege*

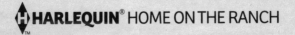

ISBN-13: 978-1-335-50712-9

Home on the Ranch: Her Montana Rancher
Copyright © 2018 by Harlequin Books S.A.

First published as Remember Me, Cowboy by Harlequin Books in 2013 and Cowboy Under Siege by Harlequin Books in 2011.

The publisher acknowledges the copyright holders of the individual works as follows:

Remember Me, Cowboy
Copyright © 2013 by Carla Daum

Cowboy Under Siege

Special thanks and acknowledgment are given to Gail Barrett for her contribution to The Kelley Legacy miniseries.

Copyright © 2011 by Harlequin Books S.A.

Recycling programs for this product may not exist in your area.

Printed in U.S.A.

HARLEQUIN®
™ www.Harlequin.com

CONTENTS

Hard to imagine a more glamorous life than being an accountant, isn't it? Still, **C.J. Carmichael** gave up the thrills of income tax forms and double-entry bookkeeping when she sold her first book in 1998. She has now written more than thirty-five novels for Harlequin and invites you to learn more about her books, see photos of her hiking exploits and enter her surprise contests at cjcarmichael.com.

Books by C.J. Carmichael

Harlequin American Romance

Colton: Rodeo Cowboy
Remember Me, Cowboy
Her Cowboy Dilemma
Promise from a Cowboy

Harlequin Superromance

For a Baby
Seattle after Midnight
A Little Secret Between Friends
A Baby Between Them
Secrets Between Them

Visit the Author Profile page at Harlequin.com for more titles.

REMEMBER ME, COWBOY

C.J. CARMICHAEL

This is for the Happy Bookers, with whom I've shared many evenings of good conversations about books and life, bottles of wine and wedges of cheese: Cheryl, Marg, Mary, Mary-Lou, Nancy, Rhonda, Shelli, Sunita and Susan.

Prologue

Where was the groom? Laurel checked her watch, not sure whether to feel annoyed or worried. Her best friend Winnie Hays should have been marching down the aisle of the Coffee Creek United Church ten minutes ago.

As young girls, growing up together in a Montana farming community about an hour from Coffee Creek, she and Winnie had planned their wedding days down to the color of the flowers and the flavor of the cake. Actually, Winnie had planned, and Laurel had gone along with her, claiming to want whatever it was that Winnie wanted.

For the longest time their friendship had worked that way. Winnie decided to take swimming lessons, so Laurel did, too. Winnie started dating a boy, so Laurel dated his best friend. After they'd finished high school and Winnie applied to college in Great Falls, no one had been surprised when Laurel decided to study at the University of Great Falls, too.

Only after they'd earned their undergraduate degrees had Laurel finally realized that she yearned for something Winnie didn't—to leave Montana. So, scared to death but determined, she moved to New York City on her own to pursue her dream of a career in magazine publishing.

To her credit, Winnie never tried to talk her out of her decision. "You have to go for it, Laurel. Or you'll always wonder *what if...*"

Good advice. From a good friend.

And now, three years later, on what should have been the happiest day of Winnie's life, the bride was starting to panic. "I don't understand. Brock promised he'd be *early.*"

The ceremony had been scheduled to start at three o'clock. Fifteen minutes to the hour a dark sedan had arrived from Coffee Creek Ranch driven by Brock's eldest brother, B.J. Dark-haired B.J., with his noble high forehead and chiseled features, had escorted his mother, Olive, into the church.

Olive, still pretty at sixty, her petite figure showcased in an ivory-colored, raw silk suit, had walked proudly on her son's arm as they made their way to the front pew. Having met her several times now during her week in Coffee Creek, Laurel still found it difficult to believe that this diminutive, soft-spoken woman ran the biggest ranch in all of Bitterroot County.

That arrival had been twenty-five minutes ago. Now the church was packed with invited guests and the organist had just started through her repertoire for the third time.

"This is *so* not a good sign." Winnie grabbed bunches of white satin, hitching up her dress so she could stand on a chair for a better view down the street. "Where the hell are they?"

"They" included not only the groom, Brock Lambert, but the middle Lambert son, Corb, who was the best man—and no doubt about that in Laurel's mind, though she'd only known him a week—and the driver, Jackson Stone.

Jackson was the quiet one. So far Laurel had been unable to engage him in any conversation lasting more than five minutes, so it was only thanks to Winnie that she knew he'd come to the Lambert's ranch as a foster child when he was thirteen. Apparently he'd taken to ranch life so well he was now considered part of the family.

"What time did Corb say they left?" Winnie asked, though she already knew the answer.

"Thirty-five minutes ago." Laurel bit her lower lip anxiously. The drive from the Coffee Creek Ranch to town normally took fifteen minutes. No higher mathematics degree was required to figure out they should be here by now.

"What's happened…?" Winnie spoke softly, her gaze still fixed to the street.

"Don't worry," Laurel soothed. "Could be they ran out of gas or had a flat."

"Or maybe they got halfway here only to realize that Corb forgot the ring." Cassidy Lambert smirked. As the only girl in a family of four boys—if you counted Jackson, and most people did—she didn't faze easily. Or conform. She'd agreed to be Winnie's bridesmaid on the condition that she would not wear high heels. "It has to be running shoes or cowboy boots," she'd dictated. "Take your pick."

Which explained the cream-colored boots in butter-soft ostrich leather that she was swinging as she sat on her perch on the ledge of the same window that Winnie was peering out of.

"But if they've been held up," Winnie reasoned, correctly in Laurel's mind, "why haven't they called?"

That was the unanswerable question. One of three men might have forgotten to charge his phone last night. But all three? Hearing tears in Winnie's voice, Laurel stepped forward to urge her off the chair.

"You're making me dizzy up there. Here, sit for a while. You heard Olive say that this would be the first time one of her boys had been to church in a decade. Maybe they got lost and, being men, won't stop for directions."

Laurel generally counted on humor in moments of tension. And she was rewarded with a wisp of a smile, before Winnie's faced creased with worry again.

The fact was, no one could miss the church in Coffee Creek. The white steeple made it the tallest building in a town of about fifteen hundred people. Damn those Lambert men. How could they do this to Winnie? They better have one hell of a good excuse for being so late.

"I'll call *them*." Cassidy jumped softly to the wooden floor. "I'll go get my phone."

As soon as she'd left for the minister's office where they'd stowed their personal effects, Winnie let out a small moan.

"I can't stand this anymore. I've been dying to tell Brock, but you'll have to be the first to know."

"Know what?" Long familiarity with her friend's

dramatic streak meant Laurel didn't overreact. She frowned at a scuff on her imitation Valentino pumps, then tried rubbing it off with her thumb.

"Maybe you should sit down. I don't want you fainting or anything."

"Fat chance, Winnie. I am *not* the fainting kind." But she abandoned the scuff. This actually sounded serious.

"I called Brock at the crack of dawn today and told him to get to the church early. That there was something I needed to tell him before the ceremony."

"So you decided to come clean about your criminal record? Good call."

Winnie didn't even crack a smile. "I'm serious, Laurel. I should have told him earlier, but I was in shock myself."

Laurel didn't interrupt this time when Winnie paused. She just waited for her friend to find the right words.

"I'm pregnant."

Laurel could feel her mouth drop open. She couldn't help it. Those were *not* the right words she'd been expecting to hear. "Holy cow. Really?"

"Yes. Two months along, I figure—"

Winnie stopped talking as the door opened. Cassidy was back, cell phone in hand, frowning.

"Brock isn't answering." She punched another button. "I'll try Corb."

No one spoke. The relentless repitition of "Ode to Joy" was getting on Laurel's nerves.

"Damn." Cassidy disconnected the call after reaching the answering service. Next she tried Jackson's number. Again, no one picked up. "If this is some sort of prank, I'm going to kill them."

But Laurel could see the worry in Cassidy's deep green eyes. She was scared. So was Winnie. Her face had gone whiter than the fabric of her wedding gown, making her brown eyes seem almost as black as her hair.

Winnie glanced out the window again. "Someone's coming! I think it's Jackson's SUV...."

Cassidy peered over her shoulder. "No. It's a County Sheriff vehicle."

The three women exchanged looks, no one saying what they were all thinking. This couldn't be good. Laurel's pulse thumped crazily in her throat as she watched the driver park in front of the church. A long-legged woman dressed in uniform, dark hair worn in a long braid to accommodate her hat, stepped out to the street. She glanced left, right, then seemed to take a deep breath before heading inside the church.

"Who was that?" Laurel wondered.

"Sheriff Savannah Moody." Winnie's voice was unnaturally low. "She's a good friend of Brock's. We were going to invite her to the wedding, but he said there was bad blood between her and B.J. I don't know the details."

Laurel's mind went blank, refusing to speculate on the reasons for the sheriff's unexpected appearance. Instead, she thought of the day, a week ago, when she'd arrived at the airport in Billings, having spent most of a day traveling to Montana from New York City.

Winnie had been called in for an unexpected dress fitting and so she'd sent the best man to collect Laurel. Corb Lambert, brother of the groom. "He'll be the cowboy with a dimple in his left cheek," was all Winnie wrote in her hurried text message.

Laurel hadn't seen him at first. She was worried about her bag, which hadn't appeared on the carousel, even though most of her fellow passengers on Delta 4608 had claimed their luggage and departed the airport at least five minutes ago.

"Please don't let them have lost my suitcase," she pleaded with the airline gods. Besides her clothes for the week, she stood to lose her bridesmaid gown and Winnie and Brock's wedding gift.

And then she saw them both, in the same second. The brown, beaten suitcase with the pink ribbon tied around the handle. And the cowboy striding toward her with a grin and a sparkle to his eye that made her automatically pat her hair and suck in her tummy.

"Sugar?" He walked right up to her. "If you're Laurel Sheridan I think Coffee Creek is about to become a whole lot sweeter."

A corny line, but, oh, how her heart had pounded.

As it was pounding now, in a much less pleasant way.

Laurel squeezed Winnie's hand, staying close to her friend, who'd started to tremble. They followed Cassidy out the door of the antechamber into the vestibule. Two wide doors stood open to the church where all the guests awaited. Chatter filled the air, along with the Beethoven.

And then, abruptly, the organ stopped and everyone turned, expecting to see the bride. A collective gasp washed over the room when Sheriff Moody stepped forward, instead. With a grim expression she said, "I need to talk to someone from the Lambert family."

A brief hesitation, then B.J. stood, tall and lean in his charcoal suit and tie. "Savannah." His grim expression grew darker. "What happened?"

Olive made her way to her feet and said what everyone in the room was fearing. "Has there been an accident?"

The silence intensified as one second stretched into two.

"I'm sorry, Olive. But yes. There's been an a-accident." The sheriff's voice broke on the last word and Laurel could feel Winnie wobble on the delicate heels of her wedding shoes. On cue, Cassidy came up on the bride's other side and helped Laurel hold her steady.

Sheriff Moody looked from B.J. to the bride, then finally back to Olive. "Jackson's SUV hit a moose on Big Valley Road, about five miles from town."

The name of the road meant nothing to Laurel. She was holding her breath, praying again, not with sharp annoyance as she had at the airport, but with total desperation. *Please let them be okay. Just a few cuts and bruises,* she bargained, *maybe a broken leg or two.*

"Brock?" Winnie locked her gaze on the sheriff, who slowly shook her head.

"I'm so sorry, Winnie. Brock was sitting in the front passenger seat—the impact point with the moose. He didn't have a chance."

Winnie made a sound somewhere between a gasp and a cry, then pulled her hands free from the supportive hold of Laurel and Cassidy and covered her face.

Laurel wrapped her arms around her friend, her mind slipping away to the party they'd had, just last night. She and Corb had been dancing. They'd had a few beers. The lights were low and her body had tingled at the touch of his hands on her waist and shoulder. When she'd stumbled, Corb said, "Tired? Let me walk you home, sugar."

He'd done more than just walk her home. A lot more. Never in her life had she fallen for somebody this hard. This fast.

"What about Corb?" B.J.'s voice was stretched tighter than a barbed wire fence. "And Jackson?"

"Jackson was driving, wearing his seat belt and the air bag was able to cushion him from the worst of it. He's badly bruised and shaken, but he's okay."

And Corb?

"Your other brother was in the backseat. He should have been fine, but I'm afraid he wasn't wearing his seat belt. As we speak he's being medevaced to Great Falls. I can't say how bad his injuries are. You'll have to talk to the doctors for that."

"Is he conscious?" Olive asked, her voice rough, eyes desperate.

The sheriff shook her head. "No."

Chapter 1

Two Months Later

Laurel was making the rounds of the Cinnamon Stick Café with a fresh carafe of coffee, when she noticed Maddie Turner's mug needed refreshing. She paused to serve the stocky, gray-haired rancher, who glanced up from the papers she was reviewing to give her a smile.

"Thanks, Laurel. Could you get me another cinnamon bun, too, please?"

"You bet, Maddie." After two months of running the Cinnamon Stick while Winnie convalesced on her parents' farm, Laurel was a fixture with all the regulars. And Maddie Turner, owner of the Silver Creek Ranch, sure did love her baked goods.

When she'd first started working at the café, Laurel had drooled over the cinnamon buns, too. Now, just the sight of one of the frosted goodies made her queasy. Laurel tried not to inhale as she plated one of the buns, then passed it to Maddie.

Back behind the counter, she put on a fresh pot of coffee. As she filled the carafe with water from the tap, her gaze was drawn out the window to the line of willow trees that grew between the café and the creek for which the town was named.

Another lovely September day. She wished she had time to get out and enjoy the sunshine, but, as usual, she was being run off her feet.

When Winnie told her, ten months ago, that she'd fallen in love with a cowboy and was going to move to Coffee Creek to open her café, Laurel had thought *how quaint.*

Now she knew better. The café was charming to look at, the food was devilishly delicious, but the work? It was damned hard. The first month she'd had so much to learn, she'd been running all day long. Then, when she'd finally found her rhythm, she'd caught some sort of bug that she still hadn't managed to shake.

What she needed was rest, but she wouldn't complain. How could she, in the face of what Winnie was going through? Thank heavens for Eugenia, Vince and Dawn, Winnie's regular staff. Without their help, and willingness to work extra hours, she could never have kept Winnie's café afloat while her friend struggled to deal with the double whammy of losing her fiancé and dealing with what had turned out to be a difficult pregnancy.

Laurel still couldn't believe what had happened.

Imagine losing your fiancé on the day of your wedding. Actually being in the church, in your gown, waiting… Laurel felt sick every time she thought back to that day.

In the awful hours following the grim news, she'd canceled her flight back to New York, and she'd promised Winnie she would stay in Coffee Creek as long as she was needed, never guessing she'd still be here two months later.

But with Winnie laid up in bed on doctor's orders, what choice had she had? She couldn't let Winnie lose her business as well as the man she'd been planning to share her life with.

With a long sigh, Laurel replaced the coffee carafe in the machine. Maddie, finished with her paper and her coffee, waved as she made her way out of the café and into the ancient Ford truck angle-parked out in front. Laurel was clearing her table when Vince Butterfield, Winnie's baker, came out from the kitchen.

She couldn't believe it was eleven o'clock already. "Time to call it a day?"

He nodded, never one to use a word when a gesture would do.

"See you tomorrow, Vince."

He tipped his head in her direction, just half of a nod this time, then made his way out the back door.

Laurel still found it amazing that this man—a weathered and scarred ex-bronc rider who looked about ten years older than his real age of sixty-two—was responsible for the bakery's rich cinnamon buns, mouthwatering bumbleberry pies and buttery dinner rolls. He came in every morning, except Sunday, at four in the morning and worked his magic for seven hours before getting on his bike and riding out to his trailer ten miles from town.

Winnie had confided some details of his past to Laurel—a former rodeo cowboy with a drinking problem, he liked the early hours at the bakery since they left him too exhausted to stay up much past eight in the evening. Early to bed meant no late nights at the bar, which meant no more drinking.

"He figures this job saved his life," Winnie told her. Laurel wondered how Winnie knew so much about him. The man had never said more than three words in a row to her, and those had been, "nice meetin' ya."

The door chimed and Laurel glanced up to welcome her next customer. The smile forming on her face froze the minute she saw him.

Corb Lambert.

She'd heard he'd been out of the hospital for several weeks now. And had wondered when she was going to see him.

It seemed now was the moment.

He looked good, though his hair had been cropped and she could see a long scar on the side of his head. His dimple flashed when he gave her a smile, though not as deeply as before. Laurel figured he'd lost about fifteen pounds.

He came up to the counter hesitantly, holding his hat politely in hand.

Through the grapevine, Laurel had kept posted on Corb's recovery from the accident. He'd been in a coma for forty-eight hours, and in critical condition for several days beyond that. All in all he'd been in hospital for almost three weeks, with visits strictly restricted to family members only.

Or so Laurel had been told when she'd called the hospital to ask about him.

She'd wondered if maybe he would phone her when he was finally released, and when he hadn't, she'd told herself she shouldn't be surprised. He'd been through a lot physically, and had lost a brother besides. He wouldn't have time or inclination to think about the woman he'd flirted with, and charmed, during the week before his accident.

But now he was here, and clearly his smile and the sparkle in his eyes hadn't been damaged one bit by his accident. She took a cloth to the clean counter, willing her heart to return to its regular standing rate of sixty-five beats per minute.

"Hello, sugar. Looks like Coffee Creek got a whole lot sweeter since the last time I was in town."

She smiled, thinking he was feeding her the same line on purpose. But when she glanced up at him, she saw no recognition in his eyes. "Corb?"

He looked puzzled. Then he frowned. "Have we met before?"

Oh, Lord. She'd heard he had some memory problems after the accident. But she hadn't been prepared for this. "I'm Winnie's friend from New York City. Laurel Sheridan. I'm so glad you're feeling better. I was meaning to—" She stopped, wanting to say so much, yet not knowing how to begin.

He didn't remember her. How was that possible? He'd touched and kissed the most intimate parts of her. They'd stayed up talking until the wee hours of the morning, sharing their deepest secrets.

She'd told him her entire life story. She hadn't intended to—normally she was quite reserved—but he'd seemed so genuinely interested in everything about her.

The bells over the door chimed again, a fact Laurel

barely registered until Jackson joined them at the counter and tapped Corb on the shoulder.

"You here to flirt? Or order coffee?" He nodded at Laurel. "Hey, Laurel. Any word on how Winnie is doing?"

"She's okay." Winnie had made her promise not to say a word about the baby. She wanted to wait until she was well enough to return to Coffee Creek and deliver the news to the Lambert family in person.

"Will she be coming back soon?"

"I doubt it. She's had some health issues, and for now it's good for her to be around her mom and dad." She glanced at Corb who was listening to the exchange intently, lines marring his high forehead and obscuring his charming grin.

"So you're Winnie's friend from New York? The one who was traveling down to be her maid of honor?"

"He doesn't remember much about that week," Jackson said by way of explanation.

Corb nodded. "Scared me at first. I guess I'm kind of glad I don't remember the crash." He swallowed. "But there's lots of other stuff that's gone, too. The specialist told me it's normal, though, so I'm trying not to worry about it."

Laurel knew she shouldn't take his loss of memory personally. But it was hard not to feel hurt that he didn't recall her at all. "Is it possible your memory will come back?"

He shrugged. "They say it could happen—but no guarantees." He stiffened his spine, and managed another smile as he offered her his hand. "Hard to believe I could forget a woman as beautiful as you. Must have been some knock to the head, huh?"

It was so weird to shake his hand, as if they were strangers making their first acquaintance. Playing along though, she kept her tone light. "Nice to meet you—for the second time. I take it you're here for coffee. Like to add a couple of cinnamon buns to your order?"

"I'll take one, sugar. How about you, Jack—" He turned to confer with his foster brother, but Jackson was already on his way out the door.

"I'll skip the coffee for now and go put in that order at the feed store."

"I'll meet you there," Corb said. Then, leaning over the counter, he added, "Say, Laurel, I was wondering if you could give me Winnie's number at her folks' place. I've been meaning to call her and see how she's doing. My family's been treating me like an invalid. Mother put me in the guest room at the main house, and until today, wouldn't let me even touch the keys to my truck. So I haven't had much chance to check in on her."

"Sure." Laurel wrote the number on an order slip, then tore it off the pad and handed it to him. According to Winnie, none of the other Lamberts had been in touch since the funeral and Olive hadn't even returned the calls Winnie made to Coffee Creek Ranch. So Laurel was glad to see at least one member of the family willing to reach out to her friend.

"Maybe I should ask for your number, too." Corb's eyes glinted with charm as he folded the paper and slipped it into the pocket of his jeans.

Gosh, this was weird. He was flirting with her as if he'd never met her before.

"You'll find me here most of the time," she answered lightly. "How's your mother doing?"

The flirting light left Corb's face. "Not so well. She's

been spending too much time alone in her room. Now that I'm stronger, I'm trying to coax her out, get her working with the horses again. That's the only thing that'll cure her, I figure."

"I can't imagine your mother on a horse. She looks so fragile."

Corb laughed. "Looks are deceptive where my mother is concerned. But losing Brock has taken a toll. When Dad died, she didn't have the luxury of isolating herself with her grief. Us kids were a lot younger then and she had to run the ranch. Now she knows she can leave all that to me and Jackson—though to be honest, it's been mostly Jackson up until now."

When Corb fell silent, Laurel passed him his coffee and bun, and Corb put a ten-dollar bill on the counter, refusing change.

He lifted the lid off his coffee and was about to add sugar, when Laurel stopped him.

"I already did that. Two packages."

He gave her a puzzled smile, then headed out the door.

As soon as he was out on the street, Corb let his smile drop. The effort of being himself these days was almost more than he could bear. All his life he'd been the easygoing Lambert, the charming one, the peacemaker. Never had his family needed him to fill that role more than they did right now. And never had he felt less like doing it.

Corb looked at the coffee and the bun he was holding. He ought to gobble it down and head over to Ed's Feed Supply, where he knew Jackson was picking up that alfalfa mix for the new palomino his mother had bought three months ago.

She'd actually bought the horse for Cassidy, though she'd never admit it. As if a new horse—even a great horse—would lure his sister back to Coffee Creek.

No, like B.J., Cassidy had decided to make her own way in the world, which meant there were only two of them—himself and Jackson—to carry on. Work was piled up so high at the ranch, he felt like they'd never catch up. He had no right to be taking a break and yet he found himself settling on one of the pine benches that flanked the café entrance.

He took out the cinnamon bun, and with his first bite, he could hear Brock saying that he was marrying Winnie for her buns. He'd always give a wink when he said this, and Winnie would groan.

Corb followed the roll with a long swig of the sweetened black coffee. It had caught him off guard that Laurel knew how he liked his coffee. Why didn't he remember Winnie's maid of honor?

Leaning back, he allowed his eyes to close for a second. Though he wouldn't admit it, not to his doctors or his family, he was suffering from some terrible headaches these days. He figured they'd ease off with time. But in a way he didn't want them to. Brock had died and he felt that he needed to pay a price, since he'd been the one to live.

Well, there was Jackson, too, but he'd joined the family when Corb was already fifteen, so it wasn't like they'd grown up together the way he and Brock had. God, he couldn't believe his baby brother was really gone. That damned moose coming out of the brush at just the wrong moment had stolen so much from so many people.

He felt especially bad for Winnie. It was too bad she'd taken off and left the county. He wished his mother would call her, but at the best of times Olive had not been fond of the woman Brock had chosen for his bride and these were definitely not the best of times.

Thankfully Winnie's friend from New York had stuck around to help her out. That had been real good of her.

But even from this one meeting, he could tell that Laurel Sheridan was that sort of person. You could see the kindness in her eyes, a warmth that gave her pretty face a special glow.

He admired her hair, too. Thick, red and long, all piled up in a luxurious mess. He wondered what she looked like with it down. The fact that he'd probably already seen her that way but couldn't remember, made his head throb.

Stop it!

What the hell was he doing, anyway, fantasizing about Winnie's friend at a time like this? His family was in mourning, damn it. Besides, it was weird that he couldn't recall meeting her when she obviously re-membered him.

Had they spent much time together in that week be-fore the wedding?

He wished like hell that he could remember.

Right after Corb left the café, Dawn Dolan showed up to start her shift, her long, fine blond hair already pulled back in a ponytail. She came in the back way, grabbing an apron from one of the pegs on the wall by the freezer as she passed by.

"Busy day?" she asked. "I hope so. I could use some good tips. I saw this top that would look perfect with that new skirt I bought last week."

Online shopping was twenty-year-old Dawn's main form of recreation. Laurel wished she would spend as much time on her college correspondence courses as she did surfing the net, but that was Dawn's choice to make.

"Lunch hour rush is sure to start soon," Laurel said. "So that'll be your big chance to wow the customers and earn big bucks."

They both smiled at this—the café did well for such a small town. But big bucks? Hardly.

"Mind if I take a little break?" Laurel checked her hair in the mirror, pursed her lips and added some peach gloss. "It's been a long morning."

"No problem." Dawn glanced at the sandwich special Laurel had printed on the chalkboard. "Should I mix up the tuna salad?"

"That would be great."

Laurel dried her hands on her apron, then slipped the strap over her head and slung it on the peg with Winnie's name stenciled above it. She went out the back way and walked around to the front. As she'd hoped, she found Corb Lambert sitting on one of the benches.

Maybe slumped was a better word. His eyes were closed; he seemed to be soaking up a little of the noon sun, but his brow was furrowed. He looked like he was in pain. Physical or mental, she couldn't tell. She supposed he had a right to be feeling both.

She sat next to him.

Though he must have sensed her presence, he said

nothing, and for a minute or so, neither did she. Instead she focused on the sun's glorious heat as it penetrated her tank top and jeans. It felt so good to rest. Why was she always so tired these days?

Across the street Laurel could see the post office and library. Though she'd only been in Coffee Creek for two months, Laurel knew the middle-aged people who worked inside each of those buildings. They were regulars at the café, too.

Tabitha, the librarian, always came to the Cinnamon Stick for her morning tea and muffin. Burt, from the post office, stopped in for his lunch. In fact, he'd be crossing the street for his sandwich and black coffee in about twenty minutes.

She turned to the man beside her. He'd opened his eyes and was now looking at her. "I'm sorry to disturb you," she said. "I just wanted to say how sorry I am about your brother."

There were many other things she'd wanted to say to Corb Lambert. But this was the most important.

"Thank you. And I'm sorry I don't seem to recall meeting you before. You're sure we did?"

"Oh, yeah."

He put a hand to his head, to the spot where his scar was barely visible under the stubble of his newly grown hair. "It doesn't seem real to me. The accident. Brock's death."

"Winnie's still in shock, too, I think."

"She and my brother were good together."

"Winnie was crazy about Brock."

"A lot of people were. Brock was a lot of fun, but a hard worker, too. My mother saw to that."

"She sounds like quite the woman, your mother."

He chuckled. "She comes across as delicate and soft-spoken. But once you get to know her you realize she has a way of controlling things from behind the scenes. Us kids used to knock ourselves out to please her. Some of us still do."

"I guess she had her hands full running a place like Coffee Creek Ranch. Must be a lot of work for her. For all of you."

"It is, but we love it. At least those of us who stayed on the ranch love it. My brother B.J. is more interested in the rodeo circuit. And Cassidy seems to be feeling the lure of the city. Mom is hoping she'll move back home when she finishes school, but Cassidy is equally determined to go her own way. I figure the two of them are too headstrong to live in the same county let alone the same house."

He put his hat back on and took the last sip of his coffee. Laurel thought he was about to leave, but then he started talking again.

"How about you, Laurel? How are you doing? I bet you never counted on spending this much time in Coffee Creek when you left the city."

"I sure didn't pack enough clothes for two months," she agreed with a smile. "Fortunately a friend of mine from work, Anna, sent me a package by bus."

"Are you missing the city? Coffee Creek is about as small as towns come, I guess."

"I grew up in a rural community, so it hasn't been hard to adapt."

"You did? Where?"

"The Highwood area. Our farm was five miles from Winnie's."

"Well, that explains how you know one another."

"We've been friends since our first day at school. Winnie helped me through some hard times back then. My mother died when I was eight. Then my father passed away the night of our high school graduation. Both times Winnie and her family were there for me."

"And now you're returning the favor."

"I wish it wasn't necessary. But yes. As long as Winnie needs me, I'll stay."

"I have to wonder. What drew you all the way to New York City in the first place?"

This was so surreal—she and Corb had had almost this exact same conversation during the drive from the Billings Airport to the ranch the first time they'd met. They'd had many follow-up discussions during the days that followed, to the point that she'd shared the most private details of her past.

And now here they were—back at square one.

"I was never all that happy living on a farm." Her relationship with her father probably played a big role in that. She and Corb had had a long conversation about this, too, but now she glossed over that part of her past. "Teachers told me I had a talent with words, so I studied English and after I graduated, I moved to New York and applied for every job even remotely related to publishing. Eventually I was hired by *On the Street Magazine* as a lowly online sales rep—but I was sure it would be just a matter of time before I was promoted."

"And were you?"

She smiled. "I was finally offered an editorial assistant job just a month before the wedding."

"I hope they're holding the job for you?"

Laurel hesitated. "They are. But to be honest, I'm

getting some pressure to come back soon or give my notice."

Across the street, the door to the post office opened. Burt waved, then started in their direction. And then a rusted pickup truck rumbled in from the west, pulling up next to Corb's black Jeep Cherokee.

Laurel stood, and as she did so, felt the now-familiar queasiness in the pit of her stomach. "I'd better get back to work. Looks like the lunch rush is about to begin."

"See you, Laurel. It was nice talking with you."

They made direct eye contact then, and Laurel felt the zap of instant attraction that had first pulled her to him when they'd met at the airport.

But this time she felt a second zap, too.

The tiredness. The nausea.

It might not be a bug or the unaccustomed work at the café.

She could be…

No. She didn't dare even *think* the word. Because being *that* was the last thing she needed right now.

And she was pretty sure it would be the last thing Corb needed, too.

Chapter 2

At five o'clock, Laurel put out the Closed sign, then wiped down the kitchen counters.

The Cinnamon Stick was a small establishment, intended to serve primarily take-out coffee and baked goods, though Winnie always had homemade soup and sandwiches on the menu, as well. For those who opted to stay—and there seemed to be plenty of people who wanted to do this—there were four stools at the counter and two big booths on the window wall.

Laurel loved the colors Winnie had chosen for the bakery—delicious hues that made her think of pumpkin pie, caramels and mocha lattes. Unfortunately the idea of eating any of those foods was totally unappealing right now.

All afternoon the suspicion that she might be pregnant had grown into a near certainty. After all, she hadn't needed to buy tampons once since she'd left the city.

And she'd been too wrapped up in Winnie's problems to notice.

Hell.

Wasn't it her luck that just as things were starting to work out for her careerwise, something would happen to set her back?

Not for the first time, she wished Winnie was here with her, which was silly, because if Winnie were able to stay in Coffee Creek and work at the café, then Laurel would be back in the city living in her cute, if miniscule apartment, working her butt off at her new job.

But even if she'd left for New York the day after the wedding, as originally scheduled, she'd still be pregnant.

Oh, Lord, she just *had* to talk to Winnie.

Once she was satisfied that the café was clean and ready for the next day, Laurel went down the hall. To the left was the customer restroom. To the right, a door that led to a staircase and the second floor of the building.

She was barely in the door of the one-bedroom apartment when the phone started ringing.

Laurel kicked off her sandals—oh, that felt good!—then dashed for the receiver, hoping it would be Winnie. "Hello?"

"Hey! How are you doing?"

Her friend sounded stronger. More like herself. "I'm fine. How about you?"

"I had a good day today. Really. Got out of bed. Showered."

Her tone was self-deprecating, but Laurel understood the effort that had been required. "That's good, Winnie."

"I gave myself a talking-to last night. Decided this baby was going to be a mental case if I didn't get a grip on myself."

"No one can blame you for grieving. It's only natural."

"It's not like I'm forgetting about Brock. That's not even possible. But I have to start facing a future that doesn't include him. Mom got me started on a knitting project. That probably sounds lame. It's really helping, though."

"Are you kidding? Knitting is cool." Laurel went to the sofa and settled in for a long chat.

"So how are things going at the Cinnamon Stick?"

"Pretty good." Laurel gave her the cash register totals for the past week, then filled her in on some of the day's highlights, omitting, for the moment, the visit from Corb and Jackson.

"That sounds great. I can't thank you enough for all you're doing for me."

"You'd do the same for me. You know you would."

"But you can't keep putting your life on hold. You have to book your plane ticket home. Tonight. I'm serious."

"And what about the Cinnamon Stick?"

Winnie sighed. "We'll just have to close it until after the baby is born. My doctor is saying work is out of the question for me. Maybe if I had a desk job. But I can't be on my feet all day long. It would be too much of a strain."

"I'll vouch for that."

"Oh, Laurel. It's exhausting you, isn't it?"

Yes. But for reasons she wasn't quite ready to explain. Not until she knew more about Winnie's plans.

"Are you going to stay with your parents until the baby is born?"

"It's looking that way."

"Well then, maybe you should rethink telling the Lamberts about the baby in person. Jackson and Corb were in town today and I felt awkward when they asked about you. They should be told. I mean, this kid is going to be their nephew."

"Yes. And Olive's grandchild. Believe me, *I know.*" Winnie sucked in a long breath. "And I *would* tell them if I hadn't had such an awful relationship with Olive."

She'd complained about Olive before. And while Laurel agreed that Olive wasn't the warmest person, she did think Winnie was exaggerating.

"How can *anyone* not like you? I mean, you're so easygoing, without any strong opinions on *anything.*"

"Exactly. I'm perfect, but Olive doesn't appreciate that."

They both laughed. Then Winnie continued, "According to Brock, my first faux pas was serving Maddie Turner at the café."

"Maddie's one of your best customers. Why wouldn't you serve her?"

"Because." She paused dramatically. "Maddie Turner and Olive Lambert are *sisters.*"

Mentally Laurel compared the two women. "Impossible." Olive was fine-boned and elegant, while Maddie was sturdy and down-to-earth.

"Yes. *Estranged* sisters. I guess it's an unspoken rule in the Lambert family that no one is to talk to Maddie or even acknowledge the fact that she exists."

"How bizarre. What happened to cause the rift? Did Brock ever tell you?"

"He didn't even know. It's like some big family secret."

"And is that the whole reason Olive Lambert doesn't like you? Because you dared to serve coffee and baked goods to her sister?"

Winnie laughed. "Not hardly. Olive had someone else in mind for Brock. A daughter of one of her bigwig ranching buddies. It made her crazy that he picked me instead."

Laurel never knew whether to believe Winnie when she talked about Olive this way. "Is it really possible, in this day and age, that a mother would think she had the right to arrange a marriage for her son?"

"It sounds crazy. Yes. But you have to see her in action. She never raises her voice or argues—she has this passive-aggressive way of getting her way. Her children—in particular, her sons—can't seem to jump high enough trying to please her."

Laurel didn't doubt that Winnie believed what she was saying, but at the same time she suspected that Winnie's point of view was biased. Because Winnie also had a very strong personality. And it was possible that they had suffered from a clash of personalities.

But how unfortunate that they hadn't been able to move past their differences after Brock's death. The two women who had loved him most should have been able to share their grief.

"Have you considered selling the Cinnamon Stick and moving closer to your parents permanently?"

"I have," Winnie admitted. "Mom and Dad have been pushing me to do just that. But this morning I called the real estate agent who sold me the property. Unfortunately, the market has softened in the past year. Even if I was lucky enough to sell the place, I'd never get back what I put into it."

Laurel took a moment to absorb this. "So you're stuck here?"

"Pretty much."

"Then you've got to make peace with the Lamberts. Living in Coffee Creek, you won't be able to avoid them. And think of what it could mean to your baby. He'd have all those uncles and an aunt and a grandmother...."

Another sigh from Winnie. "What you say makes sense. I *will* try to make nice with Olive. I promise. Just...not quite yet."

"Don't put it off too long, okay?"

"I won't. As long as you promise to get your butt back to New York and that fabulous new job of yours."

"About that." Laurel hesitated. Putting this in words was going to make it seem so real. But she had to face up to facts. And who better to trust than Winnie? "I'm not so sure that I *can* go back to New York just yet. I've come up against a bit of a speed bump."

"What are you talking about?"

"You know how I said I've been tired? Well, I've also been nauseous. And today I realized that I haven't had my period since I left New York."

Winnie's soft gasp was audible. "Really, Laurel?"

"Afraid so. I believe I'm about two months pregnant."

"So it must have happened right before you left New York. But I didn't think you were dating anyone seriously back there."

"I wasn't." Here was the tricky part. "Actually, it happened on the night of your rehearsal dinner."

"Shut up. It did not."

Laurel let her friend process for a few moments.

Sure enough, it didn't take Winnie long to come up with the right answer.

"That must mean Corb is the father? The two of you seemed awfully cozy that night, but I never guessed—"

"You were too busy being crazy in love with Brock to notice."

"Yes. I suppose I was." Pain registered briefly in Winnie's voice before she returned to the subject under discussion. "Have you told him?"

"I can't, Winnie. He doesn't remember anything."

"Are you serious?"

"It's called retrograde amnesia. Apparently he doesn't recall anything much from the week before the accident. When he came into the café today, he didn't know my name. He acted like we had never met!"

"How awful for you."

"It was bizarre. He started asking me questions—the same questions he asked when he was driving me home from the airport. At times I thought he had to be faking it, but he really doesn't remember me, Winnie. How can I tell him that he got me pregnant?"

"Back up a minute. Are you sure you're pregnant? Have you taken a test?"

"No. But—"

"You've got to take the test."

"I already checked the general store. They don't carry those pregnancy test kits. The next time I'm in Lewistown I'll—"

"No need to wait that long. I bought a couple boxes when I took my own test. In case I screwed it up or something. Look under the bathroom sink."

Laurel suddenly felt shaky and weak. She realized she was scared silly. It was one thing to suspect you were pregnant.

Quite another to know for sure.

"Want me to call you back?" she asked Winnie.

"Are you kidding? I'll hold," answered her friend. "Now get in the bathroom and pee on that stick."

The next morning, Corb took a little longer with his chores than usual. Partly because of the nagging headache that he just couldn't shake. And partly because of a certain redhead that he wished he could remember.

On his way toward the ranch house, where breakfast would be waiting, he came across Jackson, carrying a sack of feed over his shoulder.

"Why don't you leave that for a bit and join Mom and me for breakfast?" Corb asked.

Before the accident, a typical day had seen him, Brock, Jackson and Olive eating together every morning after chores. But since Corb had been released from hospital, Jackson hadn't joined them once.

"Nah. I'd rather finish with the horses. I'll eat later."

Jackson was a quiet guy. Though lately he'd been more quiet than usual. Corb paused, wondering if he should insist that Jackson take a break and get some food.

But Jackson had already ducked into the far barn with the special feed they'd purchased for Lucy. They had another equestrian barn on the property for the American Quarter Horses which they bred for sale. The purebreds and the working horses were never allowed to mingle.

Then there was the cattle barn, clear on the other side of the yard, where Corb spent most of his time.

Coffee Creek Ranch was a big operation requiring lots of work—and while they hired several wranglers and part-time help in spring and fall, all the key positions stayed with the family.

With Brock gone, though, there was going to have to be some reshuffling of responsibilities.

Corb entered the main house from the back entrance, kicking off his boots in the mudroom, then washing his hands in the stainless-steel sink next to the coatrack.

Bonny Platter, their housekeeper for the past three years—a record tenure for the position—came to the doorway with her hands on her ample hips.

"I have pancakes and sausages waiting, but first you better get your mother out of bed. It's time she joined the land of the living."

Corb was damned hungry, having started the day three hours earlier on just a package of oatmeal and a cup of instant coffee. But he shared Bonny's concern about his mother.

"I'll round her up," he promised.

"What about Jackson?"

"Just spoke to him. He's giving breakfast a pass."

"Again?" Bonny sounded annoyed.

"Again. I'll go get Mother." Corb crossed through the kitchen to the hall that led to the master bedroom. After his father's death ten years ago his mother had redecorated the room with a bunch of flowery fabrics and pinkish colors. Now he always felt awkward when he was called to enter the feminine space.

For that reason, or perhaps out of habit, he hesitated at the door after knocking. When a full minute passed without any answer, though, he finally cracked the door open.

"Mom? Are you awake?" Ten o'clock on a weekday morning and she was still in bed. Prior to Brock's death, this behavior would have been unthinkable.

"Yes, Corb. Please shut the door. I'm not ready—"

He ignored her and strode inside, stopping abruptly in the near darkness. "Jeez, you can't even tell it's daylight in here. Why didn't Bonny open the curtains?"

He made his way toward the outline of the windows at the far wall, then pulled back on the fabric, allowing in the brilliant morning sunshine.

"Bonny didn't open the curtains because I asked her not to," his mother answered tartly. Normally she styled her hair in a sleek bob, but it was looking lank and gray today. An appointment at her hair salon was long overdue.

She squinted at him and frowned. "The sunshine gives me a headache."

Feeling the scar on his scalp throb, Corb could relate. But he didn't admit it. Instead he checked the tray on the table beside his mom's bed. The toast and coffee were untouched. "What's this? Mom, you have to eat. Come on, Bonny will serve you something fresh in the dining room."

Her expression turned contrite. "You're a sweet boy to worry about your mother, Corb. I'm just not hungry."

"At least sit at the table with me." He stood by her bed, until finally she sighed and sat upright. He waited until she swung her feet to the ground, then held out his hands to her.

"You're kind and patient, Corb. Just like your father."

Being compared to his father was about the highest compliment his mother could give. It was curious, Corb thought, that while his father had treated all of them pretty much equally, his mother seemed to have a unique relationship with each of her children.

B.J., as the eldest, had always been the son that Olive expected the most from—until he'd decided to become a full-time rodeo cowboy. Now Olive rarely mentioned his name.

Brock had been the doted-upon youngest son, while Cassidy, the baby of the family and the only daughter, seemed to take the brunt of their mother's criticism.

He'd gotten off easy as the middle child, Corb expected. Often ignored, but that was okay with him. And if he suspected that his mother would have traded his life if she could have spared Brock's, that didn't bother him, either.

Frankly, he would have given his life for Brock's, as well.

He led his mother to the dining room, pulling out her chair and waiting for her to sit, before settling at his own spot at the gleaming oak table. Bonny emerged from the kitchen with two hot platters of food, pancakes and sausages for him, a boiled egg and toast for his mother.

Corb was reaching for a second helping of pancakes, when the house phone rang. A moment later, Bonny brought him the receiver. "It's Laurel Sheridan."

His heart flip-flopped at the mention of Winnie's pretty friend. He reached for the phone, at the same time rising from his chair and heading for the patio door leading outside.

"Hi, Corb. I— This is going to sound strange but I was wondering if you could come by the café tonight after closing time?"

"That shouldn't be a problem. You close at five?"

"Yes. I— The thing is, I have something to tell you. Something that happened during the week before the wedding. I know you don't remember. But…"

Lord, but she sounded nervous. Was she worried he'd say no? But he was certainly keen to spend more time with her. And he was also anxious to fill in some of the missing blanks in his memory, as well.

He paced to the edge of the deck then stared beyond the outbuildings and pastures to the profile of Square Butte, the mountain that flanked the south side of their property.

In between were hundreds of acres of rolling hills covered with wild grass and dotted with patches of brush, aspen and ponderosa pine.

Usually the sight of the land—his family's legacy— filled Corb with a profound sense of calm and peace.

Today, he felt anything but peaceful.

There's something about this woman, he realized. Something he should be remembering.

"We'll talk at five," he promised, wondering what she had to tell him.

When the fact of her pregnancy had been confirmed yesterday, Laurel had spent most of the night wondering how she would break the news to Corb.

She'd spent the better part of the day thinking about the very same problem. During a lull in business, around 9:00 a.m., she'd called the ranch to ask Corb to come into town.

He'd sounded surprised to hear from her.

Of course he was. In his mind they had only just met yesterday.

"My pie, Laurel?" Burt, the postmaster had finished his sandwich and was looking expectantly at the pie on display just twelve inches from his nose.

"I'm sorry, Burt. My mind is somewhere else today, I'm afraid." She lifted the glass cover off the stand and slipped a wedge of the juicy bumbleberry pie onto a plate, then grabbed a clean fork and set it down, too.

The door chimed and she snatched a quick look.

A couple of young mothers with strollers headed for the corner booth. Laurel smiled at them, then turned to the cash register so she could get the bill for the elderly couple who'd been waiting to pay for five minutes now.

Corb wasn't due for another four hours. She had to relax and focus on the present instead of fretting about what she was going to tell him. So what if she didn't have a plan? She'd just have to trust that she'd know the right words to say when the time came.

By five minutes to five Laurel was rethinking the wisdom of meeting Corb right after work. She should have given herself an hour to rest and get cleaned up. Every time she caught a glance of her reflection in the mirror by the sink, she thought she looked drawn and pale. Her feet and lower back ached. And she was tired. You'd think her body would have adjusted to being on her feet all day by now, but the job seemed to wear her out more and more each day.

If this was pregnancy, then it sucked.

And she still had seven more months to go....

And then she'd have a baby.

It was too much to think about. Better to focus on one day at a time.

The door opened, setting off a cheerful tinkle from the bells.

Expecting Corb, she was surprised to see a balding, middle-aged man looking hungry and cranky.

Right behind him was Corb.

Yesterday the cowboy had been wearing work clothes. Faded jeans and a shirt that had seen so many washes that the fabric was threadbare at the cuffs and collar.

Not today.

Today he was in dark, pressed jeans and the shirt he'd worn at the rehearsal party the night before the wedding day.

He came up to the counter, right next to the balding, cranky man and she waited to see what he would say. If it was anything about the town getting sweeter, she would know that she was stuck in an endless loop of *Groundhog Day.*

"Hey, Laurel. How's it going?"

"You remembered my name this time."

"No bumps to the head in the past twenty-four hours. Generally—and you'll have to take my word on this—I'm pretty good with names." He gave her a warm, approving look. "And faces."

Not five minutes had passed since he'd walked in the door and already she was feeling it. Sizzle. For whatever reason this cowboy totally did it for her.

God help her.

"Excuse me," said the balding cranky man. "I don't remember your name, little lady, but I'm pretty sure I was here first. Doesn't that entitle me to some service?"

"Of course, sir. What would you like?"

"Two coffees and a half dozen of those sticky buns to go."

"Cream or sugar?" she asked, all too aware of Corb watching her.

"Nope. Black like the creek."

This seemed to be a standing joke in the town, since it had been named for the creek that ran through the town with water the same color as a weakly brewed pot of joe.

As she boxed up six of the cinnamon buns, Corb settled himself on a bar stool.

Laurel willed her hands to be steady as she poured the coffee. A few minutes later, she sent balding cranky man on his way, locking the door behind him and putting the Closed sign in the window.

Turning, she removed her apron and gave Corb a nervous smile. "I'll just clear off the dishes from the back booth, then we can sit down and talk."

Corb was off his seat in a flash. "Let me help."

They each carried some of the mugs, plates and cutlery to the dishwasher. When it was loaded, Laurel started a wash cycle, then stood awkwardly.

The kitchen seemed a lot smaller when Corb was sharing it with her. They stood so close that she could smell the scent of his soap.

"You must think it's pretty strange that I asked you to come here."

"Not strange," he insisted. "I was glad." He looked at her intently. "Since we met yesterday, I haven't been able to stop thinking about you."

His words gave her a warm, sweet thrill, and she was reminded of why she had fallen so hard for this cowboy, so fast. He was totally sexy and a terrible flirt. But he had a soft side, too. And could be disarmingly honest.

She poured them each a glass of water, then led the way to the back booth. She slid onto one bench and he settled in on the opposite side.

He looked at her expectantly.

Nervously, she sipped the water. "I see you're wearing your lucky shirt."

"I am." His eyes widened. "But how do you know that?"

Their eyes met and held. His, dark green and fringed with thick short lashes, were oh so familiar to her. But what did he see when he looked into *her* eyes? Did any of the memories of their time together come back to him?

Like their first dance, when he'd held her in his arms and told her he was glad he'd worn his lucky shirt because that night was turning out to be one of the best of his life?

"Laurel, ah, just how well did we get to know each other in that week before the wedding?"

Chapter 3

Despite the water, Laurel's mouth was suddenly too dry to form words. Here was her opening. But she still had no idea what to say.

Suddenly she wondered if it was even safe to tell him the truth. Weren't you supposed to be careful when dealing with people who'd suffered traumatic memory loss?

But the trauma was the accident—not their affair. No, she had to tell him the truth.

Absentmindedly Corb put a hand to his scar, then quickly withdrew it when he noticed Laurel watching.

"Is your head hurting?"

He nodded.

"Can I get you anything? I have over-the-counter painkillers."

"Took a couple of those before I came here. I'll be

all right. The headaches aren't as bad as they used to be. I'm fine."

But he wasn't. Laurel could tell by the forced quality of his smile. It was just so weird to be talking to him like this—as if they'd truly just met. Could he really not remember kissing her? Looking into her eyes as they made love?

He shifted uncomfortably, and she realized she'd been staring at him. She turned away, pretending to check the view out the window. Anything to keep from staring at him.

Finally Corb asked, "Are there things about you and me that I ought to know?"

"Yes."

"Then fill me in, please. You can't know how strange it feels to have a whole chunk of your life gone totally missing."

"I hardly know where to start."

"How about when we met?"

"Okay. That's easy enough. It was at the airport. Winnie had an appointment so she sent you to pick me up."

"Really? Seems like I ought to remember that."

She smiled. "When you saw me you said it looked like Coffee Creek was about to get a whole lot sweeter."

He groaned. "Sorry. Usually I try to use that line only once per woman."

"We talked nonstop during the drive home from the airport. You took me straight to your ranch for a family dinner."

He shook his head, his eyes reflecting his inner torment at his inability to recall any of this. "Was I wearing this shirt that night? Is that why you knew about it?"

Laurel traced a pattern on the table with her finger-nail. "Not that night, no. You wore it at the rehearsal party the night before the wedding." She raised her eyes to his, briefly. "When the music started, you asked me to dance. And when I said yes, you replied that it was a good thing that you'd worn your lucky shirt."

"So. We *danced* together?"

"Yes." *And a whole lot more.* But how on earth was she going to tell him? She could see that he was already blown away by just the few things she'd already shared.

"Wow. This is so freaky. It feels so unreal."

Yeah. Tell me about it. "Maybe one day you will re-member. When the headaches stop, perhaps your mem-ory will come back."

He gave her his charming smile. "I'd love to recall the feeling of you being in my arms. But I'm not so sure I want to remember the accident."

Pain resurfaced on his face, and Laurel could tell this wasn't the physical kind. Suddenly she went from feeling nervous to nauseous.

She put a hand on her stomach and took a deep breath. As much as she wished Corb remembered ev-erything about their affair, she, too, was glad he had no recall of the accident. "The doctor told Winnie that Brock didn't suffer. That he probably didn't even reg-ister what was happening."

"Yeah. That is some comfort."

He didn't look comforted, though, and she realized that she wasn't going to tell him the rest today. He'd been through enough. Let him absorb the fact that they'd spent quite a lot of time together, first.

To be hit with the fact of her pregnancy right now just

wouldn't be fair. Besides, maybe he'd remember their affair on his own if she gave him a chance.

"Thanks for filling in those blanks for me, Laurel."

"No problem. I thought you should know. But I should probably finish closing up here and getting the place ready to open in the morning."

He took the hint with grace, getting up from the booth and heading for the door. She followed him outside, where the day was still warm and sunny. Once he was gone, she'd take a walk along the creek, see if fresh air would help her feel better.

"It was good to see you again, Laurel." Corb had been carrying his hat. Now he settled it on his head, preparing to leave, but for some reason, not heading for his Jeep.

Laurel couldn't answer. Since she'd stood up, her stomach had not been happy. Now it was threatening to heave the contents of her water glass all over the front sidewalk.

The feeling would pass. It always did. She put a hand on her stomach. Closed her eyes. *Please...*

But the feeling didn't go away. In fact, it grew worse. She needed a restroom. *Now.*

Cupping a hand over her mouth, she raced back inside, desperate to make it in time. Behind her, Corb called, "Are you okay?"

No. She sure wasn't.

Corb didn't know what to do. He couldn't just drive away without making sure Laurel was all right. Tentatively, he headed back inside the café and stuck his head down the short hallway that led to the restroom. He could hear retching on the other side of the closed door.

Jeez. That didn't sound good.

He waited for the noise to subside, then called out, "Can I get you anything?"

"I have everything I need here. Fresh water. Towels. A solid door between us so you can't see how embarrassed I am."

He grinned, glad that she wasn't so ill she had lost her sense of humor. There was the sound of flushing. Then her voice again, from behind the closed door. "You can go now. I'm fine."

"Hey now. No need to be embarrassed. If I worked in this place, I'd overdose on cinnamon buns, too."

"Ugh." Water splashed from the sink, a few seconds passed, then the door opened and a pale-faced Laurel stepped out. "Sorry about that."

His smile vanished as soon as he saw her. Despite her flippant commentary, she was obviously ill. "You look like hell. You'd better lie down."

"I will." She glanced pointedly at the door. "After I lock up behind you."

"I'm not sure you should be left alone."

"Believe me, I'm fine. I've had this bug for a few weeks now."

"That's a long time to have the flu. Have you seen a doctor?"

She gave him the oddest look. Then her face went superpale again. She put a hand to the wall, balancing herself.

He immediately sprang forward, placing his arm around her shoulders. "Maybe I should drive you to the clinic in Lewistown right now."

"No. No. That isn't necessary. I'll just head upstairs and lie down."

She didn't say anything more about shooing him out the door Corb noticed. So he stayed right behind her as she climbed the stairs that led to Winnie's apartment above the café. He could see right away that Laurel had been sleeping on the pullout couch in the sitting room. Sheets were folded on the chair beside the couch and a pillow with a white cover laid on top.

"I'll make up the bed for you."

Laurel didn't turn down his offer, just collapsed into a second chair, looking pretty much like death warmed over. What was wrong with her?

Quickly he removed the top cushions, pulled out the bed, then put on the sheets.

"You make a cute housemaid," Laurel commented.

She couldn't be *too* sick if she was still making wise-cracks.

"Yeah, but I don't do windows." He tossed the pillow on the bed, then pointed at her. "Lie down."

Obediently as Cassidy's old border collie, Laurel did as told, only pausing to kick off her sandals before sinking gratefully onto the bed.

"Good girl," he said. "I'll get you some water."

"Woof, woof."

He laughed, then gave her a quizzical look. Funny how she almost seemed to be able to read his mind at times. He went to the small galley kitchen and found a glass on the draining board which he filled with cold water from the tap.

"Anything else you want while I'm in here? Crackers or something?"

"Water is fine."

He handed her the glass then watched as she took a careful sip. Even though she was sick and pale, she still looked pretty. The freckles dusting her slender nose was just about the cutest thing he'd ever seen. He had an odd sensation of déjà vu, then realized he'd probably admired her freckles when they were dancing. Holding her in his arms, standing a good six inches taller than her, he would have had a perfect view of them.

"Was it a slow dance?" he asked.

She didn't meet his eyes. "Yes."

"I thought so."

Her lashes flew up as she looked at him. "You remember?"

"Just your freckles." He had the strangest urge to lean over the bed and kiss them. Once the freckles had been taken care of, he'd move to those rose-petal lips of hers. Why was it redheads always had the most kiss-able mouths?

Not that he'd dated so many redheads in his life. In fact—Laurel was pretty much the first.

This woman. She had a pretty strong effect on him. He'd better get out of here before he said or did something really stupid.

"If you're okay, I guess I'll be going."

"I'm fine," she assured him.

"Don't worry about locking up behind me. Coffee Creek is a safe sort of place."

"Really?" Laurel said softly. "Could have fooled me."

"I'm not going to be able to tell him, Winnie. I just can't."

Fifteen minutes after Corb left the apartment, when she was sure her stomach had settled enough that she wouldn't be sick again, Laurel had called her friend.

For the past two months all her focus had been on helping Winnie.

But now she was the one who needed help.

And, as usual, Winnie didn't let her down.

"Okay, let's say you don't tell him. What are your options?"

"I—I'm not sure."

"Well, how about this? Abortion."

Laurel's answer was instinctive. "No way."

"Fine then. Option two—you have the baby and give it up for adoption."

"No way." That answer had come out of nowhere, too, and Laurel was surprised at how sure she felt about it. She had been adopted by her parents, and she'd always wondered about her biological mother and father. Why had they given her up? She'd sworn that she would never do the same thing, no matter how dire her circumstances.

Well, these circumstances were pretty dire, but at least she was twenty-six, not sixteen as her own birth mother had been.

"Well, then. That leaves only one alternative. You're going to have a baby, Laurel. Just like me. We can be single mothers together. We'll be like a same-sex couple except for the sex part."

Reluctantly Laurel laughed. In some ways the picture Winnie was painting was almost appealing. But there was one big problem with it. "I'm not moving to Coffee Creek."

"Oh, I know. I was just teasing. But isn't it a good thing you got that job promotion? The extra money is bound to come in handy now."

In theory, yes. But she'd already tested her employer's patience with an extended leave of absence. What would her editor say when she told her she was going to have a baby?

"Oh, Lord, this is so complicated...."

"And you haven't even factored Corb into the equation yet," Winnie pointed out.

"But if I don't tell him…"

"If you're keeping the baby, you have to tell him. Can you really imagine any other way?"

Laurel realized Winnie had just talked her around in one big circle. They were back where they'd started, with no other option in sight.

Feeling as if she'd been saddled with a thirty-pound weight, she sank back into the pillows that Corb had plumped up for her.

"You're right. I have to tell him."

The first time Corb had driven past the location of the accident had been the day Jackson chauffeured him home from the hospital. A plain white marker had already been placed in the spot where Brock had died.

This was to be expected. In Montana, sites of traffic fatalities were identified in this way to remind drivers to take caution when behind the wheel.

What wasn't to be expected was the wreath of purple daisies that had been hung over the marker.

No one in the family had any idea who had put the flowers there.

Until now.

Corb pulled over to the side of the road, behind a familiar, rusted old truck. When he got out from the driver's seat and crossed over to the other side of his

Jeep, he saw Maddie Turner. His mother's sister. The woman none of them were supposed to talk to.

His earliest recollection of the feud between the two sisters was when he was around six years old. His dad had been driving him home from his first day at school, and they'd stopped to get an ice cream from the freezer out front of the gas station.

A truck much like the one at the side of the road here, had been parked at the pumps. He remembered the woman looked old to him then, but he'd thought she had nice eyes.

For some reason, though, his father had ignored her.

This struck him as wrong. He was used to his dad smiling and chatting with all sorts of folk, whether he'd met them before, or not.

"Who was that lady, Dad?" he'd asked on the drive home, in between licks of his chocolate-covered ice cream.

"That woman is your mom's sister. Her name is Maddie Turner."

"Why— Then she's my aunt, isn't she, Dad?"

"Well, yes, but you shouldn't think of her that way. Long ago she and your mom had a big disagreement. That woman hurt your mom pretty bad."

His little-boy heart had been stricken by the very idea. "What did that lady do to her?"

"Your mom doesn't like to talk about it, and neither should you. Corb, next time you run into her, in town, or wherever, you just quietly go about with your business. Got that?"

"Got it, Dad."

Following family protocol, as established all those

years ago, Corb supposed he ought to get back into his truck and drive away.

But screw family protocol. His dad had died a long time ago. Now Brock was dead, too. Why was this woman, who the family had disowned, setting out flowers for him?

Corb leaned against his truck to watch. The new wreath had been hung. Now Maddie Turner took the dead flowers and stuffed them into a black garbage bag. Then she started wading through the tall grass back toward her vehicle, without even glancing in his direction.

She was going to get into her truck and drive off without saying a word. And suddenly Corb knew he couldn't let that happen.

"Why?" he asked.

She stopped and stood still for a few moments.

She was about the same height as his mother, but built much stockier, carrying at least twenty-five extra pounds. Her gray hair was cropped bluntly at her chin, and her features were thick, her skin heavily lined.

She had none of Olive's delicate beauty.

Except for her eyes. Even at her age, which must be around sixty, he figured, they were large and a lovely shade of green.

"You are breaking the unwritten code, Corbett."

He couldn't say what shocked him more. Her speaking voice which was soft and refined. Or the fact that she not only knew who he was but used his full name, which almost no one but his mother ever did.

He decided to ignore the comment. "Why are you putting out flowers for Brock? Did you know him?"

"Just let it be, son." She blinked and a single tear rolled down the side of her face. Then she tossed the garbage bag in the back of her truck before driving away.

Corb watched, puzzled. Technically, Brock had been Maddie Turner's nephew. She had every reason to leave a tribute to him if she so desired.

But he couldn't help wondering if there was more to this than just that simple explanation. If perhaps Brock had broken the unwritten rule, too.

Corb got back into his Jeep and followed Maddie Turner farther along Big Valley Road, up to the point where the road forked. When she headed right, toward Silver Creek Ranch, the place where she and his mother had been born and raised, he turned left. He'd never been to the Turner place. Once it had been on par with his father's spread. But his mother had inherited a good chunk of the land with Grandpa Turner's death, and so now Coffee Creek was the much bigger property. Still, Silver Creek had to be a big operation for a single woman to handle on her own.

Corb was thinking about that as he continued on his way toward home. He knew that Maddie hired help, but no one lived out on the ranch with her, other than her animals. Word was, she had only her dogs and cats to keep her company.

Maybe the explanation for why she'd laid that wreath was simply that she'd gone a little squirrely in the head.

Corb drove past the entrance to the main ranch house, sticking left on the road to Cold Coffee Lake. Back in the days before Jackson came to live with them his father had commissioned three cabins to be built on the north shore of the small lake, one for each of his sons. The two-bedroom cabins weren't large, but they'd been built with plenty of space between them so they could easily be expanded, should any of them marry and decide to have children.

Corb had never thought to ask where his sister was supposed to live. He supposed his parents had the old-fashioned expectation that Cassidy would stay in the main house with her parents until she married, at which point she would move in with her husband.

He wondered if it had annoyed Cassidy that a cabin hadn't been built for her. If maybe that was the reason she was so determined not to move back to Coffee Creek after she graduated. He made a mental note to speak to her about the apparent inequity. There was more room along the lake for another cabin, after all.

Like his mother, he hoped his sister would eventually move back home. While he admired the drive that had led her to tackle the Accounting Master Program at Montana State, he wasn't sure she was on the right path. Cassidy had a way with animals that was almost spooky. Could she really be meant to spend her life working on computer reports and attending boardroom meetings?

Corb slowed his speed as he neared the cabins. The first one had been built for B.J., but as he was rarely home, he'd gladly relinquished it to Jackson years ago.

The next cabin was Brock's. Corb slowed to get a look at the porch, then sighed when he spotted Cassidy's dog, Sky, sleeping on the top stair, right in front of the door. With a heavy heart, Corb stopped the Jeep and got out. When Cassidy left home to go to college, her dog had moped like crazy for months.

Finally, she'd given her heart to another Lambert—Brock.

The two of them had become a team. Any time Brock was heading to the barn, Sky would be sure to be one step behind him. Nothing that dog loved more than keeping busy. But she was almost fourteen now, and most days she was content to lie in the sun and sleep.

Corb perched on the step next to the old dog. Slowly Sky raised herself to her feet and moved closer, dropping down again and settling her head on Corb's thigh. Corb obliged by giving her head a good scratch. Sky's beautiful black-and-white coat was showing more than a hint of gray.

"Poor old Sky. First Cassidy deserts you. Now Brock. But it isn't Brock's fault, you know. He'd be here with you, if he could."

Sky gave him a sad look. Corb knew she'd picked up on the names "Cassidy" and "Brock." But what he couldn't expect the dog to understand was that Cassidy would be coming back. While Brock never would.

Corb put a hand to the source of the pulsing pain in his head. How could he expect a dog to understand what he, himself, found so unbelievable.

Brock wouldn't be back. Ever.

He fought against the urge to lie down with the dog and give in to the grief. But that was Brock's mother's prerogative. The rest of them had to carry on.

He patted Sky's neck. "Change is hard, isn't it, girl? But you've got to stop doing this. My porch is just as comfy as Brock's, you know."

Sky tilted her head, as if considering the idea. Then she sighed, and sank back down onto Corb's thigh.

"Too tired to move?" Corb interpreted. "Let me give you a hand." He picked up the dog, thankful that due to the healthy food mix she'd been fed since her first day on Coffee Creek Ranch, and a lifetime of fresh air and exercise, Sky hadn't put on any excess weight in her old age and was still a trim thirty-five pounds.

Still, she was heavy enough, Corb thought, as he carried the dog and settled her in the passenger seat of the Jeep. Corb got back into the vehicle and drove the remaining distance to the third and final cabin: his.

He had work to do at the barns, but first he was going to grab a light meal and make sure Sky was comfortable in one of the chairs by the window overlooking the lake.

There was always work to be done on a ranch, but Corb liked being busy. While Brock had been in charge of the quarter horse breeding end of their operation, Corb was the cattleman.

As a teenager and young man, he'd worked under his father. After his father's death, however, when Corb was in his twenties, he'd taken charge of the entire one-thousand-head operation, with Jackson dividing his time between the horse and the cattle.

Corb wondered if his foster brother would be interested in working full-time with the horses now that Brock was gone. Someone would have to talk to him about that. He couldn't see his mom doing it, even though she was officially the one in charge. Still, he'd have to get her okay before he spoke to Jackson.

"Too much to do and not enough time," Corb told Sky as he settled the old dog on a blanket-covered chair that had been used for this same purpose every night since Corb was released from the hospital. He wondered how long it would take before Sky finally accepted this was her new home.

He hoped soon. It broke his heart every time he saw her waiting so faithfully on Brock's deserted porch.

Corb wiped away the tear that had managed to creep

up in the corner of one eye, and went to the kitchen to fry bacon and cook up some eggs. As he worked, his thoughts drifted from the ranch back to town, and the pretty woman he'd left resting in the apartment above the Cinnamon Stick.

It had been news to him that they'd shared a dance at the rehearsal dinner. He strained to remember, but nothing from that day came back to him. Nothing at all. Laurel said he'd picked her up from the airport, as well. And he did have a vague remembrance of the drive to Billings. But he didn't remember meeting her, or chauffeuring her back to Coffee Creek.

It all defied belief.

How could he forget a woman like her? He found her fascinating to watch and loved her sense of humor. Something just felt right when he was with her.

And at just that moment, his phone rang. When he saw the number he smiled. This wasn't the first time they'd been on the same wavelength.

Chapter 4

"Um. Hi, Corb. It's Laurel."

She sounded nervous again. Maybe she was getting up her nerve to ask him out. Right. He should be so lucky.

"Feeling better?" With one hand he removed a package of bacon from the fridge, put the skillet on medium-high, then tore open the package and dumped the meat in to fry.

"Yes. No. I'm not sure. It's complicated."

"Well, actually, it's not *that* complicated. Have you gotten sick to your stomach since I left?"

"No."

"Are you still dizzy? Weak?"

"No…"

"Then you're feeling better," he pronounced, adding, "And I'm real glad you called to tell me. 'Cause I was worried about you."

"Y-you were?"

"Sure. Goes against the cowboy code to leave a woman when she's in distress."

"This cowboy code. Is that a real thing?"

She sounded so tense and serious. What had happened to that sassy sense of humor he liked so much? "Look, Laurel, let's cut to the chase. Are you calling to ask me out? 'Cause if you are, let me do the honors. Are you free for dinner tomorrow?"

"Oh. Well, yes, I am. But that wasn't why I was calling."

His head was fairly aching now, and he wished she'd get to the point. That anxious pitch to her voice was making him feel pretty edgy, too. He stepped back to the fridge to grab the eggs. "Would you just spit it out, already?"

He heard a long sigh from the other end.

"You know how I asked you to come to the café because I had something to tell you?"

"Yeah. And then I came to the café and you told me all the things I didn't remember. Like picking you up at the airport. And dancing together at the rehearsal party." He shut the fridge, egg carton in hand. "Wait a minute. You did tell me *everything,* right?"

But even as he asked the question, he suspected she hadn't.

"Actually, I left out some important bits."

"Such as…?"

"I thought this would be easier over the phone. It isn't, but here goes. Corb, I'm pregnant."

Corb swore his heart stopped cold in that second. At the same time, he lost his grip on the carton in his hands. It flew open as it fell, and all seven eggs splattered on the tile floor. Egg whites and yolks were everywhere, along with tiny bits of shattered eggshells.

"Hell!" he exclaimed.

"I'm sorry. I shouldn't have told you over the phone."

"I'm not yelling at you. It's the eggs."

"My eggs?"

"Not yours. Mine."

"But Corb, you provided the sperm, not the eggs."

He knew he should have seen it coming. A woman didn't call a man to tell him she was pregnant if she wasn't also calling to tell him he was the father. And yet, her words hit him like a splash of glacier-fed water to the face.

He stepped over the mess in the kitchen and collapsed in a kitchen chair. The bacon was burning on the stove. He didn't care.

He needed to catch his breath here. Gathering his wits would be a good idea, too.

"So, I guess we did more than just dance the night of the rehearsal dinner?"

"Yes."

He rubbed a hand over his face. "Why didn't you tell me earlier?"

"I don't know. Maybe I was afraid you wouldn't believe me."

He could hear the hurt in her voice. He only wished he could see her expression.

"This is way too complicated for the phone. I'm coming back to town so we can talk face-to-face."

As soon as Corb ended their call, Laurel phoned Winnie. "I just told him. I don't think it went very well."

Winnie made a sympathetic sound. "What did he say?"

"Hell. He said hell."

"Really? That doesn't sound like Corb."

"Now he's coming back to town so we can talk."

"Probably a good idea."

"I'm not so sure." Laurel's stomach was queasy again. She hadn't had time to adjust to the reality of being pregnant, herself. It had been too soon to tell Corb.

Thank you, Winnie.

But now the news was out, and she was going to have to deal with the aftershocks. She wished she had time to come up with a plan before she threw Corb into the mix. For sure, he'd have opinions—she was especially worried about that stupid cowboy code he'd mentioned.

"It was too soon to tell him. I should have waited a few weeks until I worked out how I want to handle things."

"And then you'd have spent the whole time being nervous about it. It's better this way," Winnie assured her.

"If that's true for me, then why not for you?"

"My situation is different," Winnie insisted. "For one thing, my doctor has ordered me to avoid stress."

Laurel couldn't argue with that point. Winnie's spotting had started the day of Brock's funeral. They'd both been terrified that she was going to lose the baby.

"Well, he's on his way here right now. What should I do to get ready?"

"I suggest you have a cup of peppermint licorice tea. It will help your tummy. And your nerves."

Tea? A shot of scotch whiskey would be nice. But that was off-limits to her now, she realized.

"I promise you one thing," Winnie added. "Corb is a

good guy. He'll help you figure out how to handle this. The two of you are in this together."

Yes. Exactly what she was afraid of.

"I hope you don't mind that I brought you here." Corb laid a plaid wool blanket over one of the flat rocks on the bank of Coffee Creek. The day was still pleasantly warm, with about an hour and a half of sunshine left in it. "I think more clearly when I'm outdoors."

Laurel settled on one side of the blanket. "It's peaceful. I like it here, too."

On the drive to town his mind had spun like a bucking bull.

What did she expect from him? More importantly, what did he *want* her to expect from him?

He had no freaking idea. And that scared him more than anything.

From his backpack he pulled out the food and drinks he'd brought from home. Cans of sparkling lemonade, a few crackers and some cheese. A couple of apples.

"You're pretty good at throwing together a picnic on short notice." Laurel took out the clip that held her hair in place for work, and let the red curls float gracefully past her shoulders. Then she selected a cracker and took a nibble.

He sat next to her, stretching out his legs and planting his arms so he could lean back a little. He'd always liked this spot. Just a short walk out of town, with a screening of willow trees for privacy and a nice view of the creek. He'd never agreed with town lore that likened the water to cold coffee. To him, it looked like liquid topaz—all gold and gleaming in the sun. When he was younger, he used to bring his girlfriends to this spot to make out.

A sudden thought hit him. "It didn't happen here, did it?"

Laurel looked confused first, then she smiled. "Taken a lot of women here, have you?"

"Mostly when I was a lot younger. I can't remember the last time. But that's the point, isn't it? I don't remember being with you." And it was driving him crazy. He could hardly wait for her to fill in the blanks. "Please tell me how it happened."

"Well, as I've already explained, we hit it off from the moment you picked me up at the airport."

He nodded. He had no trouble believing *that*.

"We actually spent a lot more time together than I let on earlier. The first night you took me to Coffee Creek Ranch for dinner to meet your family and then you drove me home afterward."

"Why didn't you get a ride with Winnie?"

"She was spending the night at Brock's cabin."

"That makes sense. So…did you invite me in that night?" he guessed.

"It didn't happen quite that fast!" Laurel reached for an apple and took a bite. Then took her time before continuing the story. "The next day was the shower. It was a Jack and Jill event and you and I helped your mother decorate the house and prepare the food."

God, but it was hard to believe that so much had happened. And he remembered none of it. "And after the shower? Did we—?"

"No! I'm just setting the stage, Corb. Trying to explain that we actually did spend quite a lot of time together."

No wonder she was so hurt that he had no recollection of her. He met her gaze and held it for a few seconds. "I wish I could remember, Laurel. I really do."

Her expression softened. "A day later we had the rehearsal party, which was held at the town hall. Again, you and I helped with preparations, then later, after the dinner, there was dancing. I've told you about that part, too."

"I was wearing my lucky shirt."

She gave a wry smile. "Maybe that shirt of yours is a little *too* lucky."

He was surprised to feel his face grow warm. "So *that* was the night?"

"Yes. That was the night. You and I slipped out. It must have been around ten at night. You took me to your cabin and...well, we made love. It was about one in the morning when you drove me back to town. Winnie wasn't there yet, but I had a key and I let myself in. Then you drove back to the ranch and as soon as you arrived home, you called and we talked on the phone for about an hour before Brock finally brought Winnie back to the apartment and we had to say goodbye."

"Sounds like we did a lot of talking." He wondered what she'd told him, and what he'd told her. He felt so clueless sitting here beside a woman who knew so much more about him than he knew about her.

But more than facts, he wished he could remember his feelings. Had he been falling in love with this woman? Or had he simply taken the opportunity for a fun affair with a beautiful woman who was only in town for a week?

"We did," Laurel agreed. She'd finished her apple. Now she reached for more cheese. Corb was happy to let her munch away on the picnic. He was more interested in feasting his eyes on her. The days were still long in Montana in September and the air held that special clarity that came just before sunset. Her hair glowed like copper and even her fair skin took on a golden cast.

Oh, how he wished he could remember how it had felt to make love to her.

Laurel, about to pop a slice of cheddar into her mouth, paused. She blinked, then shifted her hazel eyes in his direction. For a long moment, the two of them simply gazed at one another. Then she put down the cheese and slid closer to his side of the blanket.

"You're giving me that look," she said, her voice low and sexy. It made him feel a little crazy.

"I am?"

"The same one you gave me that night."

He leaned closer. Irresistible. That's what she was. "And after I looked at you this way, did I do this next?" He put a hand to the back of her head, threaded his fingers through the silky, rich strands of copper, then lowered his lips to hers.

Sweetly, slowly, he savored the kiss. Then he withdrew a few inches to check her reaction.

"Yes, you did. And then, I did this." This time she reached for him, placing a hand on his shoulder, then angling her face as she leaned in for another kiss.

She parted her lips this time, and their kiss deepened, lengthened, sweetened, until time lost all meaning for Corb. He felt like he could kiss this woman forever, and never have enough of her.

But no kiss can last forever.

"So?" she asked.

He stared at her, his mind blank. Then he understood what was happening here. She'd let him kiss her—encouraged him to kiss her—in hopes that he would remember what had been between them.

Part of him was angry at her for the ploy.

But, on another level, he supposed it had been worth a try. "Sorry to disappoint you. That was a great kiss, but I still don't remember. All I can say is it must have been a hell of a knock to my skull for me to forget something that wonderful."

She smiled at him sadly. "It's starting to look like you never will remember, isn't it?"

"The doctors did say that was likely." Then he asked her something he had wondered about on the drive over. "If you hadn't found out you were pregnant, were you going to return to New York without telling me about—us?"

She shrugged. "What point would there have been?"

"So…we hadn't made any promises or commitments?"

"It was only a week," she pointed out.

Only a week. "And yet long enough that you got pregnant."

Laurel gazed pensively at the creek burbling at their feet. "It doesn't seem fair, does it? That it would happen after just one time. I mean, what are the odds?"

Yeah, he'd been wondering that, too. "Didn't we use protection?"

She looked affronted. "Of course we did. Though you did mention at the time that you weren't sure how old the condoms were." A hint of humor brought out the gold flecks in her eyes. "On a bit of a dry spell, were you?"

"You could say that. A few months ago I split with a girl I'd been seeing a long time. I haven't dated anyone since her."

"Jacqueline."

"Yes." When was he going to stop feeling this shock of surprise every time she revealed some new fragment of knowledge about him? "I guess I mentioned her?" God, but this was messed up.

"You said you were together for about five years. But that when Brock and Winnie announced their engagement, she started wondering when the two of you were going to get married."

He hadn't realized, until Jacqueline put him on the spot, that he wasn't ready to take that step. And when he couldn't even give her a date when he *might* be ready, she'd decided to end their relationship.

He'd been sad and out of sorts for a while. But not brokenhearted.

Which had been reassuring in a way. At least he'd known for sure that she wasn't the right one.

"So, back to the condoms," Laurel said. "Do you figure they were about six months old?"

"More than that. Jacqueline was on the pill and we were committed to one another, so we didn't bother with condoms. Those were pre-Jacqueline condoms."

Laurel's eyes went huge. "Are you saying that package was *five years* old?"

"More like six." He looked at her sheepishly. "God, I'm sorry, Laurel. I guess this is even more my fault than I thought."

She shook her head, then gracefully got to her feet and went to watch the water gurgling along in the creek. She tossed in a stone, then another and another.

"Try this." He passed her a stick and they watched it bob along in the water until it was out of sight.

"What about your love life?" he asked. "Is there anyone significant in New York?"

"I had been dating a couple of guys before I left for Montana. Neither relationship was serious. One of the guys is from work, so that's problematic. The other I met at the coffee shop where I always stop for my morning Americano. Nice enough, but as far as I could tell he didn't have a job and that kind of worried me."

Corb found he didn't like the idea of Laurel dating other men. Not even from a time when the two of them hadn't even met.

And then another thought hit him.

"Any chance one of those guys could be the father?"

Laurel stared at Corb, unable to believe he would ask such a jerky question. If she thought there was a chance he wasn't the father, she wouldn't have told him that he was.

Besides, she'd just told him that those relationships were casual. He ought to know her a hell of a lot better tha—

Wait a minute. She kept making this same mistake, assuming that he knew her as well as she knew him.

He didn't. To him they were virtual strangers.

Still, it had been a pretty nasty accusation to make. Rather than lash out, she cloaked her anger in sarcasm. "Gosh. I never even thought about that. Silly me. Maybe Mitch or Ethan is the father of this baby."

Corb looked confused. Then sheepish.

"You can't blame me for asking."

"No? Watch me." It had taken them about fifteen minutes to walk from Winnie's place to this spot. Laurel figured she could make the return trip in half that time if she hurried.

"Hang on. We're not done talking about this." Corb started to gather their picnic supplies, then changed his mind and ran after her.

"Actually, I think we are. Having established the questionable paternity of this fetus, your work is done. Why don't you go home to your ranch and ride a horse or something."

"It's going to be dark soon. I can't ride a horse in the dark."

He tried to step in front of her to force her to stop, but she brushed past him. "You just said it's going to be dark soon and I don't know this area very well. Please let me pass as I'd like to get home while there's still enough light to see."

"Hell." He let his hands fall to his side and stepped out of her way. "I didn't mean to insult you, Laurel."

"Really? So that was supposed to be a compliment, I suppose?" She didn't know which was worse. That he thought she would be sleeping with three men at the same time. Or that she would tell him that he was the father of the baby when she wasn't sure.

Both were pretty bad, in her books.

"Surely you have to understand that it was a natural question. From my point of view."

"You know what? I'm not a fan of your point of view."

"Laurel…"

His voice sounded fainter. In another minute or two he'd be out of hearing range completely. She was glad he was no longer following her. She had to get out of here before she either lost her cool…or dissolved in tears.

Chapter 5

Could it be true?

Corb stared up at the exposed beams of the ceiling in his loft bedroom. He had no curtains on the two-story-tall windows looking out at the lake and an almost-full moon cast so much light in his room he could see a cobweb dangling from one of the rafters.

The cobweb swayed with the airflow from the slowly moving ceiling fan. First one way. Then the other.

Just like his thoughts.

Was he really going to be a father?

The idea filled him with terror.

But also with hope.

In the wake of Brock's death, the world was a different place. When people you loved could be snatched away in the amount of time it took to draw in one breath, the birth of a new child seemed like a tremendously wonderful thing.

Despite questioning Laurel about other men she might have slept with, he didn't really doubt that he was the father. Her reaction alone had given him the answer he needed.

But at a high cost. He'd wounded her with his lack of trust.

Of course, it was a lot easier to trust someone if you could remember sleeping with them.

When dawn finally lightened the dark shadows in his room, Corb got up. He let Sky out for her morning constitutional, then grabbed a packet of organic dog food from the fridge and emptied it into her bowl on the porch. He freshened the water from the outside tap, then went round to the side of the cabin that bordered the lake.

A drenched Sky was just emerging from a short invigorating swim. In years gone by, she would be coming at him with a stick in her mouth, anxious to play.

But now she just walked slowly toward the cabin for her breakfast. Corb gave her a friendly pat as she passed by. Sky had frightened away the loons that often swam here at dawn, but the view was still beautiful, more so than usual now that the aspen were turning. He loved this time of year. Soon they would have to move the cattle in closer for the winter. This was a job that everyone in the family usually enjoyed. Even Cassidy and B.J. had been known to make special arrangements to take time off from their work and studies to participate.

It was the one time of the year, other than Thanksgiving and Christmas, when the entire family could be counted on to be together.

Only this year Brock wouldn't be among them.

As Corb went about his morning chores—Saturday was just like any other working day on a ranch—his melancholic mood lingered. He nodded to a few of the hands out working with the horses, but didn't stop to chat as usual.

There was only one man he wanted to talk to this morning.

He found Jackson in the office, checking something on the computer. His foster brother had been a part of the Lambert family since he was thirteen years old and had come up on charges of theft in juvenile court. Bob Lambert had been a good friend of Judge Danvers and he'd volunteered to take the kid in—father unknown, mother incarcerated on a drug-related robbery charge—as part of the state foster parent program.

Why Bob Lambert had decided to reach out to this one particular kid, no one knew.

Initially Olive had been resistant. Bob, who usually ceded to his wife's opinions in most matters, somehow prevailed, and Jackson had proven worthy of his benefactor's faith, never causing the family a lick of trouble since.

In fact, he'd soon become an invaluable contributor to the ranch thanks to his solid work ethic and an almost eerie gift with numbers. By the time he was eighteen, he'd taken over most of the bookkeeping, fitting in the office work after long days working with the cattle and the horses.

Despite all he did around here, though, Olive never had, and probably never would, hand over control of the checkbook.

Corb paused at the doorway to the office. When

they'd built the new barns six years ago, Jackson had taken on the office as his own project, designing a bank of oak filing cabinets, the desk and a floor-to-ceiling bookshelf himself. He'd done all the carpentry, staining and painting, as well, and the final result was worthy of a magazine spread in Corb's opinion.

Right now Jackson was sitting in the oak chair he'd purchased to go with the desk, staring vacantly at the computer screen with an expression of deep misery.

Corb had seen too much of that expression since his release from hospital. He slipped into the upholstered chair across from Jackson's. "So what's up with you? Why aren't you joining us for breakfast anymore?"

Jackson—whom Corb had heard described by the ladies as the "dark, handsome, brooding sort"—shrugged. "I'm not that hungry these days."

Corb flattened a hand over the papers Jackson was shuffling. "Look, I know it's hard. But we have to move on. You think Brock would want us to grieve forever?"

"Easy for you to say. You weren't driving."

He'd guessed this was about guilt, but hadn't wanted to be the first to bring it up.

"And what if I had been? I wouldn't have been able to avoid that moose any more than you could."

"Yeah, well, tell that to your mother. You know she blames me." Jackson stood abruptly, took a sheet of paper from the printer, filed it, then slammed the drawer closed. Then, as if the rare act of aggression had exhausted him, he bowed his head and closed his eyes.

Corb didn't bother to deny the claim. He had a vague recollection of sharp words spoken between Olive and Jackson while they'd been visiting him at the hospital.

They'd assumed he was asleep, or unconscious, but he'd heard enough to know that what Jackson said was true.

"You have to forgive Olive. Brock was her favorite. She's hurting."

Jackson snorted. "You don't get it. I *don't* blame her. This is one time when I totally agree with her."

Corb had hoped to discuss his dilemma with Jackson, but seeing his foster brother in such a miserable state, it didn't feel right to dump his problems on the guy, too.

So he went to the house, washed up and joined his mother for breakfast, once more trying to entice her to leave the house and get some fresh air. Maybe go for a ride on that pretty new palomino.

But Olive wasn't interested. She was staring out the dining room window, listlessly, when he left, and he shut the back screen door with more than a hint of frustration.

His family was falling apart and there didn't seem to be a damn thing he could do about it.

Except maybe solve his own problems. A plan was starting to take shape in his head, a vision of the future that included a little boy or a little girl. He was surprised at how easily the picture came into focus.

A baby he would carry in his arms.

Then a toddler, riding on his shoulders as he walked around the property.

He'd teach the kid to ride, to love the land, to care for the animals....

Corb drove one of the ranch ATVs back to his place. He resisted the urge to call Laurel, thinking it might be a good idea to let her cool off a bit more, before presenting her with his new idea.

Instead, he'd catch up on a few chores around here, so tomorrow would be free to spend with her.

He showered, then went looking for clean jeans and a T-shirt.

Nothing. When was the last time he'd done laundry?

He couldn't remember, and that had nothing to do with his injury and everything to do with his lax housekeeping skills.

Corb sorted through his piles of dirty clothes, trying to find something that wasn't too bad. His favorite blue T-shirt didn't have any stains. When he pulled it over his head he caught a whiff of a fragrance—sweet and subtle—that made him think of Laurel. Had he worn this when he'd spent time with her? He must have.

On his way to load the washer, he glanced at his unmade bed and tried to recall the last time he'd done the sheets.

Hmm. A long time.

He went back to strip the sheets, first pulling off the duvet, then tugging the bottom sheet from the box spring.

Out tumbled a pair of black undies. Much too tiny and silky to be his. Another tug and a matching bra was lying on the floor, too.

Well.

If he'd needed any more proof that he'd slept with Laurel—beyond the affronted expression she'd given him last night—here it was.

What to do?

Give them back to her, obviously. But should he wash them first?

He had a feeling the hot, regular cycle along with the sheets would not be a good idea. Maybe gentle with cold water? It seemed a waste to do an entire load with only two tiny items of clothing, but that's what Corb decided to do. When the cycle ended, he set the wisps of silk and lace on a towel in the sun to dry.

God, he wished he could remember what Laurel looked like in these. Even more, what she looked like with them off.

Sunday. Glorious Sunday.

It was almost noon and Laurel was only just out of bed. She took a sip of the decaf coffee that she had just made with Winnie's French press, then a bite from one of the day-old cinnamon buns left over from the café.

The food tasted great, for a change.

She was feeling much better than she had all week. She almost wanted to take another pregnancy test in case the other had been some sort of mistake.

Logically she knew this was crazy.

Probably her body was just enjoying the blissful pleasure of a day off work.

Sunday was the only day of the week that the Cinnamon Stick was closed and Laurel was looking forward to a quiet day of contemplation. Time alone to adjust to the reality of pregnancy. She put a hand on her flat stomach and tried to imagine what was going on in her uterus right now. Cells dividing and multiplying. Hmm. That was a bit of an oxymoron, wasn't it? How could they be dividing *and* multiplying at the same time?

Laurel lifted her mug for another sip, only to realize that she'd emptied the cup. The cinnamon bun was all gone, too. She was padding back to the kitchen for refills of both, when the doorbell rang.

There were two entrances to Winnie's upper-floor

apartment. One was through the stairway that led to the café on the main floor. There was no buzzer on that door, just a simple door handle lock.

The other was via an exterior staircase that provided an alternate exit in case of fire. And it was this door that Laurel cautiously approached.

"Hello?" she called, without unlocking the dead bolt.

"Laurel? It's Corb."

Oh, hell. She was dressed in gray yoga pants and a baggy, striped T-shirt. Her hair was pulled up in a messy knot and she hadn't even brushed her teeth yet, let alone washed the sleep from her eyes.

Besides. She was still mad at him.

"Go away."

"I have something of yours."

And I have something of yours, she thought grouchily. *It's called a baby.*

"Laurel?"

Part of her was dying to open the door. The other part was still holding a grudge. "I'm thinking."

"I *do* have something for you. But it's really just an excuse to see you. I'm sorry about Friday. I'd like to apologize in person for being such a jerk."

That was better. She twisted the dead bolt, then opened the door about six inches. Corb was wearing jeans and a white T-shirt that showed off his upper-body build to perfection. In his hands he held a paper bag. She wondered if he really did have something in there. It looked pretty weightless to her.

"I'm listening."

"Good. Thanks. So, um, I apologize and I'm sorry for what I said about those other guys maybe being the father. You wouldn't have told me I was if you weren't sure."

She let the words soak in a minute. They felt good. "Apology accepted." She opened the door wide to let him in, and as she felt him take in her appearance, she held out a hand in warning. "No judging. This is Sunday, technically still morning if only by a few minutes, and you dropped by without notice."

"Actually, I was thinking you looked pretty good."

Oh, man, she loved this guy. Not just for the things he said, but for the honest way he looked when he said them. Like he meant them.

"So...what's in the bag?"

A grin teased up the corners of his mouth. "I washed my sheets yesterday and guess what I found?" He pulled out her missing bra and panties.

"Oh, my lord."

"If you don't mind trying them on, so I can verify that their yours..." He dangled the garments in front of her.

"Good try. But that line works better with glass slippers." She snatched them out of his hands, catching a whiff of fabric softener as she did so. "You washed them?"

"Gentle cycle. And I laid them on a towel to dry."

Adorable. This guy was something else. All the reasons she'd fallen for him came crashing in on her. She supposed she could excuse his jerky reaction to her news on Friday.

It must have been a hell of a shock.

"Well, thank you. That was nice."

"If I could ask a question?"

"Sure."

"Why weren't you wearing those when I drove you home?"

She could feel her face growing hot. "We tried to find them, but it was getting late. We agreed that I would come back the next night and…we'd look for them again."

"Damn." No mistaking the regret on his face now. "We sure had us some fun, didn't we?"

"Yes, we did."

"Do you think we could start over? You and me?"

"Start over in which way?"

"Like—go on a date together? Try to forget the past—well, I'd have an easier time with that than you would—but just enjoy one another's company. Simple as that."

She almost said no. But he was being so charming. And it couldn't hurt to try to establish a good relationship with the father of this baby inside of her. "I suppose we could try. What did you have in mind?"

"My favorite thing to do on a beautiful Sunday afternoon is go on a trail ride."

"I'm not very good with horses." She glanced away, and he immediately picked up on what she was thinking.

"You told me that before, right?"

She nodded. "But that's okay. We're starting over. I'll try to pretend I know as little about you as you know about me."

"And you'll come on the trail ride? My mom has a pretty palomino named Lucky Lucy. A real gentle mount and she's in desperate need of a good workout."

"Give me fifteen minutes to get ready?"

"Take twenty if you need them. I'll wait outside in the Jeep."

* * *

Thirty minutes later Laurel was in the barn at Coffee Creek Ranch helping Corb tack up two horses. Lucky Lucy, the palomino he'd told her about, was even lovelier than she had expected. She was calm, too, standing cooperatively as Corb put on first her saddle blanket, then the saddle.

"Want to attach the girth?" he asked.

"Sure." She moved slowly toward Lucky Lucy, introducing herself to the mare before gradually fastening and tightening the girth straps. As she got acquainted with her mount, Corb tacked up a sturdy quarter horse called Chickweed. He had a small pack he'd picked up from Bonny in the kitchen that he tied to the back of his saddle.

As they led their mounts outside, Laurel felt a flicker of anticipation for the afternoon ahead. It was true that she'd always been nervous of horses, but Lucky Lucy did seem very well mannered, and the day was so sunny and beautiful it was hard to resist, as well.

"What a gorgeous place this is."

Corb smiled proudly. "It's home. And I feel damn lucky to call it that. Let's keep the horses to a walk. You and Luce can get to know one another."

And maybe she and Corb could do the same, Laurel thought. She was determined to give this "fresh start" idea of his a fair shake.

After about fifteen minutes of riding single file, Corb brought his mount up alongside of hers. "So tell me," he said, "How is it you're nervous around horses? You sure look like you know what you're doing."

"Why thanks, cowboy." He looked pretty good himself. At one with his horse and his surroundings. She hadn't seen him this relaxed or at peace since the accident.

Surprisingly, Laurel could feel her own blood pressure dropping. She hadn't been on the back of a horse since she'd left home for college. Her memories of riding as a kid were pretty tense. Yet somehow she'd remembered the skills she'd learned back then, without any of the nervousness.

"Who taught you to ride?"

"My father." She could feel the muscles along her spine tighten as she said this. She glanced at Corb's face, the part not shaded by his cowboy hat, and saw, not the commiseration she'd expected, but simple curiosity.

Fresh start, she reminded herself. *Pretend you never talked about your family with him before.*

"My dad and I didn't have the best relationship. He wasn't mean or anything. Just sort of disinterested. When I was out riding with him, I was anxious not to make any mistakes."

Because, if she did, a weary look would come over his face, a look he would quickly mask as he patiently explained where she'd gone wrong and how to correct it.

He'd been that way no matter what he was teaching her to do, or helping her with, whether learning to ride a two-wheeler bike, driving a car, or filling out her college application form.

"What about your mom? Were you closer to her?"

Funny. That was exactly what he'd asked her the first time she'd told him about her dad. "Yes. Mom and I were close. But she died when I was eight. Want to hear the whole story or a condensed version?"

Two months ago, Corb had asked for the whole story. He did the same today.

"Okay. Stop me if you get bored."

He tilted his hat up so she could see his eyes. "Not going to happen."

Okay, then... "First thing you need to understand about my family is that my father was totally crazy about my mom. Nothing about my life makes sense unless you understand that."

"Let me guess. She had red hair and freckles, too?"

The compliment made her smile, but she went on as if he hadn't interrupted. "No. I was adopted. About two years after they were married my mother developed uterine cancer. They caught it early and she survived, but the surgery left her unable to have children."

"That must have been a lot to go through."

"Yes. Shortly after that my mom convinced my father that they should adopt a baby. I was only three months old when they brought me home."

"I bet you were a beautiful baby."

"Actually, I was kind of homely."

"Impossible."

The look he gave her made her spine tingle pleasantly. Suddenly she didn't mind telling her story for the second time. "I remember my early years being very happy. But then Mom's cancer came back. And this time she didn't make it."

Corb pulled up his mount. "Damn. That must have been so hard."

"It was. Especially since I was older and beginning to understand some things. Like why my father always seemed cool and aloof. It was especially noticeable because he loved Mom so much. Yet he was so different with me. What I figured out later was that he'd agreed to the adoption to make my mother happy. It wasn't something he'd wanted, at all."

"But surely—"

She held up a hand for him to pause. "I remember one day near the end. My mom was in bed—too weak to do much other than sleep. I overheard her ask my father to promise to take care of me. And love me."

"Which he, of course, said he would do."

"Sort of. He said he would take care of me for her sake. But he didn't say anything about the love part. Even though I was so young, I understood that he hadn't been willing to promise something he knew he couldn't deliver."

Chapter 6

Corb looked stunned, as if it was beyond his imagination that a father could not love his only daughter. But it *was* true, Laurel thought sadly.

"We should take a break," Corb said.

Only then did Laurel notice that they'd come upon the bank of a creek. She let Corb help her dismount and was surprised at how mushy her legs felt. "Gosh. I can hardly walk."

"Your muscles are in shock. Try moving around while I tie up the horses near the water."

Once he'd done that, Corb took off his hat and knelt by the creek to splash his face. The temperature was edging toward eighty already and Laurel decided to do the same, not realizing quite how unsteady her legs still were.

Corb caught her before she face-planted in the cold, mountain-fed stream.

"Thanks."

He gazed down at her face for a few seconds before releasing his hold. "Let's sit in the shade and keep talking."

They rested their backs against two tree trunks facing one another. Colt had pulled food and lemonade out of his pack and they opened their drinks and shared squares of chicken sandwiches.

"So what was life like once your mom was gone and you were alone with your dad?"

"Much different. Quiet. Lonely. I started spending more time at Winnie's. Her parents were kind enough not to complain even though they must have felt like they were raising two daughters, not just one."

"I'm beginning to understand why you feel so close to her."

She nodded. "I was lucky to have a friend like Winnie. We were at our high school graduation party the night I found out my dad died in a car crash. The police told me he'd fallen asleep behind the wheel and drove straight off the road into a tree."

"Jeez. What horrible luck to lose a second parent so tragically."

She hesitated. She'd told him more the first time they'd had this conversation, but maybe she'd been too candid then. "Yes, it was horrible. Once again Winnie and her family came to my rescue. I lived with them that summer while the lawyers arranged to sell my father's land and auction off the animals and equipment."

"That must have been overwhelming."

"Actually, between Winnie's parents and my dad's lawyer, I was pretty insulated. And I had college to look forward to. Winnie's father drove us to Great Falls and helped us move into residence. Winnie and I were roommates, so the adjustment to college life was pretty painless."

"So you left your hometown and never looked back?"

"I'd always dreamed of being a journalist and living in New York City. The farm was sold and even after the debts were paid off, I had enough money to go to college and study English. After that I moved to New York City, just the way I'd always wanted to."

"And you're happy there?"

"I have a cute studio apartment. And a really fun job. I do like it a lot." She hesitated before adding, "Winnie says it's time for me to go back. So I went online yesterday and booked a flight."

"You did?" He looked more than surprised. More like shocked.

"Yes. I'm leaving two Sundays from now."

Corb fought off the panic stampeding through his veins. He had to convince her to cancel that ticket. If Laurel went back to New York, he'd never see their baby. Never walk around the ranch with the munchkin on his shoulders, never teach the kid to ride or give him a chance to know his grandma and aunts and uncles.

No. He could not let this happen.

What was so great about New York anyway? So what if he'd never been there. He'd visited Billings plenty of times and could never get out of the place fast enough.

He had trouble picturing Laurel as a city girl. She looked perfect the way she was right now in faded jeans and riding boots, her hair wild and curly, and her face devoid of makeup.

Be calm, he told himself. *Take a deep breath. You can fix this.*

He waited for Laurel to finish her sandwich. "How are you feeling?"

"Like an eighty-year-old chimney sweep." Gingerly she got back to her feet, then immediately groaned.

"What about your stomach? Food staying down okay?"

"Thanks. Yes."

"So you're okay to head back?"

"Not sure. Maybe we should hail a cab."

"Smart-ass." He untied Lucy, then walked the mare over to where Laurel was standing. *Very smart ass, indeed,* he couldn't help thinking, as he helped her back into the saddle.

They rode back to the barn in under an hour and Laurel insisted on helping as he cleaned and put away the tack, then brushed down the horses.

By the time they were done it was almost six and Corb was starving.

And he still hadn't figured out what he was going to do to make her stay.

"Want to come back to my place for dinner? I have some steaks we could throw on the barbecue."

"Sure. I'll even make a salad if you have some greens on hand."

He opened the door to his Jeep for her, then drove the lakeshore road toward his cabin. As he passed by Brock's place, he was discouraged to see Sky on the porch again.

"Hell. That poor old dog just doesn't learn." He stopped, and was surprised when Laurel got out with him. She went to the old border collie, sitting on the stair and crouched low beside the dog.

"Hey, Sky."

He was startled that she knew the dog's name, then realized since she'd been to dinner at the main house, she'd probably met the dog then.

Sky lifted her head, as if to return the greeting. Then she sighed.

"Poor thing. She looks heartsick."

"She used to be Cassidy's dog. Then she bonded with Brock. Ever since I moved out of the guest room at the house and back to my cabin, I've found her here every afternoon."

Laurel's response was to lay her cheek against Sky's soft fur. "Poor girl," she murmured.

"I'm trying to train her to accept that my place is her home now. But you know what they say about old dogs and new tricks."

"Hmm." Laurel patted the dog's head then looked deeply into the border collie's dark eyes. After several minutes of this silent communion, she glanced up at Corb. "Could we go inside?"

He glanced at the door to his brother's cabin. He hadn't been in there since before the accident. "Are you serious?"

She nodded. "I think that's what Sky wants."

It was the last thing Corb wanted to do. Seeing his brother's empty home was just about the most depressing sight he could imagine. But how could he say no?

He looked for the key hidden under an empty terracotta flowerpot, then used it to open the door.

Sky watched all this activity with eyes that were suddenly bright, and as soon as the door cracked open an inch, she was on her feet, nosing her way inside.

Corb gestured for Laurel to go next. He followed.

The smell hit him first. Never before had he noticed that Brock's home had its own individual scent. But he noticed now. He took a few steps into the hall.

His mother had asked Bonny to have Brock's cabin cleaned and his clothing boxed and donated about a month after his death. Since then, no one had been near the place. There was a little dust, but not as much as Corb would have expected. His eyes skirted over the passport and travel documents lying in wait on the hall table for the honeymoon that would never happen.

Bonny must not have known what to do with them.

He swallowed, then stepped forward into the living area.

Sky seemed to be taking Laurel on a tour of the place. She'd started in the bedroom, then had gone to the bathroom. Now the dog and the woman brushed by Corb as they checked out the living room with its floor-to-ceiling windows and river-rock fireplace, then the attached eating area and kitchen.

The house was just like his. But in so many ways Brock had made it his own. Not the least was the vinyl record collection that filled an entire shelving unit made for the purpose. Brock insisted the sound was superior to CDs.

"Sky seems to be looking for something," Corb noticed. "Maybe a favorite old bone or chewing toy?"

Laurel came up beside him and smiled sadly. "I think she's looking for Brock."

He felt as if his heart had been squeezed, flattened and stomped on. Damn. Laurel was probably right, Corb realized, wondering why he hadn't thought to let Sky have a good sniff around the place. Dogs had their own way of collecting information and processing change. And now that she'd been over every square inch of the cabin, Sky seemed satisfied.

She went to the door, and as soon as he opened it, made her way down the stairs, then along the path to his Jeep.

Sky was the first one in the house when they arrived at Corb's cabin. She went straight through to the living room where she settled herself in her blanket-covered chair with the view of the lake.

"She's claimed the best seat in the house," Laurel said, amused.

"Never said she wasn't a smart dog." Corb showed Laurel around his home as if she'd never been there before. She made no objection, enjoying the chance for a second tour of the place.

It was absolutely charming. The floor plan was identical to his brother's, except for the furnishings and artwork. Laurel had been impressed on her first visit with the framed photographs on the walls. She knew he'd taken them all on the ranch, that photography was his hobby, and a pretty serious one at that.

But she admired the photographs as if she'd never seen them before. Loons on the lake at sunrise. A moose knee-deep in the water, nuzzling the calf standing beside her. A cow emerging from frost-covered branches in winter with a dusting of snow on her hide.

He had other pictures that captured the beauty in the little everyday things, as well.

In the bathroom was a series of wildflowers. In the

hall, a photo of river rocks that stretched six feet across and only two feet tall.

"Can I get you a glass of wine or a bee—" He caught himself as he was asking her what she'd like to drink. "I guess the choice is soft drink or water, huh?"

She made her way back to the kitchen. "Yeah, I'll have to stop smoking, too, I guess."

At his startled look, she laughed. "Kidding." She opened the fridge and took out a lemonade. He popped the tab and poured it into a glass, with ice.

Then he touched her glass with his bottle of beer. "A toast?"

"To—?"

"A healthy baby?"

She nodded. She could definitely drink to that. And it did help to put their problems into perspective. If they managed to have a healthy baby, wasn't that the main thing? Surely everything else could be worked out with a little time and understanding.

Corb took one drink of his beer then set it down. "That was good, but I'd better go light the barbecue. Take a look in the fridge and see what you can find. I don't think I have salad fixings, but there should be some potatoes and carrots."

As she puttered in the kitchen, Laurel thought about Corb and the day they'd spent together. He was different. His brother's death and his own injury had changed him. He was no longer simply the charming, carefree, artistic cowboy who had swept her off her feet the very second she'd met him.

This Corb had layers of sadness around his heart. He weighed his words before speaking. And smiled a whole lot less often.

She knew his grief would eventually lessen. But he would always be a changed man.

Life did that to people. It knocked them around, sometimes to the point where there was no more telling what was up and what was down.

Twice she'd been there herself. After the death of her mother. And then her father.

Because, despite the fact that he had never loved her, she *had* loved her father. And his death had been a major loss.

She ate the steak that Corb grilled to perfection, and he complimented her on the veggies.

When the meal was over, they moved to the living room to watch the sun set into the lake. Or that was how it looked, anyway, as if the orange globe was slowly submerged into the calm, peaceful water.

What a life it would be. To live in a place like this. With a man like—

Corb was gazing pensively out the window. He could have any number of worries on his mind. But what Laurel saw was a strong man with a good heart. Two months ago, she'd thought she was falling in love with him, even though she'd only known him a week.

Now, she knew she had.

Just as she also knew that he didn't feel the same way. She—and her unborn baby—were just one more worry, one unneeded complication. What made it so much more maddening was remembering how different he'd been before.

When Corb had asked her if they'd made promises to one another, she hadn't answered, because it had hurt too much to know that he didn't remember holding her close and telling her there was no way he was letting her go back to New York. He'd never met anyone like her. *"I know you feel it, too, Laurel. This is a once-in-a-lifetime chance. Stay."*

Before she'd met Corb she would have laughed at anyone who said she would leave New York to go back to living on a ranch in Montana. But when he'd asked, she'd promised she would think about it.

She sighed.

The sound pulled Corb's thoughts back to the present. He got up from the sofa, full of apologies. "You must be tired."

She was. But he was looking at her intently, reminding her of that moment when he'd kissed her by the creek. And even though her muscles still ached, and she was weary, and ought to be asking to go home, all she wanted was for him to kiss her again.

Why did he have this pull on her?

He rested his hands lightly on her shoulders, then slid them up, along her neck, until he held her face gently between his palms.

His touch was like magic.

She wanted to fold into him, to feel his strength enclosing her tightly. And she ached to hear his voice whisper into her ear, saying all the words that had seemed to come so easily from him before.

Before his brother died.

Before he'd lost his memory.

Before she was pregnant.

Could lightning strike between them a second time?

She looked into his eyes, trying to mine their depths to find the answers she was searching for.

The green flecks sparkled, then slowly disappeared as he closed his eyes and touched his lips gently to hers.

After a few seconds, he shifted his kiss to her cheek, and then to the lobe of her ear, where he said in a soft but heated voice, "You know what we should do?"

She nodded, imagining him taking her hand and leading her up the stairs to the loft, much like he'd done two months ago. She'd go more than willingly, remembering what a sweet and passionate lover this cowboy had been.

"We should get married," he said.

Chapter 7

"This isn't—I mean you're not—" Corb's proposal had left Laurel breathless. "Are you serious?" she finally managed to blurt.

Corb looked hurt. "I'm not likely to joke around when I ask a woman to marry me."

"No. I'm sorry. I'm just surprised." In more ways than one. Surprised that he had asked her. And even more surprised at how her heart had leaped with joy when he did it. She'd always wondered at that expression, but it was true. When you were very, very happy your heart truly did feel physically lighter.

But that reaction faded all too quickly. Because she knew that duty and responsibility lay behind Corb's proposal. True, he'd said some lovely things about her, today and other times, as well.

But he wasn't in love with her. Not the way she was

with him. And to say yes when there was such an imbalance in their emotions was surely a mistake.

But he might grow to love me....

It had happened before. So it could happen again. Couldn't it? She was the same person, after all.

But Corb wasn't. The accident had changed him. The question was, how much?

Corb took her hands. "Well?"

"Part of me wants to say yes," she admitted frankly. "But I'm scared."

"Me, too. It's a big step. And we haven't known each other very long. But I figure if we marry now we'll have some time for just the two of us before the baby comes."

He'd obviously thought this through, which gave her some comfort. And he seemed sincerely determined to make their relationship work.

The urge to say yes was growing stronger. Her feelings for Corb aside, the idea of having a baby on her own was frightening. She had no family in New York, or close friends like Winnie, the kind you could call in a pinch if you needed a sitter, or in the middle of the night if your baby was sick and you didn't know what to do.

But was she ready to leave New York? She loved her job. And she'd worked so hard for that promotion. If she gave up on her dream of being an editor for one of the big magazines now, she'd probably never have a second chance.

But she might never have a second chance with Corb, either.

"I think we both might be crazy. But I'm going to say yes."

She saw him swallow and wondered if the cause

was nervousness. But the smile he gave her next looked genuine.

"You won't regret that decision," he promised her. Slowly he pulled on her hands until she was close enough to kiss.

And then he claimed her lips, the way he'd just claimed her future. She sank into the kiss, trusting him and loving him and ignoring the tiny warning voice in the back of her head and the pit of worry at the bottom of her stomach.

He'd only intended a quick gentle kiss to seal their deal. But he hadn't counted on how sweetly Laurel would fit into his arms, or how absolutely hot her luscious lips would feel pressed next to his.

Her skin was the silkiest of magnets—he was drawn to touch every lovely inch.

"Laurel…" He looked at her in amazement, taking in her flushed cheeks, swollen lips, dewy eyes. She was incredibly beautiful.

They kissed again and he could feel her lovely, thick hair brushing against his face and neck as he delivered kisses to her petal-soft neck and collarbone.

Scatterings of freckles lay over her creamy skin, and the desire to see more—and *feel* more—was overwhelming.

Her quiet, responsive moan both inflamed him and brought him back to his senses. She was pregnant. And he'd never been with a pregnant woman before.

"Is it safe to go further? I don't suppose you've talked to a doctor?"

"I made an appointment for next week." She drew a ragged breath, then smiled with lips that quivered just a little. "I think it's probably fine."

He smoothed her hair back from her brow. During their make-out session her hair had seemed to develop a life of its own, growing thicker and wilder and framing her face so that she looked totally bewitching. His body responded with a deep, urgent ache that was part pain and part pleasure.

He satisfied himself with a gentle kiss to her cheek.

"Just to be sure, we should probably wait." He tucked another wild curl behind her ear. "But I have to say, that was a sensational kiss."

"I'd have to agree, cowboy."

He was relieved to see that they were on the same page with this. Marrying Laurel to secure his child's future was something he was prepared to do, no matter what. But it sure helped that his bride-to-be was beautiful and passionate.

It actually helped quite a lot.

Corb drove Laurel to her doctor's appointment the next week. Laurel had been referred to Winnie's doctor, who had a practice in Lewistown.

She left the Cinnamon Stick in the capable hands of Eugenia Pyper, Winnie's oldest and most experienced employee. Eugenia was in her mid-fifties, a widow with a grown son who lived in Billings. She had a part-time catering business of her own and helped out in the kitchen as well as serving customers.

Laurel didn't tell Eugenia the reason for her doctor's appointment, but she suspected Eugenia had guessed.

"Must be something in the water around here…."

The comment made Laurel wonder if Eugenia also knew that Winnie was pregnant. She probably did. And since word hadn't spread around the town, that also meant that Eugenia knew how to keep her mouth shut.

She gave Eugenia a thankful smile. "Maybe the town should post a sign warning of the danger."

"All I can say is I'm glad those days are over for me, honey." She patted Laurel's hand. "Now get off to that appointment. Your man is out there in his truck waiting for you."

She and Corb had said nothing of their plans to marry yet, either. But obviously, where there was a baby there had to be a father, too, and Eugenia had everything all worked out.

Laurel checked her purse to make sure she had her insurance information, then hurried out to the truck.

Corb was standing by the open passenger door of his Jeep. He had on a dark green shirt with his jeans, and his left dimple was in full evidence as he gave her one of his most charming smiles.

As Laurel stepped on her toes to kiss him, she put a hand on his hard, muscular shoulder. "You didn't have to do this. I could have driven myself."

But she thought it was a good sign that he'd insisted. She liked the idea of marrying someone who was thoughtful. A streak of gallantry went a long way in smoothing out the bumps of any relationship, she figured.

The appointment itself was over quickly. The test was positive and she was given a prescription for vitamins and also an appointment for a follow-up in one month's time. The doctor assured them that sexual relations would not hurt the baby and then a nurse had them select dates for prenatal classes. Again Corb impressed her by agreeing right away that he would attend with her.

She'd thought some men—probably most—were squeamish about labor and delivery, but Corb sure wasn't.

"You better believe I want to be there when this baby is born," he said, placing his hand on her still-flat stomach.

Ten minutes later they walked out of the red brick building that housed the doctor's office together, blinking as the late-afternoon sunlight hit them.

The everyday world of downtown Lewistown looked so different to Laurel.

"Is this really happening?" She sank onto a wooden bench in the shade of a leafy tree. Corb settled next to her and meshed his fingers with hers.

"It's official," he said. "March 28, we're going to have a baby."

Laurel hesitated, wanting to admit something, but not sure if she dared. Finally she just said it. "I'm terrified, Corb."

"Me, too!"

Then they laughed, and went for ice cream, and Laurel was filled with a crazy optimism that maybe the two of them could actually get through this together.

On the drive home, Corb brought up the subject of their wedding.

"So what would you like to do? I know most girls dream of having a big wedding. But I was hoping you wouldn't mind if we kept it quiet and just invited immediate family?" He reached over the gearshift to grasp her hand. "Given that we're still grieving and all."

"I wouldn't want a big wedding anyway," she assured him. Maybe it was because she'd lost her mother so young and her father so tragically, but she'd never fantasized about a special wedding day the way Winnie had.

That didn't mean she hadn't yearned for love. She had. And did. She wanted to marry and have lots of children. Maybe even adopt a few, as well. A big, happy, noisy home was what she dreamed of. Not a fancy dress and a towering cake and a bunch of speeches.

"I can't even offer you a honeymoon," Corb admitted. "Fall is a busy time. In a couple of weeks we're going to start moving cattle in from the high country. It'll mean long days in the saddle."

Though she'd grown up on a small mixed farm, Laurel had had friends who'd lived on ranches and she understood what Corb was saying. The Lamberts owned a lot of land and a lot of cattle. Moving them closer to home for the winter wouldn't be easy.

"What if we combined our wedding and honeymoon into the same weekend? We could go to Vegas or Reno, just the two of us."

He looked intrigued by the idea. "You'd be happy with that?"

She nodded. "It would be good for us to have a few days to be alone together without the distractions of your ranch or Winnie's café."

"I like that idea a lot." He gave her a happy grin. "Now that everything's all decided and official, what do you say we swing by my mother's and give her the good news? She's already asked me to come by for dinner. This way we can make it a sort of welcome-to-the-family celebration."

"Oh." That was faster than Laurel had expected. "Maybe you should call her and make sure she doesn't mind another person for dinner."

Corb laughed. "It won't be a problem. Bonny always cooks way too much food."

Laurel wasn't so sure. "At least drop me off at the apartment first? I'd like to change into a skirt and clean up a little."

"You look great just the way you are."

"Thanks for saying that, but I'd also like to follow you in Winnie's car so you don't need to give me a lift back to town when dinner is over."

She'd been feeling perfectly wonderful just minutes ago. But the mention of telling their news to his mother had made her stomach tighten and churn. Just in case she needed to make a fast escape, she thought it would be good to have her own car.

Scarcity of food wasn't the issue when they pulled up to the ranch house thirty minutes later, Laurel a hundred yards behind Corb driving Winnie's RAV4 with Cinnamon Stick Bakery painted on both sides. Though Winnie had encouraged her to use the vehicle whenever she wanted, this was the first time Laurel had taken her up on the offer.

Not used to a standard gear shift, she had a little trouble at first, and she was sure Corb was laughing at her as she stalled in the middle of the first intersection leading out of town.

She'd changed into a dress and touched up her makeup, wanting to make a nice impression on the woman who would be her mother-in-law. As she drove, she thought about Winnie's contention that Olive didn't like her.

She sure hoped Olive didn't take exception to her, too.

The irony of the situation didn't escape Laurel. She'd come to this town expecting to witness Winnie's marriage into the Lambert family. Instead, she was the one who would become Olive's daughter-in-law.

She still couldn't quite believe it. Didn't think it would seem real until their vows had been spoken and the ring was on her finger.

By the time she reached the main ranch house, Laurel's stomach was very unhappy. Whether from nerves or the pregnancy, she had no idea. She waited until Corb had pulled up beside her before she got out of the car.

But just as she was gathering her courage to approach the front door, a third vehicle approached, pulling in behind Corb's Jeep. The woman driver, a blonde, took a moment to gather a few things before stepping out of her car.

Laurel turned to Corb, who had joined her outside the entrance to his family home. One look at his face and she realized he knew this person. And wasn't happy to see her.

The front door to the house opened then, and Olive, dressed and made up to her preaccident standard, appeared with a welcoming smile. She smiled at her son, but the instant her gaze shifted to Laurel all the warmth froze out of her face. She put a hand to her throat, as if under threat of attack. Then narrowed her eyes at Corb.

"What in the world is going on here, Corbett?"

Corbett? Was that his real name? That trivial bit of information was pushed to the side as Laurel struggled to puzzle out the situation.

The blonde woman, close to her own age, Laurel guessed, was out of her car now. Her hair was sleekly styled and she wore a lacy black blouse with a short black skirt that showcased amazingly long, slender legs.

Yikes. Was this—

"Jacqueline." Olive's voice sure sounded warm now. "It's so good to see you again."

Her worst fears were confirmed. Corb's ex-girlfriend had been invited to dinner. Judging from the shock on his face, he'd had no idea. Clearly his mother had been doing a little matchmaking.

And Laurel's unexpected appearance put a very big wrench into her plans, which explained the chill Laurel felt every time Olive glanced in her direction.

But Olive didn't say a word. Ignoring Corb and Laurel as totally as if they were shrubs planted on either side of the large walnut door, she held out her hand to the newcomer, accepting a bottle of wine with admirable grace.

Frozen in place, Laurel turned to Corb for guidance. He gave her a smile, but she could tell it took some effort. Then he, too, greeted the blonde.

"Hey, Jacqueline. This is a surprise. Mom didn't tell me we were having guests."

"The invite was last-minute," Jacqueline explained. "Your mom happened to be out at the ranch talking to Dad about an upcoming auction this afternoon. I saw her and went out to see how she was doing, and we just started chatting…."

"I told Jacqueline that I missed having her around the ranch and invited her to join us for dinner." Olive lifted her chin, speaking in a somewhat haughty tone. "I saw no need to inform you, Corb, given that this is my house and I'm the one who makes the arrangements for dinner."

The unspoken accusation was, of course, that Corb should have informed his mother about inviting Laurel. Olive was right on that point, and Laurel could do nothing but regret that she hadn't insisted Corb call before she agreed to come.

Her mistake. There were lots of families—and Winnie's was one of them—where a last-minute invite was no big deal. The Lambert family might have been that way usually, too. But not tonight.

Jacqueline hadn't been expecting another woman to be on the scene, either, and Laurel stiffened under her laser-sharp appraisal as they shook one another's hands.

"Come in, everyone," Olive said. "We'll have a glass of wine on the back patio before dinner. Bonny's left us a very nice baked salmon and spinach salad in the kitchen."

It would have to be a very nice salmon indeed, to turn this dinner party around, Laurel reflected. Corb's body language was awkward as he served drinks out on the cobblestone patio, at his mother's request.

Scattered around the patio, pots of mixed annuals were still blooming as recklessly as they had two months earlier in the summer at Winnie and Brock's shower. A table placed near the kidney-shaped pool had been set for three.

Laurel wanted nothing more than to turn and run.

Olive didn't want her here. Even Corb, she was certain, now regretted his invitation. And she couldn't help but wonder how he felt at seeing Jacqueline again. He'd never described the woman to her and she definitely hadn't expected his ex-girlfriend to be quite so beautiful. Except for the blond hair, she was a ringer for Katie Holmes.

And, clearly, she was Olive Lambert's choice for her son's future wife.

"So, Laurel, you must be planning to return to New York City soon?"

The question came five minutes into the meal, after Olive had adjusted the place settings and Corb had been sent to fetch a fourth chair for the table.

For all that the query was worded politely and asked in a mellifluous voice, Laurel understood the underlying meaning quite clearly. Basically Olive was telling her that it was *time* she left. That her presence at Coffee Creek Ranch was no longer welcome.

Across the table from her, Corb raised his eyebrows, a silent question asking if he should make their announcement now.

She gave a desperate, but tiny, shake of her head. She couldn't imagine a more awkward moment to tell Olive that she and Corb were planning to get married.

Other than that one question about returning to New York, which Laurel dodged, Olive didn't address any more of her comments toward her. Most of the dinner conversation centered around people Laurel had never met, events from the past she hadn't been involved in and plans for a future that she was not expected to be a part of.

When dessert—a blackberry cobbler—and tea were finally served, Laurel looked forward to her imminent escape with relief. The salmon and salad had done nothing to settle her stomach and her refusal of wine either before or after dinner had earned her yet another disapproving frown from her hostess.

Olive chose that moment to address her second comment of the evening to Laurel. "What a shame that you don't care for your dessert. Jacqueline, I'm so glad you enjoyed yours. We had a bumper crop of blackberries this year."

"Oh, I'm a big fan of dessert," Jacqueline replied.

"Yet you're so slim." Olive seemed surprised and impressed. "You must have wonderful genes."

Laurel took a surreptitious look at her watch. When, oh when, would this dinner from hell finally end? One thing was for certain. She now had a lot more sympathy for Winnie. In fact, she could hardly wait to call her friend. They certainly had a lot to talk about.

Corb knew his mother had had good intentions when she invited Jacqueline to dinner. But he sure wished she'd given him a heads-up about it. Having Laurel and Jacqueline at the same dinner table was damned awkward. Now he was obliged to make polite chitchat with his ex-girlfriend, all the while dodging cutting glances from the woman he was planning to marry.

It was an exhausting balancing act for him.

And he was pretty sure Laurel was feeling pretty miserable, too.

So he wasn't surprised when, the moment she'd finished her last sip of tea, Laurel put down her cup and made a move to get up.

"I really should be running since we open the café at the crack of dawn."

"My chores come early, too," Jacqueline agreed, folding her napkin and placing it next to her empty plate.

"Oh, but you can stay a few more minutes, can't you? It looks like we're going to have a beautiful sunset. I'll make a second pot of tea and we can have a glass of brandy to go with it…."

Corb didn't think his mother realized that her invitation sounded like it was meant for Jacqueline, only. He got out of his chair and went over to Laurel, who was already up from the table.

"Stay?" he asked. Maybe once Jacqueline left, they would have a chance to deliver their news to his mother. But Laurel just shook her head.

"It was a lovely meal. Thank you so much Mrs. L—"

Suddenly her hand went to her mouth and her eyes widened. Having experienced this once before, Corb had a good idea what was happening next.

"This way." He took her elbow and led her to the patio doors. "First door to the left," he instructed as she raced ahead of him into the house. He intended to follow and make sure she was okay, but his mother stopped him with a question.

"I hope that wasn't what I think it was?"

Holy crap. Had she guessed so easily? He paused to scrutinize her expression, which seemed peeved and slightly scornful.

"I've heard this is how those city girls stay thin."

Corb was shocked when he realized what she was thinking. Shocked and a little angry, too. "Laurel isn't bulimic, Mom. She's pregnant."

As soon as the words were out, he wanted to yank them back in. But unfortunately a conversation with his mother wasn't like catch-and-release fishing. There was no stepping back, so he might as well keep blundering forward.

Taking advantage of Olive's and Jacqueline's stunned silence, he spilled out the rest of it.

"I'm the father and we're getting married."

Chapter 8

"Laurel, you in there?"

It was Corb at the door. Finally. What had he been doing all this time? Laurel rinsed her face, then blotted it dry with a tissue rather than use one of the immaculate white towels hanging near the sink.

Seriously. White linen hand towels? On a ranch?

"Laurel? How are you?"

Poor guy was starting to sound quite worried.

"It's a good news, bad news scenario, Corb."

"What's the good news?"

"Whoever cleans the toilet bowls around here does a real nice job."

"That would be Bonny." He paused. "And the bad news?"

"I'm still pregnant." She released the lock on the door and let him open it.

He put his hands on her shoulders and studied her face like it was the periodic table and he was getting quizzed on it in ten minutes. "Is there any situation where you won't make a wisecrack?"

Then he didn't give her a chance to answer, just hugged her nice and tight. "You're so pale. I'm sorry you have to go through this. Guys really get off easy when it comes to making babies, don't they?"

"So far I'd say yes. And I have a feeling the hardest part is yet to come." Delivery. She hadn't even thought about that yet. And now wasn't a good time to start.

He laughed and eased back from her a little. "Now my turn for the good news/bad news routine."

"What do you mean?" She felt a lot better after that hug. Seriously, Corb should get a patent on his hugs, they were that awesome.

"Bad news first? When you got sick all of a sudden, Mom took it into her head that you had some kind of eating disorder."

Laurel had to think for a moment before she realized what he was saying. "She thought I was bulimic?"

"Yeah."

"That's crazy. People with bulimia sneak off to the washroom to empty their stomachs. They don't make a big scene and do the twenty-yard dash."

"Well, Mom's never actually known anyone with bulimia. She just reads about it in magazines and stuff. But of course I couldn't have her thinking that about you, so I—"

"Told her I wasn't feeling well," Laurel said hopefully.

"More like mentioned you were pregnant."

Oh, Lord. Laurel closed her eyes. Olive's impression

of her had undoubtedly fallen another couple of notches after that announcement.

"On the plus side, we don't need to worry about breaking our news to her anymore."

Laurel's eyes flashed open. "What else did you tell her?"

"Pretty much everything. That I was the father. And that we were getting married." Corb's words flew out so fast she could hardly follow what he was saying.

When the meaning finally hit her, she was sorry it had. "Wow. Not exactly subtle, are you?"

He looked contrite. And he did a good job with it, she had to admit, managing to look so adorable it was difficult for her to be truly angry with him.

"That was a lot to hit her with at once. How did she react?"

"She fainted."

"Seriously? Your mother fainted?"

"Yup." Corb scratched the top of his head, as if the whole thing puzzled him more than he could say, then gave her another contrite smile. "I caught her before she hit the ground, so that was good."

"That *is* good," Laurel agreed, thinking of the stone patio. "Where is she now?"

"On the sofa. Resting."

"Oh my. And what did Jacqueline make of all this?"

"Well, I think she's given up on Mother's matchmaking plan, that's for sure."

Laurel put a hand to her mouth to stop a very odd inclination to giggle.

"As soon as Mother's eyes were fluttering open, Jacqueline took off. She's probably on her cell phone right now, telling everyone within forty miles of Coffee Creek about our news."

"Oh, dear. I need to call Winnie. And you should talk to Jackson and the others." She didn't want Winnie to hear about her plans to marry Corb via the grapevine. And he probably didn't want his siblings finding out their news that way, either.

She covered her face with her hands. "Oh, Lord. What a mess. Are we doing the right thing?"

"No doubt about it." Corb's voice was firm and assured. "Our family will be onside once they've had a chance to absorb everything. But I don't think now is a good time for us to talk to my mother."

Laurel was relieved. She didn't feel up to talking to Olive, either. "I agree. If you don't mind, I'd like to go home now."

"Sure you're okay to drive?" When she nodded he took her hand. "I'll walk you out to your car."

"Thank you." She could hardly wait to leave. Hopefully Corb was right and in time his mother would adjust to the news and become, if not warm, at least a little more cordial.

Corb saw Laurel off with some misgivings. He could tell she was weak and tired and he would have preferred to be the one driving. But she'd insisted on bringing her own vehicle and if he drove her back in that, then he'd be stuck in town with no way home.

So he waved her off, and stood in the driveway watching as the little white SUV—with the decal of a steaming cup of coffee in the back window—booted up the gravel drive on the way to the main road.

Not until the dust had settled did he head back into

the house. He wasn't looking forward to talking to his mother. But it had to be done.

Olive was still on the sofa where he'd left her, sitting now, and gazing pensively out at the land. He settled in a chair near the window, resting his arms on his thighs and leaning forward.

"Sorry for hitting you over the head with all that, Mom. We meant to tell you together. And gradually." He'd lost his cool when his mother had called Laurel bulimic. And Corb didn't lose control often, so he didn't have much experience in reining himself in.

"I still can't believe it." She shook her head slowly. "Can it really be true? Are you sure she's pregnant?"

He nodded. "I drove her to the doctor's office myself and was with her when they gave her the news."

"And you're the father?"

Corb hesitated. "Yes."

"But—how can this be? You hardly know this woman."

Corb was sure his mother would find it even more unbelievable if he confessed that he didn't remember sleeping with Laurel. Not that he was going to do such a thing. His mother knew he didn't remember the accident, but he hadn't told her that his memory loss extended to the week prior, as well. When it came to his mother, Corb had a habit of minimalizing problems.

But it was hard to make light of this one, and he could see why she was so doubtful. He'd felt the same, at first.

Still, he'd found Laurel's underwear in his bed, which made it pretty clear that they'd slept together at least.

Not that that constituted proof of paternity, but his gut told him that trusting Laurel was the right thing to do. Not the least because the alternative—losing out on a chance to be a part of his child's life—was just too much to risk.

Realizing his mother was going to need some convincing, however, he moved to the sofa and started the story as Laurel had relayed it to him.

"I fell for her as soon as I met her at the airport. With all the focus on Brock and Winnie in the week before the wedding, Laurel and I found plenty of time to…be together."

There. That was as blunt as he could put it. And by the frown marring his mother's forehead, he could tell she'd found it plenty blunt as it was.

"So, Laurel is about two months along?"

He nodded.

"Oh, Corb. And you're absolutely sure that you're…" She let the sentence trail delicately, as if even speaking the words was too much for her.

He nodded again.

"But you will insist on DNA testing when the baby is born?"

"Mom, no. I'm not going to ask that of Laurel, and you sure as hell better not suggest anything like that to her, either."

His mother had been stronger the past few days and it was time he set her straight on this. "I won't have Laurel insulted like that."

The words had needed to be said, but he couldn't help wondering if he'd been too harsh when he noticed tears glimmering in his mother's eyes.

"Son, I so wish your father was here right now to give you advice. But I have to ask. Are you certain that marriage is…the right solution?"

"What other solution is there?"

"I'm not suggesting you shirk your duty. There are such things as child support payments."

Corb couldn't believe she was saying this. He'd been certain that once she understood the situation his mother would stand by his decision. That she, like him, would believe it was the honorable course of action to take.

"I just worry about the long-term feasibility of your marriage. Of all my children, you're the one who feels the strongest connection to the land. You could only be happy here, on Coffee Creek Ranch."

He wouldn't argue that point. "And this is where we plan to live. At the cabin. At some point we'll add on an extra bedroom or two…." Something he hadn't had time to discuss with Laurel yet. But he would.

"Are you sure she'll be happy? She may have grown up on a farm, but she's a city girl now, Corb. And not just any city, but New York. After a while, aren't you afraid she'll get bored of our simple way of life?"

"We don't get bored. Why should she?" But Corb knew his mother had a point and it was one that he'd already found vaguely troubling.

"You and I love the cattle ranching business," his mother said gently. "And Jacqueline does, too, which is why I invited her to dinner, as I'm sure you've guessed."

"Mom—"

She put up a hand to stop his objection. "B.J. and Cassidy both moved away because they wanted more. And they're family. Don't you think it's likely that eventually Laurel will feel the same way?"

He wanted to argue. But he had no facts to counter with. So, miserably he sat there and let his mother continue.

"You've only known her a few months—and most

of that time you were in bed recovering from the accident. How can you possibly know her well enough to take this big step?"

"I do know her. Look how she's stuck by Winnie since the accident. Not many people would drop everything to help a friend in trouble. She's a good person and besides—"

He moved over to the sofa, putting a hand on his mother's shoulder and looking her square in the eyes. "You said you wished Dad were here to give me his advice. Well, I don't need to hear him say the words to know what he would tell me. Family comes first. I must have heard him say those words a hundred times."

"That's true."

"Laurel's unborn child is going to be a Lambert, Mom. One of us. If I have to marry her to keep her and the baby here in Coffee Creek, that's exactly what I'm going to do."

Corb made his mother a cup of tea before he left her for the night. It was almost dark now and the amber glow from the sunset was reflecting in his rearview mirror as he drove from the main house down the graveled lake road.

He was pretty sure he'd convinced his mother that he was taking the right course here.

But he wished he could understand why he didn't feel more at peace about it himself.

Clearly he and Laurel had the sexual attraction thing happening. He couldn't look at her without wanting her. And she must feel the same way, or she wouldn't have spent that night with him.

Besides, he liked her. Really liked her. She was fun to be with, interesting. And a good person.

His mother's well-intentioned concerns notwithstanding, he thought they had a damn good shot at making their marriage work.

So why the knot in the pit of his stomach?

He didn't think it was Brock's death or his lost week of memories that was plaguing him. No, this feeling was more like the awful churning in his gut that he would get when he was a boy and knew he'd done something wrong.

But he hadn't done wrong here.

Oh, making that mistake with condoms had been wrong. But he'd taken responsibility for that.

As he approached Brock's place, Corb eased off the accelerator and craned his neck for a look at the porch. No Sky. Interesting. He continued to his own place, where he found the border collie lounging on his porch.

So Laurel had been right. All Sky had wanted was the chance to check out Brock's place. Whether to make sure he was truly gone, or as a final gesture of farewell, Corb couldn't be sure.

He guessed Sky, so smart, and so tuned in to the feelings of this family, was capable of both.

"Good girl, Sky. You know where home is now, don't you, girl?"

She scrambled to her feet, gave him a good sniff, then looked hopefully at the empty food bowl next to the door.

"I'll get right on that," he promised her as he let himself inside.

He was glad that Sky was no longer keeping vigil at Brock's cabin, but it made him kind of sad, too. Life was going on, and while that was only natural, it still kind of hurt to see it happen.

* * *

"Winnie? I hope I'm not calling too late?" Laurel was cuddled under the covers of the pullout couch, a cup of peppermint licorice tea beside her. Even though her friend had offered the use of her bedroom, Laurel hadn't made the transition. Moving into the bedroom would have seemed too permanent. Besides, she'd been hoping that Winnie would get the all-clear from her doctor soon and come home.

But that wasn't likely to happen for a long time.

"It's only nine," Winnie scoffed. "Of course it isn't too late. Am I ever glad you've called. At first it was nice having Mom fuss over me. But I've caught up on all my favorite shows, my eyes are strained from reading and I've got calluses from knitting too much…."

For Laurel, who'd lost her own mother so young, getting fussed over didn't sound like something she could ever tire of. Especially not with a mother like Adele, who knew how to be caring and supportive without crossing the line into meddlesome and manipulative.

Now, if Olive was her mother, that would be a different question….

"There have been no dull moments here, trust me."

"Did you book your flight back to New York?"

"I did. And I just canceled it."

"Why?" Winnie asked, her voice animated with curiosity.

Laurel took a deep breath. "Because I'm staying in Coffee Creek. Corb asked me to marry him."

"Wow."

"Yeah. It is kind of a wow thing, isn't it?"

Winnie's reaction was reassuring. "Oh, I'm glad! It's

going to be great to have you in Coffee Creek. Our kids are going to grow up to be best friends, just like we are."

Those were things Laurel wanted, too. So very much.

"I'd love to live close to you again, Winnie. But—it's weird, isn't it? I mean, *you* were the one who was supposed to be living on Coffee Creek Ranch. Not to mention have Olive Lambert for your mother-in-law."

Winnie laughed. "I'm guessing you've seen her other side by now? The one she only shows prospective daughters-in-law that she doesn't approve of?"

"She invited Corb's ex-girlfriend to dinner tonight. Totally fawned all over her. And froze me out."

Winnie groaned sympathetically. "Sounds like Olive. Did Corb notice?"

"Not really."

"Brock, either. Those boys have a real blind side when it comes to their mother."

Laurel agreed, uneasily. Marrying Corb meant signing up for a lifetime with Olive, too. Now that was something grim to think about.

"Have you told your boss at the magazine that you won't be coming back?"

"Not yet. Corb just proposed. It's going to take a bit of time for all of this to feel real."

"It must be hard when you just got that promotion, huh? I know how much that job meant to you."

"It really was a great job. But getting pregnant was going to change everything, even if I hadn't accepted Corb's proposal. First there'd be maternity leave and then the problem of finding child care when I was ready to return to work."

"Having a baby makes life a whole lot more complicated," Winnie agreed. "I hate being away from the

Cinnamon Stick, but I won't come back until I know it's the right thing for me and my baby."

"I'm glad, Winnie. You have your priorities straight."

"At the same time, I don't want you to feel locked into managing the café for me while I'm gone. Anytime you want to shut it up and go live with Corb on the ranch, please do so."

"Thanks, Winnie. I must admit there are times when I wish I had more freedom. But I can't imagine not having a job of any kind. Plus I worry about the staff. Eugenia has her catering, at least. But Dawn has an internet shopping habit to support."

Winnie laughed.

"And what about Vince. Didn't you tell me that this job has helped him stay sober?"

"It's true. Maybe one solution would be to hire another staff member, so you wouldn't have to continue to work so hard."

"I'll have a staff meeting and we'll talk about it," Laurel promised. "As long as you follow doctor's orders, and take care of yourself."

"Will do." Then, just before they said goodbye for the evening, Winnie added one last comment. "And Laurel? Congratulations on your engagement. I always thought Corb would be perfect for you. It wasn't a coincidence that I asked him to pick you up at the airport."

The next morning at ten o'clock, Laurel was presented with the perfect opportunity for an impromptu staff meeting. Vince was nearing the end of his shift and Eugenia had just shown up for hers, when Dawn came in to see if she could get an advance from her next paycheck.

Business was at a lull, so Laurel made the decision to flip over the Closed sign and lock the door for fifteen minutes.

"Look, guys," she said without preamble. "We have some decisions to make. Winnie's health is still an issue. She won't be coming back in the foreseeable future."

Dawn stopped chewing her gum—a habit she never indulged in when she was working, thank goodness—and looked worried. "Is she okay?"

"She will be." Laurel avoided looking at Eugenia, hoping the older woman wouldn't share her suspicions about Winnie being pregnant. It wouldn't be right for the staff at the Cinnamon Stick to hear about Winnie and Brock's baby before the Lambert family did.

Fortunately, Eugenia didn't say a word.

"Which leaves us with the problem of how to keep the café running during her absence. Unless you all just want to close shop until she returns?"

"Not an option." Vince looked grim. "I'll work a twelve-hour day, six days a week, if need be."

Laurel had never heard him say so much at one time. Which only went to show how much this job did mean to him.

"I'm sure Winnie would appreciate that, Vince. But that shouldn't be necessary. We could always hire a fourth staff member. Or…divvy up the extra hours between all four of us."

"*I'd* love some extra hours," Dawn said.

Eugenia was less enthusiastic. "I could handle a *few* more."

"Put me down for two extra hours every day," Vince said. "I can take care of some of the supply ordering and bill paying."

"Awesome. You guys are the greatest." Laurel got out the calendar and without much fuss, they were able to come up with a working schedule that would keep the café open and suit everyone's needs.

Once she'd finished writing down everything, Laurel gave her staff a grateful smile. "Thanks for pitching in this way. I know Winnie is going to be very grateful."

Business was brisk at the Cinnamon Stick from eleven until one-thirty. Then, just as they were experiencing their second lull of the day, an unexpected customer popped in. Jacqueline was dressed in jeans and a simple T-shirt, but even in such everyday wear she looked stunning.

Laurel gave her a closer look, searching for flaws. Unless it was possible to have teeth that were too white, she couldn't find any.

Then she scolded herself. Jealousy was a very unattractive emotion. *Be friendly. Smile.*

"Hi, Jacqueline."

"Hey, Laurel. Beautiful day, isn't it?"

Jacqueline slid up on a stool and Laurel marveled anew at the length of her legs. When Laurel sat on those stools, her toes barely reached the ground. Jacqueline's boots—a serviceable tan color—were planted flat on the wood plank floor.

"I want to apologize about last night," Jacqueline announced.

"You do?"

"If I'd known Corb had a new girlfriend I would never have accepted Olive's invitation."

"Right. Well…" It was odd hearing herself described

as Corb's girlfriend. But she was more than that now. She was his fiancée.

"I wasn't even expecting Corb to be there," Jacqueline continued. "Olive made it sound like it would be just the two of us and she seemed so sad and lonely, I couldn't say no."

Not only beautiful, but nice, too. Laurel could feel her smile tighten.

Then Jacqueline leaned in a little closer and lowered her voice. "Also, I wanted to reassure you that I haven't told anyone your news. Not about the baby or the engagement. Though I must admit both caught me by surprise."

Put Corb and herself in that camp, too.

"Thanks, Jacqueline. I appreciate your discretion. Let me get you a coffee and a cinnamon bun for the road."

"I won't say no."

While Laurel was pouring the coffee, Eugenia poked her head through the opening between the kitchen and the counter. She'd been in since eleven o'clock, first helping with the lunch hour, then making the soup for tomorrow's menu.

"Hello, stranger," she said cheerfully. "Haven't seen much of you lately."

"It's been a crazy summer." Jacqueline smiled ruefully. "Dad's leased a bunch more land and is working on expanding our herd. Not much time for making unnecessary trips to town."

"All work and no play…" Eugenia wagged a finger at her. It was clear that she liked Jacqueline and Laurel could understand why. Ten minutes later the other woman was on her way, having left Laurel lots to think about.

Why hadn't Corb wanted to marry her? She seemed perfect to Laurel. She was beautiful, not to mention kind and friendly. And she came from a ranching family so she would fit in at Coffee Creek Ranch perfectly.

No wonder Olive had invited her to dinner. If Laurel was Corb's mother, that's who she'd want her son to marry, too.

Corb called Laurel fifteen minutes after closing to see how she was doing. She'd just locked the door when her cell phone chimed.

"I'm fine," she assured him. It was true her stomach was queasy, but that was a feeling she was learning to live with.

Still, she was touched that he'd thought to call. As soon as she'd seen his name and number light up on the display, she'd felt her spirits lift. "Guess who dropped by to talk this afternoon?"

"Jacqueline?"

"Right on the first try," she said, a little surprised.

"She came by the ranch to see me, too."

Laurel's heart lurched a little to hear that. Jacqueline hadn't said anything to *her* about talking to Corb. "Oh, yeah? What time?"

"About an hour ago. I could smell cinnamon on her breath, so I figured she'd been to the café, first."

"You were close enough to smell her breath?"

He laughed. "Nah. I was kidding about that. She told me she'd spoken to you, apologizing for her awkward appearance at dinner last night. I told her it wasn't her fault—she had nothing to be sorry for. She was just trying to be kind to a grieving woman."

"Right." But Laurel wondered. Had the trip to the ranch really been necessary? Maybe Jacqueline's intentions weren't quite so admirable as she'd thought. After all, she'd dated Corb for five years, hoping the relationship would lead to marriage. It couldn't be easy for her to see him agreeing to marry someone else after such a short period of time.

"I imagine she told you that she's keeping our little secret?" Laurel asked.

"She did. Which is decent of her."

"Yes." She waited to see if he had anything more to say about Jacqueline. He was quiet for so long she wondered if their connection had been lost.

"Corb?"

"I'm still here."

"The line sounds funny."

"That's because I'm using my Bluetooth."

"So you're in your Jeep?"

"I am."

"Driving somewhere?"

"It's what I usually do in my Jeep."

Was she silly to hope? But she couldn't stop herself. She went to the window and parted the wooden slats for a view of the street, just in time to see his dusty Jeep slide into a parking space near the front door.

"Let me in?" he asked. And then the line went dead.

Laurel smiled and closed her phone, tucking it into the pocket of her jeans before unbolting the door and opening it wide.

Corb took one step, then gathered her in his arms and kissed her. Thoroughly. Not sweetly or tentatively, but as if he had only one thing on his mind and it didn't involve clothing.

He kicked the door shut with his booted foot, then kissed her again, somehow managing to release the clip holding up her hair at the same time.

"Wow, Corb…"

He smiled. "I was just thinking…. We did get the green light from the doctor…."

"That's true."

"Then how about we go upstairs?"

Her body was on fire. She needed no persuading. Taking his hand she led him up the staircase and into the upper apartment. She'd slept late that morning and hadn't bothered folding up the pullout coach. Or straightening the bedding.

"I'm sorry about the mess."

"What mess?" His eyes locked with hers, and then he kissed her again.

Chapter 9

Corb hadn't driven to town planning to make love to Laurel. After Jacqueline's surprise visit to the ranch, his mother had cornered him for another little talk.

She'd helped him see that an elopement wasn't what the family needed right now. And his plan had been to open a discussion with Laurel about it.

But somehow, when she'd opened that door, kissing her had moved to the top of his agenda.

And he'd been blown away.

All fine and well to talk about getting married because it was "the right thing" to do.

But here was the baser truth. He wanted her.

He'd made a baby with this woman. Shouldn't he know what it felt like to make love to her?

And when she led him willingly upstairs, all rational thought left him. Maybe, in a corner of his mind, he hoped having sex with her would bring back memories of the night they'd conceived their baby.

It didn't happen, though.

He felt as if he was exploring the lush, magical wonders of her body for the very first time. Only at the end, when he was gazing into her flushed and smiling face, was there a whisper in the back of his head. *I've seen her like this before.*

He closed his eyes, waiting for more memories to come flooding in. When that didn't happen, he opened his eyes to find her watching him intently as if waiting for him to say something. But he stayed silent not wanting to admit that it hadn't worked. The past was still locked away in some isolated section of his brain.

When he gathered her into his arms to hold her close, he knew that he had done this the first time, as well. He felt her soft face pressed against his chest and he wondered what she was thinking.

And an odd question occurred to him.

How had he stacked up…compared to the first time?

"Corb?"

He hadn't had a headache all day. But suddenly he felt the familiar tension in his skull. He was happy holding her. Very happy. But he didn't want to talk. He didn't want to admit that even after making love to her, he still couldn't remember the time before.

He considered pretending he was asleep. But Laurel had already shifted up on her elbow and was looking at him. He studied her beautiful eyes, golden-brown and flecked with copper. His gaze shifted lower, to the freckles on her nose. Also copper. He kissed them.

"Are you okay?" he asked.

"Very okay. But I need to talk to you about something."

His gut tightened.

"I know you can't remember this—"

The tension in his head turned to a pulsing pain.

"—but that first week we spent together, you talked quite a bit about Jacqueline."

Jacqueline? Why the hell was she talking about Jacqueline?

"You sounded so done with her. So sure that you'd made the right decision not to marry her."

God help him, he had *no* idea where she was going with this. "It's true. Don't tell me you have a problem with that?"

"The only problem I have is believing you. I hadn't met her back then. Now that I have—well, Corb, frankly she's gorgeous. And nice and friendly. Plus she's a rancher, just like you. Wouldn't she fit in perfectly as your wife?"

He propped his head up and stared at her. "Did my mother somehow brainwash you into asking that?"

"Of course not."

"Are you trying to get out of our engagement? If so, just tell me. You don't have to try to rekindle my feelings for Jacqueline."

"No, no." She placed her hand against the side of his face. "I don't want out. I was afraid you felt trapped. Even before I met Jacqueline I was worried about that."

He took her hand from his face, and kissed it. "I imagine you feel trapped sometimes by the baby growing in your body."

The look she gave him was inscrutable. He wondered if she was thinking about her life back in New

York City. He would never know exactly what she was giving up by staying in Montana and marrying him.

He wished he could have seen her there, even just once. To see how well she had fit in, how happy she'd been.

But maybe it was better this way. He could pretend that he was giving her everything she wanted, and not just selfishly taking over her life so he could be near their baby.

"So we're *both* trapped," she said. "Is that what you're saying?"

"I'm just being honest. You know we wouldn't be talking marriage if it wasn't for the baby. To say that we're trapped might be going too far. How does 'gently corralled' sound?"

Awful. It sounded just awful to Laurel. But she didn't say that. What was the point? Corb wasn't trying to hurt her. He was just being perfectly logical.

Which she hated.

She had wanted him to tell her he loved her. He'd been looking into her eyes as if he could see her very soul, and she'd longed to hear him say the words that were all but bursting to be free from her heart.

But he hadn't and so she'd held her words in, too. It hurt, though, knowing that she could well spend the rest of her life waiting for something that he might never tell her.

What would that be like? Living her life with a man who didn't really love her?

She already knew the answer to that.

"Laurel?" His voice was gentle. "Are you *sure* you're okay?"

She desperately wanted to say something funny, to ease the tension and take his focus off her. But for once her sense of humor let her down.

"I'm good, Corb. But hungry. We pregnant women need to eat." At least she'd managed to lighten the mood a little. She could feel his muscles relax and see the relief in his eyes.

"Now that you mention food, my original plan was to take you out to dinner. I know a great place in Lewistown. Want to give it a try?"

"Gosh, I can't remember the last night I went out on the town. That sounds wonderful."

He got out of bed, giving her a nice view of his muscular cowboy body—still leaner than it had been two months ago. He hadn't put back all the weight he'd lost after the accident. She knew the story behind the scar on the left side of his abdomen. Also knew that when he turned around, his butt would be firm and round.

She'd tried to be subtle, but he noticed her checking him out. "What do you think?" He flexed his biceps. "Do I pass inspection?"

"Hmm." She tilted her head and put a finger to her lips. "Quite nice, but a little on the skinny side…"

He whooped, then tackled her, taking her right back onto the bed, where he leaned over her and kissed her firmly on the lips. "I may be scrawny, but I'm tough."

"Uncle," she conceded. When he'd released her she turned her back to him and slipped on her bra and top. She knew she had nice curves, but no one would ever call her skinny and she wasn't about to parade her body in front of him to invite his commentary.

But as she was zipping up her jeans, he came from behind her for a hug and planted a kiss on her neck. "You're a beautiful woman. And I feel like a very lucky man."

It wasn't *I love you.*

But it was very nice.

Corb took her to a restaurant that specialized in Montana beef and they both ordered a steak and salad. As they waited for their meals to arrive, Corb broached the subject of their wedding.

"What do you think about getting married right away?"

Laurel felt thrilled and panicked at the same time. "Really?"

"It's a good time for me right now. In another month I'll be so busy moving cattle I won't have time to think."

But was he taking enough time to think now? "We could wait until winter to get married. Would that be a better time?"

"I'm not a fan of waiting. Getting cold feet?"

"Not at all." Honestly? Yes. But she took comfort from the fact that Corb seemed so sure they were doing the right thing. "Want me to go online and look for flights to Vegas?"

He was quiet so long that she wondered if he'd heard her. But finally, he spoke. "About that. Are you dead set on eloping? Because I talked to my mother today. And she has other ideas."

"Oh, does she?"

He nodded, not seeming to sense the new tension in her voice. "Weddings are family matters. You don't mind if we let her have a little input?"

Yes, was her first, gut reaction. *I would mind.* But if she was hoping to have a decent relationship with her mother-in-law, it wouldn't be wise to antagonize her from the start.

"I suppose we could talk to Olive." What could it really hurt? With the recent death in the family, surely her mother-in-law would see that a quiet elopement was the best way to proceed.

After they finished dinner, Corb encouraged Laurel to order tea and dessert. She was surprised by this because he'd started checking his watch so often she'd assumed he was in a hurry to leave.

After the waiter headed for the kitchen with her request for peppermint tea and chocolate mousse, and Corb's coffee and brandy order, Laurel leaned across the table.

"Tell me more about what happens on a ranch during the fall season."

If she was going to be a rancher's wife then she had a lot to learn.

"Once we have the cattle in the pastures close to home, we have to sort and wean the cows and calves, doctor them up and get them preg tested."

She assumed he meant "pregnancy" tested. "Why do you do that?"

"To have an idea when the calves will be coming next spring—sometimes it's March, but it can be as late as April or May."

Her chores on the farm as a young girl had included feeding the chickens and collecting the eggs and that was pretty much it. Her father and his hired man had taken care of the fields and the cattle.

"Do you think you'd like to take an active role on the ranch? My mother always did."

"I'd need a lot of training, I guess."

He gave her a warm, approving smile. "I have a feeling you'll catch on quick."

Something beyond her field of vision seemed to catch his eye then. His intimate smile vanished, and he rose from his seat. Laurel noticed a woman at a nearby table glance at him, then look again.

Lick your lips, why don't you?

But Laurel didn't blame the woman for admiring the view. Corb was the finest-looking man in the room and any woman with a pulse would notice.

Laurel shifted to see who Corb was looking at. And wasn't it Olive, dressed in a tailored pantsuit and clutching a black patent bag. As she neared their table Corb commandeered a third chair.

"Hey, Mom, why don't you join us? We just ordered dessert."

Everything happened so fast that Laurel hardly knew what to think. Had the meeting been planned? She couldn't imagine why else Olive would have happened by their table at this moment.

But it turned out that Olive did have an explanation.

"I hope you don't mind if I interrupt, Laurel? I just finished a business dinner with an old friend of Bob's. He's interested in purchasing horses and he'd rather not wait for our fall auction."

"Not at all," Laurel said, while Corb signaled the waiter, who noticed the new addition to the table and quickly came to take Olive's order.

"Black coffee is fine for me." Olive gave her son a warm smile, then shifted her gaze to Laurel. "I understand congratulations are in order, dear."

Tacking on that "dear" at the end of her sentence was

a brilliant touch, Laurel thought. Corb noticed, too, and smiled. She could guess what he was thinking.

Good. Mom's warming up to her.

Laurel wished it could be true. But she had her doubts. She still felt a chill every time Corb's mother looked in her direction.

Never had a smile been so difficult to force. "Thank you."

Conversation paused as beverages and Laurel's chocolate mousse were delivered to the table. As soon as the waiter was gone, Olive said, "A baby. *And* a wedding. Quite a lot to celebrate. Too bad you can't drink or I'd order a bottle of champagne."

"It is exciting," Laurel agreed. "But also overwhelming—for me, and it must seem so to you, too."

"Well." Olive arched her finely drawn brows, which drew attention to her beautifully made-up gray-green eyes. "These things happen when we're not careful."

Laurel shot a glance at Corb, who stepped in quickly. "It's more my fault than Laurel's, Mom."

She was glad he'd defended her, but wished he'd simply declared the topic too private to discuss.

"Our baby may not have been planned, but he or she will be loved and wanted," Laurel said.

"But of course. By all of us. But first we must have the wedding."

What was that look passing between mother and son? Worried that she might be losing control of the conversation, Laurel stepped in quickly. "Given the unfortunate timing with your family's recent loss and everything, Corb and I thought a discreet elopement would be the best."

Olive couldn't argue with such a sensible plan, could she? And yet, she did.

"For sure, the timing could be better, but we're talking about the first wedding in our family. A big celebration is out of the question, but we simply must have a dinner for immediate family. Imagine how hurt Cassidy and B.J. would feel if they were excluded."

Laurel doubted that. Cassidy and B.J. had busy, happy lives of their own. And both of them liked to keep trips back to the family ranch down to the minimum. She hadn't known the family for long, but she had at least that much figured out.

No, this had to be about what Olive wanted.

And Corb?

She studied her cowboy's expression and wasn't mollified at his artless smile. He was pretending this had nothing to do with him. But she still couldn't help suspecting he had set her up.

"We could always have a party later, after the wedding." She wasn't giving up on the elopement plans without a fight. She and Corb *needed* that time, for just the two of them. Especially since he'd already explained there could be no honeymoon.

If they waited until later, after all the fall work was done, she'd be five months pregnant. And she wanted some time alone with him before that stage.

"It's *your* wedding," Olive said. "And you should certainly do whatever you prefer. I just thought that it would be nice for the family to have a happy reason to get together."

Olive lowered her eyes then, but not before Laurel had seen the sheen of unshed tears. Corb had noticed, too, because he reached across the table to cover his mother's hand with his.

"We aren't that set on our plans, are we?" His eyes were pleading with Laurel. *Look how upset my Mom is,* they seemed to say. *Won't you do this to make her happy?*

"Nothing is booked yet," she agreed, begrudging each word as she saw her lovely weekend with Corb dissolving into a gathering out at the ranch with his family.

"Well, then." Olive batted her tears away and produced a tentative smile. "That's fine then. You can get married at the ranch and save some money and we'll have a nice family get-together at the same time. How does that sound?"

Laurel shrugged and left the talking to Corb, who was quick to concur with his mother. Next thing she knew, Olive had removed her PDA from her purse and was looking at dates. "If you want to steer clear of the fall roundup, may I suggest Sunday of next week?"

"So soon?" Laurel voice squeaked, betraying her nervousness.

"Why not take the plunge and get it over with?" Corb countered.

Wow. How romantic. Really, Corb? Take the plunge and get it over with? "What about *two* weeks from next Sunday?" She didn't really care about the timing. She just wanted to feel like she had *some* input on the planning.

Olive considered the request, then nodded, as if it was her place to approve the date. "If it's a nice day, you can say your vows by the lake."

The fall colors would be at their peak by then. They'd have beautiful wedding pictures, at least. "Okay."

"And we can have lunch after, on the patio."

"I could ask Eugenia to cater," Laurel suggested.

"Whatever you want, dear." Olive's smile couldn't have been sweeter.

Laurel reached for her cup of lukewarm tea and downed half of it. Silently, she envied Corb the coffee and brandy that he'd ordered. If ever she could have used a drink, now was the time.

She'd just gone her second round with her mother-in-law-to-be. And come out the loser, again.

Chapter 10

The next week passed in a whirl of planning and organizing. On Monday Corb and Laurel headed back to Lewistown to get their wedding license. They also purchased wedding rings—matching bands of eighteen-karat yellow gold.

On the drive back to Coffee Creek, Corb filled her in on how his calls to his siblings had gone.

Cassidy and B.J. hadn't been as surprised as Corb expected. He smiled at her ruefully. "I guess they remember all the stuff that I forget."

Laurel squeezed his hand, wanting him to think it didn't matter. She'd given up hoping, at this stage, that he'd ever remember anything of that special first week. And he must have done the same.

"Can they come?" she asked.

"Cassidy said she wouldn't miss it. B.J. was supposed

to be heading out to a rodeo in Arizona, but he said he would withdraw his name."

Like Jackson, Corb's oldest brother, B.J., was a bit of an enigma to Laurel. Unlike Jackson, though, who tended to hang back at family gatherings, B.J. had a natural air of authority that she supposed came with being the firstborn. "How long has B.J. been on the rodeo circuit?"

"Since he was eighteen. Dad and Mom were both pretty choked up when he announced he was going on the road. He's made quite a name for himself, including several World Championships. But he hasn't had a fixed address for almost half his life now." Corb shook his head as if such a thing was unimaginable to him. "I keep thinking he's going to get tired and want to come home, but it hasn't happened yet."

"I bet your mother would be happy if it did."

"We all would. Especially with Brock gone."

"Do you think there's any chance your sister will come back to Coffee Creek when she finishes her degree?"

"She says no, but I have my doubts. You should see the way Cassidy is with animals. She has a special gift that'll be wasted if she decides to work at some accounting office all her life."

"Maybe she has a gift for accounting, too."

Corb gave her a look that told her what he thought about that idea. But maybe it wasn't her natural talents that were driving Cassidy from Coffee Creek. If Olive was *her* mother, Laurel figured she'd be looking to put at least a hundred miles between them, too.

But that wasn't kind. She had to stop thinking of Olive in such a negative way. The woman might have her flaws, but she was Corb's mother.

As they turned onto Coffee Creek's Main Street, Laurel asked if he had told Jackson about the wedding yet.

Corb's forehead creased with worry. "Been meaning to. But it's like the guy is avoiding me. I am for sure going to track him down tomorrow morning."

He pulled up to the Cinnamon Stick, leaning over the gear shift to give her a kiss. "You haven't invited Winnie yet, have you?"

"I'm going to call her tonight," she promised, giving him one more smile before hurrying back to relieve the staff at the café.

Corb started to drive away, then paused and unrolled the passenger window. "Almost forgot to tell you. Mom says she set aside a dress for you at Sapphire Blue in Lewistown. Said to tell you that it would look great on you."

Really? Olive was selecting her wedding dress now?

Corb must have seen that she was annoyed. He gave her that *please be kind to my mother* look again. "Just try it on, sugar. Okay? You don't have to buy it if you don't like it."

When Laurel called Winnie later that evening, she vented about the way Olive had taken over her wedding, right down to choosing her dress.

"You have to stand up to her. Or she'll walk over you for the rest of your life."

"I know. And believe me, I'd love to tell her where to shove her wedding plans. But then Corb gives me this look that I call his *please be nice to my mother look*. Honestly, Winnie, I can't resist him when he turns on his charm."

Winnie laughed. "Oh, you have it bad, girl. Real bad."

"I know. Just about the only thing that could make this whole Coffee Creek Wedding thing tolerable for me, is if you could come. Do you think you can?"

"I'm so sorry, but no. I had another appointment today and the doctor was real stern. He said I could lose my baby if I wasn't careful."

Laurel told herself it was selfish to be disappointed. "You better listen to him."

"Believe me, I am. This baby…" Winnie's voice weakened, then grew stronger again. "At first I really resented being pregnant. But now I think I would have just dissolved with grief if it wasn't for Brock's baby. I'm going to love this child so much—" Her voice caught again. "I already do."

Corb could cook when he had to. Besides eggs and bacon, he also made stew, in huge batches that he froze in plastic tubs on the top shelf of his freezer. He grabbed one of the tubs that evening when he finished work, transferred it to a roasting pan and stuck it in the oven to heat.

Then he went looking for Jackson. There were no lights on at his foster brother's place, so he figured Jackson must be at the office.

Corb made his way back to the home barn, pausing at the doorway to the office. Jackson was behind the desk, staring at the computer screen.

"Hey. Haven't you put in enough hours today? Come up to my place. I've got some stew in the oven and some cold ones in the fridge. I guarantee you one thing. You're not likely to get a better offer tonight."

He slipped into the upholstered chair across from Jackson's. "I have good news for a change."

"Yeah? I could use some."

"Laurel and I—we're getting married."

Jackson looked as stunned as if he'd pulled out a gun and threatened to shoot him. "Winnie's friend from New York? I thought you didn't remember her? That you'd forgotten pretty much everything that happened around the time of the accident."

"That's true, but let's keep that part between you and me, okay? The thing is—" He brushed his hands against his jeans. Telling B.J. and Cassidy his news over the phone had been a cinch compared to this. "The thing is, she's pregnant. It happened the night before—"

He stopped, not sure what to say. The night before the wedding that never happened? The night before the accident that took the life of his baby brother?

Jackson was staring at the ground. From the expression on his face, the same emotions were churning within him. But when he finally lifted his gaze, he had managed a small smile.

"You're right. That *is* good news. Congratulations, buddy."

As soon as she saw the exterior of the Blue Sapphire, Laurel could tell that the store catered to an older, wealthier clientele. The two-story, wooden Victorian had been painted a lovely, rich blue, with white trim. The display window had several smartly coordinated outfits with matching handbags and shoes.

More encouraging was a sign announcing a blowout sale with prices marked down from fifty to seventy-five percent.

If she had to buy a dress she didn't like, at least she'd be getting it at a good bargain.

Squaring her shoulders—all she'd promised was to try it on—she walked up the stairs and into the pot-pourri-scented shop.

Inside, three salesclerks were trying to keep up with the demands of about a half-dozen customers. "It's the first day of our sale," one of them explained to Laurel as she rushed by with her arms full of clothes, heading to the till to ring them up.

Laurel browsed through a rack of dresses as she waited to be helped. After only a few minutes, a woman in her fifties, stylishly dressed and very well-groomed, came up to her with a smile.

"Thanks for your patience. May I help you find something?"

"I'm getting married soon and my fiancé's mother spotted something here that she thought I would like."

"You must be talking about Olive Lambert."

When Laurel nodded, the older woman beamed.

"Olive is one of our best customers. I have the dress put away for you, dear." She put a hand on Laurel's back and led her to the curtained change rooms at the rear of the store. "My name is Lisa. You wait right here while I get the dress."

Less than a minute later she returned with a strapless sheath in an ivory silk with flattering ruching around the waist.

"This is our last one. I'll bet it's going to look fabulous on you. Olive has quite the eye."

Laurel examined the dress with begrudging admiration. It was actually quite nice.

Lisa hung the dress on the hook in the change room. "You call me if you need help with that zipper, okay?"

And then she was off, helping another customer.

Laurel pulled the curtain closed, then removed her T-shirt and jeans, taking off her bra, as well, so the straps wouldn't show. She had just put on the dress and was contorting her body in an effort to get the zipper all the way up, when she heard a familiar voice in the change room next to her's.

"Here, Mom, I found this for you to try on, too."

It was Jacqueline. Laurel was sure of it.

"Thanks, love," was the reply. "I sure hope one of these works. I hate shopping for dresses."

"Try this one first," suggested the woman who had helped Laurel earlier. Lisa. "Your daughter can sit here and wait, if she wants."

Laurel was about to step out to say hi to Jacqueline and to ask for help doing up the dress properly, when Jacqueline's mother said something intriguing.

"So are the rumors true? Help me with these buttons, love."

Amid rustling from the change room, Jacqueline said, "Which rumors?"

"Don't pretend you don't know what I'm talking about. Is Corb Lambert marrying that woman from New York City?"

Laurel sank into the chair, on top of her discarded clothing.

"Yeah. She was a lot smarter than me," Jacqueline replied. "She got pregnant."

Oh my God. Laurel stared at her reflection in the mirror, horrified. And she'd thought Jacqueline was *nice.* Boy had she been fooled.

"You can't be serious. You wouldn't have—"

"No. Of course I would never have stooped that low. But the Lamberts, for all their unassuming ways, are one of the richest ranching families in Montana. So, I suppose it must have been tempting. For a certain type of woman."

Her mother tsk-tsked. Then there was the sound of curtain rings scraping against a metal rod. "Oh, that is totally awesome on you, Mom. You have to get that."

"I think I will. I'm not even trying on the others."

Thank God, Laurel thought. She needed them gone. And soon. Her phone beeped then, and she pulled it out of her purse to see a text message from Winnie.

Did you try on the dress? she'd asked. Is it awful?

Something was awful all right. But it wasn't the dress.

Laurel covered her face with her hands, and tried to compose herself. Even though she'd only met Jacqueline a few times, it still hurt to hear her pass on such malicious gossip. Probably what hurt the most, though, was the kernel of truth at the heart of it all. She, too, had felt as if she might be trapping Corb into this wedding.

But she'd given him the chance to back out, hadn't she?

And it wasn't as if this was any easier for *her.*

Laurel forced herself to take deep, slow breaths until she felt her heart rate level out to normal.

Then she pushed back the curtain.

Lisa was right there.

"Oh, my, look at that fit. It doesn't need a single alteration."

If she noticed the stunned expression on Laurel's

face, maybe she put it down to shock at finding such a wonderful dress.

"Turn around, honey, and I'll get that zip...."

Obediently Laurel swiveled, and then felt the woman's warm fingers tug the zipper up the final inch.

"Lovely. Would you like a picture to show Olive?"

Laurel's phone had fallen to the floor at some point. Lisa picked it up and expertly snapped a couple of photos—obviously she was used to performing this service for her clients. Then she handed the phone back to Laurel.

"Olive will be so pleased. I've seen that dress on many women, but it's only been perfect on one of them—and that's you."

Obligingly Laurel texted the photo to Olive and Winnie. And she bought the dress. Olive replied right away. I was right! It's perfect. Laurel rolled her eyes, but she couldn't deny that it wasn't true.

She didn't hear back from Winnie until she'd returned home to the apartment over the Cinnamon Stick.

You look like a vision in that dress! read the text message. Did you buy it?

Laurel sat on the sofa, and punched in her reply. Yes. But I wish you'd been there. Oh, did she ever. She could just imagine her more assertive friend pushing back the curtains of that changing room and giving Jacqueline a good dressing-down. She might have done it herself if she hadn't been so shocked.

As if sensing Laurel's need to talk to her, Winnie didn't text a reply. She phoned instead.

"Are you okay?"

Laurel gushed out the story of what had happened at the dress shop.

"That bitch. I wish I had been there. I'd have torn a strip off her."

Laurel laughed, knowing this was no idle threat.

"She's just jealous, Laurel. Think about it. She dated Corb for *five years*. And you've known him for what— just three months?"

"Yeah, I know. But, she is right about one thing. Corb wouldn't be marrying me if I wasn't pregnant."

"Are you sure about that? This isn't the 1950s, Laurel. People don't *have* to get married anymore. There are all sorts of options. You and Corb are getting married because you're awesome together. So stop letting that woman get to you, okay?"

Laurel let the words sink in for a few seconds. "Winnie?"

"Yeah?"

"You're the best."

Thursday Corb was driving home from town with a case of beer, two bottles of champagne and a bottle of nonalcoholic wine for the wedding, when he noticed Maddie's old Ford puttering at half his speed on the road ahead of him.

He eased off the accelerator, not wanting to overtake her on the narrow country road. Going slower wasn't a bad idea anyway. He had a lot on his mind.

Like the wedding, which was a little over a week away. He'd thought he would be nervous as the day grew closer. But he wasn't, and that confused him.

Also, he was thinking about Jacqueline. Laurel's questions the other night had stuck in his head and he found himself wondering why it was that just a few months ago the idea of getting married had seemed out of the question, whereas now, he was kind of excited about it.

Was it the baby? If Jacqueline had gotten pregnant, would he have felt okay about marrying her, too?

He didn't think so. But sorting out his true feelings for Laurel was difficult. He was too busy focusing on keeping her and the baby in Montana.

Brock was gone, but the Lambert family lived on, and so did Coffee Creek Ranch. His child was part of it—the family and the land were all part of a way of living that Corb treasured. Maybe one day his son or daughter would opt out the way Cassidy and B.J. had done.

But his child had to be given the choice.

Marrying Laurel was his chance to give their child that choice. And he didn't want to spend the rest of his life regretting that he hadn't taken action to make sure that happened.

Corb slowed as he approached the fork in the road. Ahead of him, Maddie turned on her indicator light and he watched as her taillights veered to the right. He took his foot off the accelerator and paused before splitting off in the opposite direction.

It struck him, suddenly, as strange that in all his life he'd never seen Silver Creek Ranch.

At the last moment he jerked his wheel to the right. The approach to his mother's sister's place was not as well maintained as their road. His Jeep jostled over deep-set ruts, and he shook his head as he imagined what the road would be like when it rained. No wonder Maddie's truck was all beaten up.

He drove for six miles before he saw the homestead. A fieldstone house with a low roof, several barns and outbuildings, a series of corrals, all nestled into a clearing that overlooked a view of Square Butte, from a different angle than he was used to seeing it. The ranch was on a much smaller scale than the one where he'd grown up. But it was settled on a pretty piece of land, he conceded.

As he drove closer, he saw that the siding on the barns needed paint, some of the shingles on the roofs were lifting and the front windows of the house had been covered with aluminum foil.

Either Maddie was short on money or she was short on help. Either way, the place needed a little TLC.

Meanwhile, his unexpected appearance had been noted by the owner. Having parked her truck in front of the house, Maddie climbed out and took a stance with her legs planted firmly and her arms crossed. She was wearing work clothes, with a bandanna at her neck and a beat-up hat pushed back on her head. Clearly she was waiting to see what he wanted, why he had done this crazy thing and followed her home.

But he had no idea what his answer would be.

Maybe he should just pull a U-turn and head home like he should have done in the first place. Instead, he climbed out of the Jeep.

Two dogs came running, younger versions of Sky. They'd spotted him, as well as their owner, and they looked at Maddie as if waiting for instructions. *Run him off the property? Or love him to bits?*

Maddie whistled, and they ran to her with impressive obedience. She put a hand on each of their heads. "Good girls," she said in a soft voice, never once taking her eyes off him.

He'd have to be the first to talk.

"Where'd you get those dogs? They look just like our dog, Sky."

"That's because they have the same lineage. Trixie and Honey are quite a bit younger than Sky, though."

Again, he was taken aback by her voice, which didn't match her rough-and-tumble appearance. And then he realized something else, too. Her voice was a lot like his mother's.

"So, you and Dad got your dogs from the same breeder?"

"I suppose you could say that."

He narrowed his eyes, trying to figure out what she was saying, or, more accurately, *not* saying. And then the lightbulb went on. "Sky was born here, on Silver Creek Ranch."

She didn't answer but Corb knew he was right.

"Did Dad buy her from you?" He'd seen his father walk right by Maddie Turner in town, not acknowledging her existence by as much as a glance in her direction.

"Corbett, you have a lot of questions all of a sudden. Why don't you leave things be? After all these years, the answers don't matter anymore."

"Just tell me one thing then. Why do you keep leaving fresh flowers on Brock's marker?"

She pressed her fingers to her right temple, as if trying to stop a secret throbbing. "Your brother wasn't as obedient as the rest of you kids. I'm sure he knew he wasn't supposed to talk to me. But he did anyway."

This rang true for Corb. Of all of them, Brock would be the one most likely to disobey the unwritten family rule. "When you ran into one another in town, you mean?"

"It started that way. But when he got older, he started

dropping by the ranch every now and then." She nodded toward a stack of new shingles. "He was planning to fix my roof for me after the wedding."

Corb was speechless. All he could think of was his mother and how crushed she would be if she knew this. He already felt guilty just for driving here and talking to Maddie. But another part of him felt badly for Maddie, too.

"You're wondering if you should help me with the roof now that Brock's gone," Maddie said. "I can see it in your face. You don't hide your emotions very well. You're like your father that way."

Again the woman shocked him. This time by how well she seemed to know his father. Corb realized there was a lot of family history that he had no clue about.

"Did you know my dad well?"

She smiled sadly at that, then waved him off. "Go home, Corb. I've got hands to help me with this roof. And your loyalty belongs with your mother."

Chapter 11

Corb wanted to hole up in his cabin for the rest of the evening. Fry up some eggs and bacon, relax and watch the sunset. Maybe later, when it got dark, he'd call Laurel to talk over the day's events.

But his sense of responsibility wouldn't let him. So when he got back to the ranch, he headed for the office in the barn to work on the schedule for the next four weeks. It was a job he should have tackled a few days ago and he knew he wouldn't sleep well until it was done.

He was updating the spreadsheet on the computer when his mother appeared carrying a tray with dinner.

"I saw the light on," she said. "It's late, Corb—have you eaten?"

"No, but that sure smells great."

"Bonny made her enchilada casserole. Enough for

at least a dozen people. She hasn't adjusted her recipes even though she's only cooking for one, now."

The plate, piled high with layers of spicy chicken, corn tortillas, salsa and cheese, was calling out to him. But his mother's words broke his heart and dulled his appetite.

He knew there was no sense reminding her that even when Brock was alive, they'd mostly eaten their evening meals at their own cabins. She was probably thinking back to the old days, when his dad was still alive and there were four kids—five when you included Jackson—around the table with her.

She'd gone through a lot of adjustments over the years. One by one, everyone had left her. That must be how she felt, anyway.

"How are you holding up, Mom?"

She managed a smile. "You've been so patient with me, son. But I am feeling stronger. Maybe planning this wedding of yours was just what I needed. It hasn't been overwhelming, since the affair is so small, but it's given me something to look forward to. Including having Cassidy and B.J. back home for a while."

Hoping he wasn't pushing his luck, but knowing that these warm moments between him and his mother didn't come along all that often, he decided to ask some questions.

"Mom, what's the deal between you and Maddie Turner? What happened to cause the rift between you two?"

In a flash it was as if his mother had become a different person. Her smile vanished and her face looked haggard and pained in the shadows cast from the overhead lighting.

"Why are you bringing that up?"

"I've—" He sensed it wouldn't be wise to mention anything about the wreath, or the border collies who were related to Sky, or the stack of shingles Brock had been meaning to replace. "I've run into Maddie a few times in town lately. It just seems strange the way we both act as if we don't even know the other one exists."

"Oh, Corb." His mother sighed, then sank into the upholstered chair. "I don't like to speak of it. I thought your father told all you kids this years ago."

He hadn't. He'd never said a word to explain the weird family divide. But again, Corb judged it was best to keep quiet and let his mother speak.

"I loved my father very much. He was a wonderful man, your grandpa Turner. But unfortunately Maddie was always jealous of me—I don't want to sound vain, but I was widely considered the pretty one, and it may be that my father favored me because I took after my mother. She died in childbirth, as you know."

"Yes." That much of the family history, he had been told.

"Maddie's jealousy got worse after I was married. She did her best to come between Father and me. So much so that she didn't even tell me when he had his stroke."

"Why would she do that?" Maddie had looked sad and lonely, but she hadn't struck him as mean. And what his mother described was more than mean. It was almost vicious.

"Who knows? Maybe she was worried I would talk him into changing his will. He left her the best and biggest share of the ranch, you know. Or maybe it was just jealousy, pure and simple. She'd always wanted all of Daddy's attention...."

There were tears in his mother's eyes, and Corb was sorry he'd raised the subject. He went to give her a hug and asked if he could walk her back to the house.

"No, I'm fine, dear. Stay here and eat your dinner then go home and get some rest." She placed a hand on his cheek.

"Thanks, Mom."

She paused on her way out the door. "Just please don't mention that woman to me ever again. Because of her, I never had a chance to say goodbye to my father or tell him one last time how much I loved him. And I will never forgive her for that."

An hour later, Corb finished with the schedule and closed up the office for the night. Outside the night air was cool and refreshing. He decided to leave the Jeep and walk the half mile to his cabin. He needed to clear his head and a sky dazzling with stars and a quarter moon was offering enough light for him to watch his footing.

Ten minutes later, he was almost at the first cabin when he heard a vehicle approaching from his rear. He moved to the side of the road and watched as Jackson slowly drove by, giving him a slight wave before turning into the driveway.

In the days prior to the accident, he'd run into Jackson several times during the day. Besides having breakfast together at the main house, they'd cross paths as they worked in the barns or out in the field with the cattle.

But since Corb had been released from the hospital,

seeing Jackson was about as rare as a sighting of the shy northern bluebird.

Corb followed the truck, catching up to Jackson just before he went in the door to his cabin.

"Hey there."

Jackson turned. He looked weary, from the set of his shoulders, to the lines bracketing his mouth and weighing down his forehead.

"Hey, Corb. Out for a walk? Nice evening."

"Haven't seen you around the last few days."

"Been busy."

Corb waited, expecting to be invited in for a beer. When he wasn't, he headed for one of the willow chairs on the porch. "Mind if we sit for a while?"

Jackson didn't look pleased, but he took the other chair. He removed his hat and started tracing the rim with the pad of one thumb.

"What's been keeping you so busy lately?"

"Getting the horses ready to move the cattle. Have you worked up the schedule yet?"

"Just did that tonight. I've been wanting to talk to you about something else, though. I was wondering if you would be willing to take over the entire quarter horse breeding end of the operation. We could hire an accountant to handle some of the office work. And maybe an extra hand to look after the working horses."

"That would suit me fine," Jackson admitted. "But it doesn't feel right to take over Brock's job."

"Don't think of it that way."

"How the hell should I think of it?" Jackson's words came out in a rush of anger. "Lately I've been considering my options. It might be healthier for everyone concerned if I found a job somewhere else."

Corb stared at him, feeling as if he'd been sucker punched. "Have you been talking to other ranchers in the area about this?"

Jackson wouldn't look at him, just kept working at his hat. "I've had a few conversations."

That was the last straw. "Damn it, Jackson. I can't believe this. I've lost one brother and now you want to make it two?"

"Don't think of it that way." Jackson was mocking him, throwing back his own words.

Corb sprang out of the chair and went to lean on the railing. "Dad always treated you like one of the family. You've been with us for almost fifteen years now. But you're going to pack your bags as if we were just another job. Is that it?"

"No. Damn it, no. You must understand why I have to go."

Suddenly Corb's anger vanished. Jackson was acting out of guilt and there was no uglier feeling. "No, I do not. Running away won't change anything. And it'll sure make things worse for me. Besides being my best friend, I need you here. You're a talented horseman and I'd be hard-pressed to replace you with two men, let alone one."

Jackson joined him by the railing and offered him his hand. "I'm sorry. I should never have said all that. I owe you and this place my loyalty."

"If that's all it is, just loyalty, then maybe you *should* leave."

"No. I feel the same way about you, like you're my brother. And I felt the same about Brock. That's what makes it so hard."

"It is hard," Corb agreed. "But it's going to get better. And life goes on. You'll see."

"Speaking of life going on…" Jackson swallowed, like he was nervous or something. "You heard from Winnie Hayes lately? Is she planning to come to the wedding?"

"Laurel invited her, of course. But apparently she's not well enough to travel."

Jackson looked sick when he heard this. "Do you know what's wrong?"

"I asked Laurel, and she said it was up to Winnie to fill us in on her health. She was real mysterious about it all."

"I hope it's not serious."

"Laurel didn't give me that impression. I told Mom she should call the Hayes family and check in with Winnie, but as far as I know, she hasn't done that yet." He paused then added, "Maybe you want to give her a call?"

"I doubt she wants to hear from me."

Corb didn't argue the point. For all he knew, Jackson was right.

The ironic thing about planning a wedding, Laurel soon discovered, was that you had no time to spend alone with the man you were intending to marry. That weekend Olive wanted to go over the menu with the caterer, so Laurel agreed they would meet at the ranch at two o'clock on Saturday afternoon.

"Why don't you come, too?" she asked—well, more like pleaded with—Corb on the phone.

"I promised Jackson I'd help him shoe some horses

today, or I would. Nothing I'd like better than to talk recipes with you and my mom."

Laurel laughed. "You liar."

She called Eugenia next, letting her know the time of the meeting and also suggesting that she come prepared with some choices for a casual outdoor barbecue.

Southwestern cuisine would be perfect for their low-key, family wedding, Laurel thought. But that was before Olive had her say.

Olive greeted them both at the door, then led them to the dining room table. Once they were seated, Eugenia handed out the menus she had printed off for the meeting. Corb's mom took one glance at the menu of ribs, baked beans, salads and corn bread, then set it aside and opened a red leather-covered notebook of her own. Slender gold pen in hand, she flipped through the pages until she found what she wanted.

"What about a shrimp salad to start?"

From her end of the table, Eugenia cast a worried look at Laurel, then focused again on Olive. "I can make a shrimp salad. That's no problem. But I thought we were going for a casual afternoon barbecue?"

"Really?" Olive already had perfect posture, but she managed to pull an extra inch out of her spine as she turned to look at Laurel. "Is that what you want, dear?"

"Everyone loves a good barbecue, don't they?"

"But this is an *occasion,* dear. Don't you want something special?"

She really didn't. But half an hour later Laurel had agreed with every one of Olive's menu suggestions, and the result was a French-inspired four-course meal.

"Are you sure you know how to cook all that stuff?" Laurel asked Eugenia as she walked her out to her car, leaving Olive in the dining room savoring her victory. "I sure couldn't."

"I can make anything—if I have the recipe. And they have plenty of those on the internet." Eugenia patted her hand. "Don't you worry—everything will be delicious."

On Sunday Olive insisted on having Laurel to dinner so they could discuss more wedding details. This time Corb was present, and Laurel noticed he was wearing his lucky shirt.

"This should be fun, huh?" she whispered in his ear as he bent to kiss her hello.

"Oh, yeah…" he said in a voice that denied the truth of the words. "More fun than deworming hogs in the springtime."

"Have you ever done that?"

"Nope. But I'd be willing to give it a try if I could get out of this."

Since Bonny didn't work on the weekend, Olive served reheated frozen pizza on china plates, with a salad starter—the kind that came in a package at the grocery store. Laurel picked up her silver fork and had to credit Corb's mother. She knew how to make fast food look good.

They'd barely finished eating when Olive pulled out the red leather notebook. First she went over color scheme suggestions for the flowers and the table linens. As soon as she said the words "table linens" she lost Corb. Laurel could see him craning his neck for a look at the baseball game playing silently in the family room.

Laurel was a fan of green, but Olive cringed when she mentioned this, suggesting instead a palette of white and silver.

"Okay," Laurel conceded. "We'll go with a white-

and-silver color scheme. And for the flowers, I've always loved carnations. I know they're simple, but that's what I like about them."

"Oh, but freesia and white roses would be so much more elegant."

Seriously? Could she not get her way on something as simple as a carnation? She gave Corb's leg a surreptitious nudge.

He winced, then sat up straight, and reengaged with the discussion. "What's that?"

"Flowers, Corb," his mom said patiently. "Don't you think white roses and freesia would be nice?"

"Yes, but white carnations are elegant, too. And much cheaper," Laurel pointed out.

Corb looked from his mom to Laurel, then back to his mother. "Can't we have all of them? The roses, that free stuff and the carnations, too?"

Olive gave him a condescending smile. "But the carnations would just detract." She shifted her gaze to Laurel. "You see that, don't you, dear?"

Laurel sighed. Did she really care about the flowers that much? No, she did not. "Whatever, Olive. Let's just leave it in your hands. That is, if Corb agrees?"

"Uh-huh," he said, eyes back on the TV.

Olive looked pleased, then moved on to the next item on her list. "We'll need to have a few speeches during dinner. I know you kids want to keep things simple, so we won't go overboard. Just a toast to the bride—perhaps you'd like to do that, Corb? After which I'd like to say a few words."

Of course she would. Laurel couldn't imagine a situation where Corb's mother *wouldn't* like to say a few words.

"*I* have to make a speech?" Corb looked like he'd rather face down a rattler. Or maybe a rabid dog.

"I can get you a book on toasts for weddings from the library," Laurel suggested. "To give you some ideas."

"A book? They must have an app for that."

"Probably." But she'd been looking for an excuse to check out the local library and this seemed like a good one.

After coffee and a slice of the bumbleberry pie Laurel had brought from the café, Olive finally closed the notebook.

"That was a very productive evening, don't you think?"

"I do," Laurel agreed, not sure if she should laugh or cry. Basically Olive had just overridden her on every single decision to do with the wedding, while Corb obliviously watched it happen.

Was this what the rest of her life was going to be like?

Or would Corb *ever* pick her side over his mother's?

Later, as Corb walked her out to her car, she shook her head. "That was interesting. Any chance you might change your mind about eloping?"

Corb looked worried. "But planning our wedding has really been good for her. She actually seemed like her old self tonight. And this afternoon she took the new palomino out for a ride. It's the first time she's been on a horse since the accident."

"That's good," Laurel had to admit.

They'd reached her car. But instead of opening the door, Corb backed her right up against it and planted his arms on either side of her. Then he leaned in for a nice, thorough kiss. "Can I talk you into staying? A sleepover would be nice…."

She was tempted. A night in Corb's arms might help all of this make sense again. Lately she'd felt as if she was on a treadmill and couldn't find the pause button.

Much as she'd tried to shake the conversation she'd overheard between Jacqueline and her mother, certain phrases still haunted her.

She got pregnant…. I would never have stooped that low.

She knew Winnie was right, that Jacqueline was speaking out of envy. But for some reason those words still stung. And she couldn't keep asking Corb if he was sure about marrying her. He'd start to think that it was *her* who wasn't sure, and that was the one thing she did know for certain.

She loved Corb.

She loved him like crazy.

Placing her mouth close to his ear, she whispered in her sexiest kitten voice, "What will your mother think?"

Corb laughed. "I admit there are times when I humor my mother—but our sex life will never be one of them. Besides—" he pulled her in nice and close so she could feel the hard refuge of his chest, the solid beating of his heart "—why do you think I wore my lucky shirt?"

Chapter 12

As soon as they were alone in Corb's cabin, there was no bothering with the niceties. Corb shut the door, pressed Laurel's back to the solid oak and unleashed his passion with the hottest kisses she'd ever experienced.

She loved his strength; she loved his ardor. And she absolutely adored the way he scooped her into his arms and carried her up the stairs to the loft as if she were a delicate damsel in distress.

He truly was the sexiest man she had ever known, and he was all hers. She could see it in his eyes, the way they burned for her, just as she was burning for him.

They kissed again, only this time they also tugged at each other's clothes, peeling back the layers, until they were skin to skin.

They made love in a tangle of desperate need, without the tentativeness of the other two times. She knew his sweet spots, and, oh my, he knew hers.

Later, he pulled her in close and traced lazy patterns with his fingers on her tummy.

"There's a baby in here. Hard to believe, huh?"

Her heart swelled at the awe in his voice. "Our own little tadpole."

"I'm so excited, Laurel. I mean it. I want to do all the things with our child that my dad did with me."

"Such as…?"

"Go fishing. Teach him to ride. Give him his first horse."

"And if he's a she?"

"The list won't change. Dad did all those things with Cassidy, too. But he did spoil her some, as well. She was the only one of the kids who got a dog for her birthday."

"I expect you'd spoil a daughter, too."

"No doubt I would." He kissed her tummy, then kissed her lips. "Thank you for agreeing to marry this Montana cowboy when you probably had your sights set on a sophisticated New Yorker."

"I never thought about it that way. I guess I just hoped I would find someone I could share my life with, someone to love and to raise a family with."

"Well, you found him." He kissed her again. "I won't be one of those hands-off kinds of fathers, either. Diapers, 2:00 a.m. feedings, marathon rocking sessions—you can count me in on all of that."

Laurel sighed, and cuddled in closer to his solid warmth.

This was such a perfect moment. Of course, the icing on the cake would have been if he'd mentioned how much he loved *her*. Or some of the things he wanted to do together, as a couple.

But a lot of cakes tasted just fine without icing.

If Laurel thought the wedding plans had been squared away that weekend, she was wrong. On Tuesday Eugenia insisted on going over the recipes she'd found on the internet. Then on Thursday Olive phoned her in a panic about the wedding cake. She'd forgotten all about it. Had Laurel ordered one?

She hadn't.

In stepped Vince Butterfield, who must have overheard her talking on the phone to Olive, then later ranting to Dawn.

"Where am I going to get a wedding cake on such short notice?"

"I really don't know." Poor Dawn seemed as distressed as if it were her own wedding. "Maybe you could make one yourself?"

"I'll do it," said a masculine voice from the back room.

At first Laurel wasn't sure she'd heard Vince correctly. She pushed through the door to the kitchen, where she found him pulling the last batch of cinnamon buns out of the oven. How a man in cowboy boots, jeans and a big white apron managed to avoid looking silly, she didn't know. But Vince pulled off the look, looking both competent and hygienic, and completely masculine all at the same time.

"Did I hear that right? Vince, did you offer to bake a wedding cake for Corb and me?"

He nodded, setting down the pan on a hot pad, then shutting the oven door with the tip of his boot.

"Have you made a wedding cake before?"

"Nope."

She stood in the kitchen, not sure what to ask next, or if she should maybe make some suggestions, like no fruitcake please, or go easy on the rosettes and the thick white icing. Vince didn't seem to be awaiting any instructions, however.

"Leave it to me. You and Corb, you've got enough on your hands."

What did he mean by that? she wondered. But Vince had already said a lot of words for one morning. As he turned back to his baking, she knew better than to try and get anything more out of him.

It was Friday by the time Laurel made it to the library. She hadn't seen Corb since the night they'd spent together the previous Sunday. The wonderful chemistry of their lovemaking, and the tender hour Corb had spent holding her and talking afterward, had reassured her at the time that they were doing the right thing.

But after five days with no contact—other than texting and the occasional phone conversation—she was getting nervous again. She wanted to blame Jacqueline, but she suspected that she would be feeling the same way even if she hadn't overheard that conversation.

While their night together had been wonderful, he still hadn't told her he loved her. At the time, she'd felt it didn't matter. He was *showing* her how he felt. And cowboys weren't exactly famous for sharing their feelings.

Vince was a prime example of that.

But she wasn't marrying Vince, and she couldn't help needing more reassurance than Corb seemed prepared to give her. As the days to the wedding ticked by, and Sunday loomed closer, it seemed to her that he might have said the words *at least once*. If he felt them.

She pulled open the door to the library, which was situated in a white clapboard building that had once been the town schoolhouse. Back in the forties and fifties, all the children in the area had been schooled together in this place. Framed black-and-white pictures on the wall in what had once been the cloakroom showed neat rows of wooden desks, with the smallest desks lined up to the teacher's left and the larger ones on the right. She couldn't imagine what it must have been like for one teacher to juggle all the grades in one room, but clearly that was how it had been done.

"Hello! Welcome!"

She followed Tabitha's voice into the main room. Here all the desks had been replaced with bookshelves. A metal desk sat in one corner, next to a computer and some filing cabinets. Across the room were a couple of wooden tables, with two more computers for the public to use. Presently both were vacant. It seemed she was the only patron in the library.

"For a change, I get to be the one to serve you," Tabitha said with a smile.

"Yes. I'm embarrassed that I've been in town for this long without visiting the library before now. I'm certainly not the regular customer that you are at the Cinnamon Stick."

Tabitha laughed. "Well, I am addicted to Vince's blueberry muffins. And the coffee is good, too."

"I'm glad—but why do you only visit us in the mornings? I've never seen you come in for lunch."

"Hasn't anyone told you? It was part of my divorce settlement."

"Pardon?"

"You know Burt and I used to be married?"

"I do."

"We used to go to the café together. Sometimes for breakfast and sometimes for lunch. When we separated, I got breakfast and he got lunch. Does it make sense now?"

"Yes. It makes perfect sense." It was lovely and heartbreaking all at the same time. But what had gone wrong between these two gentle souls? "You'll probably find this funny, but a few times I've thought to myself that the two of you would make a good couple."

"Well, it was true for a while. But it's never a good thing for a marriage when one partner does all the loving."

"Oh. I guess not." Laurel waited, wondering which had loved more and which had loved less. But Tabitha was finished confiding for the day.

"So," she prompted. "May I help you find something or are you just here to browse?"

"I'd love some help. I'm looking for a book with examples of wedding toasts."

"Ah!" Tabitha beamed. "That's right. Tomorrow is the big day, isn't it?"

And then, so subtly Laurel wasn't sure if she was imagining it, Tabitha checked out Laurel's waistline.

She knows I'm pregnant?

How was that possible? She hadn't even told Vince or Dawn, and she was pretty sure Eugenia had kept the news quiet.

Which left Jacqueline. Despite her promise to keep their news to herself, she must have talked. Silly her to be surprised.

If Jacqueline was blabbing about her in a dress shop in Lewistown, she wouldn't have drawn the line about spreading the word here in Coffee Creek.

Not that it really mattered what people knew. In a few months she wouldn't be able to keep her secret anymore. But she sure hoped the whole town didn't see the affair the same way that Jacqueline did—as some sort of ruse to get Corb to marry her.

Laurel left the library with the book of wedding toasts under her arm, no longer certain that Corb was going to need it.

"Winnie, were you nervous the night before your wedding?" Laurel was sitting on the floor in the apartment, sipping ginger ale and wishing, badly, that she could add something a lot stronger to the glass.

It was seven o'clock on Saturday evening. She'd received a text from Corb a few hours earlier telling her that Cassidy and B.J. had both arrived at the ranch. They were going to have a big welcome-home dinner, and did she want to join them?

She'd begged off, claiming there was too much for her to do to get ready for tomorrow.

And there *had* been a lot to do, but she'd done none of it. She hadn't filed her nails or painted her toenails. She'd also planned to have a bath and give herself a mini facial. Also not done. She hadn't even taken her dress out of the garment bag she'd brought home from the shop.

She was freaking out.

She wished Winnie was here, in person. But Winnie was at home with her feet up, doing her best to keep the baby that she and Brock had made together.

"I was more excited than nervous," Winnie said now, which did not make Laurel feel better *at all*.

"Oh."

"Are you okay, Laurel?"

"Yes. No. Oh, Winnie, what if I'm making a terrible mistake?"

"I don't know what to say to that. Other than to follow your heart. Do you love him, Laurel?"

"Yes."

"Well then? Seems pretty simple to me. Look, sweetie, I'm sorry but I've got to go. I haven't had the best day, myself."

Laurel felt like the most insensitive person possible. All her talk about the wedding must be bringing back so many painful memories for Winnie.

"I'm sorry. I've been so busy thinking of myself. I haven't been a very good friend to you, lately, have I?"

"Don't say that. You're a terrific friend. I just have bad days, when I can't help—" The rest of her sentence was lost as she choked over a soft sob.

"Go ahead and cry, Winnie. I'm sure a few tears won't hurt your baby."

And Winnie did cry. But only for a minute. Then she spoke again, her voice fortified with determination. "I'm going to rest now, Laurel, and I want you to go to sleep, too. Things will look brighter in the morning. I know your wedding is going to be beautiful. Try not to worry and just enjoy it."

Don't hang up, Laurel wanted to plead. But she knew it wasn't fair to keep Winnie from her rest when there wasn't anything her friend could say to help her, anyway. This was Laurel's life and her decision to make.

"Thanks, Winnie. We'll talk soon."

Laurel put away her phone, then eyed the pullout couch, which was all made up and ready for her to crawl into. But she knew she would never sleep. Instead she went to the suitcase she'd packed almost three months ago, when she'd thought she was coming to Coffee Creek for just a week.

No matter where she went in life, even if it was just a weekend away in the country, Laurel always took a velvet-covered box with her. It was about as big as a legal-sized envelope and two inches deep. Inside she kept her family—or what was left of them.

A picture of her and her mom taken when Laurel was two years old. She was sitting on her mother's lap and her mother was looking at her with such tenderness that it always brought a tear to Laurel's eye. She did remember her mother, but looking at this picture helped keep those memories strong.

Also in the box were her parents' wedding bands—one of which, the larger one, had about ten years more wear and tear than the other. She held them in her hands and wondered about her parents' wedding day. She knew they'd loved one another deeply. But had her mother felt any nerves the night before?

If only she could ask her.

The final item in the box was a letter. She didn't often read it. It made her too sad. But on this momentous night, she felt she needed to see those words again.

The letter was from her father—written in his familiar scrawling style. It had been left with his lawyer, along with his will, to be given to her in the event of his death.

The single page was wrinkled from repeated readings—and more than a few tears that had spilled from her eyes.

She took a deep breath. Then plunged on.

Dear Laurel, If anything should happen to me, I want you to let Mr. Wilson sell the farm on your behalf. He'll take care of everything and you'll be left with enough money to put you through college and maybe buy yourself a house later, or help you through any rough patches you encounter later in life.

I'm sorry I wasn't a better father. I did try to do my best, and you made it easy on me. You were a good kid and I thank you for that. Remember your mother, always. She loved you so much.
Dad

No matter how many times Laurel read the letter, it always wounded. Not that she hadn't known, growing up, that her father didn't love her. He was a kind man and he always made an effort, but there was always a faraway look in his eyes when she spoke to him that made him seem as if he wasn't really present.

She'd tried so hard to make him happy. She'd earned good grades at school. Learned how to cook and do laundry and help keep their home neat. She'd never indulged in "moods" and tried to say funny things to make him smile at the end of a long day spent in the fields or handling the cattle.

And what had been her reward?

You made it easy for me...thanks for that.

She'd wanted love. Not gratitude.

And her father had only wanted...release. He'd

waited until she was eighteen. He'd waited until she'd graduated from high school, and then he'd died in an automobile crash.

Later, the police told her that they couldn't determine the reason he went off the road that day. He must have fallen asleep at the wheel.

But she'd known the truth. His promise to her mother fulfilled, her father had wanted to die that day.

It had been duty, not love, that bound her father to her.

Just like Corb.

Laurel's heart started pounding too fast, her breathing was off. Putting a hand to her chest, she wondered why she hadn't seen the parallel earlier, between that early parental relationship and this new one with Corb.

If he was marrying her out of duty and not love, then one day she might have to expect a letter like this one from him.

Thanks for being cheerful and funny and making our years together easy. But I think it's time we went our separate ways....

What was it Tabitha had said? It wasn't a good thing for a marriage if one partner did all the loving. Had she shared that bit of wisdom with her because she suspected that Laurel and Corb were about to make the same mistake that she and Burt had made years ago?

She'd asked Winnie if she was making the right decision, but all she'd had to do was open her eyes. The signs were everywhere that she hadn't. Even in the way that Corb always put Olive's wishes ahead of hers.

She'd kept telling herself that it didn't really matter.

Only, one day, there would come a disagreement that was important to her, and when she needed her husband to have her back. But by then, the precedent would already be set. Olive's wishes came first. Hers second.

She'd spent the first eighteen years of her life trying to earn the love of a man and failing. Did she really want to repeat that mistake with Corb?

Laurel sat at the kitchen for a long while, trying to work out what she had to do. End it now?

Her heart shrieked *No*.

Maybe she should give Corb one more chance to prove that he really did care. Before she could change her mind, she dialed his cell phone. Even before he spoke, she could hear the sounds of conversation and laughter in the background.

"Laurel? Did you change your mind? Are you coming over?"

"No. Actually, I was hoping you could come here. I really need to talk to you right now."

"Tonight?" There was a pause for a second. In her mind she could picture the torn expression that would be on his face. "But Mom made this big meal. And with Cassidy and B.J. home, it doesn't feel right to run out on everyone."

"I see."

"Please change your mind and come over. We can grab some time for ourselves later on, once everyone's had dessert and coffee."

Maybe a reasonable person would have said yes. But Laurel didn't have it in her to be reasonable tonight. This, on top of everything else, just seemed like too much.

"I don't think so, Corb. It's just too late."

"It's only eight," he said.

But she wasn't talking about the time.

Chapter 13

Corb had made certain that Sky was at the main ranch house when Cassidy arrived home for the weekend. His sister had given their mother a kiss, then dropped to her knees and thrown her arms around the dog.

"Oh, you good girl. You haven't forgotten me, have you?"

The adoration in Sky's dark eyes was her answer and they'd been inseparable ever since. Corb guessed that Cassidy had even let Sky sleep on her bed—a definite no-no in this house when they'd been growing up.

They'd all gone to bed late last night. And now, a few hours before the wedding, Corb checked in at the house thinking lunch would be a good idea, since he hadn't had any breakfast. He found Cassidy curled up on the sofa eating a sandwich, Sky at her feet, accepting the odd discreetly offered piece of chicken or cheese.

His sister looked good, he thought. She'd always been cute. A long-legged blonde with the kind of skin that tanned easily every summer, and the greenest eyes of all of them, she'd never gone through an awkward adolescent stage that he could recall.

But now, in the final semester of her MBA, his sister was starting to look like a woman. The transition was kind of scary and he wondered how his mom felt about it.

Corb took his plate loaded with chicken sandwiches and carrot sticks and sank on the sofa next to her.

"So? Any men in your life these days, sis?"

"When I get engaged, I'll let you know." Having grown up with only brothers, Cassidy knew better than to give him a straight answer.

"That's a lot of sandwiches on your plate," B.J. commented, entering the room after his own foray into the luncheon buffet set out on the dining room table.

Cassidy and Jackson had done the work of making sandwiches, chopping veggies and piling Bonny's homemade cookies onto a plate. Their mother was still in her room, claiming to need the rest to prepare for the busy day to come.

"I'm surprised you have an appetite, considering that in less than two hours you're going to be signing your life away." B.J. settled into the big leather armchair that had once been their father's, and that everyone but him still did their best to avoid.

"If you knew Laurel, you'd understand why I'm not nervous," Corb retorted. Lobbing insults and challenging statements to his big brother was habit to him. But the truth was, his stomach had been feeling a little queasy.

It had started last night, after the strange phone call from Laurel. She hadn't sounded like herself, and he wished she would have agreed to join them at the ranch rather than hole up in that apartment, all by herself.

The big, noisy family dinner had included some quiet moments and more than a few tears as they recalled the last time they'd been gathered together—for their brother's funeral.

Corb hadn't been there, of course. He'd still been in the hospital, only one day out of his coma. At that point he hadn't even known his brother was dead.

They'd waited until the day after the funeral to tell him.

So at dinner, he'd listened to his family talk about the service as if he were an outsider. Then later, B.J. had pulled out a DVD of family movies and they managed to have some laughs—and shed more tears—with a trip down memory lane.

The party hadn't wrapped up until after midnight, when Olive finally put her foot down. She'd turned off the music and switched off the lights and everyone had received the message loud and clear and gone to their respective beds.

Alone in his cabin, Corb found he couldn't sleep. He'd missed Sky sleeping in her bed in the corner.

And he missed Laurel.

Too late, he'd wished he'd driven into town like she'd asked him.

He welcomed his chores the next morning, but he couldn't deny that the nervous feeling in his gut just got worse as the day progressed. Now he wondered why he'd bothered putting the food on his plate in the first place. Habit, he supposed. He held out a piece of chicken toward Sky, but even for her favorite food, the loyal dog refused to budge from her spot at Cassidy's feet.

"She's been missing Brock something awful," Corb told his sister. "I hate to think what she's going to be like when you go back to school."

"I wish I could bring her with me." Cassidy gave Sky's head a good scratch. "But she'd hate apartment living. I'm on the third floor and I don't think she could manage the stairs."

Corb leaned over, dangling the chicken right in front of Sky's nose. Finally she deigned to accept it.

"Did you guys know," Corb asked, "that Sky came from Silver Creek Ranch? She was bred from the same dog that used to belong to our Grandpa Turner."

Grandpa Turner was someone they knew only by name, since he had passed away before they were born.

"That's not true," Cassidy argued. "I found him in a basket at the front door on my fourteenth birthday. Mom was so annoyed, I figured Dad was behind it. And he never would have bought a dog from Maddie Turner. Mom would have killed him."

"I know what you mean," B.J. said. "One of my most vivid memories as a kid is going to town and having Dad walk right by Mom's sister as if he couldn't even see her. That was so not like Dad, I've never forgotten it."

"I have the exact same memory." Corb wondered if maybe he and his brother were remembering the same incident. "Still, I happened to drive up to Silver Creek the other day. Maddie Turner has a couple of border collies the spitting image of Sky. She admitted that Sky was from the same lineage."

"That can't be," Cassidy said again.

"What were you doing driving there, anyway?" B.J. asked.

"The old family feud has been bothering me lately. I noticed Maddie Turner putting a wreath on the road where the car crash happened. It just got me thinking about the fact that we're all related, even though we hardly know her."

"Well, for Mom's sake, I think we better let sleeping dogs lie. Figuratively and literally." B.J. turned to Cassidy. "By the way, is your cell phone charged?"

"Why do you ask?" Cassidy transferred her plate to the coffee table, then pulled her phone out of the front pocket of her jeans. When she saw the blank screen she gave him a puzzled look. "How did you know?"

"Some guy called the house half an hour ago. You must have been in the shower."

"And you're only telling me now?" She scrambled up from the sofa.

"His name was Josh," B.J. teased as she ran off toward her bedroom, with a confused Sky struggling to keep up. No doubt she wanted to plug in her phone and call the guy back, in private. "He sounded really nice. I can't wait to meet him."

"Oh, shut up, B.J.," Cassidy shouted back at him.

Corb smiled. Just like old times.

B.J. leaned back into the sofa. "That girl is starting to worry me," he said. "She's getting way too pretty for her own good."

"I agree. But what about you, bro?" Corb countered. "Any woman in your life right now?"

"Hell, yes. It's all work *and* all play for me on the rodeo circuit. You should have tried in when you had the chance."

"There's enough real cowboy work here on the ranch. Don't you have enough trophies, belt buckles and prize money by now?"

B.J. looked at him as if he was stupid. "It isn't about the winnings."

"Then what?"

"Not everyone finds Coffee Creek the most wonderful place in the world."

Corb decided to let the conversation end there. He and B.J. had had this same argument before and he never won. Besides, today he had weightier matters on his mind. He carried his plate to the kitchen where he scraped the food into the trash, then placed the plate in the dishwasher.

"Not hungry?" Jackson had been present last night and for most of today, but he kept a low profile and didn't talk much. This morning he and Cassidy had gone out riding for a few hours and he and B.J. had spent some time talking in the tack room afterward.

That was Jackson's way. He preferred to deal with people one-on-one rather than in large groups. Now he was hanging out in the kitchen, looking almost as nerve-racked as Corb felt.

"Big day," Jackson said, his eyes trained on the view out the kitchen window. "You sure Winnie won't be coming to the wedding?"

"Positive. She's just not up to it."

Some of the edge seemed to leave Jackson's face then. "What time is Laurel coming over?"

"The justice of the peace will be here at two-thirty. Laurel and Eugenia will be coming fifteen minutes later." Corb glanced at his watch, surprised to see that it was already past one. "Hell. I better get back to my place and take a shower."

Jackson nodded. "A shave would be a good idea, too."

Corb knew it was supposed to be bad luck for a groom to see the bride before the ceremony on their wedding day. He didn't think there were any rules against talking on the phone, though.

So why wasn't Laurel taking his calls? He'd tried her that morning, after chores, then again after lunch, and once more when he came out of the shower.

All his calls went straight through to messages.

"Where are you, sugar? I hope you slept well. Give me a call when you have a minute."

But either she didn't have a spare minute, or she never checked her messages, because by three o'clock that afternoon he still hadn't heard from her.

The justice of the peace, a friendly woman in her forties who'd driven down from Lewistown and was dressed for the occasion in a light brown suit, had arrived right as scheduled. She was in the kitchen now, sipping tea and chatting with his mother.

Laurel and the others should have been here fifteen minutes ago. Finally, Corb grew tired of pacing the length of the family room and he went out to the yard to wait. Cassidy, Jackson and B.J. came with him.

It was the last day of September. A warm, sunny day that promised only good things.

So where the hell was she?

His stomach knotted as he remembered another wedding when part of the wedding party hadn't arrived on time. Could fate be that cruel? Had she been in an automobile accident?

He could tell other members of his family were anxious, too. Jackson was fiddling with his truck, pretending to check the oil and the tire pressure, all the while keeping one eye on the laneway.

Cassidy and Sky were sitting on the front porch. His sister was wearing the same ivory-colored cowboy boots she'd bought for Winnie and Brock's wedding. At one minute past three, she took them off and flung them angrily in the grass. "Maybe we should call the sheriff."

"No. Hold off. It'll be okay." B.J. was the voice of reason, but Corb could tell that even he was feeling tense. B.J. always went still and calm when he was nervous. A trait he'd either inherited, or picked up from their father.

Then, finally, at five minutes past three, a vehicle came into view. No one relaxed until it was close enough that they could be sure this wasn't an official vehicle, but Eugenia driving an old gray station wagon.

She was alone.

What the hell?

Eugenia was out of the car a second after she turned off the ignition. "I'm so sorry I'm late. I've been trying to call, but maybe someone left the phone off the hook?"

Cassidy came running, barefoot, from the porch. "It's my fault. I unplugged the house phone because I needed to charge my cell. I meant to plug it back in, but I forgot."

Corb waved off her explanation. "Where's Laurel? Is she okay?"

Eugenia's crestfallen expression was not encouraging. She was still wearing an apron, as if she'd left in a hurry.

"I had the food ready to go and stopped to pick up Laurel at two o'clock, just as planned. I was going to help her get into her dress, then drive her here to the ranch."

Corb nodded. Laurel had gone over this with him last Sunday. Which was the last time he'd seen her, he realized, kind of surprised. How had an entire week gone by without them getting together?

"But Laurel wasn't there," Winnie continued. "All her stuff was gone. She left me a note. And this letter for you." She passed Corb an envelope then and he stared at the name written in blue pen on the front.

His name. In Laurel's handwriting.

He folded it in half and tucked it in the back pocket of his pants. He'd have to be someplace private to read it. But first he wanted to know what she'd told Eugenia.

"Did you bring the note she wrote for you?" His voice sounded as though it was coming from someplace faraway. He couldn't believe this was happening to him. Last time they'd made love, he'd thought they were so happy. What had happened to change all that?

And why had Laurel opted to tell him in a letter rather than in person?

She tried last night...you didn't have time.

"I have it," Eugenia said, her gaze traveling to the family members slowly circling around him. Cassidy and Sky on one side, B.J. on the other, Jackson standing slightly behind them all. And then, the only one missing came out of the house.

"Is she finally here?" His mother stepped out of the house, into the sunshine. She was wearing a dress Corb had never seen before. Her hair had been freshly colored and styled, and she'd put on makeup and proper shoes. Not as gussied up as she'd been for Brock's wedding, but she was mother of the groom—no one would mistake her for anything less.

Not wanting his mother to come to the wrong conclusion, Corb spoke quickly. "It's okay, Mom. Laurel seems to have changed her mind. Eugenia didn't find her at the apartment. But she left a note."

Olive took a few seconds to process all this. Then she pushed her way to the center of her family and stood next to Corb. She sized up Eugenia, then her gaze moved to the note in her hands.

"What did she say?"

Olive sounded fragile, and Corb put a hand around his mother's waist. B.J. moved in closer, too, and Corb wondered why it was that his family never seemed to be able to support one another except in moments of crisis.

Eugenia's hands were shaking as she unfolded the piece of paper.

Eugenia, I'm sorry to do this to you, but I've decided I can't go through with it. Would you please call off the wedding for me? I know I've left this to almost the last possible moment, but I figured this out myself just a few minutes ago.

I've written a letter to Corb explaining everything to him. Please make sure he gets it.

I cleaned the apartment before I left and you'll see I've borrowed Winnie's car to drive to Billings. I'll leave it in the airport parking lot and I'll courier you the keys as soon as I arrive in New York. Please arrange to have someone go and collect it. I'm sorry for the inconvenience. And I'm sorry I won't be there to help with the Cinnamon Stick anymore.

Eugenia stopped. She looked up from the paper to Corb's face. "That's all she wrote. I imagine the rest is in your letter."

He nodded, then turned away and started walking.

"Corb, honey, don't run off." Olive sounded as torn up as he felt. "She never was good enough for you."

Corb kept moving. He headed up Lake Road, his head in a fog.

Suddenly Sky gave a sharp bark. He turned back to look at her. Her eyes fixed right on him, Sky got to her feet, took a few steps in his direction, halted and looked back at Cassidy.

His little sister was crying. She blinked, then nodded at her dog and finally managed to say, "It's okay, Sky. He needs you more. Go."

And Sky went—her lope betraying a slight limp as she advanced toward Corb. When she caught up to him Corb didn't stop but he did pat her briefly on the top of her head. And then they rounded a bend in the road and his family was out of sight.

He stayed numb for a good while. He'd initially planned to hole up in the sanctuary of his home, but he ended up by the lake, sitting in one of the cedar chairs lining the shore. It was peaceful here. Beautiful. A shimmering upside-down version of the golden aspen, sage-green ponderosa pine and crisp blue sky was reflected in the water.

His camera, safely ensconced in its black case, was sitting on the chair next to his. He'd planned on asking Jackson to take some photographs of the ceremony, which should have happened right here, about fifteen minutes ago now.

Corb sank deeper into his chair. And Sky, faithful

Sky, settled patiently at his feet, her head resting over one of his boots.

Time passed. Maybe half an hour.

He started thinking again. Slowly. First he thought of her. Where was she right now? In a plane? Already in New York? What did she look like, how did she feel?

He shifted in his seat then pulled his phone and her letter out from his pockets. First he checked the phone. No missed calls. No messages.

Then he opened the letter. Took a fortifying look at the beauty around him, then started to read.

Dear Corb,

I'm so sorry for canceling our wedding this way. It's cowardly, I know. But I was afraid if I told you in person that you would change my mind. You're a persuasive guy, you know, or at least I find you that way.

Because why else did I agree to this crazy plan of ours? It isn't fair to either of us. You've had such a tough time lately and I know you want to do the right thing, but these are modern times and getting married isn't always the only solution.

We can raise this child without getting married. I know we can make it work.

As for me, I'm not ready to give up my dream of living and working in New York City. So I'm going home. But I will be in touch, and you and I will work out a way for us both to spend time with our child.

Then she signed off. He thought she'd written "Love Laurel" but there was a smear on the word before her name, a little round spot about the size of a teardrop.

So maybe she hadn't written love. Maybe it was "best wishes" or something like that.

Corb ran his thumb over her words, trying to imagine her penning this letter in the wee hours of the previous night.

And he'd had no idea. He hadn't even entertained the possibility that she might not show up today.

Now what?

He contemplated the day before him. The week. The month. The year. It all seemed to be just a whole lot of time to get through somehow.

Eventually he remembered his camera. He hadn't used it since before the accident. There were probably pictures on it that he'd taken during the week that he no longer remembered.

Curious, he unzipped the case and pulled out his Nikon. He turned on the power and shifted his body to protect the viewfinder from the sun.

One by one he scrolled through the pictures. There were dozens of them.

And yes, some of them were of Winnie and Brock. And it hurt to see how happy they were, with no clue of the tragedy that would soon end it all.

But most of the pictures were of Laurel.

He'd clearly been entranced with her. There were pictures she posed for, but even more that he'd taken when she wasn't looking.

One of her crouched next to Sky, rubbing the old dog behind her ears.

Another of her with Winnie, laughing like the lifelong friends they were.

And still more of her listening quietly at the dinner table, one with her tucking a strand of her hair behind her ear, and finally a silly shot of her sticking her tongue out at him for taking too many pictures.

At one point he'd wondered if he'd viewed that week as a fun affair with a beautiful woman, or if he'd actually been falling in love.

Looking at all these pictures, the answer was obvious.

There were even some that he must have taken in his bedroom, the night they'd made love, the night she'd become pregnant. She was wearing his shirt—the blue one that had smelled faintly of her perfume. Her hair was long and disheveled and her complexion was pink and her hazel eyes glowed like liquid gold.

He knew that look. There could be no doubt what had happened before those images were captured.

"Wow." He scrolled through the pictures a second time. And a third.

And slowly it hit him. The reason this was hurting so much was because he loved her.

He'd loved her then.

And he loved her now.

More time passed. Eventually Corb heard footsteps approaching from behind. Then his brother handed him a beer, and settled with his own drink in the chair to Corb's right.

"Are you okay?" B.J. stared at the lake, then he turned to Corb, his dark grey eyes full of worry.

"I don't know. I was kind of numb at first. Now I'm starting to feel pretty crappy."

"This came out of the blue? You hadn't fought or anything?"

"No fight." He sighed. "But I can't say it came out of the blue. A few times lately Laurel asked me if I was sure we were doing the right thing. Last night she called and said she wanted to talk. I told her to come to the ranch, but she wanted me to go to her."

"And you didn't."

"I knew Mom would be disappointed…." He stopped and thought about what he'd just said. "Hell."

"Mom is tougher than she looks. You can say no to her now and then and she won't break."

Corb shook his head. "I haven't said no to her at all lately." He'd been trying to be a good son. But every time he'd put his mother first, he'd been putting Laurel second.

Laurel hadn't mentioned anything in her letter about that. She'd made it sound like she'd chosen New York and her career over him.

But he couldn't remember her once talking about her job and how much she missed it.

What he could remember her talking about was his feelings for Jacqueline. And was he sure they were doing the right thing?

"This getting married idea was a little rushed," B.J. said. "Maybe Laurel made the right decision going back to New York."

Corb wanted to howl. "She's thousands of miles away from me, man! How can that be the right thing?"

"So, it's more than the baby," B.J. replied, his voice insufferably calm in the face of Corb's distress. "You love her."

"I— Yes! I do love her."

"And she knows that?"

Corb didn't answer. Instead, he leaned forward, wrapping his arms around his head, like it was aching, when the truth was only his heart was in pain.

"We were talking up at the house, after you left," B.J. said.

"I'll bet you were."

"Hey, don't sound bitter. We all want what's best for you. Mom said something that didn't make sense to me at the time."

"What else is new?"

B.J. ignored his attempt at a joke. "She said that you must have done something to scare Laurel off. Mom said the way that woman looked at you, reminded her of the way she felt about our father."

Corb sat up straighter. Olive's love for Bob Lambert was the stuff legends were made of. And his father had been just as devoted to her.

"When she said that, I thought to myself that she had to be wrong. If Laurel loved you that much, she'd never have left. Unless—" He glanced at Corb.

"Unless she didn't know I felt the same way about her." Corb thought with regret of the opportunities he'd had. When he'd asked her to marry him. After they'd made love. On the drive home from buying their wedding rings and the license.

The wasted chances seemed endless now.

"I don't know why I never said those words. I was so focused on the baby, and wanting the kid to grow up in Montana. That's why I asked her to marry me in the first place."

"I guess that's a good reason for some people," B.J. replied. "But it obviously wasn't enough for Laurel."

Chapter 14

It was seven in the evening in New York, which meant it would be five o'clock in Montana. On a regular weekday, Laurel would be closing the café and battling the nausea that always seemed to hit her around this time of day.

So maybe it was pregnancy, and not the swaying and lurching of the taxi as the driver wove through Manhattan traffic, that was making her feel so terrible.

Laurel had brought the barf bag from the plane with her, just in case. She had it close at hand, beside her purse. And if things got much worse, she might need it.

Above her queasy stomach, another one of her internal organs was in pain, too. Her heart felt twice its usual size, as if a heavy weight had been inserted inside.

No pregnancy hormones were to blame for this problem, though. She'd just severed ties with the most amazing man she'd ever known. And what a mess she'd made of it. They'd be calling her the "flyaway bride" back in Coffee Creek. Maybe someone would make a movie. She hoped they got Amy Adams to play her role. Ryan Reynolds could play Corb—only he wasn't nearly cute or sexy enough for the role.

Laurel leaned her head against the windowpane. Everywhere she looked there were buildings and lights, taxis and cars. And people. People out walking their dogs, mothers holding the hand of a child, couples arm in arm, businesspeople striding while talking on the phone or texting, glancing up to orient themselves every now and then.

New York.

Once she'd wanted it so badly. And now it was all hers.

The taxi jerked to a stop. The driver put his arm over the seat and turned so she could see his hawkish profile. "Forty-three dollars."

She had the money ready and passed it to him. "Keep the change."

Her old brown suitcase with the pink ribbon on the handle was in the trunk, but he didn't get out to help her with the luggage, just pressed the button to release the trunk. She unloaded the case to the sidewalk herself, then stood in front of the three-story apartment building where she lived, trying to remember how she'd felt the first time she'd seen it.

Excited and full of hope. Open to adventure, but a little nervous, too.

She wished she could be that girl again, rather than her own nauseous and heartsick self.

Oh, stop feeling sorry for yourself. She gripped her

suitcase in one hand, her carry-on and purse in the other and climbed the stairs slowly, planting both feet on one step before heaving the suitcases ahead of her. Her neighbors would think a three-hundred-pound man with mobility issues was on his way up.

The usually musty hallway smelled sweetly of turmeric and coriander. One of her neighbors must be cooking a nice curry for dinner. Laurel set down her cases by the door marked 2C and pulled out her keys.

The place was just as she'd left it, clean and neat, the stale smell almost completely masked by the orange blossom scented infusion sticks she'd left sitting on the table.

She didn't unpack, simply pushed her suitcases against the wall, then looked around the three-hundred-square-foot studio apartment. She'd taken a lot of trouble to decorate the place nicely and make it feel like a real home.

Once she'd thought she'd succeeded.

But now she knew she hadn't. This wasn't her place. Not really. She'd tried New York, and it was exciting and different, but she'd been born in Montana and that was where she truly belonged. Once she'd had a few days to recover and organize she would move to Billings, find a job and rent a bigger apartment—one with room for a baby.

She'd be close to Winnie and also to Corb, who would be able to spend a lot more time with his child than if she chose to stay in New York City.

The decision came to her in a rush, and she was amazed at how right it felt. She'd figured on needing at least a month to figure out the next step in her life.

But now that she knew where she wanted to be, she

was anxious to get her plan in motion. First thing was subletting her apartment. She had a good idea who to call.

She dug out her phone, then went to stand by the window as she waited.

"Laurel? Is it really you?" It was her friend Anna from work.

"I'm finally back in the city."

"Oh, good. I've missed you. We all have. The extra work has been insane, even though they hired a temp. Blair was assigned your stories and he's such a pain! He walks around with his nose so high in the air, like he's Anderson Bloody Cooper or something, but his writing totally sucks. Will you be in the office tomorrow?"

She'd forgotten how much Anna liked to talk. But she had to admit it was rather ego-repairing to hear that she'd been missed.

"Actually, I'm not in New York to stay. I've decided to tender my resignation and move back to Montana."

She didn't mention being pregnant. Or her almost-marriage to Corb. What was the point? She and Anna had grown to be pretty good friends in the two years they'd worked at the magazine together. Still, once she moved to Montana, Laurel knew they would eventually drift apart. Not like her and Winnie. No matter what, they were friends for life.

"Seriously?"

"Seriously. I'm here to pack up the rest of my stuff and find someone to sublet my apartment."

Anna sucked in her breath. "Oh—I've always loved your cute little walk-up. And the location! Right by the L train in the East Village."

Laurel smiled, not insulted—well, not much—that

Anna was more interested in her studio walk-up than in the fact that she was moving.

"I have nice neighbors, too. And the good news is they have the mouse problem almost under control."

"Very funny." Anna paused. "That was a joke, right?"

"Yes." They made plans to go for dinner on Monday evening to finalize the details. Laurel ended the call feeling curiously empty inside.

She didn't really care about any of it. Not her old job. Not even Anna, that much.

She dropped listlessly to the daybed that also doubled as her couch. She ought to order in some food. Had she eaten anything at all today?

But fatigue caught up to her before she could place another call. She closed her eyes and drifted off....

It was Monday, almost noon, when Corb finally arrived at the address he'd conned out of Winnie without too much difficulty. Getting into the locked main entrance of Laurel's apartment building wasn't difficult. The door was stiff and hadn't closed properly, which meant the lock hadn't caught.

Corb slipped inside. He paused to get his bearings, then, noticing a bank of letter boxes, checked the name for 2C.

Laurel Sheridan. He was definitely at the right place. *Thank you, Winnie.* Her directions had gotten him this far.

The rest was up to him.

He climbed the worn wooden stairs, his boots sounding loudly on each step. When he reached her door, he pulled a paper bag out of his pocket, then knocked.

It took a while for her to come to the door, but he knew she was home, because he could hear sounds. Footsteps and running water and then suddenly the door opened two inches and he could hear her voice.

"Who's there?"

"Me."

"Corb?" Her voice was a squeak, initially. Then she said a louder and more uncertain, "Corb Lambert?"

"Yup. Would you let me in? I have something of yours."

She closed the door so she could release the safety chain. Then opened it wide and put her hands on her hips, staring at him in disbelief.

She was wearing the same yoga pants and striped shirt that she'd had on the last time he'd dropped by unannounced. Her hair was in the same messy bun, and her eyes had that sleepy, muddled look.

He wanted to kiss her.

But first he'd wait to see if she invited him in.

"How did you get here?"

"Red-eye. A couple of them. I missed a few connections and had to do a little scrambling or I would have been here earlier." He looked past her to the apartment. It looked small. But pretty. Walls were painted a color that looked like fresh butter and there were paintings of flowers on the wall, and cozy rugs on the wooden floors.

"Come in," she said finally.

Three steps put him pretty much in the center of the room. There weren't any bedrooms, just a galley kitchen, a bathroom, and this. Feeling claustrophobic, he went to stand by the window, which was open a few inches.

"So what's in the bag this time?" Laurel asked, crossing her arms over her chest, looking uncomfortable and so damn adorable, all at the same time. "Don't tell me I left my underwear behind again?"

"Not this time." He didn't show her, though. It was too soon. "How are you?"

"I'm okay. Feeling kind of stupid, though. I'm sorry for leaving that way, Corb. I should have talked to you."

"Yeah. You should have."

"And now you've traveled all this way— Oh, I am really sorry, Corb."

Tears shimmered in her eyes. He knew she wasn't crying to make herself more attractive to him, but that was the result just the same. He looked away from her to the street, and the view of the brick building that had been built about six inches from this one.

Why would anyone want a view like this when they could be looking at a lake and mountains and trees?

"I wish you would have talked to me before you left, because there's something I would have told you. Just to see if it made any difference."

She moved closer, as if she could tell how difficult this was for him, and knew that he needed a little encouragement.

"What would you have told me?"

"I would have said that I don't remember falling in love with you the first time." He glanced sideways. Saw her mouth tighten with pain.

"But I *do* remember falling in love with you the second time," he continued. "And I suppose that if somewhere down the line I happened to get another major crack on the head and lost my memory again, I'd fall in love with you a third time, too."

He turned to her then, looking in her eyes for his answer. He was prepared to be shot down. But he knew he had to take this risk rather than spend his life wondering what her answer would have been.

Her eyes were filling with tears again. But he could tell these were the happy kind, and as his heart started lifting, he held out his arms with hope.

And she came to him. Putting her arms around him, too, then laying her head against his chest. "You don't know how badly I wanted to hear you say that."

"I was an idiot. I was hung up on trying to remember the past, not realizing that it was the here and now that mattered most."

"I love you, too, you know. Just in case you were wondering."

"That's nice to hear. Given that you ran off on our wedding day and all."

"I really am sorry about that, Corb."

"It's okay now. I have an apology of my own. I'm sorry I put my mother's preferences about our wedding ahead of yours. Looking back, I can't believe I was so stupid."

"You love your mom. And you're a good son, Corb."

"But I want to be an even better husband." His hand slid down to her belly. "And father."

"You will be. I know it."

He wrapped his arms around her and pulled her in close, wanting no space between them. None at all.

He rested his face against the wild curls on the top of her head. Then he released the clip, setting them free.

She arched her neck back and finally they were kissing. Softly and gently, like two people who still couldn't quite believe this was happening to them.

Eventually he pulled away, needing a little more reassurance. "Does this mean you'll marry me? And come back to Montana?"

"I will," she said solemnly. "I promise."

"And you won't miss the city too much?"

"We can always visit."

"Then it's time you looked in here." He held out the paper bag which had gotten crumpled quite badly while they were kissing.

"It looks empty," she said, but on trust, she slipped her hand inside and felt around.

His heart skipped anxiously when she didn't find anything.

And then her eyes grew wide and her lips parted with a soft "Wow. Oh, Corb."

She pulled out the ring, then passed it to him, holding out her left hand so he could slip it on her finger. It seemed to fit quite well.

"It's beautiful! Corb, where on earth did you get this?"

"They have this store here in New York City. Tiffany's? I told them we wouldn't need the box. We don't, do we?"

"No. Because this ring is never going to leave my finger. I love it, Corb and I'll wear it proudly. But the wedding bands we bought in Lewistown would have been enough."

"No, they wouldn't. I came here to do things right this time, and an engagement ring was part of the package. But I do have a favor to ask of you."

"Anything."

"I'd like to stay a few days and get married here."

"But—I thought you wanted to have our wedding

at the ranch. And I do, too. It's so beautiful…it's the perfect place."

"We have our entire lives to enjoy the ranch. Think of the story we can tell our kids, about how I chased you all the way back to New York City, then whisked you off to City Hall to tie the knot."

"That would make a great story," she admitted. "But your mom. She'll be crushed."

"She'll recover. This is *our* day, after all." He pulled her back into his arms, working his hands under her sweatshirt as he leaned in for another kiss. "'Course there are going to be parts of this story we never tell our kids."

She urged him back a few steps, then toppled him down to the daybed with her right on top of him. Her face just inches from his she whispered, "I'd like to get to those parts right now if you don't mind."

He sure didn't.

Epilogue

Since her mother-in-law had been denied the wedding she wanted, Laurel graciously allowed her to organize the baby shower.

And Olive, in her own inimitable style, took the ball and ran with it.

B.J. and Cassidy were home for the event, of course. Also invited were all the local ranchers—excluding Maddie Turner, of course—and Vince, Eugenia and Dawn from the café.

Never had the Lambert family been so badly in need of spring as they were this year. Rebirth was all around them. Fields full of sturdy, dark-faced calves and wobbly-legged foals. And best of all, a new baby in the family—two if you counted Winnie's new son, but the Lamberts didn't know about him yet.

None of this made the loss of Brock any easier to handle, but it was a reminder to celebrate the precious gift of life when you could.

Corb felt serenely happy, almost blissful, in the middle of the organized chaos of the event. The house was decorated with fresh tulips and daffodils, as well as balloons in the pastel shades his mother had selected.

Matching napkins and streamers had been purchased in the same watered-down shades—though he'd only noticed this because Laurel had pointed it out to him earlier.

He was holding one-month-old Stephanie in his arms, his gaze following Laurel as she circulated among the guests, sipping sparkling apple juice and turning every now and then to look at him and smile.

He wondered how it was that everyone else in the room wasn't staring at her, too. The only times he could tear his gaze away was when he glanced down at their perfect little daughter, resting against his chest, where he could offer her the warmth and security she needed in the face of all the noise and commotion.

All his life he'd thought his calling in life was to be a rancher. But now he knew it was so much more. Being a husband to Laurel and a father to Stephanie were the roles that meant the most to him. He'd been happy before, but now he felt fulfilled. He knew they were still in the so-called *honeymoon phase* of marriage, but he had no doubt that he and Laurel had what it took to make their relationship last.

Respect, trust…and humor. Somehow even when they were both up at two in the morning dealing with dirty diapers and colic, Laurel could still make him laugh.

She was putting her sense of humor to use in other ways, as well. She'd started a blog a few months before the baby was born. She called it *Rancher's Wife 101* and in it she chronicled the ups of downs of adjusting from life in New York City to being a hands-on wife of a cowboy in Montana, and a new mother to boot.

She had her hands full, that was for sure. But so did they all, and being busy just meant the quiet moments were treasured all the more.

"I see you've found yourself a nice quiet spot here in the corner."

"Busted." He grinned at Vince, the crotchety old baker from the Cinnamon Stick. "Say, I saw you talking to my mother earlier. I didn't know you two were acquainted."

"Oh, we grew up together. I used to know her and her sister real well."

"Maddie."

Vince hesitated, then nodded. "Yes, Maddie."

He slipped off then. Maybe for another soft drink, maybe to get some fresh air.

Corb had been thinking of his aunt more and more lately. In fact, he'd mentioned to Jackson that he was hoping to swing by one day and put on a new roof for her, when Jackson had surprised him and told him he'd handled the job himself.

There were undercurrents in his family that he'd never understand, Corb figured.

Including the whereabouts of Winnie. She still hadn't made it back to Coffee Creek and Laurel refused to discuss this mysterious ailment that apparently wasn't life-threatening, but that also seemed to make travel impossible.

* * *

Laurel was munching down an oatmeal cookie when Cassidy came to join her at the buffet table. The pretty blonde had Stephanie in her arms—and she looked like a natural.

"I can't believe you managed to wrestle her away from Corb." Laurel chased the cookie down with a sip of apple juice. "He'd hold her all day long if he didn't have so much work to do."

"Yeah, I always knew Corb would make a great dad. But I told him he has to share." Cassidy smiled down at the tiny baby snuggled in her arms. "She's so adorable. I wish I didn't have to leave tomorrow."

"Your final exam is next Friday?"

"Yes. And then I'll be done."

"So then what? You know your mother is hoping you'll move back home."

"Oh, right, like I went to all the work of getting my master's so I could work on a ranch for the rest of my life." Cassidy wrinkled her nose. "Sorry. That sounded bitchy. I'm sure I *will* come home for a few weeks at least, just to take a break before I start working full-time."

"That would be nice." Laurel was looking forward to the opportunity to get to know her new sister-in-law a little better. "Do you have a job lined up?"

Anxiety creased Cassidy's fine brow. "I have a few prospects, but no firm offers."

Laurel touched her arm sympathetically. "Give it time. I'm sure the offers will come soon enough."

The baby's eyes suddenly popped open. She gazed up at Cassidy with a worried frown on her forehead.

"What's the matter, sweetie? Don't recognize me?"

Despite Cassidy's loving tone, the baby started to cry, and Laurel happily helped Cassidy transfer the bundle to her.

"Stephanie is such a pretty name."

"We named her after my mother," Laurel explained. After both mothers, actually. She hoped her daughter didn't one day complain about the middle name Olive. But it would have been impolitic not to include both grandmothers as namesakes.

Corb joined them then, slipping an arm over Laurel's shoulders, then bending over to give his little girl a kiss.

"You two are sickeningly happy," Cassidy said, the harsh words tempered with a reluctant smile.

"Maybe one day you'll be so lucky," Corb replied mildly.

"I doubt it."

"What about that Josh fellow? You still seeing him? Farley will be pretty disappointed if you are."

"Isn't Farley the vet?" Laurel had been following the banter up to that point. Now she gave Corb a look of total confusion.

But Cassidy had no trouble deciphering his meaning. "Stop it, Corb. You're supposed to be the nice brother, remember?" Face flushed and eyes bright, she turned and disappeared into the crowd.

"What was that about?" Laurel asked her husband, leaning a little against his solid chest.

"It's a long story." Corb nuzzled the side of her neck. "Is this party going to break up soon? I want to take my girls home. I'm tired of sharing."

Laurel smiled, more to herself than anything. She was so, so lucky to have found this man.

And this family, too. For the most part, she was enjoying being a new member of the Lambert clan. Once she'd been an orphan with no siblings or extended family. Now she had, not only a husband, a daughter and the best friend in the world, but also two new brothers and a sister, as well.

Plus a mother-in-law, of course. Olive was a challenge but the new baby had softened her. Hopefully the changes would be permanent.

And if they weren't, Laurel wouldn't complain. She'd never expected perfection. But here, in Coffee Creek, Montana, she'd come darn close.

* * * * *

RITA® Award finalist **Gail Barrett** always knew she wanted to be a writer. After living everywhere from Spain to the Bahamas, earning a graduate degree in linguistics and teaching high school Spanish for years, she finally fulfilled that goal. Her books have won numerous awards, including the National Readers' Choice Award, the Book Buyers' Best Award, and RWA's Golden Heart® Award. Visit her website, gailbarrett.com.

Books by Gail Barrett

Harlequin Romantic Suspense

Fatal Exposure
A Kiss to Die For
Seduced by His Target
High-Stakes Affair
High-Risk Reunion

Visit the Author Profile page at Harlequin.com for more titles.

COWBOY UNDER SIEGE

GAIL BARRETT

To John, my own Montana hero.

Acknowledgments

I'd like to thank the following people for their extraordinary help with this book: Elle Kennedy and Judith Sandbrook for their invaluable input and critiques; René Tanner at Montana State University for explaining how their library system works; Caroline Sullivan and Dorothy Archer for their nursing help; Russ Howe for information on pharmaceutical companies; Rebecca May-Henson and Mary Jo Archer for patiently answering my questions about horses and bloat; Piper Rome and John K. Barrett for information about weapons. Please note that any mistakes are definitely my own!

And a very special thank-you to Patience Bloom, Keyren Gerlach and the rest of the Harlequin family for including me in this project. Marie, Beth, Carla, Elle and Cindy—you ladies rock!

Chapter 1

The sharp report of a gunshot cracked through the afternoon stillness, the echo reverberating through the rolling rangeland and scattering the sparrows on the barbed-wire fence. Cole Kelley jerked up his head and fixed his gaze on the parched brown hills marking the southern boundary of his ranch. Four more shots barked out in quick succession, execution-style. Then a deep, ringing silence gripped the land.

Cole stood dead still, every sense hyperalert, his attention locked on the hills. Nothing moved. No wisp of dust blurred the cloudless sky. Only the dried grass rippled and bowed, paying homage to the perpetual Montana wind.

But coming close on the heels of his sister's abduction, those shots could only mean one thing—trouble.

His pulse kicked into a sprint.

Cole released his hold on his fencing pliers, yanked off his leather work gloves and tugged the cell phone from the back pocket of his jeans. He speed dialed the bunkhouse, relieved he could pick up a signal on the twelve-thousand-acre ranch.

"I just heard gunfire," he said when one of his ranch hands, Earl Runningcrane, answered the phone. "I'm in the south section along Honey Creek. Who've we got working nearby?"

"Nobody. They're all in the northeast section, stacking the rest of the hay."

Just as he'd expected. *Then who had fired shots on his land?*

"All right," he said. "I'm going to investigate. Stand by in case I need help."

A profound sense of uneasiness unfurling inside him, Cole gathered up his fencing tools and whistled softly for Mitzy, the border collie chasing rabbits nearby. He loped through the grass to his pickup truck, the tension that had dogged him for the past two weeks ratcheting higher yet.

There was an outside chance those shots had come from a hunter, but deer season didn't start for another week. And with the danger currently stalking his family...

Cole yanked open the truck door, waited a heartbeat for the dog to leap inside, then slid in beside her and turned the key. "Hold on," he warned as she pointed her nose out the open passenger side window to scent the breeze. "We're moving out fast."

He shifted into gear and gunned the engine, causing the pickup to fishtail on the gravel road. Then he stomped his boot to the floorboard and sped toward the

Bar Lazy K's southern boundary, giving rise to a billowing plume of dust.

Those shots could be a coincidence—someone shooting at targets, local teens fooling around. But Cole's gut warned him that he wasn't going to like what he found. Ever since his father's infidelities had hit the tabloids, creating a national media sensation, his family had been under siege.

Dealing with the press was annoying enough. Reporters tramped over Cole's land for a glimpse of the senator. Paparazzi massed outside the ranch gates like flies over roadkill, their numbers swelling every time another of Hank's mistresses came to light—six so far, proving his father had ignored his wedding vows as easily as he'd forgotten his kids. Photographers had even hovered over the house in helicopters, vying for a shot they could sell to the tabloids, until Cole took out a restraining order to stop them from terrifying the cows.

But there was a darker, far more sinister element seeking his father, unknown enemies who'd threatened his life. And two weeks ago, in a bid to force the senator out of hiding, they'd abducted Cole's sister, Lana, throwing the family into a panic and dramatically upping the stakes.

His jaw clenched tight at the thought of his kidnapped sister, Cole sped up the hill at the corner of his ranch. At the top he hit the brakes, waited for the dust to clear, then scanned the surrounding terrain. Antelope watched from a rise in the distance. Gnarled fence posts stood at the edge of his property like sentinels against the cobalt-blue sky. The gravel road ribboned across the hills toward the Absaroka Mountains, the wide-open rangeland giving way to clusters of pines.

There wasn't a person or vehicle in sight.

His nerves taut, Cole leaped from the truck, grabbed his rifle from the gun rack behind his seat, and chambered a round. Then, keeping Mitzy beside him, he waded through the grass toward the fence. The wind bore down, carrying with it the faint sound of lowing cows.

He reached his barbed-wire fence, and Honey Creek came into view below him, a sparkling streak meandering through his neighbor's unmowed alfalfa fields. *Still nothing.* His heart beating fast, he ran his gaze over the treeless hillsides, then turned his attention to the grass trampled down around the gate. Someone had recently been here, but who?

The foreboding inside him increasing, he unhooked the barbed wire gate and dragged it aside, then followed the line of crushed grass to the slope of the hill. He swept his gaze to the river bottom where he'd pastured his cattle—stalling on three black cows lying motionless in the sun.

He curled his hands. Anger flared inside him like a wildfire on a brush-choked hill. Someone had deliberately slaughtered his cattle. *But why?*

Furious at the senseless loss, he searched the grass around his feet and found a brass casing glinting in the sun. He examined the markings—300 RUM. Powerful enough to take down big game—or several defenseless cows.

Struggling to control his temper, he stormed down the hill, scanning the slopes for the remainder of his herd. Insects buzzed in the midday heat. The warm wind brushed his face. He glanced upriver and finally caught a glimpse of the scattered cows. They'd crashed through the barbed-wire fence and crossed the creek into his neighbor's alfalfa. Now he had to chase them out before they died of bloat.

Disgusted, he tugged out his cell phone and called the bunkhouse again. "It's me," he said when Earl picked up. "We've got several dead cows."

"Someone *shot* them?"

"Yeah." And then the coward had run away. "The rest of the herd broke through the fence and got into Del Harvey's alfalfa. I need several men here fast. Have them bring extra barbed wire and stomach tubes, just in case. And tell Kenny to bring the front loader to haul away the dead cows."

"Kenny went to the Bozeman airport," his ranch hand said. "He's picking up Rusty's daughter. She's flying in from Chicago for a couple of weeks."

The muscles of Cole's stomach tightened. *Bethany Moore.* This was all he needed. He swore and closed his eyes. But Bethany was no longer his business. Their affair had ended years ago.

"You there, boss?" the cowboy asked.

"Yeah, I'm here." Cole blew out his breath and massaged his eyes. "Just make sure someone brings the front loader. And call the sheriff, Wes Colton. I want him to take a look at this."

Cole disconnected the call, determined to keep his mind off Bethany and the past. She'd made her choices. She'd left Montana. *She'd left him.* But he hadn't expected anything else. He'd learned early in life that people never stayed. The only thing he could depend on was his land.

Turning his thoughts firmly back to his herd, he returned to his truck, placed his rifle in the gun rack, and climbed into the cab. He had to work quickly to drive the surviving cattle back across the creek. Mitzy could keep them safely corralled until the men repaired the fence.

Still furious, he cranked the engine. He glanced in his rearview mirror, waited until Mitzy jumped into the open truck bed, then steered his pickup off the road. He bumped and jostled across the field and through the gate, still barely able to keep his temper in check.

He didn't understand this senseless destruction. And he sure as hell didn't need it. Not when his foreman had broken his leg, leaving him shorthanded. Not when his sister had been abducted and the FBI didn't have any leads. And not when he was smack in the middle of the fall roundup, when the future of the Bar Lazy K Ranch—and the livelihood of a dozen men—depended on him getting a thousand healthy cattle to market in the next two weeks. An entire year of work boiled down to this single paycheck, and every cow, every pound they gained or lost, could make or break the ranch.

He splashed the truck through the shallow creek bed and drove up the opposite bank. Even worse, he still had a hundred head stranded in the mountains he leased for summer pasture. He needed to hightail it up there to rescue them before the predicted snowstorm moved in, instead of wasting time hauling dead cows.

Scowling, he steered around the trio of carcasses, appalled again by the pointless waste. And fierce resolve hardened inside him, an iron vise gripping his gut. He'd put up with the paparazzi. He'd put up with his self-absorbed father and his bodyguards hanging around. But this was different. This was personal, a direct assault on his ranch.

But whoever had done this had underestimated him badly. The Bar Lazy K meant everything to Cole. This ranch was what he did, who he was. It wasn't just his livelihood, it was his soul. And anyone trying to harm it had better watch out. Because if they wanted war, they'd get it.

But he intended to win.

"What do you mean, she *died?*" Bethany Moore stood at the luggage carousel at the Bozeman airport, her cell phone pressed to her ear. "How? When? She was fine last night when I gave her the evening dose." Her seventy-year-old patient had been smiling, showing off photos of her granddaughter. How could she have suddenly died?

"They're looking into it," Adam Kopenski, the lead doctor administering the trial, said. "I'll let you know what I hear."

"Poor Mrs. Bolter. Her poor family." A lump thickened Bethany's throat. "I'll come right back. I'll have to check the flights, but I'm sure I can get there by tomorrow morning."

"There's no point returning," Adam said. "There's nothing you can do here. The hospital is looking into it, and I can answer any questions they have."

"I know, but—"

"Bethany, forget it. I told you, I've got everything under control. There's no reason for you to come back."

Bethany sighed. Adam was right, but she still felt torn. As head nurse in the drug trial, the patients' safety was her chief concern. "All right, but promise you'll call as soon as you hear anything. Day or night. Don't worry about the time difference."

"I will. And try not to worry. I'm sure it's just one of those things. Now enjoy your vacation. Eat some buffalo burgers and relax."

She forced a smile, trying not to think of Frances Bolter's kind blue eyes. "It's beef on a cattle ranch. Not buffalo."

"Whatever. Just have fun. You work too hard. And I promise I'll keep you informed."

"Thanks, Adam." She meant it. She owed her friend big-time. Not only had he put in a good word for her, helping get her appointed head nurse on the study—a huge advance to her career—but his lively wit had kept her entertained on many a lonely night.

But despite Adam's reassurance, she couldn't put the woman out of her mind. She clicked off her phone and stuck it in her purse just as her hunter-green suitcase pushed through the carousel's plastic flaps. She couldn't imagine what had gone wrong. The Preston-Werner Clinic had a stellar reputation. Adam had screened the patients meticulously for the trials. And Bethany's fellow nurses were all top-notch.

She sighed and pressed her fingertips to her eyes, gritty from the 3:00 a.m. wake-up to make her flight. Adam was right, though. There wasn't much she could do about Mrs. Bolter's death now. And she wasn't naive. She'd lost an occasional patient during the years she'd been a nurse. Still, it was never easy, especially with a patient that sweet.

Besides, her father needed her here in Montana, even if he'd insisted he was all right. He'd fallen off his horse and broken his leg—not an easy injury to recover from at sixty-eight years of age.

Her suitcase began to draw closer. Bethany skirted a

man in cowboy boots, hefted it from the carousel, and wheeled it across the luggage-claim area to the tall glass doors. Once outside, she blinked in the afternoon sunshine, Bethany walked past the stone pillars to the end of the sidewalk where she stopped to wait for her ride.

Relax, Adam had told her. She inhaled, filling her lungs with the dry mountain air, and willed her tension to ease—not hard to do since Bozeman's small regional airport had none of the frenzy of O'Hare. There were no shuttle buses spewing exhaust, no constant stream of traffic, no frantic people rushing to catch their flights— just a deserted parking lot dotted with rental cars and an occasional passenger strolling past.

She scanned the mountains ringing the horizon—the Bridger Mountains to the north, the Madison front of the Rockies to the west—their huge peaks dusted with snow. It always amazed her how far she could see out west without humidity hazing the air. Looking up, she spotted a lone hawk riding the currents, and a soothing peace settled inside. She loved the wide open spaces of the land where she'd grown up.

Then a man drove past in a pickup truck and shot her a hostile glare. She stiffened, trying not to let it affect her, but her fleeting sense of harmony disappeared. That right there was the reason she'd moved back east—because of people like him. To them, she was a Native American first, an individual second. Even having a Caucasian mother hadn't helped her fit in. At least in the anonymity of Chicago, she had the freedom to be herself.

And frankly, there'd been nothing to hold her here after high school. No family, aside from her father. No man, not after Cole Kelley made it clear where his priorities lay.

Her stomach turned over at the thought of Cole. In the past she'd managed to avoid him during her visits home to Maple Cove—but that was before her father had become the foreman on his ranch. Now that her father lived in a cabin on the Bar Lazy K, she was bound to run into Cole.

But maybe not. October was roundup time, the busiest time of the year. Cole would be loading cattle, shipping them to market. If she was lucky, she'd never see him around.

And if she did… So what? Cole was ancient history. He'd made his choice—his land over her—and she no longer cared. She had a great life in Chicago—a cozy apartment, good friends, a fabulous job despite the current setback. If she'd hoped for more at one time—if she'd longed for a family and marriage to Cole—she'd learned the futility of that. There was no point dreaming for things she couldn't have.

A new Ford pickup pulled up to the curb, and she waved to the driver, Kenny Greene, a former high school classmate and a cowboy on Cole's ranch. Determined to forget Cole—and her worries in Chicago— she tossed her suitcase into the back of the shiny pickup and climbed into the passenger seat.

For the next two weeks she was on vacation. She would bake her father chokecherry pies, sit on his porch swing and read and go for long rides on his horse while he napped. The Bar Lazy K had twelve thousand acres to get lost in, more if she rode onto government land. She'd never see Cole Kelley or even give him another thought.

She hoped.

* * *

Late that evening, Cole pulled into his yard and parked in the fluorescent halo pooling from the pole light next to the barn. More light poured from the ranch house, glinting from the floor-to-ceiling windows like honeyed-gold.

He cut the engine, a deep weariness seeping through his bones, and sighed. Damn, he was tired. He'd put in another sixteen-hour day. He tossed his leather work gloves onto the dashboard and massaged his throbbing temples, still unable to believe that he'd lost those cows.

It made no sense. None of his neighbors would have done it. They were all on friendly terms. In fact, the neighbor who owned the alfalfa was trying to sell Cole his thousand-acre spread—if Cole could swing the down payment when he sold his cows.

And he couldn't imagine his father's mistresses shooting the cattle. Shooting Hank, definitely. Cole was surprised his mother hadn't done that years ago. But to kill the cows?

Still, he'd bet his ranch the killings were related to his father. He couldn't prove it, but given the problems plaguing his family, no other explanation fit.

His back aching, Cole climbed out of the truck and rotated his stiff shoulders, then bent to pet Domino, who'd joined Mitzy in circling his feet. He'd reported the shooting to the sheriff. He'd herded the surviving cows back into their pasture and strung new wire on the fence. And tomorrow, he'd have his men check every cow on every inch of the twenty-square-mile ranch.

He just hoped he could get those cattle to market before that predicted cold front moved in—or anything else went wrong.

A soft whine drew his gaze. "Hey, Ace." He stooped and scratched the gray-muzzled, fifteen-year-old border collie who thumped his tail and licked his hand. Ace had retired from chasing cows when his eyesight failed and now spent his days in the house, pampered by the ranch's cook and housekeeper, Hannah Brown. But, retired or not, the old dog still faithfully greeted Cole whenever he came home.

The other two dogs, not to be ignored, leaped against Cole and butted his hand. Cole laughed and ruffled their fur. When he straightened, they bounded off, heading for their food bowls, no doubt.

His own stomach growled, and he shot a longing glance at the ranch house, wanting nothing more than a cold beer, a hot meal and some long-overdue oblivion in his king-size bed. But he had a lame colt to check on first.

He strode to the barn, the sight of the freshly painted corral easing his tension a notch. His grandmother had built the lavish ranch house on the family homestead, its soaring ceilings and two-story windows more suited to Aspen than Maple Cove. But the barn... Fierce satisfaction surged inside him. That was Cole's contribution, the first thing he'd remodeled when he and his brother Dylan had bought the place. He'd added a dozen horse stalls, created more heated space to birth calves. He'd also upgraded the pens and loading chutes, satisfied that he now had a modern outfit to tend his stock.

He opened the wide barn door, greeted by the familiar scent of hay. A soft light came from the nearest stall where his ranch foreman kept his horse.

"Rusty?" he called out, his exasperation rising. The stubborn man was supposed to be lying in bed with his broken leg propped up, not fooling around with his horse.

He swung open the gate to the stall, expecting to see his old foreman hobbling on his crutches and cast. Instead, a woman stood with her back to him, brushing Rusty's chestnut mare.

Bethany Moore. Cole abruptly came to a stop. Even after a dozen years, the sight of her straight black hair shimmering in the lamp light and those long, slender legs in her tight blue jeans knocked his heart off course.

She whipped around, and her black, fathomless eyes met his, giving his pulse an erratic beat. He scanned her full, sultry lips, her high, exotic cheekbones, the feminine curves of her breasts. And damned if she didn't still get to him, even after all these years. From her dusky skin and erotic mouth to the intelligence in her sooty eyes, she called to something inside him, appealing to him in a visceral, primitive way.

And memories flashed back before he could stop them—Bethany riding beside him into the mountains, her satiny hair streaming behind her like a sensual flag. Bethany digging with him for arrowheads, her white teeth flashing as she laughed. Bethany poised above him, her tawny skin bathed by moonlight as they made love beneath the stars.

As a teenager, she'd burned him alive. She'd sparked a craving in him he couldn't resist. And he'd never experienced anything remotely like it since.

Realizing he was already half aroused, he scowled. After the day he'd had, Bethany was the last person he needed to deal with. "What are you doing here?" he said, his voice roughened by fatigue.

Her full mouth flattened. She flicked her head,

swinging her long, straight hair over her back. "Brushing my father's horse."

Obviously. His frown deepened. She lifted her chin, her eyes sparking fire, a sure indication that he'd ticked her off. Then she hung up the brush on a peg in the stall and pushed past him out the door, her soft scent curling around him like a taunt. "Bethany…"

She spun around. "I'm only here to take care of my father, okay? I'm not going to bother you."

The hell she wouldn't. Just seeing her stirred up feelings he didn't want to deal with, memories he had no desire to relive. His temples suddenly pounding, he crossed his arms. "I was just surprised to see you. I never expected you to come back to Maple Cove, considering how anxious you were to leave."

"Anxious?" She shot him an incredulous look. "I had no choice. You knew I couldn't stay here."

She meant she *wouldn't* stay. But no one ever did. His own temper rising, he lifted one shoulder in a shrug. "It was none of my business what you did."

"Yes, you made that clear." She shook her head, and a weary look replaced the temper in her eyes. "Don't worry, Cole. I'm only here for the next two weeks. I'll be sure to stay out of your way." She turned on her heel and stalked from the barn, her boots rapping the cement floor.

He watched her go, a dull ache battering his skull. *Hell.* He'd screwed that up royally, putting the perfect cap on an already lousy day.

He pinched the bridge of his nose and exhaled. He hadn't meant to hurt her feelings. And he hadn't meant to dredge up the past. She'd just caught him off guard.

He was exhausted, hungry, worried about his ranch and his sister. He'd needed time to prepare.

But maybe it was for the best if she was mad. He didn't need more complications in his life—and she'd only leave again. Besides, they weren't exactly friends, despite the attraction he still felt. They were former classmates, former lovers...former everything. Whatever they'd shared was over, and there was nothing left to say.

Nothing except *sorry.* He dragged his hand over his face with a sigh. He owed her an apology, all right. No matter what his mood, she hadn't deserved to have her head chewed off. But he'd deal with that in the morning.

And then he'd stay as far from Bethany—and temptation—as he could.

Chapter 2

So much for not giving Cole Kelley another thought.

Bethany stood in the pharmacy in the neighboring town of Honey Creek the following morning, berating her lack of control. She'd spent the entire night tossing and turning, reliving every nuance of that strained encounter in the barn. She'd overreacted. She'd let Cole's vibrant blue eyes demolish her composure, bringing back a flood of rejection and pain. But she hadn't expected to see him so soon—or that he'd look so impossibly good.

Disgusted with herself, she exhaled, determined not to spend more time thinking about Cole. If she'd learned anything in the years since high school, it was that there were things she couldn't change. So she'd moved on. She'd made a good life for herself in Chicago. And she had enough to worry about without obsessing over him.

"I've got it in stock," the pharmacist said, returning to the counter where she waited. "But it will be about twenty minutes before I can get to it."

"That's fine." Pulling her mind back to her father's prescription, Bethany glanced at her watch. "I'll do some shopping and come back."

Dead tired from the lack of sleep, she strolled up the narrow aisle of the pharmacy and pushed open the door to the street. It was early, barely nine o'clock, and nothing else was open in Honey Creek except the ranch supply store and Kelley's Cookhouse, the town's most popular place to eat.

Yawning, she glanced up the empty main street toward the restaurant, debating whether to get some coffee while she waited for the prescription. She could definitely use the caffeine boost. But Cole's aunt and uncle owned the cookhouse, and she'd gone there on dates with Cole—memories she didn't need to stir up.

Another yawn convinced her. She started up the tree-lined sidewalk just as a black, four-wheel-drive pickup pulled up to the restaurant and parked. Cole Kelley climbed out, and Bethany came to a halt.

Her heart somersaulted as he turned toward her. Their eyes met in the morning sunshine, and her traitorous pulse began to race. She shifted her weight, the urge to flee surging inside her, but she forced herself to stay put. She wasn't going to spend the next two weeks bolting like a startled rabbit whenever she ran into Cole.

He started toward her, his long, determined strides devouring the distance between them. She pasted a neutral expression on her face, refusing to let him see how rattled she felt. But it was hard to feign indifference

when the lanky, rangy teen she'd once loved had turned
into an impossibly virile man.

She skimmed the wide, thick planks of his shoulders,
the intriguing fit of his faded jeans. Years of ranch work
had broadened his neck and back, erasing any hint of
softness, turning his powerful biceps to steel.

She swallowed around the dust in her throat, her
blood humming as he drew near. Cole had certainly
aged nicely. And he was no vain Chicago businessman
with muscles toned in front of a mirror. He was the
real deal, a rugged Montana cowboy, a one-hundred-
percent-natural male.

He stopped close enough to touch her, and his startling blue eyes captured hers. Her pulse beating wildly,
she scanned his sensual mouth, the strong angles of his
rock hard jaw, the lean, tanned planes of his face. Sunshine slanted through the branches of a nearby maple,
highlighting the sun kissed streaks in his espresso-col-
ored hair.

"Listen, Bethany…" His deep voice rumbled through
her, and she rubbed her arms, trying to quell her response. He had the sexiest voice she'd ever heard, a
deep, gravelly rasp that tempted a woman to sin. And
when he'd whispered to her in the dark…

She shivered again, battling her reaction. It was con-
ditioning, nothing more, like Pavlov's dogs. One look
at Cole and she instantly thought of sex—which was
inevitable, considering the molten affair they'd had.

But she knew that wasn't quite accurate. Any woman
would react to him the same way. Cole's blatant masculinity attracted women like a lone tree drew lightning
during a violent electrical storm.

"I'm sorry if I was rude last night," he continued. His

lips edged into a grimace, making sexy dents bracket his mouth, and she found it hard to breathe. "I had a bad day. I didn't mean to take it out on you."

"That's all right."

"No, it's not. Not really." His intense eyes skewered hers. "How about if we start over? I'll buy you a cup of coffee."

"Oh." Her gaze shot to Kelley's Cookhouse, where two elderly ranchers limped out the door. "Thanks, but I don't think—"

"Come on, I owe you that much. And you can fill me in on Rusty's progress." He tilted his head. "I was heading there anyway. I need to talk to my Uncle Don."

Her instincts warned against it, but she never did have any willpower around Cole. A whispered word, one glance from those hypnotic eyes had convinced her to abandon every inhibition—with the most erotic results.

But that was then. Surely she could have a cup of coffee with him now without falling apart. And maybe it would put their relationship on a more casual footing. Then she could simply nod and wave when she saw him on the ranch—and *finally* get him out of her head.

"All right. Coffee it is." She just hoped she wasn't making a mistake.

"So how is Rusty?" Cole asked, adjusting his longer stride to hers.

"He's in a lot of pain. He won't admit it, but I heard him groaning all night." While she was lying awake thinking about Cole. "That's why I'm here. The pharmacy in Maple Cove didn't have his prescription and I didn't want to wait another day."

"It was a nasty break."

And an even odder accident. "He didn't tell me what happened, just that he fell off his horse." Which was bizarre. She's seen her father stick to the back of unbroken mustangs. She couldn't imagine him getting thrown from his steady mare.

"He was out riding fences in the pasture that borders Rock Creek, near the old Blackfoot teepee ring. He'd stopped there on his way back up to the mountains to find my missing cows. He said his mare spooked and dragged him a ways."

"Dragged him?" Horrified, Bethany stopped and gaped at Cole. "He didn't tell me that."

"He probably didn't want you to worry."

Or insist he stay off a horse, especially at his age. But she knew better than to suggest it. Behind her father's quiet, laid-back facade lurked fierce stubbornness and pride.

"I can't believe his horse dragged him. That mare never spooks. What on earth set her off?"

"He didn't see," Cole said as they resumed walking.

"He's lucky he wasn't killed." Shaken that she could have lost him, Bethany climbed the wooden steps to the cookhouse. While she'd been oblivious in Chicago, her father could have died.

Cole pulled open the door, jangling the welcoming cowbell, and she preceded him inside. The restaurant hadn't changed in the past twelve years. The same red-checkered cloths still covered the tables. The old, planked bar still dominated the room, flanked by square wooden stools. Cattle brands and horseshoes decorated the walls, along with photos from local rodeos. The familiar scents of coffee and bacon permeated the air.

She didn't know how many hours she'd spent here in

high school, hanging around with Cole. But it brought back a rush of longing, a poignant reminder of the hopes she'd left behind.

A reminder she *definitely* didn't need right now. She was trying to gain some distance from Cole, not remember the good times they'd shared.

The saloon-style doors to the kitchen swung open. Cole's aunt Bonnie Gene came bustling out, her face wreathed around a smile. "Why, Bethany Moore! Aren't you a sight for sore eyes." She hurried around the bar, her shoulder-length brown hair swinging, her light brown eyes shining with warmth, and Bethany couldn't help but smile back.

"It's about time you came back here," Bonnie Gene scolded. "And aren't you as gorgeous as ever!" She gave her a hard hug and turned to Cole. "Isn't she gorgeous, Cole?"

Bethany's face burned. She braved a look at Cole. His eyes met hers, and a sudden sizzle of awareness stopped her breath. So he still felt it, too.

"Yeah," he said, his voice gruff. "She's gorgeous."

Her heart skittering, she jerked her gaze away.

"Sit right here." Bonnie Gene ushered her onto a stool. She pulled another seat close and pushed Cole into it, maneuvering him faster than a border collie herding cows. "Coffee?" she asked Bethany.

Still struggling to regain her composure, Bethany managed to nod. "Sure, I—"

"Don't you dare move. I'll get Donald and be right back."

Bonnie Gene rushed off. Cole's thigh bumped hers, putting Bethany's nerves on further alert. "I see she hasn't changed," she said in the suddenly awkward silence.

"Yeah. Sorry about that." He rose, dragged his stool a foot away, and she battled back a sliver of hurt. But he was right to put some space between them. Bonnie Gene was a notorious matchmaker—and the last thing Bethany wanted was to encourage her. This was just coffee between old friends, not the rekindling of their high-school romance.

Then the kitchen doors sprang open and Cole's uncle came out, accompanied by Bonnie Gene. Donald had added a few pounds to his midsection over the years, but his friendly blue eyes hadn't changed. And he still wore his short, white hair in that oddly lopsided style, which gave the renowned businessman a deceptively guileless look. "Bethany, it's good to see you again."

"It's nice to be here." She realized, with surprise, that it was true. In Chicago, she was always surrounded by strangers, an anonymity and freedom she liked. Still, there was something comforting about running into people she knew.

Bonnie Gene filled their cups with steaming coffee. "Now tell me, how is your father doing?"

"Not great," Bethany admitted. "He's in a lot of pain. That's why I'm here, to fill his prescription."

Bonnie Gene clucked. "A man his age shouldn't be on a horse."

"Can't keep him off it," Cole said, his deep voice rumbling through her nerves.

"That's right," Don cut in, sounding belligerent. "A man's got a right to live his life the way he wants no matter how old he gets."

Bethany sipped her coffee to hide a smile. Everyone

knew that Bonnie Gene kept her husband on a short leash, especially when it came to his beloved cigars.

Bonnie Gene rolled her eyes at her husband and turned to Cole. "And how about Hank? How's he doing?"

Cole made a sound of disgust. "The same. Still hiding in the house, leaving the rest of us to deal with his mess."

Bethany stole a glance at Cole's handsome profile, a reluctant spurt of sympathy twisting inside. She'd heard about the senator's infidelities. His mistresses had been popping up like gophers in a hay field, dominating the tabloids for weeks. And the media was having a field day, relishing the California senator's spectacular fall from grace—especially given the "family values" platform on which he'd built his career.

She could imagine how the scandal affected Cole. Hank had been a lousy, self-centered father from the get-go, ignoring his wife and children to pursue his political career. His absence and indifference had wounded Cole deeply, turning the neglected child into a wild and rebellious teen—until his desperate mother had sent him to Montana to live with his Uncle Don.

Donald and Bonnie Gene's patience had subdued Cole's anger. The rugged Montana land had given him a reason to live. Now just when Cole had put his life together, his father had come back—creating havoc Cole surely didn't need.

"Has he told you any more about what's going on?" Bonnie Gene asked him.

Cole shook his head, the furrow deepening between his dark brows. "I was hoping he'd said something to you."

"You mean about La—" Bonnie Gene glanced at Bethany and clamped her hand over her lips. The men exchanged uneasy looks, and a strained silence fell over the group.

There was something they didn't want her to know.

Bethany pretended to study her coffee, experiencing a sudden feeling of hurt—which was ridiculous. Cole had no reason to confide in her. She hadn't been part of his life in years.

"About anything," Cole finally said. "You heard that someone shot three of my cows?"

"*Shot* them?" Bethany snapped her gaze to Cole. "Are you serious?"

He nodded, his grim gaze shifting to hers. "I found them by Honey Creek."

Bethany's heart tripped. Another wave of sympathy surged inside. That ranch meant everything to Cole. He'd slaved for years to buy it with Dylan, working with a single-minded intensity, sacrificing everything for the land—even his relationship with her.

His uncle leaned on the counter. "You called the sheriff?"

"Yeah. Wes Colton came out to look, but there wasn't much for him to go on. I doubt it's a coincidence, though. All this trouble started when my father showed up. That's why I was hoping he'd talked to you."

Donald's face flushed. "No, he hasn't called me."

Bonnie Gene turned to her husband and frowned. "Then why haven't you called him?"

"Why should I?"

"He's your brother, your family. And he needs you, no matter what he did in the past."

Cole grunted. "Family or not, I wish he'd go hide

somewhere else. Bad enough I've got the paparazzi tramping through my fields, leaving the gates unlocked. Now I've got someone killing my cows."

"That's not Hank's fault." Bonnie Gene topped off Bethany's coffee. "Not that he's a saint—not by a long shot. What he did to your mother and you kids…" She pursed her lips in distaste. "He deserves to be horse-whipped for that. But no one is all good or all bad, not even Hank."

She turned to her frowning husband. "And you need to forget your blasted pride for once and talk to him. He's your brother, for Pete's sake. He needs your help."

Donald's expression turned mulish. "He can call me if he wants to talk. I have nothing to say to him. Now I need to check on the food." He pushed through the swinging doors to the kitchen and disappeared.

"Stubborn man," Bonnie Gene muttered under her breath.

Bethany took a swallow of coffee. Cole's father was a piece of work, all right. He'd alienated his wife and children, and had been estranged from his half brother, Donald, for years. Now even his mistresses appeared fed up.

The soft chimes of a cell phone interrupted her thoughts. Cole reached back, the motion showcasing the impressive definition in his biceps, and pulled his phone from the back pocket of his jeans. He frowned at the display. "I'd better take this."

He rose and walked a few steps away. His broad shoulders stiffened, and Bethany knew instantly that the news was bad. "How many?" he asked, his deep voice clipped. "All right. I'll be right there."

He slipped the phone back into his pocket and turned

to face them, tension vibrating off his muscled frame. "I've got to go. Someone dammed up Rock Creek, just above the northeast pasture, cutting off water to the cows."

Bethany's heart squeezed. Without water, cattle died fast. "Are they—"

"I don't know how many we've lost yet. No one has checked that pasture since your dad got hurt, so they might have gone without water for several days." He angled his chin toward the bar. "Sorry to run."

"Don't be silly. You've got more important things to do than sit here and talk to me."

"Yes, go on," Bonnie Gene urged him. "Just let us know what we can do to help."

He nodded, his mind obviously elsewhere, then strode across the wooden floor to the door. He flung the door open, making the cowbell clank, and stomped across the porch outside.

Filled with compassion, Bethany watched him go. He'd be torn up about the suffering animals and furious that someone had attacked his ranch—not to mention angry at the financial loss.

"He's a good man," Bonnie Gene said, echoing her thoughts. "And a lonely one. He just needs the right woman to soften him up."

Warning bells clanged. Bethany swiveled back to Bonnie Gene, determined to nip that train of thought. "Don't look at me. Cole and I are old friends, nothing more."

"Of course. I know that." Bonnie Gene gave her an innocent look. She pulled a small photo album from her apron pocket, set it on the bar, and flipped it open, turning it so Bethany could see. "You haven't seen my granddaughter yet. Eve's daughter, Patience. My little angel is four months old."

A darling, red-haired baby girl smiled up at her, softening Bethany's heart. "Oh, my. What a doll." She slowly flipped through the pages, remembering when she'd dreamed of forever with Cole.

She straightened, shocked at the direction of her thoughts. She had no future with Cole. He'd never marry her, no matter what his aunt believed—a lesson she'd learned years ago.

And no way could she delude herself—because that would only bring pain. It had taken her years to get over him the first time, years to resign herself to harsh reality and finally move on with her life.

And no matter how cute Bonnie Gene's granddaughter was, no matter how much Cole still made her pulse pound, she couldn't succumb to dreams.

She was older now. Definitely wiser. And she would only be here for two short weeks. She had to keep her emotional distance, not allow herself to get swept up in Cole's problems and begin to care.

Because that was a surefire path to heartbreak—an experience she refused to repeat.

Determined to hold fast to that resolution, Bethany drove through the towering log entrance to the Bar Lazy K Ranch an hour later and headed to her father's house. The main ranch buildings were clustered around a large, grassy triangle a quarter mile in from the gate. The barn, workshops and machinery sheds formed one end of the complex. In another corner stood the foreman's log cabin, where her father currently lived, with the ranch hands' bunkhouse beyond that. Cole's house—a lavish, two-story stone building with floor-to-ceiling windows—stood apart from the other buildings, taking advantage of the mountain views.

She parked the truck beside her father's cabin, then got out and glanced around. Several men worked near the machinery shed, loading a backhoe onto a flatbed trailer. Others strapped shovels to four-wheelers, preparing to deal with the dammed-up stream. She didn't see Cole, but his truck was parked by the tractors, so she assumed he was still around.

She climbed the wooden porch steps, her father's prescription in hand. Then she hesitated by the porch swing and took another look at the men. Even from a distance she could feel their tension, which was easy to understand. Ranchers worked hard under tough conditions—from winter blizzards reaching forty below to sweltering summer heat. Seeing their work destroyed would infuriate them.

Troubled, she pulled open the door and went inside. Her father sat reading the newspaper in a recliner near the window, his broken leg propped up, his crutches lying beside him on the braided rug.

"Hi, Dad." She bent and kissed his leathered cheek, careful not to bump his bruises and scrapes. "I've got your pain medication. Have you had breakfast? You want me to scramble you some eggs?"

"I can do it," he grumbled. "I don't need you to wait on me."

"I know that." She stifled a sigh, remembering Bonnie Gene's comment about stubborn men. "But since I'm up…"

"Fine." He set his paper aside. "But just get me one

of the sandwiches Hannah brought by. She put them in the fridge."

"All right." Still thinking about Cole's cattle, Bethany entered the kitchen and took the medicine out of the bag. Maple Cove had its share of crime—domestic disputes, meth labs, occasional thefts. But to deliberately destroy someone's livelihood...

Incredulous, she shook out a pill, then went to the sink to fill a glass from the tap. Above the sink the white lace curtains fluttered around the open window, framing a view of the old-fashioned clothesline in the small backyard. That was Maple Cove—sheets drying in the sunshine, kids playing baseball in their grassy yards— not cold-blooded killings and sabotage.

Still unable to believe it, she returned to the living room with the pill. "Here you go. Take this while I get your food."

He leaned away. "I don't want to be all drugged up."

"It's only for a couple of days until the worst of the pain is gone. You need to rest," she added when he opened his mouth to argue. "I heard you thrashing around all night." She set the glass on the side table and handed him the pill.

"Since when did you get so bossy?" he muttered but dutifully gulped it down.

Leaving him to his morning newspaper, she crossed the wooden floor to the kitchen and readied his food. But his comment sparked a sliver of guilt. She didn't visit her widowed father as often as she should. And he was getting older; his thinning white hair proved that. But she led a busy life in Chicago and could rarely get away.

Still feeling guilty, she put the sandwich on a plate

and carried it out. She rearranged her father's pillows, making sure he was comfortable, then sat on the adjacent couch. It wasn't just his advancing age that bothered her, but that she'd lost touch with the everyday happenings in his life—his accident, the trouble on Cole's ranch…

"I saw Cole Kelley in town," she said. "Why didn't you tell me your horse dragged you?"

Her father swallowed a bite of sandwich. "It wasn't important."

"How can you say that? You could have been killed. Don't you think I deserved to know?"

"What was the point? There was nothing you could do about it." He returned his attention to his food.

He was right, but she still wished he'd told her. She drummed her fingers on the couch. "So how did it happen? Cole said Red—"

"It was an accident, that's all. So just drop it."

Bethany blinked, shocked by his testy tone. Her father never lost his temper. He was the most even-keeled man she knew. But pain put everyone out of sorts.

She studied his craggy face, the deep lines testament to a lifetime spent working in the wind and sun. "Cole told me about the cattle getting shot," she said, changing the subject. "And now the stream's dammed up."

Her father paused in midbite. His gaze shot to hers. "What stream?"

"Rock Creek. He just found out a little while ago. The cows couldn't get any water. He doesn't know how many head he might have lost." She leaned forward. "You think it has something to do with his father? Cole said the problems started when the senator showed up."

Her father paled. "I don't know."

"You must have an opinion. You're here every day."

"I said I don't know." Rusty's voice turned defensive. He scowled and tugged his ear. "How would I when I'm stuck in here with a broken leg?"

He was lying. The realization barreled through her, stealing her breath. No one else would have noticed, but she'd played cards with her father for years—and that pull to the ear invariably gave him away.

But why would he lie? What could he possibly have to hide? Surely he wasn't involved in the sabotage. He was the most honorable man she knew.

Still scowling, he got up, grabbed his crutches and hobbled away. Bethany slumped on the couch, stunned by his behavior, questions spinning through her mind. Her father would never harm an animal. And he would never hurt Cole. It was insane even to have doubts.

But then what was he hiding? Why hadn't he told her the truth? Was he merely embarrassed about his accident or something more?

Her thoughts and emotions in turmoil, she rose and walked to the window and gazed out at the busy men. One thing was clear. Something bad was happening at the ranch. And her father might know more than he'd let on.

Cole stalked past on his way to the ranch house, his broad shoulders rigid with tension, anger quickening his stride. She hugged her arms, knowing she shouldn't care. Cole and his ranch weren't her business. She had her own problems to deal with—namely Mrs. Bolter's death. She didn't need to worry about Cole.

But as he passed, a sinking feeling settled inside her, her heart winning the war it waged with her head. She couldn't just stand here and do nothing. Cole was in trouble, his ranch under attack. And no matter how badly their relationship had ended, it wasn't in her nature to withhold her help.

She stepped away from the window, her mind made up. She'd settle her father down for a nap, then ride his horse to the stream. On the way, she could stop in the pasture where he'd had his accident and search for clues.

If her father *was* hiding something, she would find out.

Chapter 3

Bethany galloped across the field on her father's mare an hour later, the brisk wind brushing her face, a heady sense of exhilaration flooding her veins. The brilliant blue sky soared above her. Wheat-colored grass carpeted the rolling rangeland on every side. Closer to the mountains, hills rose like gnarled fingers, their ancient, glacier-carved valleys shadowed with aspens and pines.

She slowed Red to a walk, her breath coming in ragged gasps, the scent of dried grass filling her lungs. The ever-present wind rustled in the silence—whispers from her ancestors, her father had said. She smiled at the fanciful thought. She'd always loved imagining her father's people traveling through these foothills, hunting for buffalo. They'd seen the same, unchanging scenery that she did, felt the same, unending wind. Even now the sheer magnitude of the wild land awed her, the beauty a balm to her soul.

Pulling herself out of her musings, she angled her hat against the midday sun, then guided the mare toward the fence marking the perimeter of Cole's ranch. She'd detoured on her way to the dammed-up stream, hoping to find the spot where her father's accident had occurred. Although she doubted he had anything to do with Cole's problems, he was lying about something—and she intended to find out what.

Keeping Red to a walk, she scanned the pasture. A gopher scurried by. The western wheat grass bobbed in the wind. She pushed up the sleeves of her long-sleeved T-shirt, growing warm in the sun. But in typical Montana fashion, a storm front was due to arrive any day now, dumping snow on the mountain peaks.

She continued riding along the fence line—past the circle of stones forming the old teepee ring, past a cluster of Black Angus cows. A dozen yards later, she spotted a churned-up section of ground and stopped. Hoof prints and tire tracks crisscrossed the dirt, but they didn't tell her much. It rarely rained this side of the Rockies, so they could have been here for months.

She slowly circled the area, trying to envision how her father's accident had played out—but there were no tree branches to spook the horse, nothing flapping in the wind. She brought Red to a halt with a sigh. She was wasting her time. She wasn't going to miraculously figure this out. She might as well do something useful and go help the men with the cows.

She reined Red around, intending to do just that when something black in the grass caught her eye. "Whoa," she told the mare and leaped down. She walked back and picked it up. It was a strip of leather, an inch wide, maybe fifteen inches long with a braided horsehair inset—a browband from a bridle, she'd guess. Not her father's, though. He didn't own any showy tack. He'd used the same plain, utilitarian bridles for forty years.

But even if it belonged to another cowboy, what did that prove? Anyone could have dropped it here.

Discouraged, she stuffed the browband into her pocket and mounted the horse. But even without any evidence, she couldn't stifle her doubts. What if the browband *did* mean something? What if her father hadn't come here alone? What if Red hadn't spooked and dragged him? But then how had he broken his leg?

A cloud passed overhead, towing a giant shadow over the earth, and a sudden sense of foreboding chilled her heart. Unsettled, she clucked Red into motion, trying to subdue her unruly thoughts. She couldn't jump to conclusions based solely on a leather scrap. And even if her father had lied to her, so what? He might not be hiding anything bad. He might have withheld the truth out of embarrassment or to keep her from worrying about him.

Moments later she reached Rock Creek, the clear glacial runoff that fed Cole's wells in this part of the ranch. Determined to focus on reality instead of conjectures, she followed the drone of a machine downstream. She skirted a jumble of boulders, passed through the shade of some cottonwood trees, then rounded another bend. When she spotted Cole wrestling a calf to the ground, she brought her horse to a halt.

Dust billowed over the men. Cows bellowed behind them, their frantic cries filling the air. Cole dug his heels into the dirt, flipped the bleating calf to the ground, and Kenny Greene raced over to help him hold it down. A man she didn't recognize crouched beside them, and began examining the suffering calf—Judd Walker, Maple Cove's new veterinarian, no doubt.

Bethany peered through the blowing dust to the backhoe, then to the corrals where they'd penned the herd. The cows lunged and cried, desperate to break out and quench their thirst. But drinking water too fast would cause their brains to swell, killing even more of the herd.

She glanced farther downstream to the dead cows dotting the bank, and her throat closed at the sight. Who would want to hurt those innocent animals—and why? Cole didn't have enemies that she knew. People liked him in Maple Cove. Sure, he came from a wealthy family, but he'd worked his heart out to buy this ranch— putting in longer hours than his men did, never shirking an unpleasant job. And people respected that.

Her gaze swung back to the busy cowboys. She recognized most of the faces—Bill, Earl Runningcrane, her old classmate Kenny Greene. But there were some new ones, too. The same hollow feeling she'd experienced in the restaurant swirled back, but she forced it aside. So what if the ranch had changed since she'd left? Her life had moved on, too.

The sick calf thrashed, knocking Cole's hat to the ground, and her gaze gravitated to him. He swore, his arm muscles bunching as he held the calf, the veins bulging in his tanned neck.

"Almost done," the vet said. "Just a few more seconds."

Cole grunted, his dark hair dampened with sweat, dirt streaking his hard jaw. And the sheer maleness of him made her heart take a crazy beat.

"Got it," the vet said. Cole nodded at Kenny. They released the calf and leaped away. The calf staggered to his feet, wobbling badly. Cole whistled to Mitzy, who instantly raced over and steered it back into the herd.

Cole wiped his jaw on his sleeve, his T-shirt plastered to his powerful torso. He reached down to grab his hat, causing his faded jeans to tighten on his muscled behind.

Bethany shifted in the saddle, suddenly restless. No matter what had gone wrong between them, Cole was still hands down the most attractive man she'd ever seen. And the thrills she'd felt in his arms…

"Well, look who's back." A cowboy trotted up on a big roan gelding, pulling her attention from Cole.

Tony Whittaker. She recoiled in distaste. As a child, he'd bullied her daily. And as a teen… She suppressed a shudder, refusing to go down that humiliating track. Fortunately, she'd learned that he would ignore her if she refused to show any fear.

"Get out of my way, Tony. I've got work to do." She tugged the reins to the right, intending to go around him, but he shifted his gelding and blocked her way.

"If it's work you want, you can work me over good." His eyes dipped to her chest, his innuendo clear.

Her mouth flattened, disgust churning through her, but she deliberately steadied her voice. "Look, I don't have time for this. Those cows need help. Now get your horse out of my way."

His lips thinned, sudden meanness flashing in his eyes. "A squaw like you would be lucky to have me. I can show you what a real man's like."

Her face burned, fury building inside her at the racial insult, and she tightened her grip on the reins. Idiots like Tony were the reason she'd left Maple Cove. But she bit down an angry retort, knowing better than to take his bait. She refused to cause trouble for Cole.

She nudged Red forward, but Tony moved his gelding closer, and her patience snapped. "What the hell is your problem? I said to get out of my way."

"Why you—"

"Tony!" Cole shouted. "Get over here and give us a hand."

"On my way." Tony shot her an even stare, making the fine hairs rise on the nape of her neck, then wheeled his horse around. Bethany didn't move as he rode off, her hands trembling, anger still pumping through her veins. Then she signaled for Red to get moving and headed downstream to join the men monitoring the thirsty cows.

So Tony was still a creep. That much hadn't changed. She frowned, wondering if he was behind Cole's problems. Killing helpless cows sounded like something he'd do.

But criminal or not, she'd be smart to watch her back. Instead of finding answers, she'd ticked off an old enemy—a dangerous one at that.

She reached the herd, then gave her father's veteran cutting horse free rein. Red sprang into action like a kindergartener let out for recess, charging across the field, dancing back and forth to head off the bolting cows.

But as she worked, her plans for a relaxing vacation crumbled fast. She hadn't found any answers. She still didn't know why her father had lied. But if there was any chance her father's fall was more than a simple accident, she had to find out.

Red pivoted sharply and changed directions, and she spared a glance at Cole. He stood with his feet planted wide, his hat tilted low, his big hands braced on his hips. His gaze connected with hers through the shifting dust, and her heart made a heavy thud.

She had to get answers, all right—which meant she had to stick close to the men. But she was doing this for her father's sake and her own peace of mind—*not* to be around Cole.

She just hoped she'd remember that.

"All right. Listen up," Cole said. He stood on the bank of the stream they'd cleared, waiting for his tired men to gather around. The vet had returned to town an hour earlier. The sheriff had taken his statement and gone. They'd carted the dead cattle to a local food bank and made sure the wells were working again.

His head pounding, he whistled again for his men. Bethany rode to the edge of the group, then leaped off her horse. She'd done an amazing job controlling the cattle, putting his ranch hands to shame. But she'd always been an expert rider. Watching her on a cutting horse was like viewing a work of art.

A fact not lost on the men. Tony hadn't taken his eyes off her all day.

Scowling, he cleared his throat. "I'm sure you've figured out by now that we've got a problem." And he was tired of being caught off guard. "So I'm moving up our schedule. We need to get these calves shipped off before anything else goes wrong."

"I thought the trucks weren't available until next week," Kenny said.

"I'll find some trucks somewhere." *He hoped.* He'd

originally planned to ship his cattle to market last week
during the round up. But his herd had splintered in the
mountains, stranding a hundred head near the divide.
He'd rescheduled the trucks, hoping to use the delay to
his advantage, getting the calves' weight up while he
rescued the rest of the herd. But now, with someone
killing his cattle, he couldn't afford to wait.

"First thing in the morning we'll start in the southern section. We also need to start patrolling at night,"
he added. "I'll draw up a schedule."

The men grumbled. Cole couldn't blame them. They
already worked long hours. But what choice did he
have? If he lost enough money, the ranch would fold,
and they'd all be out of a job.

"If you know anyone looking for work, let me know."
He scanned the group, but no one answered. His gaze
stalled on Tony, who was staring at Bethany again.

Cole's mood darkened. He didn't care who she dated.
He had no claim on her. But he didn't need her distract-
ing the men.

Bethany swung up on the mare and trotted off. Tony
vaulted into his saddle a second later, turning his gelding to go in pursuit.

"Tony," he barked. "Take my truck and drive into
Maple Cove. Leave word at the bars that we're looking
for extra men. Do the same in Honey Creek. I'll ride
your horse back to the barn and check fences along the
way." He glanced around at the men. "The rest of you
get something to eat. I'll bring the schedule by later."

The ranch hands began to disperse. His eyes sim-
mering with resentment, Tony dismounted and handed
Cole his gelding's reins. Cole fished his keys from his

pocket and tossed them his way. "Tell them I'm paying overtime," he added.

He hoisted himself into the saddle, then took off after Bethany, ignoring the men's speculative looks. He needed to check his fences—nothing more. And if Bethany happened to be riding the same way...

He caught up with her a few minutes later as she climbed the hill. "Thanks for helping today."

Her eyes met his, and a familiar jolt changed the rhythm of his pulse. She'd always had the damnedest effect on him. One glance across the cafeteria in high school, and he'd fallen for her hard.

"I enjoyed it," she said, her throaty voice conjuring up erotic memories he'd tried for years to forget. "It feels good to be on a horse again."

"I'll bet." They'd spent some of their best moments together on horseback, racing across these hills. He guided the gelding toward the fence, checking the barbed wire for problems as he rode along, but his eyes kept returning to her. A flush tinged her sculpted cheeks. Her straight black hair fluttered against her back. She looked good riding beside him. *Right.*

But she hadn't cared enough about him to stay.

"I'm sorry about the cows," she said.

"Yeah." He shifted his gaze to the land bordering his fence. "I was hoping to turn a profit this year, enough for a down payment on Del Harvey's place."

"He's selling?"

Cole nodded. "He can't make a go of it anymore, not with property taxes so high." Ever since celebrities had discovered the valley, real estate prices had soared.

"How big is his ranch?"

"A thousand acres. The land's good. Lots of native

grasses, year-round herds of elk. There's a movement underway to get cattle off federal lands," he explained. "If that goes through I could lose my BLM lease. Del's ranch would provide me with summer pasture, enough so I wouldn't have to reduce my herd." But every dead cow—and dollar lost—jeopardized that plan.

Bethany looked toward the mountains, a small crease bisecting her brow. "How long will he hold on?"

"I don't know. He's been getting calls from developers. They're offering him a lot of money. He wants to keep the ranch intact, but if I don't come up with the down payment soon..."

His chest tight, he scanned the huge granite peaks scraping the sky, the aspens glimmering in the waning sunlight like burnished gold. He inhaled deeply, soaking in the beauty of the land. He couldn't begin to express his feelings for this place. This wild land touched something inside him, giving him a reason to live.

And he'd do everything in his power to preserve it, to make sure future generations could breathe the crisp, clean air and absorb the majestic views. In his mind, he didn't own the land; he was its steward—a privilege he felt honored to have.

For several minutes, they rode without speaking. Shadows inched over the fields. White-tailed deer crept from a grove of trees. They crested a hill, startling a herd of antelope. The animals sprinted toward a pine-sheltered meadow where he and Bethany had first made love.

His pulse thudded fast at the memory. He'd been nineteen, and so tortured by lust for her that he could barely ride his horse. And when she'd stripped off her clothes amidst the wildflowers, baring her sleek, ripe curves to his gaze…

"That gate's open," she said.

Cole dragged his attention to where she pointed. "You're right." Grateful for the distraction, he tugged on the reins and trotted to the open gate. Bethany joined him a second later, and they both dropped to the ground. He handed her his reins, then strode over and secured the gate.

He paused to study the tire tracks in the grass. "They must have come through here on the way to the stream." Which made sense. They weren't far from a forest service road.

"You have any idea who's doing this?" she asked.

"My father's enemies, I guess."

"Why do you think that?"

"Because ever since he showed up we've been having problems—windows smashed, fences cut." One of his father's mistresses, Gloria Cosgrove, had even attacked him at the bank in town.

Her brows furrowed. "But why? I don't understand the point."

He tipped back his hat and sighed. "I think they're trying to make him leave. Security's tight at the ranch house. My grandmother was a little paranoid and had it rigged like Fort Knox. So if someone wants to hurt him, they need to get him away from the ranch.

"It's no secret that we don't get along." Hell, he despised the man. His father had never kept a promise in his life—not to his wife, not to his children, and certainly not to the gullible constituents who kept voting him into power. "They probably figure if they make my life miserable enough, I'll boot him out."

But unlike the senator, Cole was a man who kept his word. He'd promised to protect his father and he would—no matter what he thought of him.

Bethany hesitated. "You don't think it could be someone else...like one of your men?"

"Why do you ask that?"

She pulled a piece of leather from her pocket and handed it to him. He studied it for a moment, examining the braided horsehair design. "It looks like part of a bridle."

"I found it in your field, not far from the stream. Any idea who it belongs to?"

He shrugged and handed it back. "Tony goes for that kind of thing. Why? You think he's causing the problems?"

"Do you?"

He turned that over in his mind. "No. He's worked for me for a couple of years now. He's reliable." He liked to booze it up on the weekends and brag about his conquests, but there was nothing criminal about that.

Her eyes thoughtful, Bethany stuffed the scrap back into her pocket. "Speaking of your men... I can help with the cattle while I'm here. My father doesn't need me to do much. As long as I check on him occasionally, he'll be fine."

He opened his mouth to agree. But the glint in her eyes brought him up short. He recognized that look— the same stubborn resolve that had made her class valedictorian and earned her a full-ride scholarship to the university back east.

She had an agenda. And if that plan included snooping around and asking questions...

"Forget it," he said. "It's too dangerous."

"I don't see how. And you said you needed more help."

She was right. This was the do-or-die moment for the Bar Lazy K, the only paycheck he'd get all year. Everything hinged on getting those cattle to market—and to do that, he needed help. Even worse, he still had those hundred head stranded in the mountains. If he didn't rescue them before that front moved in, he could lose even more of the herd.

But he refused to put Bethany in danger. And the thought of working beside her made everything inside him rebel. She dredged up too many memories, stirred up longings he'd worked too hard to subdue.

"You know I can do the work," she said.

"That's not the issue." She could run rings around most of his hands.

"Then what is the issue?"

"Whoever's killing my cows is armed. Dangerous." And if she'd come across that shooter in the field… His belly contracted with dread.

"They haven't hurt any people, have they?"

They'd kidnapped his sister. But he couldn't tell her that.

When he didn't answer, she stepped closer. "Listen, Cole, if my dad's in danger, I deserve to know."

"He'll be safe in the house. You both will. I've had the alarm repaired, and there are plenty of people around, including my dad's bodyguards."

"Safe from what?" Exasperation tinged her voice. "Exactly what do you think is going to happen?"

He folded his arms, refusing to say. It wasn't that he didn't trust her—at least in this case. She wasn't the gossipy type. But his father had insisted they keep this mum.

"There's something you aren't saying," she said slowly. "Something else has happened, more than the cows. Something your aunt Bonnie Gene didn't want to say."

He exhaled, knowing he might as well tell her the truth. She was smart. She'd eventually figure it out. And he couldn't take the chance that she'd nose around, asking questions that could get her killed.

He released a sigh. "All right, look. No one outside the family knows this. You have to promise you won't tell anyone, not even your father. I can't let this leak out."

"I promise."

He nodded. "Lana's been kidnapped."

Her face paled. She pressed her hand to her throat. "Kidnapped? When? What happened? *Oh, Cole.*"

"We don't have many details. She's been in Italy, studying art history, getting her master's degree. A few weeks ago she went to Paris on vacation…and disappeared."

He bit down hard on his jaw, suppressing the terror swarming inside him. His sister had to survive. "My dad got a call last week, and she's alive, thank God. But we don't know where she is."

Still looking shaken, Bethany hugged her arms. "What does the FBI say? You've called them, right?"

"My dad has. He has some high-level contacts. All I know is that we're supposed to keep this under wraps."

"What do they want? Money?"

"That's my guess, but they haven't said." More panic ballooned inside him, but he ruthlessly tamped it down.

Lana was fine. The kidnappers would call and demand the ransom. His father would pay it and bring her home.

"Cole… I'm so sorry." Bethany rested her hand on his arm, her soft, feathery touch a balm to his nerves. "I can only imagine how tough this is. And your poor sister!"

He met her eyes. Her sympathy tugged at something inside him, kicking off a wave of warmth in his chest. Bethany had always understood him. She'd connected with him in a way no one else ever had. They'd been the best of friends, explosive lovers. He'd been so damned crazy in love….

He dropped his gaze to her lips. Time ground to a sudden halt, as if they'd been transported to the past. And any thought of danger flitted away.

She was so close. So beautiful. And the soft, satiny feel of her had burned him alive.

His blood turned heavy and hot. Hunger rose inside him, the need to feel her again in his arms. He widened his stance and shifted closer, his pulse beating fast.

His cell phone chirped. He froze, then straightened, appalled at what he'd been about to do. He couldn't kiss Bethany. He couldn't get anywhere near her. She was the one woman who had the power to make him need her—a risk he couldn't afford.

Determined to keep his mind on track, he whipped out his cell phone and checked the display. The ranch house. He clicked it on with a frown. "Cole here."

"It's your father," his housekeeper, Hannah Brown, blurted out. "You need to come quick."

His heart faltered. "What's wrong?"

"He got a phone call…he looks terrible…all gray… I've phoned the doctor but—"

"I'll be right there." He shoved his phone back into his pocket and launched himself onto the horse.

"What is it?" Bethany swung up onto Red.

"My father." He wheeled the gelding around, then spurred him into a lope. Bethany instantly caught up.

They streaked through the field in silence, taking their mounts to the limit, anxiety pounding his nerves. His father was generally healthy, but the stress of the last few weeks had taken its toll. And if something terrible had happened to Lana...

He cut off that train of thought. His sister had to be all right. He refused to believe the worst.

They reached the county road. Cole leaped down to open the gate.

"Go on," Bethany urged him. "I'll close the gate. Call me if you need help with your dad. Otherwise I'll see you in the morning when we get those cows."

Grimacing at her tenacity, he led his horse through the gate. He didn't want her around. He had enough on his mind with crises erupting at every turn. But nothing mattered more than the ranch.

And as much as it galled him to admit it, he needed help.

"All right." He swung back onto the horse and caught her eye. "You're hired. But you'll stick close to me. You understand? I'm not taking a chance with armed vandals roaming the ranch."

He nudged the horse into a lope, then galloped toward the ranch house, but even the steady drum of hoofbeats couldn't banish his feeling of doom. He would save his ranch. And he'd keep Bethany safe; he'd make damned sure of that.

But could he do the same with his heart?

Chapter 4

Senator Hank Kelley slumped on the sofa in the great room, a clammy sweat moistening his brow, his hands trembling so hard the ice cubes clinked in his highball glass. He knocked back a gulp of Maker's Mark whiskey, feeling the burn scorch straight to his gut.

But even the triple shot of ninety-proof liquor couldn't erase the terror of that call. *They're going to kill Lana. You have to turn yourself in now.*

"You shouldn't drink that. Not until the doctor says it's all right." Hannah, Cole's housekeeper, hovered by the sofa, watching him with the same rabid attention the border collies trained on rebellious cows.

"I told you I'm fine."

"No, you're not. Your face still looks like chalk."

"I had a dizzy spell, that's all." Thanks to the threat

he'd just received. The secret society would kill Lana if he didn't surrender; they'd execute *him* if he did.

He took another long swallow of bourbon and shuddered hard. None of this should have happened. Joining the top-secret, ultra-exclusive Raven's Head Society had been his ticket to wealth. He'd felt privileged, powerful, proud.

Until he'd found out they were plotting to assassinate the president of the United States.

He gulped down another slug of whiskey, then wheezed in a shaky breath. He wasn't a murderer, for God's sake. He'd tried to quit the Society, but he knew too much and they refused to let him go. He'd gone to ground, tried to hide, but they'd kidnapped Lana to flush him out.

"Just sit right there," Hannah said. "Don't you dare move. The doctor will be here soon."

He opened his mouth to protest. He was a *senator,* by God. She couldn't order him around. He had a staff to do his bidding, voters clamoring for his attention, beautiful women vying for a turn in his bed.

Senator or not, he'd managed to muck up his life. His doting wife had left him. He'd become a laughingstock in the media, the brunt of late-night comedians' jokes. And instead of fighting back he was hiding out in Montana, cowering behind his bodyguards, while his political enemies attacked him like feral dogs.

And Lana… His stomach went into freefall at the thought of his kidnapped daughter. He'd never dreamed they'd go after her. And where was the mercenary he'd hired? Instead of rescuing her as he was supposed to, the man had gone AWOL for the past two weeks.

Cole's old dog wandered over, then whined and

nudged his knee. His lips curling, Hank jerked his leg away. "Get this damned mutt off me. I don't want him slobbering all over my clothes."

Hannah shot him a reproachful look. "Here, Ace. Come on, sweetie. Let's go get you a treat."

The dog turned and trotted off. Annoyed, Hank flicked the fur off his pants. He grabbed the bottle of whiskey from the end table and slopped more into his glass.

The door to the porch burst open. He jumped, his pulse racing off the charts, but Cole strode in, his gaze arrowing straight to him. "What happened?"

Hank gulped down another mouthful of bourbon, hissing as it seared his throat. "Nothing."

"Is it Lana? Did something happen to her?"

"No, nothing happened." *Not yet.*

"Then who called?"

"Nobody. Just Mickey. Mickey O'Donahue."

"The rancher?"

"Yes." O'Donahue owned a ranch near Hank's California estate. He was also a member of the Raven's Head Society, but no one outside the group knew that.

Cole's eyes narrowed, his suspicion clear. "What did he want?"

"Nothing important," Hank fudged. "He just had a suggestion about a business concern."

"And that made you collapse?"

"I didn't collapse. I just got a little dizzy. Hannah overreacted. I told her not to call anyone."

Cole folded his arms, his gaze hard on his father's. Uncomfortable with the scrutiny, Hank mopped the sweat from his brow. The motion made his sore ribs twinge, reminding him of his recent attack in town.

Another frisson of guilt slithered through him. He'd done more than endanger himself and his daughter. He'd brought the Society here to Maple Cove. "I heard about your cows. I... I wish that I could help."

Cole's eyes slitted. Anger vibrated off him in waves. "I don't need your help. I don't need anything from you at all."

"I know." Cole *didn't* need him. He'd built an impressive business on the family homestead. It wasn't a lifestyle Hank wanted, but it seemed to suit his son. And he'd done it on his own.

An empty feeling spread through his belly, mingling with pride for his son. While he'd been busy working, Cole had grown into a man deserving respect.

"I just..." Hell, this was hard. He wasn't used to apologizing. "I just wanted to say I'm sorry."

"You think that helps?" Hostility rang in Cole's voice. "Your words don't mean a thing. They never have. They aren't going to help Lana, and they're not going to save my ranch." He stomped from the great room into his office, his boots clipping the hardwood floor.

Hank exhaled. Cole was right. He'd been a piss-poor father, making promises he never kept. Not to the voters, not to his children or his wife. It hadn't seemed important. Who had time to attend a kid's birthday party when he had a government to run?

And now... Now it was too late.

He studied the ice cubes melting in his highball glass, aware that he'd screwed up. He'd driven away his family—and someday he'd make amends. But first he had to figure a way out of this mess and bring his daughter home.

But how? He couldn't tell anyone about the Raven's Head Society—not his family, not the police or the FBI.

Not if he wanted to keep his daughter alive.

But if the Society murdered the president…

If anyone got wind that he was involved…

And if that mercenary failed…

"The doctor's here," Hannah announced, hurrying to open the door.

Thoroughly rattled, Hank polished off the bourbon and set aside his glass. And dread burrowed inside him, a chill lodging deep in his gut.

Because he had the terrible feeling events had spiraled beyond his control—and they all would pay the price.

Bethany stood in Red's stall an hour later, still struggling to process Cole's revelation as she brushed the mare. *Kidnapped.* The enormity of it made her reel. She couldn't imagine the terror Lana must be experiencing, the horror of the dreadful ordeal.

She shuddered, wondering how the family was holding up. Lana's mother would be devastated, of course. Cole was obviously furious, especially since his father was at fault.

Was hers?

That thought shot out of nowhere, and she paused with her hand on the horse. No. She refused even to consider it. Her father would never harm an animal, let alone a human being. The idea went against everything she knew of the man.

But if he'd gotten caught in some sort of difficulty, maybe found himself in over his head…

Striving for perspective, she exchanged the currycomb for a softer brush and continued grooming the mare. He was hiding something, she knew that. But it was a huge leap from refusing to answer questions to conspiring to commit a crime. She was letting her imagination run away from her, looking for trouble where it didn't exist.

Still, it was time she demanded answers. She didn't like knowing her father was keeping secrets from her. And if he *was* caught up in something shady, he could be in danger. If the senator's enemies had kidnapped Lana, who knew what else they might do?

She gave Red a final swipe. "All right, time for your grain." Then she needed to talk to her dad.

She set the brush on the corner shelf and moved toward the door of the stall, but a sudden thud reached her ears. She stopped, her heart missing a beat, and whipped her gaze to Red. The mare had her head raised, her ears pricked forward.

The horse had heard it, too.

Her pulse began to race. She stood stock-still, listening intently, hardly daring to breathe. Who was there? Cole? One of the cowboys? But long seconds passed without another sound. She was imagining things. No one was in the barn. The hands were all in the bunkhouse, eating dinner. Besides, Cole had said they were safe near the house.

Chiding herself for her overreaction, she continued to the door. But then another thud came from outside the stall. She froze again, sharp fear blocking her throat. She hadn't imagined that noise. It had come from the direction of the tack room farther down the aisle.

Her hands trembling, she cracked open the door. She peeked out, her throat dust dry, and glanced past the row of stalls. Nothing moved. A horse snuffled from a nearby stall.

Then a cat streaked past in a blur of black, and Bethany pressed her hand to her chest. *The barn cat*. He'd probably knocked something over while hunting—and she'd instantly suspected the worst.

Rolling her eyes at her wild imagination, she went down the aisle to get the grain. She didn't usually jump at shadows. She lived in Chicago, for heaven's sake—and it had a lot more crime than Maple Cove. But learning about Lana's kidnapping had put her nerves on edge.

Still jittery, she scooped out Red's grain and lugged the pail back to the stall. She gave the mare's water a final check, then made herself walk slowly from the barn, refusing to give in to her fears and run.

But she scoured the deepening shadows as she crossed the deserted yard. The pole light blinked on, casting a silvery gleam over the ground, but did little to dispel her nerves. She'd always loved the country at night—the hooting owls, the brilliant canopy of stars, the profound silence gripping the land. But tonight the ranch seemed sinister, empty, exposed.

She glanced at Cole's stone house with its wide, welcoming veranda, and her traitorous thoughts swerved back to him. She didn't want to obsess over Cole. She didn't want to worry about his problems or spend her vacation trying to find out who'd killed his cows.

And she certainly didn't want to think about that moment in the field when she'd thought he was going to kiss her. *Talk about an overreaction!* Her face flamed at the thought. He'd looked at her with those dazzling blue eyes and she'd gone off the deep end, letting her memories sweep her away.

She shook her head in disgust. So Cole still attracted her in a major way. That was hardly a surprise. But she absolutely could not start fantasizing that they had any sort of future. Their relationship had ended. They'd both moved on in their lives.

And she had other problems to worry about—such as discovering why her father had lied.

She found him a few minutes later at the kitchen table, reading the Bozeman paper. "Hi, Dad." Careful of his injuries, she bent down and gave him a hug. "How's your leg?"

"Not bad."

The pallor of his face contradicted that. "You don't look good."

"Don't start hassling me about those pills. I'll take one before I go to sleep."

She sighed at his testy tone. She'd hoped he'd be in a cooperative mood. But maybe a meal would sweeten him up. "What would you like for dinner?"

"I already ate. Hannah brought a tuna casserole by. It's on the counter."

So much for that approach. She went to the sink and washed her hands. "Did Cole call?"

"No. Why would he?"

She exhaled. Lord, he was touchy tonight. "He said the senator wasn't well. I thought he might have needed my help."

"No, no one called."

She dried her hands. "He's probably all right then." Surely they would have heard if the news were bad. She reached up, closed the window above the sink, and caught her father's frown in the glass. "What's wrong?"

He grunted. "What isn't?" He folded his paper and

shoved it aside. "That storm front's closing in, and we've got hay to haul, calves to ship to market, cows still stranded in the mountains—and here I sit with this danged bum leg."

She understood his frustration. As foreman, her father should be in the thick of things, directing the work. She scooped some casserole onto a plate, put it in the microwave, and set the time. "So what happened in the mountains?"

Her father leaned back in his chair with a sigh. "A hundred head splintered from the main herd and went up a ravine. I rode in a ways, but they'd disappeared. They've probably holed up in a meadow near the divide. We brought the others back, figuring we'd return in a couple of days to find the rest."

But then he'd broken his leg, and someone had started killing Cole's cows.

She sat in another chair at the table, carefully choosing her words. "Cole wants to start shipping the calves out tomorrow. I told him I'd help."

"I don't want you getting involved."

She blinked, stunned by the vehemence in his voice. "Why not? You don't need me to do anything here— you even said so. And I feel guilty sitting around when Cole's shorthanded. You raised me better than that."

"He can find someone else to help. You stay out of this."

"But why? You have to give me a reason."

He crossed his arms, his mouth set in a stubborn line. "It's not safe."

She leaned her forearms on the table and frowned back, tired of being warned away. She'd grown up around cowboys. She could rope, ride and shoot with the best of them. She could do anything Cole needed on this ranch—drive a truck, deliver calves, castrate and brand a bull. And her father knew that; he'd taught her those skills himself. So what was he afraid of? The men?

"Not safe *how?*" she asked.

When he didn't answer, her exasperation rose. "Come on, Dad. You're not making sense. Cole's short-handed. He needs help, and he can't find anyone else—not this time of year. And you know I can do the work. So what's really bothering you?"

"Nothing."

"I don't believe you."

"I'm telling you, it's just not safe. Now leave it alone." Still scowling, he tugged his ear.

Her heart plummeted. So he still refused to tell her the truth—but why? What didn't he want her to know?

She tapped her foot, her frustration growing. This wasn't like her father. If he really did know something, how could he justify not speaking out? What if something happened to the men? How could he live with the guilt?

Tempted to mention Lana, she bit down hard on her lip. Cole had sworn her to silence, and she couldn't betray that trust.

Instead, she pulled the browband she'd found from her pocket and tossed it to her dad. "Any idea who this belongs to? I found it in the field."

His gaze flicked to the leather strap. "No."

"Cole thought it might be Tony's."

He shrugged. "It could be. He has some fancy tack. Hang it in the tack room. Someone will claim it."

Frowning, she picked it up. "So what do you think of Tony? He was a troublemaker in high school."

"He does his work. That's all I care about." His gaze sharpened. "I'm warning you, Bethany. Don't start sniffing around the men, stirring up trouble for Cole. He doesn't need more headaches, especially from you."

She sat back, stung. "What do you mean by that?"

"I'm not blind. I may not talk much, but I can see what's going on. You caused that boy a whole pile of heartache when you left, and he doesn't need you to come back here, meddling in his affairs."

Her jaw went slack. Fierce hurt welled inside. Her father never criticized her. And he'd never questioned her decision to leave.

"He hurt me, too."

He shook his head. "You don't know the half of it. You've got a stubborn streak a mile wide, and when you think you're right, you don't budge."

"I wonder where I got that trait?"

He wagged his finger at her. "I'm warning you. Mind your own business. That boy doesn't need more grief. Stay out of his affairs."

Rising, he grabbed the crutches propped against the wall. "I'm going to watch TV."

Stunned, she watched him hobble away. The microwave dinged, but she ignored it, her appetite suddenly gone.

She hugged her arms, feeling gutted, trying to figure out what had gone wrong. She'd only wanted answers about the sabotage. Instead her father had attacked her and accused her of hurting Cole.

But he was wrong. Cole had shut *her* out at the end.

He'd clammed up, refusing to discuss any options, even to consider leaving the ranch.

And she'd *had* to leave Maple Cove. Her father should have understood that. He knew what people around here were like. Some were all right, like Donald and Bonnie Gene. But there were plenty who had disapproved of her—even threatened her when she'd dated Cole. And she couldn't ignore the insults; she had too much pride.

Her stomach roiling with emotions, she put her plate in the refrigerator and grabbed a jacket, needing air. She went to the front porch and sat on the swing, then stared into the dark. Light from the main house shimmered from the massive windows, spilling out over the lawn.

She'd spent her whole life having proving herself, always having to work harder than anyone else. And by the time she'd graduated from high school, she'd been fed up. She was tired of battling stereotypes, tired of people judging her by her race. She couldn't even enter a store without clerks following her through the aisles, afraid she would steal their goods.

She'd wanted to live where her skin color didn't matter, where people judged her for herself. Where people didn't assume she'd only succeeded because of quotas, or that she hadn't earned her success.

And she'd found that place in Chicago. She had friends, a rewarding job where she could make a difference in people's lives. No one stared at her with suspicion or called her names on the streets.

She sighed, a headache building behind her eyes. She hated to argue with her father. He so rarely lost his temper that it left her shaken and hurt.

And he was dead wrong about Cole.

She rocked the swing, tilted her head back, and closed her eyes. Then, suddenly remembering her patient, Mrs. Bolter—and needing to put something to rights after the debacle with her father, she speed-dialed Adam on her phone.

"Hi, Bethany," he said, picking up.

She sagged back in relief. "Adam. I'm glad I caught you. I've been waiting for your call all day."

"How's Montana? Round up any buffalo?" His words were as light as always, but his joviality sounded forced. Her belly flip-flopped.

Something was wrong.

"No buffalo, just a bunch of ornery cows." She'd fill him in on the danger dogging the ranch when she returned. "So what's going on? Did you find out anything about Mrs. Bolter?" The official report wouldn't come out for weeks, but as lead doctor in the trial, Adam would be the first to know.

"Yeah, but it's not good."

"Not good how?" He didn't answer, and the anxiety in her belly grew. "Come on, Adam. You're making me nervous and I've already had a bad day. What happened?"

The silence stretched. Her forehead began to throb. "Adam? What's going on?"

He cleared his throat. "I probably shouldn't tell you yet, but there was a problem with the dose."

"She overdosed?" Incredulity washed through her. "How? We didn't change anything, and she's been tolerating that level for weeks."

"You're right. It shouldn't have changed. But when we checked the records, it looks like you doubled the dose."

"What?" She sat up straight. "I did not." She scrupulously followed the "five rights" she'd learned in nursing school, reciting them like a mantra every time she administered a drug: *right patient, drug, dose, route, time.* She even checked everything twice. "You know how anal I am about that. There's no way I gave her the wrong dose."

"Hey, I believe you. You don't need to convince me of that. I'm just telling you what they found."

"I'd better come back and clear this up."

"Don't panic. Let me see what I can do first. The investigation has just started."

Her throat closed. "They're investigating me?"

"It's routine, you know that."

"But—"

"Bethany, don't worry. I'll sort this out. I know you wouldn't have made a mistake. That's why I recommended you for the job. Give me a chance to talk to some people and inventory the drug supply, and I'll call you in a couple of days."

Not panic? When the investigators thought she'd made a mistake and caused her patient's death? Adam continued to reassure her, and she ended the call, but she still couldn't catch her breath.

She should fly back tomorrow and defend herself. Her father didn't need her here—and after warning her away from Cole, he'd be happy to see her go. Besides, she'd probably imagined his involvement in the sabotage just as she'd exaggerated that noise in the barn.

But what if she hadn't misjudged him? What if he needed her help?

She pressed her fingers to her forehead, trying to reason this out. Adam could handle the investigation at the clinic. They would check the study-drug supply, see that she hadn't made a mistake. And surely they'd do an autopsy which would further back her up.

Still, she hated being under suspicion. And it felt wrong to sit here idly with her beloved career on the line. She'd worked too hard to let anything derail her now.

She rose, still dithering, when a man emerged from Cole's house. He stood on the porch for a moment, the light shining from the windows silhouetting his powerful build. Gage Prescott, one of the senator's bodyguards. His military bearing gave him away. Then he continued down the steps and disappeared into the night, merging with the shadows like a pro.

She swallowed hard, the feeling of menace she'd experienced in the barn winging back full force. And she knew she couldn't leave. Not yet. Not while danger threatened her father. Not while armed men lurked in the shadows and attacked Cole's ranch.

Shivering, she pulled her jacket's collar closer around her throat. She'd vowed to keep her distance from Cole, sworn she wouldn't get involved. But she couldn't leave here with unanswered questions.

Even if she didn't like what she found.

Chapter 5

"The security system is down again."

Cole took a long swallow of desperately needed coffee, then dragged his attention to his father's bodyguard, Gage Prescott, who stood by the kitchen door. *Great.* Another problem already and the sun had barely come up. "What happened? I thought they just fixed it."

"I don't know, but the entire system is out."

"Any signs of intrusion?"

Gage shook his head. "Not that I could tell."

"So maybe it's just a glitch."

Gage's expression stayed neutral. "Maybe."

Or maybe it was more sabotage. Cole closed his eyes and swore. His ranch had become a war zone.

But it was a war Cole intended to win.

He huffed out a weary sigh. "All right. Call the company, see if they can send someone out right away. They should be open by eight."

He downed the last of the coffee, then glanced out the window at the still-shadowy yard, the thought of someone lurking in the darkness chilling his blood. But Prescott knew what he was doing. He'd keep the senator safe.

And come hell or high water, Cole would protect his ranch.

He strode through the great room, his boots ringing on the hardwood floor. He opened the door for Ace, then paused on the front porch, his breath turning to frost in the air. That front was fast approaching. He had to hurry and get his calves shipped off, then hustle back up to the mountains. If he didn't rescue those cows before the snow set in, he'd lose even more of his herd.

His border collies circling his heels, he crossed the yard to the staging area by the barn. His men stood by their horses and four-wheelers, drinking coffee and warming their hands. No one spoke. None of the usual banter filled the air.

He felt like snarling himself.

He scanned their sullen faces and frowned. "Where is everyone?"

Earl Runningcrane stepped forward. "They rode ahead to get the corrals set up."

"Good." His gaze landed on Bethany. She stood apart from the men, holding Red's reins. She'd donned a vest over her long sleeved T-shirt in deference to the cold. The rising light drew hollows beneath her high cheekbones and dark smudges under her eyes.

His belly tightened, his ingrained response to her beauty ticking him off. He didn't need this distraction.

He had enough on his mind without his libido leading him off course.

Determined to rein in the unwanted reaction, he turned to Earl, the seasoned wrangler by his side. "Wait here for the trucks, then direct them to the pasture. Call me on my cell as soon as they show up."

"Right, boss."

Kenny brought over his quarter horse, Gunner. Careful not to look at Bethany, Cole took the reins and leaped astride. "We've got a long day ahead. Let's move out."

"Cole, wait!" He groaned when he heard the shout. His housekeeper ran from the house, waving for him to stop.

"Hold on," he told his men. He clucked to his horse, then rode across the yard, bracing himself for bad news.

Hannah came to a stop. "The trucking company just called. There's a problem with the trucks, a scheduling glitch, and they can't get them here today."

"You're kidding." How the hell had that happened? He'd spent hours on the phone last night making sure it was all arranged. "When can we get them?"

"Tonight, if you can send your own drivers to pick them up. Otherwise you'll have to wait another week."

"A week!" His mood plummeted. No way could he wait that long. He'd lose more cows if he did.

He pinched the bridge of his nose, the dull ache behind his eyes turning into a full-fledged throb. "All right. Tell them I'll send some men up there tonight." He didn't have much choice. But neither could he afford to waste the day.

He wheeled Gunner around and rejoined the men. "Change of plans. We can't get the trucks until tonight, so we're driving the cattle to the barn instead." That would speed up the loading later. But he'd have to dip into his winter hay supply to feed the cows overnight—another unwelcome expense.

Exhaling, he turned to Earl. "Make sure we've got enough hay on hand for tonight. We'll bring them all in except the ones by Rock Creek. They need more time to recoup."

"Got it."

The men began to move out. Cole fell in beside Bethany, a bad feeling swirling inside. Dawn had barely broken, and trouble had already struck twice. He glanced at Bethany astride her horse—her long, black hair shimmering in the rising light, her exotic eyes firing his blood.

And he suspected his problems had just begun.

Bethany trailed the last group of cattle to the barn that afternoon, so tired she could hardly think. Fatigue pounded her skull. Her thighs ached from hours astride the horse. Dust clogged her throat, covering every inch of her with grit.

But even that discomfort couldn't take her mind off Cole.

He loped up the side of the strung-out herd, attracting her attention, just as he had all day. His shoulder muscles rippled beneath his T-shirt. Sweat streaked his dusty jaw. Her gaze lingered on his big hands gripping the reins, the tendons roping his powerful arms, and her body began to hum. Cole was the quintessential cowboy—tough, determined, sexy as all get-out. And there was something about a man doing physical labor that appealed to her in a primitive way.

At least this particular man.

A calf lunged from the herd. Glad for the distraction, Bethany went in pursuit, but the border collie beat her to it and steered it back into line.

"Tony," Cole shouted above the lowing cows. "Get up to the front and start turning them toward the corral." While Tony trotted off, Cole spun around and continued monitoring the herd.

He glanced her way. His amazing blue eyes captured hers, and her heart made a crazy lurch. His strong neck glistened with sweat. Afternoon beard stubble darkened his jaw. And the utter maleness of him rolled through her, inciting a riot of nerves in her chest.

All day long it had been the same—her eyes seeking him out. Their gazes colliding, then skidding away. His incredible sexual appeal winding her tighter than barbed wire on a brand-new fence.

But as he rode off to chase a cow, she had to admit something else. More than his animal magnetism kept drawing her thoughts to him. She couldn't forget her father's accusations, making her wonder if she'd hurt Cole.

And whether it mattered now if she had.

Renewing her resolve to ignore him—and stop obsessing about things she couldn't change—she wiped her forehead on her sleeve and surveyed the herd. They'd worked since dawn, driving hundreds of cows to the corrals by the barn, and now they were nearly done. In a few minutes she could escape into the cabin, take a long, hot bath and *finally* forget about Cole.

Bill swung open the corral gate, and the cows began filing inside. The men watched from their horses and four-wheelers, staying within the cattle's flight zone, but not so close that they'd make them bolt. Bethany glanced at the corral and spotted her father talking with Kenny Greene. He'd hobbled from the cabin on his crutches to watch the calves arrive.

Another calf broke free from the herd, and Bethany nudged Red forward to head it off. Then she swung around, intending to give the calves some space, but Tony rode up, his big gelding crowding her in.

"Back off," she said, fatigue adding an edge to her voice. "You're going to spook the calves."

"The hell I will." His flat eyes narrowed on hers. "I've been handling cows all my life. I don't need a squaw like you telling me what to do."

She flushed at his favorite insult, but held her ground. "Tell me that when you've scattered the herd."

As if on cue, the cattle behind her panicked. Several lunged for freedom, prompting even more to break from the herd.

Earl Runningcrane trotted up on his quarter horse, dust coating his angry face. "Tony! What the hell are you doing? Give them some space."

Tony glared back. "You're not my boss. I don't take orders from you." But he jerked on the reins and rode off.

"Idiot." Earl turned her way. He asked her something in the Blackfoot language.

Still unsettled, she shook her head. "Sorry. I don't speak Blackfoot."

"Why not?"

"Why should I?"

He studied her for a moment, something that looked a lot like disappointment in his eyes. "No reason." He kicked his horse and went after the fleeing cows.

Exasperated, Bethany turned her attention back to

the herd. What was with everyone these days? First her father criticized her decision to leave after high school, now Earl insinuated that she'd ignored her roots.

But why should she speak Blackfoot? She'd never lived on the reservation; she'd grown up in Maple Cove. And so what if she had Indian ancestors? She had Caucasian ones, too.

Still fuming, she trailed the herd to the barn. That was the problem with Maple Cove. Everyone wanted to box her in and label her according to some stereotyped notion they had. No one accepted her for herself.

Especially not Tony. Her belly tightened as he rode past her and shot her a vicious look. She raised her chin and held his gaze, refusing to back down. He was nothing but a mean-spirited bully who thrived on his victims' fear.

But did that mean he'd killed Cole's cows?

She was still mulling that over as she unsaddled and brushed the mare. She wanted to pin the sabotage on Tony. He'd made her childhood hell, and she'd love to see him pay. But she couldn't prove he'd done anything wrong yet. And aside from his nasty personality, why would he want to hurt Cole?

Unable to come up with an answer, she joined her father at the corral. He leaned heavily on his crutches, his face gray, pain adding more lines around his mouth. "You've been on your feet too long," she scolded. "You'd better get back to the house."

"I guess. The calves look good, though."

She slowed her pace to his, only half listening as he discussed the herd. At least he'd stopped arguing about her helping Cole. But the sight of Earl Runningcrane heading to his truck reminded her of the conversation they'd had.

Not sure how to broach the subject, she waited until her father had finished critiquing the calves. "Say, Dad," she began, feeling awkward. "I was wondering—why didn't we live on the reservation?"

For several minutes he didn't answer. He kept maneuvering his way toward the house, his head bowed, the exertion making him breathe hard. "It would have been too hard on your mother," he finally said.

"In what way?"

"I took her to Browning a couple of times when we first met. My parents didn't accept her any more than her folks accepted me. In the end, it was easier to live in town."

She frowned at that. It hadn't occurred to her that intolerance went both ways. "That couldn't have been easy for you."

"I didn't mind." He stopped when he reached the porch and released a sigh. "I was nearly forty years old when I met your mother. I'd waited all my life to find a woman like her, and when I did... I didn't care where we lived."

"So you sacrificed your happiness for hers."

"Who said I wasn't happy? I just wanted to be with her. And sacrifices come easy when you love someone."

Guilt trickled through her, and she crossed her arms. "It still must have been hard. Living with the prejudice, I mean."

He shrugged. "Sometimes, but people were different back then. And most folks come around if you give them time."

She doubted that. Jerks like Tony never would. And

as for the others…she didn't intend to stick around to find out.

Her father hobbled up the porch steps, but his words lingered in her mind. Should she have stayed in Maple Cove? Should she have sacrificed more for Cole? Had she run because she had to—or out of wounded pride?

Feeling uneasy, she cast another look toward the barn. Cole stood outside it, talking to a couple of ranch hands. She studied his steely jaw, the implacable set to his massive shoulders, and slowly expelled a sigh.

No, she'd had to leave. Cole had made his rejection clear. And love went both ways—he could have come with her if he'd cared.

But for the first time since she'd left Maple Cove, she couldn't quite banish *her* doubts.

It didn't help that Cole stopped by that evening to discuss ranch business with her father. Unable to avoid him in the tiny cabin, she retreated to the porch swing while she waited for him to leave. But the deep, sexy timbre of his voice carried in the still night air, further unsettling her nerves.

She still didn't believe she'd hurt him. Her father was wrong about that. But if she *had* made a mistake…

The front door swung open, and he stepped onto the porch. His eyes met hers, and she rose. "Is everything all right?" she asked.

"At the moment." He gripped the back of his neck, and the weary motion tugged at her heart. "But I keep expecting the other shoe to drop."

"I know what you mean. This is the first quiet day since I've arrived." It was almost *too* peaceful. They'd driven the calves to the barn without problems. No one had killed any cows. She glanced into the darkness beyond the yard light, feeling apprehensive at the sudden lull.

"I'm going to check on the calves by the barn." He angled his head to meet her eyes. "You want to come?"

Her heart stumbled. Warnings went off in her mind. She should decline. A walk in the moonlight was too cozy, too seductive, *too intimate.*

But she'd never been able to resist Cole.

"Sure," she heard herself say.

She followed him down the porch steps, wondering if she'd lost her mind. She should be avoiding Cole, not strolling with him beneath the stars.

Shaking her head at her lapse in judgment, she stuffed her hands in her jacket pockets to keep them warm. "Where is everyone? The ranch seems deserted tonight."

"I sent four men to Butte to get the stock trucks. The rest are on patrol." His gaze swiveled to hers, and the impact ripped through her, rattling her pulse. "I wanted to let you know that the security system is down. They'll fix it tomorrow when the part comes in, and I've stepped up patrols around the house. But I thought you should know."

She flicked her gaze from the shadows surrounding the barn to the profound darkness cloaking the fields, and a chill scuttled down her spine. Someone was out there, watching their movements. Someone wanting to do them harm.

Suddenly the barn cat flitted past, making her heart race even more. Should she mention the thuds she'd heard in the barn to Cole? But what would be the point?

He had enough on his mind without her wild imaginings adding to his stress.

But with the security system down…

Still uncertain, she walked beside him around the barn, her feet crunching on the gravel path. The cold wind gusted, and she zipped up her jacket against the chill.

"Are you cold?" Cole asked.

"Not too bad."

His gaze ran over her face, a crease forming between his dark brows. "Something's bothering you, though. You've looked preoccupied all day."

Surprised he'd noticed, she stopped beside the corral and propped her forearms on the fence. She didn't want to discuss their breakup—at least not yet. Not until she had a better handle on exactly what had gone wrong. And she couldn't mention her suspicions about Tony since she had nothing to base them on.

"I've just had some problems at work, that's all," she finally said.

"What kind of problems?"

She studied his eyes, tempted to tell him. Standing together like this, cocooned in the quiet darkness, it was easy to forget the heartbreak and remember the camaraderie they'd shared.

And he'd revealed his sister's kidnapping to her.

"I work at a research clinic," she said. "The Preston Werner Clinic in Chicago. We've been conducting a trial for an experimental rheumatoid arthritis drug called Rheumectatan. The night before I came here, one of my patients died."

"That's tough."

"It gets worse." She pressed her hand to her belly to

settle her nerves. "They think I administered the wrong dose, that I made a mistake that caused her death."

"You'd never do that."

She looked at him in surprise.

He shrugged. "You're too careful. I spent enough time studying with you to know that."

They hadn't always studied.

Awareness arced between them. Sudden heat flared in his eyes. And she knew he was remembering the same thing she was—the hours they'd spent in erotic exploration, touching, kissing, making love...

Her pulse scrambling, she jerked her gaze back to the cows. The past was gone. She was not going to dwell on their sex life or how madly in love she'd been.

Struggling to gather her composure, she cleared her throat. "Thanks. I appreciate the vote of confidence."

"It's a fact. You're the most conscientious person I know."

She braved another glance his way. Light spilled from the barn, dusting him with a silver sheen, highlighting the hard, male planes of his face. Their eyes locked again, and something else shimmered between them, something beyond the lust—a feeling of friendship, warmth, *trust*.

But hadn't that been an illusion? Hadn't he callously shut her out?

He propped his boot on the fence and looked away, breaking the spell. "So what do you think happened?"

She dragged in a breath, trying to marshal her scattered thoughts. "I don't know. Maybe the drug caused a bad reaction or interacted with an underlying condition she had. But Adam would have screened her for that. He's the doctor running the trial."

Cole's gaze traveled back to hers. "Can you check her records?"

"Yes." She knew the password and could access the system online. "But I doubt I'll have to. When they inventory the study drug, they'll notice the discrepancy and see that they made a mistake.

"By the way," she added. "I haven't mentioned this to my father. I don't want him to worry." Or think she'd failed at her job. "I'd appreciate it if you keep this quiet for now."

"Sure." Cole turned his gaze to the cows, his expression thoughtful. The calves shuffled and lowed in the pens. A moment later, he straightened, and they started back toward the house.

"Tell me more about your life in Chicago," he said.

She nodded, grateful for the change of subject. "Well, I love my job. And I've got a great apartment near the lake. No view to speak of." Nothing like the stunning mountain vistas on his ranch. "But I'm close to all the action, so there's always a lot to do."

But somehow, walking beside Cole in the moonlight with millions of stars glittering above her, Chicago didn't seem that great.

"So you like it?" he asked.

"Yes." Of course she did. "It's just what I'd hoped it would be."

"I'm glad." They stopped at the steps to her porch. His eyes stayed on hers, and time seemed to disappear. How many nights had they spent like this—walking in the moonlight, gazing into each other's eyes?

The moment stretched. She knew she should step back, climb up the steps and say good-night. But emotions tumbled inside her—longing, regret.

Desire.

His eyes narrowed. Heat radiated from his muscled build. And his raw masculinity rolled through her, making her heart rate spike.

And suddenly, she wanted desperately to feel him, to stroke her palms down his stubbled jaw, to feel his hard, warm lips devouring hers.

He wanted to kiss her, too. She couldn't mistake the hunger in his eyes this time.

But that was insane. Nothing good could come from a kiss. They had too much baggage between them, and they couldn't change the past.

Cole reached down, tucked a loose strand of hair behind her ear, and her heart began to thud. Then he cupped her jaw with his work-roughened hand, sending thrills rushing over her skin.

"Cole…" she whispered, but whether as a plea or a warning, she didn't know.

His gaze dropped to her mouth. Her heart tried to burst from her chest. And a fierce sense of yearning mushroomed inside her, the need to lose herself in the strong, solid feel of him making her sway.

Then he dipped his head, and his lips took hers— hard and potent and warm, sending a hot blast of need sizzling and skipping through her veins. She gripped his rock-hard arms, her knees suddenly buckling, a moan forming deep in her throat.

She'd missed this. *Missed him.* Nothing had ever felt so right.

But, way too soon, he ended the kiss. He stared down at her for a moment, their ragged breaths dueling in the night. Then he stepped back and cleared his throat.

"I'm glad you found what you were looking for," he rasped. He turned on his heel and strode away.

Her heart pounding, her entire body trembling, she grabbed the porch rail for support and watched him go.

He reached his house, paused to pet Ace waiting beside the steps. Then he bent down, gently picked up the arthritic dog, and carried him inside.

And, as a deep hush settled around her, Bethany couldn't help but wonder—if she'd found everything she'd wanted in Chicago, why did she feel bereft?

Cole didn't often have regrets, but that kiss ranked up there as one of the biggest mistakes he'd ever made.

He sprawled in his bed hours later, his sheets tangled and sweaty, so wound up he couldn't sleep. What in the hell had he been thinking? He'd spent the entire day trying to avoid her, only to blow it at the end.

He'd had no business walking with her in the darkness, no business asking about her life. He should have told her about the broken security system on the porch, then marched straight back to his house. But she'd looked so damned beautiful standing there in the moonlight, like every fantasy he'd ever had.

He punched his pillow and sighed, knowing that more than her looks had caused him to cave. Her beauty he could have resisted, although everything about her still turned him on. It was that sense of connection, that *rightness* she'd made him feel that had caused him to lose his mind.

So he'd messed up and succumbed to a moment of weakness. Somehow he had to forget it and make sure he didn't do it again. There was no point torturing himself with needs he couldn't indulge.

He rubbed his scratchy eyes, glanced at the clock beside his bed, and groaned. Two o'clock. If he didn't get some shut-eye soon, he'd never make it through the day.

Hoping a drink would take the edge off, he rolled out of bed, and pulled on his shirt and jeans. Then he strode down the hall toward the great room, detouring to the wet bar off to the side. Ace padded toward him and whined, and Cole reached down to scratch his ears. "Hey, buddy. You having trouble sleeping, too?"

Still whining, Ace turned and trotted toward the door.

"All right, give me a minute and I'll let you out." He opened the bar, pulled out a bottle of Scotch and splashed some into a glass. Then he knocked it back, hoping the fiery drink would deaden the lust.

The dog yipped and pawed at the door. "All right. I'm on my way. You don't need to wake everyone up." He poured more Scotch into the tumbler, then stuck the bottle back into the bar. His glass in hand, he headed toward the front door.

A glow in the windows caught his eye. His heart stopped, a sudden feeling of *wrongness* surging inside. He slammed down his glass on a nearby table, bolted to the door, and flung it open.

The barn was engulfed in flames.

Chapter 6

Cole gaped at the bright orange flames leaping across the barn in the darkness, twisting and curling like macabre dancers into the sky. Horses screamed from inside the burning building. The fierce fire crackled and roared. Cole launched himself back into the great room in a burst of adrenaline, then sprinted full out down the hall.

Veering into the guest wing, he whipped his cell phone from his pocket and pounded on his father's door. He needed to alert his ranch hands. He had to get those horses out fast. It would take the volunteer fire department half an hour or more to get here, and he couldn't afford to wait.

Speed-dialing the bunkhouse, he hammered again on the door. The noise drew Bart, the bodyguard on the night shift, from the adjacent lounge.

"The barn's on fire," Cole barked into the phone, but he kept his gaze on Bart. "Get everyone on it. And call the fire department in Maple Cove."

Comprehension crossed Bart's face. His father's other bodyguard, Gage Prescott, raced from his bedroom with his weapon drawn, just as the senator flung open his door.

"Take the senator and Hannah into the safe room," Bart told Gage, referring to the wine cellar, the most secure spot in the house. "I'll scout around outside."

Gage nodded, his eyes grim. "Be careful. It could be a trap, an attempt to lure the senator outside."

Cole's belly tightened. Trap or not, he had to fight the fire.

Leaving the bodyguards to deal with his father, he raced into the mudroom and jerked on his boots. Then he hurtled out the back door and sprinted flat out toward the barn, desperate to save the animals inside.

Heavy smoke rolled from the roof now. Vivid orange flames spiraled upward, sending sparks shooting into the sky. His eyes watered and stung as he neared the barn, and he coughed on the acrid smoke. He had to free the horses, then try to move the calves. They were in the worst possible place, penned in the corral behind the barn.

He charged toward the barn, his breathing ragged. Someone darted ahead of him through the billowing smoke. *Bethany.* His heart stopped when she ran inside.

"Bethany!" he shouted, but she didn't hear.

Swearing, his throat tight with fear for her safety, he plunged after her into the barn. Burning wood rained from the rafters. The roar of the fire filled the air. He coughed, his eyes stinging from the heavy smoke, searching frantically to see where she'd gone.

He spotted her ahead of him, flinging open Red's stall. "Go on! Get out!" she yelled at the horse, who was prancing and neighing with fear.

The crazed horse burst from the stall. Cole flattened himself to the wall as the mare thundered past, her eyes wild with terror as she fled the barn.

Flames crackled and hissed around them. Dense smoke hung in the air. Cole launched himself into action, lunging from stall to stall, helping Bethany throw open the doors. Several horses instantly bolted to safety, but the rest refused to budge.

He suddenly lost sight of Bethany, and panic slammed through his nerves. But the smoke shifted, then parted, and Bethany appeared, towing another horse toward the door. A beam fell nearby, and the thoroughbred started trotting in tight circles, his ears flat to his head.

"Stay outside! I'll get the rest," he shouted to her as she hurried past, battling to control the terrified horse.

With no time to waste, Cole darted into the nearest stall. Tony's roan gelding reared up, his eyes rolling back as sparks sizzled and popped nearby. Cole tried to throw on his halter, but the gelding pawed and tossed his head.

"Come on, damn it! I'm trying to save your life!" Coughing, his eyes streaming from the pungent smoke, Cole lunged again at the horse. He managed to toss on his halter, then hauled the skittish horse from the stall. They burst from the barn, the gelding rearing and kicking, and Cole let go of the lead. The horse raced into the night.

Cole wiped his eyes, then straightened and hauled air to his searing lungs. Men now shouted and ran around him, using shovels and hoses to fight the fire. He glimpsed Rusty through the smoke, balancing on his crutches, hosing down the cabin to keep the sparks from igniting the roof. Others leaped aboard tractors and balers, rushing to get the machinery out of harm's way.

Earl Runningcrane dashed over, his face covered with soot. "Boss! I opened the gates and let the cattle out. They were starting to stampede."

"Good." Cole was grateful he'd thought to check. "Take charge of the men. I'll get the rest of the horses out."

Bethany darted past him, then ran back into the barn, and his belly went rigid with fear. The fire was mounting, pushing sparks over the yard, threatening to explode. He had to get her back out!

Swearing, he ducked into the barn behind her, choking in the roiling smoke. The air had become a furnace, and sweat streamed down his face and back. Horses whinnied above the roar. His heart banged against his chest. Bethany came from a stall with a thrashing horse, determination etched on her face.

"Wait outside," he shouted, hoping she listened this time. "I'll get the final two."

He hurried into Gunner's stall, then circled behind him, trying to force the horse to move. But Gunner balked and kicked, narrowly missing Cole's chest.

"Come on, come on!" he urged. Knowing every second counted, he grabbed the halter and flung it over Gunner's head. Then he hauled the panicked horse from the stall and got him moving toward the open door.

But a section of roof crashed nearby, flinging up

ashes and sparks. Gunner reared up, threatening to strike him with his flailing hooves. Cole gritted his teeth, using all his strength to pull him from the burning barn.

He let go of the horse and turned back, heaving air to his fiery lungs. He coughed, gagging on the pungent smoke, but couldn't take time to rest. He had one more horse to get out.

But the fire was growing stronger, more volatile, fanned by the gusting wind. Embers shot from the roof, torching spot fires. Flames roared with deadly menace, the barn on the verge of collapse.

Bethany dashed back inside. Cole's heart halted, stark fear strangling his throat. She'd never make it. The rest of the roof was about to collapse!

Terrified, he went in pursuit. Flames crackled around him. The tack room had become a raging wall of fire. Dodging falling timbers, he sprinted toward the remaining stall.

The air vibrated as the fire gained fury. Black smoke streamed from the flames.

And a wild feeling of panic churned inside him. No horse was worth Bethany's life.

"Bethany!" he hollered, but he couldn't see her through the stinging smoke. His urgency at a flash point, he vaulted a burning log, then plowed through the wall of heat. Flames hissed and crackled on every side.

Then Bethany appeared with Bill's horse, Blaze, her eyes wild in her blackened face. She'd thrown a halter on the horse, and had a towel draped over his head.

The flames grew more erratic. The fire boiled up behind them, roaring like a freight train in the trembling air.

They only had seconds left.

He grabbed the lead from her hands. "Go!" he shouted, relieved when she listened and ran toward the door.

Another beam broke free and fell. Blaze reared, and Cole battled to hang on to the lead. His pulse rocketing, his muscles straining, he pulled the frenzied horse outside.

A deafening boom came from behind him. Men shouted and sprang away. Cole released the horse, then whipped around as the roof of the barn collapsed.

Sparks shot over the yard. Coughing and wheezing badly, Cole hauled air into his scorched lungs. They'd made it. They'd gotten out safely.

But Bethany had nearly died.

Desperate to find her, he searched through the chaos in the yard. He spotted her off to the side, bent over double, her hands braced on her knees. Swamped with relief, he closed his eyes and struggled to control his rioting nerves. But he couldn't calm down, couldn't contain the emotions careening inside. He could have lost her inside that barn.

Urgently needing to touch her, he strode across the yard. She straightened, and their eyes connected through the drifting smoke. He caught the telltale wobble of her mouth, the vulnerable sheen in her eyes and suddenly lost control.

He reached her and grabbed her arms. "What the hell were you thinking? How could you risk your life like that?"

Her full lips parted. Her eyes turned huge in her face. "I had to save the horses. I couldn't let them die."

So she'd risked her life instead.

Men sprinted around them. His lungs heaving, Cole grappled to regain control. He didn't want to care about her. He didn't want to feel these emotions bulging inside. He tightened his hold on her slender arms, the fragile feel of her making him angrier yet.

She bit her lip, her eyes uncertain in her sooty face. Shudders wracked her slender body—shock from the near-death experience setting in.

Swearing, he pulled her close and enveloped her in his arms. Then he closed his eyes, absorbing the tremors running through her, inhaling the smoky smell of her hair. And despite his fury, despite his terror that she could have died, he couldn't help but admire her courage in entering that barn.

Firebrands dropped around them. Embers sailed past in the wind. A hot spot took off beside them as the fire made a run across the dried grass.

"Watch out, boss!" someone shouted.

Jolted back to reality, Cole pulled Bethany to safety farther away from the barn. Then, not trusting himself around her, he forced himself to let her go and step back. But his gaze continued to devour her, sweeping the delicate line of her jaw, the ashes clinging to her unbound hair, the vulnerable curve of her lips.

"I… I'd better go help my dad," she whispered, her voice raspy from breathing smoke.

Too overcome to speak, he didn't answer. She turned, and he watched her go, shaken to the core by the feelings she'd evoked. Like ripping a bandage from a wound, she'd bared feelings he'd kept buried for years, leaving him vulnerable, raw, exposed.

And no way could he let that happen. He couldn't

care. He couldn't let himself like her again. Because caring would lead to heartbreak when she left.

And he refused to give her the power to destroy him again.

Gathering his scattered defenses, he turned to face his barn. All that remained was a heap of burning rubble—a bonfire blazing in the night. His men stood motionless beside it, knowing nothing would save it now.

Suddenly depleted, he watched the bright flames twirl against the sky. Everything he'd worked for—the safe, reliable world he'd built—had just gone up in smoke.

And he feared that nothing would ever be the same.

Several hours later, as dawn broke against the eastern sky, Cole once again stood by his barn. Exhaustion hammered his skull. The acrid stench of burnt wood stung his sinuses, filling the air with a murky haze. He took a pull from a bottle of water, the extent of the destruction making him numb.

The barn was toast. The pumper truck from Maple Cove's volunteer fire department continued to douse the water on smoldering logs, but there was nothing left to save.

He rubbed his stinging eyes and exhaled, struggling to make sense of the fire. He doubted an electrical problem had caused it; he'd upgraded the wiring when he'd renovated the barn. He'd also installed a state-of-the-art sprinkler system—which had failed to come on.

He hardened his jaw, unable to avoid the conclusion that had been dancing on the periphery of his mind all night. The fire had to be arson. Anything else was too coincidental, given the recent attacks on his ranch.

One of the volunteer firefighters walked over, drawing Cole's gaze. "The fire inspector is on his way," he said. "I'm sending the trucks back now. We'll keep one here in case there are any flare-ups."

Cole nodded. "Thanks, Bob. I appreciate the help." Although it wouldn't do any good.

Grimacing, he returned his gaze to the rubble. His cows were scattered across the fields, his horses traumatized from the ordeal. He could only thank God that none of his ranch hands had been hurt.

His thoughts veered back to Bethany and that nerve shattering moment when she'd entered the collapsing barn. He shuddered, not wanting to remember the terrifying ordeal. Because the thought of her risking her life…

He quickly blocked off the thought. She'd survived. *She was fine.*

But he knew one thing. He had to keep his distance. He couldn't let down his guard. There'd be no more intimate talks. No more moonlit walks. And he definitely wouldn't kiss her again. He would stay far away from Bethany until her vacation was up and she returned to Chicago where she belonged.

Earl Runningcrane jogged up, his hair wet from a recent shower. "Hey, boss. Just to let you know, we've rounded up the horses. They're in the pasture behind the house."

Cole ran his hand through his filthy hair, dislodging ashes and soot. "Any injuries?"

"Not that I could tell. We'll check them better once the trucks leave and the commotion dies down. They're too nervous to let us close." He paused. "How are the cows?"

Cole exhaled. "Several got injured in the stampede. The vet's on his way." He hoped they didn't have to put them down. It would be his own damned fault if they did. If he'd left them to graze in the fields, if he hadn't insisted on saving a few hours of work by penning them close to the barn....

"The fire inspector's on his way, too," he added.

"I'll wait for them if you want to get some breakfast," Earl offered. "I already ate."

Cole nodded, suddenly aware of his gnawing hunger. "I won't be long. I'll grab a shower and something to eat. Call me as soon as they show up."

His steps weary, he trudged toward the house. He skirted the porch, then veered toward the mudroom around the back, knowing Hannah would skin him alive if he went traipsing through the great room covered in soot.

He inhaled, his chest still fiery from breathing smoke. He didn't need the inspector to tell him the fire was arson. He had no doubts about that. What he didn't know was whether one of his ranch hands was to blame.

A sick feeling broke loose inside him at the thought. He knew his men. He'd worked beside them for years. He'd even attended high school with some and played on the same sports teams. And they'd never given him a reason to doubt their loyalty.

But he couldn't ignore the facts. Whoever had torched his barn had known that he was shorthanded. He'd known that Cole had sent men off last night to get those cattle trucks. And he'd managed to set the fire, disabling the security system and sprinklers, without anyone noticing him hanging around—or tipping off the dogs.

Cole tightened his jaw, the idea that he had a traitor in his midst was a kick to the throat. He didn't tolerate betrayal.

And anyone who abused his trust would pay the price.

He neared the mudroom door and glanced up, then spotted a mound of clothes on the stoop. No, not clothes, something covered by a blanket. He slowed to a stop and frowned. That hadn't been there when he'd left the house.

Sudden trepidation gripped him. He scanned the bumpy mound, his heart beginning to thud. Then he spotted something peeking out from beneath the blanket.

A human hand.

His lungs closed up. His blood coursed hard in his skull. He skirted the pile and made out a pair of boots. Military boots, he realized with a jolt, belonging to a man wearing camouflage clothes.

His heart slamming against his rib cage, he whipped back around and scanned the yard. The horses still stood in the field beyond the windbreak. The branches of the cottonwoods swayed, their leaves fluttering in the morning breeze. The muted roar of the pumper truck droned from near the barn.

Nothing else moved. Nothing seemed out of place.

But someone had dumped a corpse.

Dread trickling through him, Cole turned back to the man. He made himself approach him, then tugged off the blanket and nudged him over with his foot.

He was definitely dead—executed, judging by the bullet hole between his eyes.

Swallowing a spurt of bile, Cole forced himself to study the bloodless face. He had dark, military-style hair, a neatly trimmed goatee. He appeared to be in his thirties, medium height with a muscular build.

Cole knew one thing. He'd never seen him before.

So what was a dead soldier doing here?

Cole pulled out his cell phone and punched in a number.

"Prescott," his father's bodyguard answered.

"We've got a problem. There's a dead body at the mudroom door."

"I'll be right there."

Cole clicked off the phone and slid it into the pocket of his jeans. He continued circling the man, then spotted an envelope tucked into his belt.

He stepped closer. The envelope was addressed to *him*.

His pulse accelerating, he crouched down, tugged a bandana from his pocket so he wouldn't erase any fingerprints, then carefully extracted the envelope from the soldier's belt.

Still using the bandana, he opened it, pulled out a typewritten note, and read the words:

Turn the senator over now—or the Indian woman will die.

Chapter 7

Cole stood beside his father's bodyguards and stared at the murdered man, feeling as though he'd crash-landed in an alien world. The kidnappers had done far worse than burn his barn or shoot his livestock. They'd executed this unknown man.

Stark fear trickled through him. A terrible sense of foreboding whispered up his spine. These same murderers were holding his sister hostage. They'd invaded his property and dropped off a corpse on his doorstep—proving how close they could get.

And they'd threatened to kill Bethany next.

The muscles of his belly tightened. He shifted his gaze to the wide-open fields surrounding his ranch, feeling like a lab rat trapped in a maze. Exactly who was he fighting? Where were they watching him from? And why had they killed this man?

His thoughts swerved to his father, and he curled his hands into fists. His father *had* to know more than he'd let on.

And it was time he revealed the truth.

His anger stirring, Cole turned toward the mudroom. But the door swung open, and his father stepped outside. "What's going on here?" he boomed with his usual bluster.

His gaze dropped to the man lying motionless on the stoop, and the blood drained from his face. "Oh, God. He…he's dead." He swayed, then clutched the porch post for support.

Cole lunged forward and grabbed his arm. "Are you all right?"

The senator's dazed eyes met his, the fading bruises standing out on his ashen face. "No, of course I'm not all right. He's dead!"

Cole went still. "You know this man?"

"Yes." The senator turned even grayer, then flicked an uneasy glance at the corpse. "He's Rick Garrison. I hired him to rescue Lana."

"Oh, hell," Gage Prescott said, his voice thick with disgust.

"He is—*was*—a mercenary. Former Special Forces. He was supposed to be one of the best."

And the kidnappers had managed to kill him. Cole's veins filled with ice.

"I hired him two weeks ago," his father continued. "I had to do something. I was desperate. I was afraid they were going to hurt Lana. But we lost contact. He didn't call or check in with me like we'd arranged." More color leached from his face. "Now I know why."

Cole dragged his gaze back to the dead man. The

hair stirred on the nape of his neck. His father's enemies had taken out a professional sniper.

Who the hell were they up against?

"Who killed him?" he asked.

His father didn't answer, and Cole's hold on his patience slipped. "Damn it, I need to know! These people have kidnapped Lana. They've shot my cows, burned my barn and now they've murdered this man. I need to know what's going on before anyone else gets killed."

He thrust the note at his father, fury vibrating his voice. *"No. More. Lies."*

"He's right," Gage said. "You need to come clean. And it's time we involved the police."

His father unfolded the note and read it. Then he sagged against the support beam, his face so ashen Cole leaped forward again to help.

His father waved him off. "You're right. I… I'll tell you. All of you. Everything." He dragged in a reedy breath. "You'd better call the sheriff and get him out here. Call Donald and Bonnie Gene. And Dylan…put him on the speaker phone."

His face bloodless, he shuddered hard. "I… I'll be waiting inside." He handed the note to his bodyguard, then stumbled into the house.

Still furious, Cole swung his gaze back to the murdered man. He intended to get answers, all right. His father wasn't evading his questions this time. Because more than his cattle ranch was now at stake.

They were fighting for their lives.

Hank Kelley slumped on the sofa in the great room an hour later, staring at the whiskey in his highball glass. *Liquid courage.* He needed it today. The moment he'd dreaded for weeks had arrived. He had to reveal what a fool he'd been.

He lifted his gaze to his half brother, Donald, sitting across from him in a chair, his wife, Bonnie Gene, at his side. Donald had barely spoken to him since he'd arrived, his disdain for him clear. And when he learned what else Hank had done…

He gulped down another swallow of whiskey as the rest of the group took their seats—the county sheriff, Wes Colton, was there, as well as the ranch foreman, Rusty, and his daughter, Bethany, who'd received the threat in the note. Cole stood between the two body-guards, his arms crossed, his face as unyielding as the rocks on the fireplace along the wall.

He was about to get angrier yet.

"More drinks, anyone?" Hannah asked, her white hair sticking up in clumps after the harrowing night.

Cole shook his head. "We're fine, Hannah, thanks." He trained his gaze on Hank. "Let's get this started."

Hank nodded, his stomach a jumble of nerves. He downed the last of his whiskey and set the glass aside. Clasping his hands, he glanced at the laptop Cole had propped on the coffee table so his son in California could listen in.

"I, um…" He cleared his throat and tried again. "I told you that my political enemies were after me, caus-ing these problems. But that's…not exactly right."

Unable to face their censure, he dropped his gaze to his hands. "A few months ago, I got an invitation to join a private society, very exclusive. Secretive, actually." He let out a nervous hum. "The members keep a really low profile. They work behind the scenes, influencing the banks, world markets. Real movers and shakers."

The kind that never made the news. "I thought they'd advise me about investments, increase my wealth...."

In truth, he'd been inflated with self-importance, convinced he'd made it to the big leagues, that he was one of the elite.

"Does this society have a name?" Sheriff Colton asked, taking notes.

Hank pressed his slick palms to his thighs. "It's called the Raven's Head Society." He flushed, realizing how ridiculous it sounded now.

But there was nothing ridiculous about their plans.

"They, um...aren't just involved in financial matters. They get involved in politics, too."

All eyes stayed on him. The clock on the mantel ticked. He sucked in a breath, fierce shame heating his face. He'd give anything not to have to admit this, but Rick Garrison's death had forced his hand.

"It turns out they have a plan. I didn't know about it or I'd never have gotten involved."

The sheriff's eyes sharpened. "What kind of plan?"

Hank closed his eyes. "They're plotting to assassinate the president."

Hannah gasped. A shocked hush fell over the group.

"President Colton?" Cole asked a moment later, his voice ringing with disbelief.

"Yes." Hank gave the sheriff an apologetic shrug. The sheriff and the president were distant relations. And two of the sheriff's brothers had married Donald's daughters, linking his family to the president, too. "I swear I didn't know. As soon as I found out their plans, I quit. Or at least I tried to."

Hank braved a glance at his brother. Donald's eyes reflected his disgust—which Hank knew he deserved.

"I really did try to quit," he repeated. "But I knew too much and they wouldn't let me go."

"I hope to hell you notified the president about this," Cole said.

"I couldn't. These people have too much power," Hank said when Cole opened his mouth to argue. "You have no idea. They've got ties everywhere—even to the president. I couldn't trust anyone with the truth, including the police."

He cringed. "The society wanted me to turn myself in to them. But they'd kill me if I did. They can't take the chance that I'll talk. That's why they took Lana, to force me out of hiding. So I hired that mercenary, hoping he could get her free."

Instead, Hank had signed the death warrant of an innocent man.

For a moment no one spoke. Looking grim, the sheriff continued to jot down his notes. Hank picked up his highball glass, realized it was empty, and set it back down.

"Wait a minute," Cole said slowly. "You said you couldn't trust anyone, not even the police. Then who did you contact in the FBI?"

Hank swallowed hard. This was the worst part, what he hated most to admit. "I never called them."

"What?" Cole exploded. "These murderers are holding Lana hostage and threatening to kill the president, and you didn't tell the FBI?"

"I couldn't. I knew they'd kill her if I did. And I thought I could handle this on my own."

"The hell you did." Cole's voice trembled with outrage. "You wanted to protect yourself and your damned career."

He was right. Hank's shoulders sagged. "My career would have been over if word of this got out."

Cole hissed. "You've been lying all this time. Lana's life's at stake and all you can think about is your job."

"I never wanted her to get hurt. I didn't know they'd go after her. And when they did... I thought Garrison would rescue her, that he would bring her home before anyone else found out. He was supposed to be the best."

He dropped his gaze to the floor. He knew he deserved their disgust. Even he was appalled by the depths to which he'd sunk.

The sheriff put away his notepad and pulled out his cell phone. "I'm contacting the FBI. They can notify the president's detail and anyone else who needs to know." His voice turned hard. "They'll need to question you. We can do it here or at the station, your choice. But from now on you're going to cooperate fully on this."

Hank nodded, knowing he had no choice. He couldn't deal with this alone anymore. Rick Garrison's murder had proven that.

"Let us know what we can do," Cole told the sheriff, his voice gruff. "We've got to get Lana back."

"That poor girl," Bonnie Gene whispered, and her husband pulled her close.

Hank stole a glance at the group. The ranch foreman and his daughter had their heads together. Cole had walked over to comfort Hannah, who stood by the kitchen, clutching her cat in her weathered hands. Even the bodyguards had tuned him out.

He experienced a sudden pang. He was the odd man out here, the one who didn't belong. He'd screwed up so many times that his family had rejected him. Sure,

Cole had taken him in when he'd needed help—but he'd done it out of duty, not love.

A heavy feeling unfolded inside him, but he knew he only had himself to blame. He'd taken his family for granted, not realizing that love came from respect— which he had failed to earn.

"I'm going to fix this," he said.

Cole scoffed. "Cut the bull. No one believes a damned thing you say anymore."

"Cole," Bonnie Gene warned, her voice sharp. "That's no way to speak to your father."

"No, he's right," Hank admitted. "I haven't given him—any of you—a reason to believe me before." But that was about to change. He was going to earn back their respect and trust.

But *how?*

He frowned, his mind running through options. He'd put Lana in jeopardy, so he had to get her out. But he needed a plan—one he carried out himself this time. That mercenary had sacrificed his life for a woman he didn't know. How could Hank do less for his own flesh and blood?

The meeting began to break up, but he sat motionless in his seat. For once he couldn't spin his way out of this mess, couldn't blame it on someone else. He had to man up, take responsibility for his mistakes, and put his life on the line to save his daughter from certain death.

But did he have the nerve?

Bethany sat immobile, the enormity of the senator's revelation robbing her of breath. A sinister society had captured Lana. They were plotting to kill the president of the United States. Now they'd murdered a man and dumped his body on Cole's back doorstep—bringing the violence even closer to them.

She shuddered, unable to believe it. This seemed like something from a Hollywood thriller, not part of her real life.

And it was all the senator's fault.

She shot a glance at Cole's father, the depth of his self-absorption boggling her mind. How any man could sacrifice his family to his career... She shook her head. And maybe he hadn't set out to endanger Lana, but his daughter had paid the price.

So had Cole.

She skipped her gaze across the great room. Cole stood near the windows talking on his cell phone, the weary slump of his shoulders tugging at her heart. She'd known Cole and his father weren't close, that the senator had ignored his children growing up, but she'd never realized the extent of his neglect. Proof of his calloused behavior came as a shock.

And, like it or not, it also forced her to rethink the past.

She handed her father his crutches, then rose. She didn't want to dredge up those memories. The past was gone. There was no point dwelling on things she couldn't change.

But her mind kept flashing back to the day she and Cole had broken up. She'd found out about her scholarship. She'd rushed to tell him the news. She'd expected him to be pleased, proud of what she'd accomplished after so many years of hard work. Instead, he'd closed down. He'd shut her out, his indifference eviscerating her heart.

But now she had to wonder... What if he hadn't been

heartless? What if he really had cared? What if he'd believed that *just like his father,* she'd chosen her ambitions over him?

She inhaled sharply, her world upended at the thought. She might be jumping to conclusions. He'd never asked her to turn down that scholarship. He'd never asked her to stay. For all she knew, he might have been delighted to see her go. But if her father was right, and she'd hurt Cole…

Cole pocketed his cell phone. His gaze snagged hers from across the room, and the turmoil in her belly grew. He headed toward her, and she straightened, her emotions running amok.

Cole reached her side a second later. "I've called a meeting of the ranch hands," he told her father, his voice still raspy from inhaling smoke. "I told them to meet us in front of the house five minutes from now."

Her father nodded. "I'll wait outside." He balanced on his crutches and limped away.

Cole hesitated. His bloodshot eyes shifted to Bethany's, and she hugged her arms to quiet her nerves. "I need to talk to you after the meeting," he said.

"Sure." He turned to talk to the sheriff, and she studied his chiseled profile, wondering what he wanted to say. Still trying to corral her unruly emotions, she followed her father to the porch.

She spotted Ace curled up near the steps. The aging dog huddled against the railing, trembling from the commotion and noise. Knowing exactly how he felt, she knelt to give him a hug. She rubbed the top of his silky head, earning a grateful kiss in return, then buried her face in his fur. "It's okay," she whispered. "The fire's gone now."

And so were her illusions. Her sense of security had crumbled. Her certainty about the past had disappeared. She was even beginning to doubt her father's honesty—the man she'd always revered.

The cold wind gusted, bringing with it the stench of burnt wood. She gave Ace a final pat and rose, utterly drained. The ambulance pulled away from the house, carrying the mercenary's body to the county morgue—a grim reminder of the violence stalking the ranch.

Still feeling off balance, she joined her father in the yard. Several cowboys headed toward them—Earl Runningcrane, Bill, and Kenny Greene. Tony walked close behind them, and she struggled to hide her distaste.

A second later Cole tramped down the steps. He frowned as the remaining ranch hands roared past in their pickup trucks, heading toward the gate. "Where are they going?"

Earl shifted his weight and cleared his throat. "They quit. They've been complaining about the workload for a while now, and this murder was the final straw. They said they hadn't signed on for this."

Cole didn't answer. He just tipped back his head and closed his eyes.

Bethany's heart rolled. *Of all the times to lose his men.* She caught Kenny's eye, and he winced his sympathy. At least Cole still had a few good men.

"All right," Cole said. "I know you're all tired, but we need to get those calves loaded up. It will probably take us a couple of days now that we don't have as many men.

"I need to make some calls and get the insurance claims started, then I'll be out to help."

"What are we going to do for tack?" Tony asked.

"Good question." He rubbed his stubble-roughened jaw, then turned his gaze to Earl. "Check the old tack shed behind the bunkhouse. There might still be some gear in there. I'll see what I've got in the house. And make a list of what you've all lost so I can file a claim."

He paused, his voice turning to steel. "From now on, no one goes anywhere alone. You hear me? Do everything in pairs. And carry a weapon with you at all times. I'm making arrangements with the sheriff to increase their patrols, but in the meantime, watch your backs. Any questions?"

The men shook their heads. "Then let's get started. I'll be out as soon as I make those calls. Tony, you're in charge of loading the calves. Rusty, hold up a minute. I need to talk to you."

The men headed toward the bunkhouse, Domino and Mitzy at their heels. Bethany stood beside her father, surprised when Sheriff Colton joined their small group.

Cole glanced at the retreating cowboys, then turned to face them again. "I didn't want to say this in front of the men, but I'm beginning to think that someone on the inside could be involved in this."

Bethany's breath caught. She whipped her gaze to her father, but he stared back at Cole, his eyes shuttered, his craggy face like stone.

"That means we can't take any chances," Cole said. "At least until the sheriff has checked things out. Rusty, I want you to move into my house until you're off those crutches. Pack up some things, and I'll send someone over to get them."

His gaze honed in on Bethany's. "And I want *you* on the next flight back to Chicago."

"What? I can't leave." Not while her father was in

danger. Not while a sinister society was threatening the ranch.

Sheriff Colton cleared his throat, drawing her gaze to him. "There was a note attached to the body."

Something in his tone evoked a shiver of dread. "What kind of note?"

He glanced at Cole, then swung his gaze back to her. "They've threatened to go after you next."

Dizziness barreled through her. She wobbled on her feet, and Cole lunged toward her and grabbed her arm. "Me?" She gaped from Cole to the sheriff in disbelief. "But…that's crazy. Why would they go after me? What do I have to do with this?"

The sheriff shook his head. "I don't know. It might be an idle threat. But we have to assume that it's real, given that they've already murdered a man."

"But—"

"We can't protect you here," Cole said. "We don't have the manpower or time. We don't even know who we're up against. You need to go back to Chicago where you'll be safe."

Suddenly chilled, she crossed her arms. She certainly didn't want to die. And Cole had enough on his mind without worrying about protecting her.

"There's no reason for you to risk your life," he added. "This isn't your fight. And Rusty will be fine in the house."

"Cole's right," her father said, his voice sober. "You need to go somewhere safe."

She struggled to absorb the revelation, to think through her burgeoning fear. They were probably right. She *should* go back to Chicago. Not only could she escape the danger, but she could investigate Mrs. Bolter's death and clear her name.

But no one was chasing her off this ranch. Not with so many unanswered questions. She owed it to Cole and her father to stay.

"You don't know that I'll be safer there," she argued. "A gunman can hide more easily in a crowd. At least here a stranger sticks out. And I don't mind carrying a gun."

"It might not be a stranger," Cole said, sounding grim.

She winced, knowing how much that had to hurt. "Even so, there's no guarantee Chicago will be any safer. They kidnapped Lana in Europe, right?"

Cole and the sheriff exchanged glances. Cole lowered his brows, obviously not thrilled to have her stay.

"I'll be careful," she added. "I won't take any risks."

Cole's steely eyes met hers. "All right, but only under one condition. You and your father are both moving into my house. You're going to stay in there with my father's bodyguards until this blows over. I mean it," he warned. "You're not leaving that house."

Her heart missed a beat. Protests crowded her throat. She'd be living in Cole's house, sharing his meals, aware of every movement he made. "But—"

"That's the rule. You either stay in the house with the bodyguards or return to Chicago tonight."

Their eyes held. Several tense seconds ticked past. Realizing he wouldn't budge, she lifted her hands. "Fine."

Cole's mouth tightened. "I'll tell Hannah to ready your rooms."

He turned and climbed up the porch steps. The sheriff took his leave, then headed to his patrol car across the yard.

Bethany trailed her father toward his cabin, her thoughts in disarray, her belly a jumble of dread. She had far more to worry about than resisting her attraction to Cole. Murderers threatened her life. Someone on Cole's ranch could be to blame.

And worse, if her father *did* know something about this, she couldn't conceal it from Cole, not with their lives at risk.

But how could she turn her father in?

Caught between opposing loyalties, she skirted a pile of ashes and choked back the acrid fumes. One thing was clear. If Cole believed she'd abandoned him once, she couldn't do it again.

No matter what the cost.

Chapter 8

Bethany gazed out the great-room window hours later, her thoughts still in turmoil, feeling as gutted as the demolished barn. Steel-bottomed clouds hung over the snow-capped mountains. A deep quiet gripped the ranch house, the methodical ticks of the clock on the fireplace mantel torturing her already pent-up nerves.

She still didn't want to believe she'd hurt Cole. All these years she'd been the injured one, self-righteous in her indignation over his rejection of her. But her insights into his father had shattered those beliefs. And for the first time, she had to consider the possibility that *she'd* acted badly—that she'd been so driven, so wrapped up in her goals and ambitions that she'd wounded the man she'd loved.

She shifted her weight, trying to steer her mind from that awful thought. Because an even more disturbing question lurked on the heels of that one: if Cole *had* asked her to stay in Montana, if he'd asked her to give up that scholarship and live in Maple Cove, what would she have done?

She pressed her hand to her belly, not anxious to answer that. Because if she did…she might not be as different from Cole's father as she'd thought.

Shying away from that unflattering possibility, she drew her sweater closer around her and searched for something to do. But Hannah had gone into town with Gage Prescott to pick up groceries. Both her father and the senator were taking naps. The house was already spotless, and Hannah would kill her if she interfered in her domain.

She could scrounge up some tack and help the men load up cattle—except she'd promised not to leave the house. But she couldn't stay cooped up inside with nothing to distract her; she would lose her mind.

She paced across the room to the stone fireplace, her restlessness increasing with every step. Hoping a friendly voice would help divert her, she pulled out her cell phone and speed-dialed Adam, but got his voice mail instead.

She tapped her fingers against the cell phone, his silence adding to her unease. It had been two days. He should have called with an update on Mrs. Bolter by now.

Unless he was trying to avoid her…

Rolling her eyes at that absurd thought, she dialed the nurses' desk at the Preston-Werner Clinic. The danger on the ranch was making her paranoid. She was inventing conspiracies where they didn't exist.

Besides, she didn't need to talk to Adam to learn the

results of the investigation. The nurse on duty could put her uncertainties to rest.

"Hi, Janeen," she said when a nurse she worked with answered the phone. "It's Bethany."

"Oh. Hi, Bethany. What's up?" Janeen's overly chipper voice—the one she used on patients when the news was bad—put Bethany on instant alert.

"I've been trying to find out about the investigation, what they've learned about Frances Bolter's death."

Janeen hesitated a beat, prompting another spurt of dread. "Didn't Adam phone you?"

"No. I just tried to call him but got his voice mail. So what did they find out?"

Janeen paused again, longer this time, and Bethany tightened her grip on the phone. "Hold on a minute," she said. "I… I've got another call."

She was lying. Bethany bit her lip, her nerves twisting higher as a pop song came over the line. But she drew in a steadying breath, determined not to overreact. Surely the clinic had cleared her of blame by now.

Janeen picked up the line a second later. "Sorry about that. Listen, Bethany. I can't… I'm not supposed to talk to you. Not while you're on administrative leave."

Her stomach swooped. "They put me on leave? No one told me that."

"Adam was supposed to notify you this morning."

Anxiety squeezed her throat and she struggled to breathe. "He might have tried. We just had a barn fire so there's been a lot of commotion here." Except her cell phone didn't show any missed calls. "But why would they put me on leave? I know I didn't—"

"I can't talk about it. I'm sorry."

"But they must have checked the reconciliation form by now and inventoried the drugs."

Janeen didn't answer, her silence damning. Bethany clutched the phone, panic mushrooming inside her, desperation threading her voice. "The inventory *must* have cleared me. I *know* I didn't give her the wrong dose. There has to be an ex—"

"I'm sorry. I can't say any thing more. I… I've got to go." Janeen disconnected the call.

Bethany didn't move, her mind reeling with disbelief. They'd suspended her from her job. They were investigating her. They thought she'd made a mistake that caused Frances Bolter's death.

She sank onto the sofa, her belly a tumult of dread. Could it be true? Might she have misjudged the dose? Horrified at the possibility, she pressed her hand to her lips. She'd been preoccupied about her father that night, in a hurry for her shift to end so she could pack for her trip.

But she was meticulous about dispensing drugs. She remembered entering the data on the reconciliation form and double-checking the dose. But then why didn't the form back her up? And why wasn't there enough of the study drug left to uphold her claim?

Then another terrible thought slammed into her, stealing her breath. *Maybe I need a lawyer.* Maybe they intended to charge her with negligence—or worse. But surely it wouldn't come to that. The autopsy *had* to support her claims. She hadn't done anything wrong.

But what if she had? What if she'd made a mistake that night…just as she'd misinterpreted the past with Cole?

Her stomach in total turmoil, she speared her hands

through her hair. She couldn't sit here idly while everything she'd worked for collapsed. Nor could she leave; she'd vowed to stay in Montana until the threat to Cole and her father had passed.

Torn, she rose and stared out the window. The yard remained deserted; Cole would be busy loading cattle for hours. She could use his computer to access Frances Bolter's medical records and try to figure out what had gone wrong.

But as she headed down the hallway toward his office, the irony of her situation struck her hard. She'd wanted to take her mind off Cole and put her conscience at ease.

Instead, her life had just gotten worse.

By nightfall Bethany had confirmed one thing. She was in one heck of a mess.

"Am I interrupting?"

Startled, she tore her gaze from the computer monitor and peered into the shadows dimming the room. Cole stood beyond the desk, the haze from the desk lamp accentuating the angles of his face. He'd showered recently, judging by his still-damp hair. A five o'clock shadow darkened his jaw.

Suddenly aware that she'd taken over his desk, she rose. "I'm sorry. I should have asked if I could use your computer. I wanted to look at my patient's medical records." She glanced at the now-black windows and winced. "Time obviously got away from me."

"I don't mind. You can use the computer whenever you want." His deep-toned voice sparked a surge of adrenaline, and her gaze swung back to him. She scanned his hard, masculine mouth, his broad shoulders encased in a white T-shirt, his flat abdomen and faded jeans. The intriguing stress spots in the denim made her face warm, and she jerked her eyes back up.

He held up a bottle of beer. "Join me in a beer? Or a glass of wine?"

She hesitated. She had no business spending time alone with Cole. He upset her equilibrium in too many ways.

He quirked a brow. "It's only a drink. And Hannah said dinner's not for half an hour."

Knowing that any excuse would look foolish, she released her breath. "Sure. Wine would be great."

"Wait here. I'll get it." He set his beer on the desk and left. Struggling to gather her composure, she shut down the computer, picked up the pages she'd printed out, and tapped them into a pile. She could handle this. They'd have a drink. He'd tell her about the cattle; she would talk about her job. She didn't need to obsess about the past and analyze what she'd done wrong.

Cole returned a moment later with the wine and a glass. "You still drink chardonnay?"

"That's perfect."

He set down the wineglass and got to work on the cork. She stood beside him, eyeing the powerful curve of his biceps, the corded sinews in his tanned arms. His clean, soap scent invaded her senses, making her heart increase its beat.

He gave the corkscrew a final twist and tugged out the cork. "So what did you find out?"

Her thoughts swerved to her patient, and her anxiety came racing back. "I phoned the clinic. They've placed me on administrative leave. They still think I made a mistake."

He paused and caught her eye. "I thought they were going to check the drug log."

"They did." She rubbed her arms, suddenly chilled. "It shows that I administered the wrong dose. And the drug inventory backs that up."

His eyes stayed on hers. "But you don't believe it."

"No, I don't believe it." She couldn't have made such a horrific mistake.

"So the drug log is wrong." His expression thoughtful, he turned back to the desk and poured her a glass of wine. "How well do you know the people you work with?"

Her jaw slackened. "You think someone set me up?"

"Do you?"

"No, of course not. I can't even imagine that. They're my friends. We've worked together for years."

He raised a pointed brow—reminding her that someone on his ranch, someone he'd known and worked with for years, could be trying to destroy him, too. And suddenly, she understood how he felt, knowing that someone he considered a friend had abused his trust.

Did he think she'd betrayed him, too?

Unnerved by that terrible thought, she forced her mind back to her job. "Even if someone *did* want to set me up, I don't see how they could do it. We keep the drug log on a computer, and whenever we enter the data, it records the time and date."

"Someone who knows computers could get around that."

"But why would anyone bother? It doesn't make sense. Everyone loved Mrs. Bolter. No one wanted to see her dead." And Bethany didn't have any enemies that she knew.

His eyes still thoughtful, Cole handed her the wine. "They'll do an autopsy, right?"

"Yes, definitely. And it should clear me of any blame. But the results might not be available for a while, depending on the backload at the lab."

And in the meantime, her reputation would be ruined.

Lightheaded at the possibility, she sipped her wine. Then she trailed Cole to a small seating group by the windows, and sat across from him in a leather chair.

"What were you looking for online?" he asked.

Inhaling, she tried to regroup. "Mostly I looked at her records."

"Did you find anything?"

"Nothing obvious. But I went back as far as I could, and saw that she did a stint in rehab years ago. At least it seems that way. There was a reference in one of her charts… I'd have to do more digging to be sure. The oldest records are probably still on paper. But they would have been archived somewhere."

"Rehab for what?"

"Alcohol abuse. But Adam should have known about that. He gave everyone a physical before the trial began. He wouldn't have let her in if it wasn't safe."

Cole shifted his gaze to the window, as if turning that over in his mind. "Then what do you think caused her death? The drug?"

She shook her head. "They do all sorts of tests on the drugs before they go to human trials. They're usually pretty safe." She paused and frowned at her wine.

"Usually?" Cole prodded

Still hesitating, she met his eyes. "But you hear rumors sometimes, that pharmaceutical companies suppress things. There's big money involved, and a new drug for rheumatoid arthritis…" She inclined her head. "You can imagine how lucrative it would be.

"In any case, it's all conjecture. The drug, her former alcohol abuse—none of that might have mattered. They might not have had anything to do with her death."

"But they might."

"Maybe." She grimaced. "I'd need to do more research. What I really need is access to a database, the kind a university library would have."

His dark brows knitted. "Would Montana State have what you need?"

"Probably." And Bozeman was less than an hour away.

"If you need to talk to someone, I still know some professors there."

"You went to Montana State?"

"At night. It took me a while, but I got an agribusiness degree. I thought it might come in handy, particularly the accounting and finance parts. The fewer people I have to hire, the more money I can funnel back into the ranch."

She drained her glass, impressed. And suddenly, winning that full-ride scholarship didn't seem like such a great achievement. While she'd had the luxury of attending school full-time, Cole had earned his degree the hard way—after putting in long days at the ranch.

Cole took her empty glass and returned to the desk. Bethany studied his powerful back, the play and flex of his muscles under his shirt, and a heavy feeling unfurled in her chest. She'd always admired Cole's strength. He didn't shirk from a job, didn't lean on anyone else. The way he'd put himself through college epitomized that.

But maybe that self-reliance came from necessity. Maybe he'd learned that he *had* to go it alone.

And maybe she'd reinforced that belief when she left.

She dropped her gaze to her hands, a sudden thickness blocking her throat. She'd adored Cole. She couldn't stand the thought that she might have hurt him. Surely she hadn't been that self-involved.

"More wine?" he asked.

Thrown off-kilter, she met his gaze. She shouldn't linger. She should go back to her room and think this out, put some badly needed distance between them before she said something she would regret. But when had she ever done the logical thing around Cole?

"All right." She rose and joined him at the desk. While he poured her wine, she studied his rugged profile—his straight, masculine nose, the sexy downward slant of his cheekbones, the virile beard stubble shadowing his jaw. She'd been so crazy in love with this man, and she'd thought she'd known him so well. Could she really have misinterpreted what he'd felt?

His blue eyes skewered hers. Her pulse abruptly sped up. She swallowed, suddenly far too aware of how close he stood. His warm, muscled arm brushed hers.

"How are the cattle?" she asked, her heart struggling to find a beat. "Did you get them all shipped off?"

"About half." He picked up his beer and leaned against the desk. "We'll finish the rest tomorrow morning and return the trucks to Butte. I'm heading up to the mountains after that."

"Do you know where the rest of the herd is?"

"Near the divide. Del took me up in his helicopter this afternoon to check. The good news is that the herd's intact." A crease formed between his brows. "I just hope the snow holds off. This first storm of the season is supposed to be a big one."

She nodded. A heavy snowfall could devastate the herd, cutting off their access to water and food. "Who are you taking with you?"

"Tony and Kenny Greene."

She wrinkled her nose. She didn't trust Tony; if anyone on this ranch was conspiring with killers, she'd put her money on him. But her predicament in Chicago had taught her one thing—it hurt to be accused of something you didn't do. And she couldn't inflict that same damage on anyone else—not her father, not even a despicable bully like Tony, not without concrete proof. She needed far more evidence than a forgotten scrap of leather or some thuds she'd heard in the barn.

"You'll need more than two people to help you if you've got a hundred head to bring in," she said. "Especially with that snow."

"I can't do anything about that. I need to leave Earl and Bill here to tend the rest of the herd."

"I'll go with you. I can go to Bozeman tomorrow morning and do my research while you finish loading the cattle and return the trucks. I'll be back before you leave."

He shook his head. "Forget it. You agreed to stay in the house."

"I'll go crazy sitting around here."

"Better crazy than dead."

Her exasperation rose. "But I can't stay inside. I told you, I need to get to a university library."

"Why can't you look online?"

"It would take too long. I can't possibly search the online library of every university in the world. I need access to an index, a database like D.A.I.—Dissertations Abstract International. I can skim through that, and if a dissertation looks promising I can go from there. It's still a long shot, but at least it gives me a chance."

"Then wait until I get back. I'll only be gone a couple of days."

"I can't. My reputation will be ruined by then. I can't just sit here doing nothing while everything I've worked for falls apart."

Cole set down his empty bottle and sighed. "Bethany, be reasonable. You saw that note. They've threatened to go after you next."

Her breath hitched, apprehension clutching her chest. "I'll be careful. I promise. The library must have a metal detector. No one's going to barge in there with a gun."

"The hell they won't." He rose and turned to face her. "Don't you understand how dangerous this is? Those people just killed a mercenary."

"I know, but—"

"He was a *professional* and he died. You don't stand a chance."

"You're not sitting back while they attack your ranch."

His mouth hardened. "That's different."

"No, it's not."

"Of course it is. For God's sake, Bethany—"

"I'm going to do this. I have to, Cole." Her eyes pleaded with his. "If I hide in the house it means the bad guys win. And I've worked too hard for too many years to let this destroy me now."

He worked his jaw, as if striving for control, his eyes never wavering from hers. And a host of emotions paraded through his eyes—frustration, resignation, respect… And something deeper. Something that looked a lot like desire.

Her stomach swooped. She turned stock-still, unable to tear her gaze from his. And her traitorous mind bombarded her with sensual memories—the erotic rasp of his jaw, the hard feel of his muscled frame. That heady rush of delirium she'd felt when he'd moved his lips over hers.

Her mouth turned to dust. Cole's eyes darkened, igniting a blast of heat in her blood. She'd seen that hungry look too many times to mistake his intent.

She dropped her gaze to his mouth. She tried to swallow, but failed. He reached out and cupped her jaw, his warm, calloused hand sending thrills racing over her skin. She abruptly lost the capacity to think.

"Stay in the house," he said, his voice rusty. "It's a bad idea to go out."

So was this. But she couldn't move to save her life.

He stroked his thumb down her throat. She trembled, the soft touch making her quiver, desire skidding and streaming through her veins.

His Adam's apple dipped. He slid his hands to her shoulders and hauled her upright, pulling her body to his. She closed her eyes, the hard, hot feel of him sparking a torrent of need.

And then he lowered his head, fused his mouth to hers, and everything inside her went wild. Pleasure curled inside her. A craving throbbed deep in her womb. She ran her hands up his arms, glorying in the muscles bulging under her palms, shuddering at the splendor of his kiss.

He shifted and widened his stance, pulling her hips

against his. His mouth ravaged hers, making her senses whirl, the thick, potent feel of him weakening her knees.

This was madness. Perfection. Bliss. She couldn't move, couldn't think, couldn't do more than yield to the staggering need. Urgency uncoiled inside her, the intense desire to strip off her clothes and feel the heaven of his hands making her moan.

"Cole, dinner's ready," Hannah called from the hallway.

He jerked up his head. His breath sawed in the air. His eyes burned into hers, almost angry in their intensity, and for one raw, unguarded moment, she saw the same naked yearning she knew he could see in hers.

But then a shield fell over his face. He dropped his hands and stepped back, his expression carefully blank. And she couldn't deny the truth. He was fighting this attraction. He didn't *want* to desire her. Whatever he'd once felt for her was gone.

Hurt twisted inside her, followed by regret. She'd caused that distrust. She'd ruined something special when she'd left. She'd caused pain to the man she'd loved. "Cole, I—"

"We'd better go. Hannah doesn't like dinner to get cold."

He was right. This wasn't the time to rehash the past. He started to stalk from the room.

"I really do need to go to Bozeman tomorrow," she said.

He stopped, stood with his back to her for several seconds, then swore and strode away.

She inched out a tremulous breath. Her hands trembling, she gathered the papers she'd printed out and clutched them to her chest.

She'd just confirmed one thing. Her father was right. She'd wounded Cole badly when she'd left.

But how she could repair it, she didn't know.

Chapter 9

He'd screwed up again, big-time.

Cole paced across his front porch in the darkness, battling to get his wired-up body under control. He never should have touched her. He'd caved to a moment of insanity and once again broken his vow. But the seductive fragrance of her skin, the fire flashing in those temptress eyes had been too much to resist.

Pulling away from her had been torture. Keeping his eyes off her during dinner had tested the limits of his self-control. The husky purr of her voice, the alluring sight of her kiss-swollen lips had kept him painfully aroused. He'd bolted down his meal, sure he'd offended her when he'd rebuffed her attempts to talk. But he'd had no choice. He either had to get out of the house or drag her back to his bedroom and finish what they'd started with that kiss.

He reached the end of the porch, then started back toward the door. He didn't need this distraction. Not now. Not when killers had captured his sister. Not when they'd threatened Bethany's life.

So what if they had chemistry? So what if she fueled his erotic fantasies—and always had? He couldn't let down his guard, couldn't allow her to burrow beneath his defenses—a surefire path to pain.

The low rumble of an approaching vehicle caught his attention, and he stopped. He aimed his gaze at the gate, welcoming the distraction. Headlights swept the yard, illuminating the mounds of charred rubble that comprised his former barn, and then the sheriff's SUV came into view. It neared the house, its tires crunching on gravel. The sheriff cut the engine and climbed out.

"Evening, Cole." Wes Colton stomped up the porch steps, rubbing his hands. "Cold night to be standing outside."

He nodded. He'd needed a blast of frigid air to cool his blood. "Yeah, that front's moving in fast." He cocked his head toward the door. "Come on in."

"Thanks, but I can't stay. I just wanted to update you on what we've found out."

"Did you find any evidence? Any idea who killed Garrison?"

"No, it's still too soon for that. Those tests will take a couple of weeks. I ran the background check on your ranch hands, though."

Cole folded his arms and steeled himself for the news. "What did you find?"

"Not much, unfortunately. Tony Whittaker had a juvenile record, minor stuff—breaking and entering—but he's stayed out of trouble since then. Earl Runningcrane got into a bar fight a few years back and was arrested for disturbing the peace. He pleaded guilty and paid a fine. The rest are clean."

So they'd come up empty. "I guess it was worth a try."

"It doesn't mean they're not involved. I just don't have any evidence to indicate they are yet. I'll keep looking. I'm going to check their bank accounts, credit reports, see if any unusual activity pops up."

"I appreciate that." Cole paused. "Sure you don't want to grab a beer?"

"No, thanks. I'm going to do a loop around your ranch and head home. I'll let you know when I've got news, though."

"Thanks. By the way, I'll be gone for a couple of days. I still need to bring down some cattle from summer pasture. I'm leaving the day after tomorrow." Assuming nothing else went wrong.

The sheriff nodded. "I'll increase our patrols. Let me know when you get back." He tramped down the porch steps and got into his SUV.

His thoughts on his ranch hands, Cole stayed on the porch as the sheriff drove off, the low whine of his engine fading into the night. No matter how many ways he examined it, his conclusion was always the same. One of his hands had to be involved—someone who knew the ranch's daily routines. Someone who'd known when his men were gone. Someone who could move around freely—shutting down sprinklers, disabling the security system—without anyone catching on.

Someone who'd betrayed his hard-earned trust.

He crossed his arms, his mind veering back to Bethany—and the flickers of guilt he'd glimpsed in her eyes. But that was nuts. Bethany had nothing to do with the problems on his ranch. And he needed to keep it that way—which meant convincing her to forget the library. She needed to stay in the house where she'd be safe.

The cold wind gusted, hastening him into the house. Unable to put off the confrontation with Bethany any longer, he headed down the carpeted hall of the guest wing, then rapped on her bedroom door.

She opened it a second later. Her cheeks were flushed. Damp tendrils of hair clung to her temples and neck. His gaze dropped from her full, sensual mouth to the loose T-shirt that stopped halfway down her thighs. She clutched a towel to her chest.

His breathing suddenly uneven, he forced his gaze back up. But her sweet, feminine scent curled around him. Her straight black hair gleamed like silk in the hazy light. He couldn't move, paralyzed by the memory of her soft, supple body, the delirium of her mouth.

Did she have anything on underneath that shirt?

He cleared his throat. "We need to talk about tomorrow."

Her eyes turned wary. "What about it?"

Still trying not to imagine her naked, he kept his gaze on her face. "I know you want to go to the library in Bozeman, but—"

"I don't *want* to go there, I *have* to. I can't sit around here doing nothing while my career gets destroyed. I have to fight back, Cole. I can't take this lying down."

She raised her chin—a gesture he knew well. And a sinking feeling took hold inside. He'd never make her stay in the house. The minute he left to load up his cattle, she'd hop in a car and go. And he couldn't blame her. In her place, he would do the same.

"Then how about if we compromise?"

"Compromise how?"

"You're probably right about the library," he conceded, although the idea still filled him with misgivings. "You'll be safe with people around. We just need to get you there and back."

Her forehead crinkled. She chewed her bottom lip, the move drawing his gaze to her lush mouth, bringing a jolt of heat to his loins. "What do you suggest?"

That you strip off that shirt right now.

He squeezed the bridge of his nose, trying to banish the thought. "We should finish loading the cattle by noon. I can go with you to Bozeman while my men return the trucks."

She shook her head, and her long, silky hair slithered over her slender arms. "I can't wait that long. The research could take all day. And it's a terrible waste of time for you."

That was true. He already had enough to do to get ready for the trip. "So I'll help you do your research."

"You can't. I don't even know what I'm looking for exactly. And there's really no need. I can drive myself."

"It's too risky. What if someone follows you there?"

She tapped her bare foot. Frustration brewed in her eyes. "Then how about this? I heard Gage say he was going into Maple Cove for breakfast. How about if he follows me to the highway and makes sure there isn't a problem? Once I'm out of town, no one will know where I've gone."

Cole turned that over in his mind. It still made him nervous, but it was better than letting her head off alone. "All right, providing Gage approves the plan. And call me when you're ready to come back. I'll meet you at the highway and escort you back to the ranch."

"Fine, but I have a condition of my own." She paused. "I'm going to the mountains with you."

"Forget it."

She huffed out her breath. "Cole, come on. That front's moving in. You've seen the reports. You're going to need help up there when it starts to snow."

She was right. Driving a hundred head of cattle down the mountain during a snow storm was no mean feat. Horses and cattle could slip. Conditions could turn deadly fast. And even if they managed to get the cattle loaded without a mishap, the trucks could roll on the icy roads.

But he had no business involving her in his problems. Bad enough that his sister was in danger. He couldn't risk Bethany's life, too. And if one of his men really was involved and followed them into the hills...

"I'll handle it," he said.

"You'll handle it better if I'm there to help. Besides, you said you don't want me going anywhere alone, so I'll go with you. Then you can keep me safe."

Safe? He snorted. She had no idea the effort it was costing him to keep his hands off her. And working— sleeping—in close quarters for days on end would strain his self-control.

But the bodyguards had their hands full trying to keep his father in line. He couldn't ask them to ride herd over Bethany, too.

"I'll be careful," she said. "I'll carry a gun. And you need the extra hand."

A feeling of defeat seeped through him. "It's not going to be a pleasant trip."

"It won't be the first time I've camped out."

Their eyes met. Awareness coursed between them.

And he knew she was remembering the same thing he was—the cattle drive they'd made with his uncle Don.

Only they'd done things far more interesting than rounding up cows.

Heat bolted straight to his groin. His breath turned shallow and fast. He devoured the feminine swell of her lips, the pulse point at the hollow of her throat, her nipples pebbling under her shirt.

She moistened her lips. Her erotic scent twined around him, reeling him in like a siren's song. And it took all his strength to keep from ripping off that shirt, hauling her naked body into his arms, and sating the heavy urges laying waste to his self-control.

"Cole," she whispered, and the soft sound flayed him like a whip.

"Close the door," he ground out. His voice sounded dragged from a cave.

Her hot gaze stayed on his. For an eternity she didn't move.

"Bethany, close the damned door *now.*"

"Right." A dull stain flushed her cheeks, and she stepped back. "I-I'll see you tomorrow." She shut the door in his face.

He stayed rooted in place, his blood bludgeoning his skull, so aroused he couldn't move. He braced his hands on the doorjamb, wrestling with the need to shoulder open that door and finish what they'd started with that kiss.

But he couldn't touch her. He couldn't surrender to this primitive hunger, no matter how hot she made him burn. He'd already learned the hard way that she would cause him nothing but pain.

But as he stalked slowly back to his bedroom, he knew one thing. That trek with her into the mountains would be the longest ordeal of his life.

She'd seriously lost her mind.

Bethany hunched at a computer terminal at the Montana State University library the following afternoon, so wound up she wanted to scream. Instead of concentrating on her research, her mind kept gravitating to Cole—his rumbling voice, his hungry eyes, the incredible ecstasy of his kiss. She'd spent the entire night reliving every sound, gesture and move he'd made, so on fire she couldn't sleep.

And it had to stop. She had too much work to do to be acting like a lovesick fool. So Cole was hot. So the man could incinerate steel with a kiss. There were plenty of attractive men in Chicago willing to take her out, and she wasn't obsessing about them.

But pitting those men against Cole was like comparing a vintage black-and-white movie to high-definition TV. They weren't even in a similar league.

But no matter how masterfully Cole kissed—even if one carnal look from those dazzling blue eyes sent her into a torrent of need—she couldn't blind herself to the facts. They hadn't resolved the past. They had vastly different goals in life. And Cole didn't want her. He'd closed right down after that torrid kiss, firmly shutting her out.

She sighed and massaged her eyes, gritty from staring at the computer all day, and tried to subdue her traitorous mind. She had to think about Cole later. She had to focus on her research and figure out why Frances Bolter had died. This could be her only chance.

Forcing her attention back to the computer, she scrolled through another dissertation on an experimental drug. She skimmed through the technical jargon, decided it wasn't what she needed, then skipped to the next one on her list.

Still struggling to focus, she glanced at the abstract, which looked promising, then paged down to the summary at the end. The drug was similar to Rheumectatan, the one they were testing. But it had been linked to renal failure, causing the researchers to abandon the trials. That side effect had been even more pronounced when the patient had a history of alcohol abuse.

She straightened, her interest suddenly caught. Returning to the start, she read the article slowly, her excitement mounting with every word. She minimized the screen, skimmed through reports on the effects of renal failure, convinced she was on the right track. Several articles later, she came across a study linking kidney dysfunction in post-menopausal women to sudden cardiac death.

Her heart racing, she sat back. Frances Bolter was the right age. And if she'd been an alcoholic, the drug could have damaged her kidneys, leading to her sudden death. But then why had Adam approved her for the trial? Unless he hadn't known…

Bethany tugged on her lip, trying not to jump to conclusions or overreact. It was just one study. The drugs involved might not be as similar as she thought. Or outside factors might have influenced the results, voiding the conclusion she'd reached. But if she *was* right…just *maybe* she could clear her name.

She closed her eyes, dizzy with relief. But then another thought occurred to her, and she sat bolt upright again. If this study applied to Rheumectatan, other conditions besides alcoholism could trigger the same results. They needed to halt their trial before another patient died.

She paged through the article, checked the copyright disclaimer, making sure it was legal to copy for educational use. Then she emailed a copy to Adam at his private address. That done, she tossed on her jacket, gathered her papers and purse and hurried to the exit, feeling as if a boulder had been lifted from her back. She couldn't get too excited—the research might not pan out—but for the first time in a week she had hope.

She pushed through the library doors, then paused, surprised that it had turned dark. She glanced at her watch. *Nearly seven.* She had to hurry. She'd spent more time in the library than she'd thought.

A cold gust of wind blasted past. Shivering, she zipped up her jacket and raised the collar, then started toward the visitors' parking lot where she'd left her dad's truck. A group of students scurried by, squealing when the brisk wind hit their backs.

Anxious to tell Adam about her discovery, she dialed him on her cell phone, hoping that he'd pick up.

He did. "Hey, Bethany," he said. "I'm on another line. Can I call you right back?"

"Sure, but make it quick. I just discovered something you need to hear."

"Give me ten minutes."

"I'll talk to you then." She disconnected the call, shuddering when a spattering of icy raindrops hit her face. She jogged across Grant Street to the parking lot. Halogen light gleamed off the vehicles, the silver sheen a reminder of the coming snow.

Hurrying even more now, she closed the distance to the truck. Once inside, she cranked up the heater, blowing on her hands while she waited for the engine to warm.

She'd just backed out of her parking space when her cell phone rang. "Sorry about that," Adam said.

"That's okay." She shifted into gear and left the lot. "Listen. I've got great news. I did some research today at Montana State University and found a dissertation that might explain Mrs. Bolter's death."

"How so?"

Maneuvering through campus and back toward the highway, she summarized what she'd found, including Mrs. Bolter's possible alcohol abuse. "I just emailed you a copy of the dissertation," she added. "I need you to look it over and see what you think. They did the study here at Montana State, so I can contact the advisor if you've got questions. I can't do it for a couple of days, though. I'm heading to the mountains tomorrow to help round up some stranded cows."

"You're becoming quite the cowgirl."

The sarcasm in his voice brought her up short. "This *is* how I grew up."

"Hey, I was joking. I didn't mean it as an insult."

Suspecting she'd overreacted, she sighed. "I know. I'm sorry. I'm just tired." She'd spent too many sleepless hours anguishing over Cole. "Listen, if I'm right about this, you have to tell the study director. They need to halt the study before anyone else gets hurt."

"That's a bit extreme, don't you think?"

"Not if it saves someone's life. My God, Adam. Any number of patients could have problems we didn't screen for. What if—"

"All right. All right! I believe you. Don't have a coronary. I'll give the report to Marge and suggest we stop the trial."

"Fine." Mollified, she pulled in a breath. But it still rankled that he hadn't instantly understood the danger. How could he be willing to take a risk? Unless he was more involved in this than she knew...

Okay. Now she was *really* losing it. Adam had no reason to sink her career. His recommendation had helped her get the job.

She stopped at a traffic light and sighed. "Thanks, Adam. I might be wrong, but I don't think so. I have a feeling about this."

"We can't take the chance regardless. Patient safety has to come first."

"I knew you'd see it that way. I wish everyone did. If the administration hadn't cut our funding we could have rolled out that new bedside medication system by now, and I wouldn't be in this mess."

"Maybe this case will spur them to fund it."

"That would be great." Then maybe some good would come of Mrs. Bolter's death. "I just wish they weren't blaming me for this."

"Don't worry. We'll get it straightened out."

"I hope so." The light changed, and she took the turn for the highway. "I've got to go. I'm nearly on the highway. But be sure to watch for that email."

"I'll take care of it as soon as I get home," he promised.

Bethany ended the call, then merged onto the highway, her hopes cautiously buoyed. This study didn't vindicate her completely. She still had to figure out why the drug reconciliation form and inventory were wrong. But it was a major start.

More sleet gathered on the windshield, and she turned her intermittent wipers on. Then a cattle truck roared past, reminding her of the upcoming trip to the mountains—and that she'd promised to telephone Cole.

Her heart beating fast, she dialed the ranch, then grimaced in disgust. She was definitely acting like a giddy schoolgirl, falling apart at the thought of Cole.

"Bar Lazy K," he said. She shivered, his deep, gravelly voice sounding far too intimate in the dark.

"It's me, Bethany. I just got on the highway. I should reach Maple Cove in about twenty-five minutes or so."

"I'll head to the highway now."

"You'd better wait. The roads are slick so I'm driving pretty slow. I'll phone again when I get to the pass."

"All right. Be careful."

"I will." Her voice came out breathless, and she stifled a sigh. This was beyond ridiculous. She had to get a grip before she made a total fool of herself.

Cole might still physically desire her, but he'd made it clear he didn't want an affair—which was good. Between their past and the current danger, they didn't need the complication of sex.

Especially if her father was involved with the sabotage at the ranch.

Dread pooled inside her. She'd been skirting that possibility for days, but it was time she faced it head-on. And the bottom line was…she still refused to believe that her father would ever harm Cole. He just didn't have it in him. And what motive could he possibly have?

Still, she knew he was hiding something. But what? Her father got along with everyone. He was the most

accommodating person she knew. He never antago-
nized anyone, never lost his temper, even when pro-
voked. He'd even endured years of racial prejudice so
her mother could live in Maple Cove.

Turning that over in her mind, she passed a slow-
moving truck, still unable to connect the dots. Then out
of nowhere came a sudden thought. What if her father
really hadn't done anything bad—but he'd seen someone else harming the ranch? And what if that someone—such as Tony—had threatened him to make sure
he didn't talk?

Electrified, she tightened her grip on the wheel. That
made far more sense. Her father might not confront a
bully. And she could certainly envision Tony intimidat-
ing an elderly man.

But if it was true, it made her dilemma worse. She
couldn't hide her suspicions from Cole. He had a right
to know what was happening on his ranch. If she didn't
speak up, and he found out later, he'd see her silence as
a betrayal, an unforgivable breach of trust.

But neither could she implicate anyone—even
Tony—without proof.

She turned up the speed on her wipers, her mind
whirling through options, but she could only see one
way out. If her father refused to talk, then it was up to
her to find some proof. She would corner Tony in the
mountains, show him that bridle browband, and force
him to confess his part—before anyone else got killed.

Certain she was on the right track now, she flicked
on the radio, picking up a station out of Bozeman, then
hummed along to a country song. She kept an eye on
the edge of the highway in case a deer or elk decided
to cross the road.

The traffic slowed as she neared the pass. She tapped on the brakes, hoping no one had suffered an accident on the icy roads, then exhaled as they came to a stop. Suddenly feeling the lack the sleep, she yawned and rubbed her eyes.

Then a car zipped past on the shoulder and exited to the country road just ahead. She frowned, thinking fast. If she left the highway, she could pick up the old gravel road that angled south toward the ranch. It took longer to drive than the highway, but if this traffic stayed stopped for long…

Making a quick decision, she pulled onto the shoulder and followed the other car. A pickup swung in behind her as she drove down the exit ramp. It stayed on her bumper as she turned onto the country road.

She lowered the volume on the radio and reached for her cell phone, figuring she'd better let Cole know that she'd changed her route—but the glare in her rearview mirror made it hard to see. She squinted at the side mirror. The idiot behind her had his high beams on—and he was tailgating her like mad.

The road narrowed, and began to curve. She eased off on the pedal and hugged the shoulder, trying to give him room to pass. She didn't need some yahoo riding her bumper all the way to the ranch.

But he slowed and stayed behind her. Alarm prickling through her, she swung back out and sped up—and he kept pace. Sweat moistened her upper lip. Foreboding breathed down her spine. What was his problem? Was he drunk? Trying to be obnoxious? Or something worse?

She slowed again, and so did he. She punched down hard on the accelerator, and he did the same.

Her heart began to thud. Trying to see him better, she flicked a gaze at the side view mirror, but the bright lights obliterated her view.

Her tires drummed in time to her heartbeat. Her palms grew slick on the wheel. The memory of the dead mercenary slashed through her mind, and she fought back an onrush of dread. Her cell phone rang, but she didn't dare try to answer. A second of inattention could send her careening off the mountain road.

The truck roared up behind her. She bit back a scream as he rammed her bumper hard. She swerved, then fishtailed wildly. Her heart thundering, she grabbed the gyrating wheel and managed to straighten the truck.

Panting, sweat stinging her eyes, she glanced in the rearview mirror. But he zoomed up behind her again. Desperate to outrun him, she flattened the accelerator to the floorboard, and sped toward the upcoming curve.

But the truck pulled even beside her. She shot a glance at the guardrail, stark fear making her numb. He was going to force her off the road.

They neared the curve. She stomped on the brakes, praying she didn't go into a skid. He shot ahead, just as another car approached head-on and blared its horn.

A wild sound formed in her throat. Her pursuer swerved back to the right, and the other car flew safely past. But her pursuer overcorrected and hit the guardrail. A terrible screech rent the air. She watched, horrified, as he veered all over the road, then somehow regained control. He disappeared around the bend.

She jerked to a halt, slamming her head back against the headrest. Wheezing, so panicked she could barely function, she executed a three-point turn. Then she pushed down hard on the pedal and raced back the way she'd come.

Within seconds, she zoomed up behind the car her attacker had nearly hit head-on. She swung out and passed him, and the driver lay on his horn.

"Sorry. Sorry." She knew she was driving like a maniac, but she had no choice. She raced toward the highway, struggling to stay on the winding road.

And hoped that she'd survive.

Chapter 10

Bethany drove through the gates of the Bar Lazy K a short time later, her heart banging against her rib cage, still struggling to catch her breath. She pulled up to the ranch house and braked, then pried her fingers from the steering wheel, so relieved she wanted to weep.

She'd done it. She'd outrun her would-be killer and made it safely back to the ranch. But now came the hardest part—hiding the attack from Cole.

Her hands trembling, she scooped up the articles she'd printed in the library. Then she climbed from the truck and waited for him to park beside her, her wobbly legs threatening to collapse. She gulped in the freezing air, determined to get her shattered nerves under control.

Because she'd realized something during that terrifying drive back to Maple Cove. She despised being a victim. She hated experiencing this horrific fear. And no way was she going to let some thug intimidate her into cowering inside the house.

Especially if the culprit was Tony. Bad enough that he'd bullied her during grade school. Bad enough that he'd threatened her in that note. But she refused to let him scare her. She would *not* show any fear.

Of course, she couldn't prove that he'd tried to attack her. *Yet.* But she'd get that proof in the mountains.

Assuming she could conceal the attack from Cole.

Cole climbed from his truck and headed toward her. She preceded him up the porch steps, the steady thuds of his footfalls a contrast to the frenzied beats of her heart. She scooted inside the house, the warmth wrapping around her like an embrace.

She closed her eyes and swayed, the horror of the attack threatening to demolish her hard-won control. But she couldn't let her mind wander back there. Not yet. Not until she'd made it to the privacy of her bedroom—and convinced Cole that nothing was wrong.

"How did it go?" he asked from behind her.

Fine, until someone tried to kill her.

She inhaled deeply and turned to face him. His blue eyes locked on hers—and she had the strongest urge to blurt out the truth.

Instead, she hugged her papers to her chest. "Good, actually. I found an unpublished dissertation that might explain Mrs. Bolter's death. I-I'll tell you about it tomorrow when we've got more time."

His shrewd eyes narrowed on hers. He cocked his head, like a hunting dog scenting the wind.

"I sent it to Adam," she continued. "The dissertation, I mean. I just called him, too… It's complicated, but—"

"Bethany."

"What?"

"What happened?"

Her chest squeezed. "What do you mean?"

His eyes holding hers, he stepped closer. He reached out and lifted her chin.

"You're rambling. You're shaking. And you're pale enough to collapse."

"I'm fine."

"Baloney." His voice held a hint of steel.

She steadied her gaze, trying furiously to project an aura of innocence—because no way could she tell him the truth.

Cole let out a hiss and dropped his hand. "For God's sake, Bethany, there's a killer on the loose. If something happened, I need to know."

Desperation surged inside her. She didn't want to lie—but he wasn't giving her much choice. "Nothing happened. I told you, I'm fine. Now can we please drop this? I'm tired. I'm hungry, and I need to pack for our trip. I assume we're getting an early start."

For an eternity, he didn't move. Frustration blazed in his eyes. She struggled to keep her composure, feeling sick about her deception, hoping she could beg his forgiveness later for having lied.

"We leave at six." Anger laced his voice. He turned on his heel and crossed the room.

Her throat closed up. She clutched her papers closer, appalled that she'd hurt him more.

"Cole." He paused, and his furious eyes cut to hers. "I—thanks for coming to get me. I appreciate it. And I-I'll tell you what I found out tomorrow."

His mouth flattened. Hostility rolled off him in

waves. "Forget it. It's none of my business what you do." He pivoted on his heel and stalked away.

She closed her eyes, her stomach a jumble of guilt. She hadn't meant to hurt him. But she couldn't tell him the truth. Not yet. Not until she'd found proof of Tony's involvement and could clear her father of guilt. And she could only do that if she accompanied them into the mountains to get those cows.

But as his angry strides receded, the pit in her belly grew. Instead of convincing Cole to forgive her for the past, she'd just made everything worse.

The morning dawned dull and gray, the leaden clouds hanging low over the mountains, sudden bursts of flurries presaging the heavier snow to come. Bethany slumped in the passenger seat of Kenny's truck, the dismal skies reflecting her mood.

She'd angered Cole. He'd barely looked at her while they'd loaded the horses. And when he did glance her way, the distance in his eyes made her heart freeze, proving she'd erased any progress she'd made.

The mountain road curved ahead. She caught a glimpse of Cole's pickup, his horse trailer hitched to the back, and couldn't quite stifle her sigh. She was beginning to think she couldn't do anything right around that man.

"You all right?" Kenny asked.

"Sure." The switch-backing road turned steeper. Kenny downshifted, his powerful truck handling the curves with ease, even with the gooseneck trailer in tow. She glanced his way, realizing she'd been so wrapped up in her thoughts of Cole that she'd hardly spoken on the two-hour drive.

"Sorry I'm not good company. I guess I'm a little preoccupied these days."

Kenny slid her a glance. "Is Tony still bothering you?"

"You noticed?"

He shrugged. "He's always been a jerk. He used to get in my face, too. He doesn't bother me much anymore, though."

Bethany's mouth edged up. "Not since you've grown, huh?"

He smiled back. "Yeah." Kenny had been a thin, puny kid during grade school—a bully's easy prey. "I took boxing lessons, too. That helped. I landed a right hook to his nose once, and after that he left me alone. Ever notice that crook in his nose?"

She laughed. "Good work."

Still grinning, Kenny turned his eyes back to the road. But his words lingered, making her think. She hadn't been Tony's only victim. He'd pushed his weight around since childhood, tormenting vulnerable kids. Had he moved on to more sinister acts as an adult? It certainly appeared that way.

But she still needed proof.

Seconds later, Kenny turned off the road at Cole's corrals. Bethany shrugged on her sheepskin vest and grabbed her gloves. From here on out, they'd ride on horseback. Once they found the missing cattle they'd drive them back here and ship them out.

Kenny came to a stop. "You might as well get out here," he said. "I'm going to back the trailer in."

"All right." She hopped out and pulled on her gloves, her breath turning to frost in the air. Cole turned away as she headed toward him, and her stomach fell. So his temper still hadn't cooled.

She waited beside him and Tony, rubbing her arms to stay warm. They'd hauled their tack and three of their horses in Kenny's spacious, slant-load trailer. But Tony's roan gelding had proven so difficult to load—even trying to bite them—that they'd finally stuck him in a smaller trailer alone.

"All right," Cole said when Kenny joined them. "Let's get to work. Bethany, you help Tony unload his gelding. Kenny and I'll take care of the rest."

She nodded, her stomach balling at his clipped tone. How much angrier would he become when he found out about her dad?

Deciding not to borrow trouble, she turned her attention to the job at hand. Tony swaggered toward her, his pale eyes glinting with malice. A mottled bruise discolored his jaw.

Her pulse hitched. She turned toward the trailer, but gave him a sideways look. If he'd tried to run her off the road last night, he might have a bruise like that. When his truck had slammed against the guardrail, he could have banged his jaw.

She opened the trailer's back doors, trying to sound off-hand. "Interesting bruise you've got. What happened?"

He grunted. "I was in a fight."

"Really? Who with?"

His eyes narrowed. "Why do you care?"

"I don't. I was just curious." She pulled down the ramp, then aimed her gaze at him. "Someone tried to run me off the road last night."

He planted his hands on his hips. His mean eyes focused on hers. "Are you accusing me of something?"

"Not at all." This wasn't the time to press for answers, not when they had to unload his horse. But sometime during this trek through the mountains she intended to get the truth.

A thud in the trailer made her frown. His gelding was already raising a ruckus, stomping and trying to get out.

"You know," she said. "If you took the time to get your horse used to the trailer, he wouldn't be such a problem to load."

"He isn't a problem. You just need to know how to control him."

Her mouth flattened. Bullying didn't work with horses any more than it did with people. "You wouldn't have to use force if you'd just work with him a bit."

"He's my horse. I can treat him however I want."

Her temper rising, she bit back a reply. She couldn't stand men like Tony, who masked their inadequacies with force. She'd learned from her father—a true horseman—that consistency and patience gentled even the most skittish horse.

"I'll get the lead on him," she said. "Hold on."

Still seething, she stalked to Cole's truck and took out the lead rope, then headed to the trailer's escape door along the side. Tony's gelding continued to butt the partition and stomp his hooves.

She climbed up on the stoop and opened the window. Then she reached for the gelding's halter, needing to attach the lead rope before she unclipped the trailer tie. But before she could grab it, Tony leaped onto the loading ramp and unhooked the restraining strap from behind the horse.

"Wait a minute," she called. "I'm not ready. I don't have the lead rope on."

But with the strap suddenly gone, the horse sensed freedom. He instantly surged backward and thrashed his head. Bethany lunged for his halter again, but missed.

"Whoa, boy," she said, trying to calm him. But the gelding pinned back his ears and pulled again.

"Settle down. Settle down." Moving slowly so she wouldn't spook him, she inched her hand toward the anxious horse. But he whipped his head and jerked back. Without warning, the quick release on the halter snapped.

Her heart stopped. The horse began to rush back. "Watch out!" she shouted to Tony. "He doesn't have the lead rope on."

But Tony ignored her warning. He climbed inside the trailer, and everything inside her froze. "What are you doing?" Didn't he know how dangerous that was? "Get out of there!"

"Shut up. I know how to manage my horse." Tony squeezed along the partition, muscling his way toward the front. The panicked gelding continued backward. His hind legs reached the ramp, and he started to swing around. Tony made a grab for the halter, but the horse's momentum bumped him back.

The impact knocked him off balance. He slipped and fell beneath the horse. Horror fisted inside her. *Oh, God. He was going to get crushed.*

Freaked by the sudden commotion, the horse sprang back—but Tony was in his way. His hoof landed on Tony's foot.

A sickening crack rent the air, and Tony screamed.

Swearing, Bethany jumped off the stoop and raced

around the trailer. Cole sprinted over to help. "What happened?"

"*Tony.*"

The horse leaped sideways off the ramp. Bethany dove for his halter, but he escaped her, then cantered toward the trees. She let him go, knowing they could catch him later on. Tony's injuries might not wait.

She hopped onto the ramp ahead of Cole and rushed to Tony's side. He lay sprawled on the floor, half crumpled against the partition, moaning and clutching his leg.

Her stomach fell away. Even from a distance, she could see the unnatural angle of his foot.

She knelt beside him, keeping her voice calm. "Lie back and stay still. Let me see what we've got."

"Leave me alone."

"I'm a nurse. Let me see."

His mouth thinned. "I don't need your help. Get your filthy hands off me."

Her face heating, she checked the size of his pupils, then scanned his scalp for bumps. She had a professional duty to help him, no matter how despicable he was. "Did he kick your head?"

"No."

"Too bad," she muttered. Anyone dumb enough to get into the trailer with an unrestrained horse...

He groaned and rolled to his side. "Stay still," she said again, her voice sharper. "Moving around is going to make it worse."

"I don't need some damned Indian ordering me around."

"You'll listen to this one," Cole said, the threat of violence in his voice. "And you'll watch your mouth—or I'll break a hell of a lot more than your foot."

Tony shut his mouth, but his eyes turned sulky. Bethany spared Cole a grateful glance. "We need the first aid kit."

"I'll get it." His jaw rigid, Cole shot Tony a warning look, then hurried off. Bethany picked up Tony's wrist and checked his pulse.

Cole reappeared a second later with Kenny in tow. "We need to cut his boot off before his foot starts to swell," she told them. "His pant leg, too, up to his knee so we can expose the wound."

Cole pulled out his pocketknife. While he and Kenny got to work, she rummaged through the first aid kit. Cole peeled away Tony's boot, then made short work of the sock. When they finished, Kenny scooted aside, and she took his place.

She swallowed hard. Tony definitely had a compound fracture. His foot dangled at a ghastly angle, and was already beginning to swell. "Can you wriggle your toes?" she asked him.

Grunting, a sheen of sweat breaking out on his forehead, he complied.

"Good. Now don't look at me." She waited until he averted his gaze, then squeezed his toe. "Which toe am I touching?"

"The little one," he gritted out.

She met Cole's eyes, relieved. "That's good. No obvious nerve damage. We need to immobilize the leg. Do you have something we can use as a splint?"

"I've got a board in the trailer," Kenny said.

"Good. Grab a saddle blanket for padding. And bring some wrapping tape to tie it down." While he darted away to get it, Bethany grabbed the scissors from the first aid kit.

Kenny returned a second later. "This is the tricky part," she told Cole. "I need you to help me lift his leg. Kenny, fold the blanket on the board, then slide it under his leg when we lift it up."

She aimed her gaze at Tony. "It's going to hurt, but you'll feel better when we're done."

She and Cole knelt across from each other. Kenny readied the board. She nodded to Cole. "Now." They raised his leg, and Tony cried out. Kenny slid the board in place. "Okay, lower it slowly," she said.

That done, she grabbed the tape and scissors. "We need to tie it in place. As soon as I cut some strips off, I'll need you two to lift the board."

She worked quickly to secure the board, then tied off the final knot. "Let me check for sensation again." She got Tony to wriggle his toes, made sure he could feel her touch.

Relieved, she sat back on her heels and released her breath. "That's all I can do. He needs a doctor now."

"We'll lie him in the backseat of your truck," Cole said to Kenny. "You've got more room than I do. You'll have to drive him to the hospital in Honey Creek."

The men hoisted Tony from the trailer, his moans filling the air. Bethany scrambled out behind them, then raced to Kenny's truck and opened the doors. She entered from the other side, cleared her gear from the backseat, then tugged her pillow from her sleeping roll.

The men laid him across the seat. She handed the pillow to Cole. "Put this under his leg to elevate it. And here's the cold pack."

Cole turned to Kenny. "We need to catch Tony's

horse and put him in the trailer with yours. Let's just hope that damned gelding cooperates this time."

Kenny scowled, obviously not thrilled with the change of plans, but didn't argue. While the men left to catch the horse, Bethany stayed at Tony's side. "You all right?" she asked, checking his pulse again.

"Yeah." He paused. His eyes flicked to hers, then veered away. "Thanks."

She nodded, knowing it cost him to be polite. She skimmed her gaze over him again to make sure she hadn't overlooked any injuries, lingering on his bruised jaw. "Tell me about that bruise."

"Why?"

"I told you. Someone followed me last night and tried to run me off the road. His truck hit the guardrail, and the impact probably gave him a bruise like that."

"It wasn't me."

"Can you prove that?"

His eyes flashed. "Yeah, I can prove it. I was at the Wagon Wheel Saloon until midnight. Everyone saw me there. If someone tried to run you off the road, it wasn't me."

She frowned at that. His story would be easy to check. "Then what about this?" She pulled the brow-band from her pocket and held it out. "Care to explain how it got in the field by the dead cows?"

"How should I know?"

"Because it's yours."

"It is not. I've never seen it before."

"I don't believe you."

"You're nuts. What…?" Understanding dawned in his eyes. "You think I killed those cows."

"You bet I do."

"I had nothing to do with that."

She leaned closer. "Then who did?"

"How should I know?"

"Because you're the one causing the problems. And you threatened my father to stop him from turning you in."

"The hell I did. You're out of your mind."

She held his gaze. He glared back, denial hot in his eyes. And sudden doubts crawled through her mind. Even though she despised him, he seemed to be telling the truth.

But if he hadn't caused the problems...

The tailgate on the trailer slammed. Cole returned to the truck, and she stepped back, confusion muddling her mind. Kenny leaped into the driver's seat and started the engine while Cole closed Tony's door. They slowly drove away.

Bethany stared at the empty road, her world suddenly tossed on its head. If Tony had told her the truth, then she'd misjudged him. She'd let her childhood memories blind her to the facts.

Her stomach dipped. Her sense of superiority disappeared. She'd always considered herself fair-minded. She'd prided herself on her unbiased judgment, railing against bigotry in any form. But she'd been just as prejudiced against Tony, allowing her resentment to cloud her thinking, even creating a vendetta against him.

Which didn't make her any better than him.

The cold wind gusted. Chilled now, she met Cole's gaze, and another realization hit her hard. She never should have lied to Cole. If she'd told him about the attack, he could have taken precautions to keep them safe.

Because if Tony wasn't to blame, someone else

was—and they'd just lost the only backup they had. They were now open targets, heading into the wilderness alone, a killer hard on their heels.

"Let's go," Cole said, sounding grim.

She trailed him to their horses, her steps heavy with foreboding, just as it began to snow. She could only hope they survived the night.

And that Cole would forgive her if they did.

Chapter 11

The snow fell steadily as the day wore on, building with the same relentless intensity as the certainty inside of Cole. If he'd needed proof that Bethany didn't belong in Maple Cove, Tony's accident had just provided it in spades.

He picked a trail through the snow-covered deadfall, then crossed a meadow in the deepening dusk. Seeing Bethany in action—her quick thinking under pressure, her obvious medical expertise—had forced him to view her in an altered light. And for the first time he understood why she'd needed to leave Maple Cove.

And why she could never stay.

Gunner stumbled on a patch of ice. "Whoa," Cole said, reining his exhausted horse to a halt. The frigid wind gusted, whipping pellets of snow at his face and bringing a chill scuttling over his skin. He turned up his collar and hunkered deeper into his saddle while he waited for Bethany to catch up.

She emerged from a cluster of trees a moment later, her black hat dusted with snowflakes, urging her tired mount up the treacherous slope. The muscles of his belly tightened, the inevitable surge of lust tempered with heavy guilt. It was bad enough that he'd exposed her to his father's attackers. Even worse, they were going to have one hell of a time driving those cows down the mountain through the snow. But all these years he'd misjudged her, blaming her for something that wasn't her fault—and he didn't like that one bit.

She came to a halt beside him, her nose pink from the bitter cold. "How much farther to the cattle?" she asked, her breath forming puffs in the air.

He twisted in his saddle and peered at the canyon ahead. "They're up that draw, near the divide."

"Can we make it there tonight?"

He shook his head, dislodging snow from the brim of his hat. "We'd better wait until daylight." He'd pushed the pace to make up the time they'd lost, but night was fast closing in. "The ride gets steeper from here on out, and I don't want to risk a fall."

"You want to camp here, then?"

He ran his gaze around the clearing. A stream gurgled nearby. Patches of grass still peeked through the blowing snow. A rocky overhang walled the northwest corner, offering some shelter from the blustery wind. "Yeah, this looks good."

"Great." She swung down from her horse, not quite managing to stifle a moan.

Wincing in sympathy, he dropped to the ground. "Sore?"

"Not too bad."

He didn't buy it. The strenuous ride had tired him out, and he spent every day on a horse. But Bethany rarely admitted to any weakness. She always suffered in stoic silence—a trait that both impressed and irritated him.

Like when she'd refused to reveal what had spooked her last night.

Too tired to summon any annoyance, he removed his gear from behind his saddle and hauled it to the rocks. "I'll take care of the horses if you set up camp and start a fire. But keep your rifle handy," he added.

"You think we're being followed?"

"No, but there's no point taking a chance."

He removed the saddles, then led the horses to the nearby creek, his thoughts still lingering on her. All this time he'd resented that she'd moved away, that she hadn't cared enough about him to stay. But there was nothing for her in Maple Cove. His expectations had been out of line.

And no matter how many grueling hours he'd spent in the saddle, no matter how relentless the pace he'd set, he couldn't outrun the truth. He hadn't been fair to her.

Not liking that blunt assessment, he hobbled the horses near their camp. Then he sat next to Bethany at the campfire and devoured a can of stew. But he could no longer deny the facts, no matter how unflattering they were. *He'd been wrong.*

Sobered by that brutal truth, he sat beside her in the flickering firelight, the welcome warmth heating his skin. His gaze kept returning to her high, sculpted cheekbones, her exotic, dark-lashed eyes. Her beauty made his heart thud. Every gesture, every graceful motion she made brought heat surging straight to his loins. And he had to admit that no matter what else had gone wrong between them, she still appealed to him in a basic, primal way.

And sitting together, snowflakes falling around them, the cold wind murmuring in the pines, it was far too easy to remember the good times, the reasons he'd once given her his heart—her intelligence, her patience, their easy camaraderie. She'd believed in his abilities. She'd encouraged him, given her unflagging support, and made him feel worthwhile.

But that was then. That time was gone. And in a few more days she'd once again exit his life. And he'd be on his ranch, just how he wanted to be.

Alone.

Pushing that thought aside with a frown, he finished his last can of stew. "You think Tony's all right?" he asked to distract himself.

She gave her head a quick shake. "It was a pretty bad break. He'll be out of commission for a while."

"Good. Then he'll have time to find a new job."

Her head came up. "You're not going to fire him?"

"Damn right I am." He didn't tolerate disrespect or disloyalty among his men.

"But…you can't. Your ranch hands just quit, and you need the help."

"I don't need it that bad." Hell, Tony was lucky he'd only escaped with a broken foot. Hearing him disparage Bethany had sent a bolt of white-hot rage blazing through him, incinerating his self-control. It had taken every ounce of willpower he had not to attack the injured man.

His belly hot with remembered anger, he surged to his feet, then returned his utensils to his pack.

Bethany rose and moved to his side. "Seriously, Cole. Don't be hasty. Wait until the problems with your father settle down before you make up your mind."

He shot her an incredulous look. "I can't believe you're defending him."

"I'm not. Not at all. I can't stand him. It's just—"

He stiffened. "None of my business?"

"No, that's not what I was going to say." The wind gusted, making the pine trees creak. "It's just…complicated."

"It seems simple to me."

"I used to think so, too," she admitted. "The thing is…everyone pretends racism doesn't exist anymore. But it does. Not everyone is a racist by a long shot. There are lots of nice people around. But it happens, more than you'd expect."

"I know that." He'd felt the disapproval of some of the townspeople when he and Bethany had dated during high school. "But that doesn't mean I've got to tolerate it on my ranch."

"I don't expect you to. I'm just saying to wait for a better time before you fire him. Tony's a bully. He always has been. The racial aspects just give him another excuse to be mean. And maybe…maybe I misjudged him. My father says he does good work, so maybe you should give him another chance."

He doubted that. But her words triggered memories of the animosity he'd always sensed. And suddenly, it clicked. "Tony bullied you?"

She turned back toward the fire with a shrug. "When I was a kid."

"How?"

She kept her gaze on the flames. "The usual stuff—calling me names, pushing me around…"

And worse. He could hear the pain in her voice. He locked his jaw around a punch of anger. "You never told me that."

"There wasn't any point. He stopped once I learned to stand up for myself." She gave him a lopsided smile. "And when you and I started dating, he probably knew better than to risk your wrath."

"You got that right." He clenched his teeth, sudden fury mixing with guilt. "I should have done something to stop it."

"I'm glad you didn't."

He raised a brow in surprise.

"It would have made me look weaker and encouraged him more."

"Maybe." All the same, Tony had a lot to answer for when they got back.

Bethany stepped even closer and laid her hand on his rigid arm. "There's nothing you could have done, Cole. I handled it myself."

"You shouldn't have had to." No wonder she acted so stoic. When had anyone stuck up for her?

He shook his head, appalled that he'd been so blind. How had he overlooked that meanness in Tony? How had he missed something so fundamental about her? First her need to leave, and now this. Had he been too wrapped up in the steamy sex to see who she really was?

Disgusted with himself, he let out a bitter laugh. "And I thought I knew you so well."

Her mouth quirked up. A deep, sensual heat flared in her eyes. "You knew me."

Their eyes locked. Awareness erupted between them, triggering the deep, prowling tension he'd battled to control for days.

He *knew* her, all right. He knew the hot, sultry taste of her skin, the sleek, moist heat of her lips. He knew her scent, her sighs, the whimper she made at the back of her throat, the dazed look in her pleasure-crazed eyes.

His heart began to pound. Blood pooled low in his groin. And memories flashed through his mind with brutal clarity—her ripe, pouting breasts, her nipples pebbling to invite his touch, the hot, tight feel of her pulsing around him, urging him to carnal bliss.

He reached out, fingered the ends of her long hair, the black silk igniting his nerves. He knew he shouldn't touch her. They had too much baggage between them. He had to step back, move away before he did something he'd regret.

But her lush lips parted. Her eyes turned luminous in the low light. He slid his hand along her jaw, her soft skin torching his hunger, and stroked his thumb down her silky throat.

"Cole," she whispered, the hoarse plea eroding his resolve.

Her pulse raced under his thumb. Her soft scent twined around him, trapping him in place. Unable to resist, he plunged his hands through her shiny hair, hauled her into his arms, and slanted his lips over hers.

Her potent mouth held him captive. The staggering feel of her overrode common sense. Warnings bleated through his mind, that this was wrong, senseless, that he would regret breaking his vow. Helpless to stop himself, he skimmed his hands down her shoulders and back, memorizing her contours with his hands. Then he tugged her tighter against him, the thrilling, feminine scent of her laying waste to what little remained of his self-control.

She moaned, and he delved deeper, his tongue mating with hers. Her round breasts pillowed his chest. Her lush hips cradled his. She was heaven, perfect, as enticing as he remembered. The answer to his erotic dreams.

And she kissed him back, her mewling sounds driving him crazy, her hands blazing a trail of lust through his nerves. She fueled a bone-deep craving inside him, torching a need he couldn't ignore.

Calling on all his remaining willpower, he managed to break off the kiss. He rested his forehead against hers, his breath sawing hard in the night. He wanted her under him, over him—any way he possibly could. He wanted to strip off her bulky clothes, expose her ripe, naked body to his gaze. And he wanted to lose himself deep inside her, taking her again and again until he was too damned sated to think.

But he had to stop. There were too many reasons this was wrong. And he was fast approaching the point of no return.

"Don't stop," she pleaded when he pulled back. Her kiss-swollen lips gleamed in the firelight. Her dark eyes burned into his. "Make love to me, Cole."

Heat stabbed his loins. His body turned rock-hard. "You're sure?" he made himself ask.

In answer, she stepped back and slipped off her sheepskin vest. She tugged her turtleneck over her head and stripped off her bra. His gaze fastened on her taut, high breasts, the flat, sleek line of her belly, the enticing indentation of her waist.

His jaw flexed. He made a low, rough growl in his

throat. He couldn't think, suddenly couldn't remember why this was wrong. He could only watch her, riveted, as she steadily burned him alive.

The wind gusted. Her long, glossy hair slithered over her shoulders, framing her naked breasts. His pulse began to pound. A sweat broke out on his brow despite the frigid air. And he was lost. She called to something primitive inside him, needs he couldn't resist.

He kicked off his boots and peeled off his clothes, while she made short work of her own. Then she unzipped her sleeping bag, spread it over his, and slipped inside. He dove in after, his heart thundering, and pulled her soft feminine body under his.

His mouth descended on hers. A furious rush of wanting scalded his blood. He gave in to the demands bludgeoning his body, her wild urgency egging him on.

He finally broke the kiss, needing air. His pulse rocketing, he bracketed her face with his hands. And for a long moment he just drank in the sight of her—her dark, slumberous eyes, the delicate sweep of her cheeks. And emotions crowded in on him—yearning, lust, a feral feeling of possessiveness. She belonged right here in his arms.

He feathered kisses over her jaw, down the silky line of her throat, her soft moans filling the air. Then he moved lower, raking his teeth gently over her breasts. He took one sweet tip in his mouth, wringing a long, low groan from her throat. She gripped his hair and tugged him back up.

"Hurry," she urged, her eyes lost in desire. "I can't wait."

He nudged her legs apart with his knees. Then he

fitted himself to her warmth, the scent of her provoking a riot of lust in his blood.

She'd given him her virginity. He'd claimed her that day long ago, branding her as his own. She'd surrendered to him, giving herself with an intimacy that went far beyond sex, beyond the mating of their bodies, to a fundamental need.

He entered her in a desperate thrust, the tight, velvet feel of her igniting a savagery inside him, the pleasure so staggering he growled. She was hot, moist, perfect. Everything he'd ever wanted.

And she was his.

She began to move against him. He took her mouth again in a hot, frenzied kiss that obliterated every thought. His heart thudded hard. Hot blood thrummed through his veins. He sank into her welcoming heat, his body picking up the ancient rhythm, needing her in a way he couldn't explain.

"Bethany," he groaned, his breathing labored.

He felt her tighten around him. Her muscles bore down, her eyes turning crazed, and then she let out a keening cry.

He couldn't stop. Completely at his body's mercy, he made one final thrust, then exploded, a hoarse shout wrenched from his lungs.

For an eternity he didn't move, the pleasure still pumping through him, his breath ragged in the quiet night. Then he kissed her, long and hard and deep, expressing everything he couldn't say. Tenderness. Admiration. Desire.

He knew he should feel guilty. He'd had no business making love to Bethany when so much between them was wrong. But it was hard to summon regrets when it felt so incredibly right.

He buried his face in her hair, the tremors slowly ebbing from his body, her warm breath fanning his ear. Wrong or not, he doubted he'd ever get enough of her. She suited him in too many ways to count.

But the world-shattering sex changed nothing. She wouldn't stay. She belonged in Chicago where she could make good use of her skills. And he could never go.

Worrying that his weight would crush her, he rolled over, taking her with him, and settled her on top. Then he dragged the sleeping bag over her naked back, protecting her from the encroaching cold.

And for a moment, he acknowledged the longing hovering at the edge of his heart, the desire to hold her forever in his arms. But that was dangerous ground to tread, a place he could never go. He had to keep his emotional distance, just as he'd vowed at the start. He couldn't fight her battles, couldn't let himself get involved too deeply and begin to care.

But as she nibbled kisses down his unshaven jaw, sparking another savage rush of desire, he feared that he'd never stopped.

Bethany awoke near dawn, cocooned in glorious heat. Cole lay on his side behind her, his heavy arm draped over her hip, his hard muscles warming her back. Her limbs felt deliciously languid, her body so limp with pleasure she could hardly hold on to a thought.

Except one. She'd made a reckless mistake. Making love with Cole hadn't solved any problems; it had only made her dilemma worse. She still hadn't told him about the man who'd tried to kill her. She hadn't revealed that her father might be harboring secrets about the ranch.

But exactly what could she tell him? Tony's fierce denial had destroyed her leading theory, throwing her beliefs in disarray. But she knew one thing. If her father *did* have any role in this, *he* should come clean and confess it. She'd already misjudged Tony, letting her resentment over his harassment cloud her mind. She couldn't falsely accuse her father, too.

But what about Cole? He deserved to know the truth. And if he found out later that she'd deceived him…

His hand moved to her breast, the rough calluses teasing her nerves, and she instinctively arched her back. He brushed aside her hair, slid his mouth down the nape of her neck, the sexy rasp of his beard stubble making her sigh.

Wrong or not, she couldn't resist him. Everything about this man appealed to her—the hard, rugged planes of his face, his utterly carnal kiss, the devastating thoroughness with which he made love. He detonated her senses, taking her to heights she'd never imagined, until he'd reduced her to wanting to beg.

But she couldn't ignore the irony. The man who electrified her nerves—the only man she'd ever loved—was exactly the one she could never have.

His hand slipped between her legs. Pleasure coiled inside her, the feel so exquisite on her sensitized skin she nearly climaxed at once.

But instead of continuing, he went still. She arched against him, already lost to sensations, her body moistening for his.

But he didn't move. "Shhh," he hissed, his urgent tone penetrating the fog of desire. "We've got company."

She froze, the torrid feelings shattered. Her heart catapulted against her rib cage; her senses went fully alert. She skipped her gaze around the shadowed clearing, the trees barely visible in the predawn light. The horses stamped their hooves. Taut silence pulsed in the air.

And fear turned her belly to ice.

How could she have let her guard down? How could she have forgotten, even for a moment, that they had a killer on their heels? And why hadn't she warned Cole about that truck?

Cole soundlessly began tugging on clothes. She did the same, her throat bone-dry, her hands trembling as she snapped her jeans.

She reached for her rifle next to the bedroll.

Just as all hell broke loose.

Chapter 12

Gunfire erupted around them. A bullet ricocheted off the rocky overhang, shearing chips of stone onto their heads. Bethany lunged for her .22 and racked a round as Cole got off a shot toward the trees.

"Get behind the boulder," he urged, still firing.

Not unless he went with her. Her pulse running wild, Bethany sighted down the barrel of her rifle and pumped a shot at the pines. Cole rolled to his feet and hauled her upright as more gunfire came from the woods. They dove for cover behind the rock.

The shooting paused. Her heartbeat frenzied, Bethany struggled to catch her breath.

Cole reloaded his weapon, his furious eyes flashing at her. "Why didn't you run?"

"I was trying to protect you."

"By nearly getting killed?"

Not bothering to answer, she chambered a round in her rifle, then peeked from behind the rock. The horses had moved to the edge of the clearing. The trees swayed in the low dawn light. The cold wind gusted, whipping up embers from their campfire and making the pine boughs creak.

"How many shooters are there?" she asked, keeping her voice low.

His jaw like granite, he shot her another scowl. "Two, I think. I'm going to circle around and check. Stay here and cover for me."

"But—"

"I mean it, Bethany." His eyes sparked at hers. "Stay behind this rock. Just keep on firing until I get into the woods."

He rose to a crouch. She stood at the edge of the boulder and aimed her gun toward the trees.

"Now!"

Steeling her nerves, she started firing. Cole sprinted full out toward the horses, then melted into the woods. Once she was certain he'd made it, she ducked behind the rock.

An ominous stillness again descended. Her heart jackhammered in her throat. Where were their attackers? Why hadn't they shot back? What if they'd ambushed Cole?

Trying not to imagine the worst, she checked the rounds in her gun. Only two left. She hesitated, then slid her gaze to the saddle bag she'd left by the campfire—containing her extra shells. She hated to leave the safety of the rock, but running out of ammunition could get them killed.

She inhaled and gathered her courage, preparing to

dart over and grab the bag. But then a movement in the clearing caught her eye.

She whipped around. A man rushed toward her—his pistol raised. Her heart rocketing, she pumped off a shot at his arm.

He reeled around and staggered backward, then stumbled back into the trees. Her hands trembling, she ejected the spent shell and racked her final round. She didn't want to kill a man, no matter what his intentions toward her.

But she might not have a choice.

Not wanting to think about that dizzying prospect, she dragged in a shaky breath. Then she shifted her attention to her bag. She had to get those extra shells *now*.

She sprinted toward the campfire. Shots rang out, hitting the rock face behind her, and she zigzagged to the bag. She scooped it up, skidded back to the boulder, then scrambled behind it again. She hit the ground and gasped for breath.

She was safe—for now. But where was Cole? What was he doing? Had any of those shots been aimed at him?

That thought threatened to unnerve her, but she ruthlessly pushed it aside. Cole couldn't be hurt. She refused even to think it. No matter what else happened, he had to survive.

Still trembling, she fumbled in her bag for the box of shells. Then she loaded the magazine on her rifle and settled in to wait for Cole.

Seconds ticked past. The wind howled in the trees. She debated going after Cole, but forced herself to stay put. But she couldn't stem the torrent of guilt. She should have told Cole about her father. She never should have lied about that truck. She'd had no right to keep the truth from him. *He could have died.*

A twig snapped nearby. Her heart racing, she raised her gun and aimed.

"It's me," Cole called out. "I'm coming in."

She inched out her breath, but kept her rifle trained on the trees to guard against any tricks. But Cole emerged from the forest alone, and she finally lowered her gun.

He strode across the clearing. His eyes connected with hers, and he came to a sudden halt. "What happened?" He rushed the final distance between them. "You're bleeding."

Bleeding? She pressed her hand to her temple. Her fingers came away sticky. And suddenly, she was aware of the moisture trickling down her jaw, the dull throb in her scalp.

He gently lifted her chin, angling his head to see. "They shot you."

"No. I don't think so." Surely she would have felt more pain. "A piece of rock must have splintered off and hit me when I ran over to get more shells."

His hand stilled. His eyes cut to hers. "You did what?"

"I needed more ammunition. I was nearly out. So I ran over to get my bag."

His jaw worked. A muscle ticked in his cheek. Then he moved his face even closer, his eyes blazing at hers. "I told you not to move. Do you have a death wish?"

"I didn't have much choice."

"The hell you didn't. You could have died."

"So could you." Their eyes dueled. She let out a

heavy sigh. "It's just a scrape, Cole. Nothing major. I'll bandage it when we've got time."

His jaw still rigid, he looked away. She could tell he was fighting his emotions, trying to keep his temper under control. But she didn't need him to worry about her.

"Did you see who was out there?" she asked.

He gave a curt nod. "Two men on horseback. No one I recognized. There might have been a third farther off. They're heading downhill right now, but they could circle back."

"I shot one in the arm." She started to tell him the details, but his furious gaze stopped her cold. Better that he didn't know how close the man had come. "But it might not hold them off for long," she added.

His mouth turned even grimmer, forming brackets in his unshaven jaw. "We'd better head out before they come back."

"Right." She hesitated. "Cole, listen. About the other night, when I went to the library in Bozeman—"

"We'll talk later. We need to get moving."

He was right. There wasn't time for explanations with the killers lurking nearby. But before this ordeal was over, she had to reveal what she knew. She couldn't withhold the truth with their lives at risk.

While Cole hurried to saddle the horses, she doused what remained of the campfire and threw together their gear. Then she sprang up on Red, keeping her .22 within reach in the scabbard, and took off with Cole up the draw.

But as they worked their way up the icy slope, night giving way to a somber dawn, the extent of their predicament sank in. The killers knew where they were now. They had no way to call for help. And once they found the cattle, they had to head back down the mountain—possibly into an ambush.

And she only had herself to blame.

They trudged through the mountains for miles, the arctic wind bearing down with a vengeance, whipping the snow sideways and reducing the visibility to nil. Shivering, Bethany pulled her wool scarf higher over her nose and hunched her shoulders in the frosty air. But even the bitter cold penetrating her bones couldn't distract her from her mounting guilt.

She'd screwed up terribly during her time in Maple Cove. She'd done an injustice to Tony. She'd failed to confront her father and lied to Cole. And instead of coming clean and warning Cole about the threats, she'd recklessly indulged in a night of passion, nearly getting them killed.

The snow swirled, and she caught a glimpse of him on his horse—his broad back straight, his head swiveling as he surveyed the terrain—and her heart made a heavy lurch. Of all the things she'd done wrong, making love with Cole had been the worst—and not only because of the danger they were in.

It had stirred up too many memories, making her yearn for things she couldn't have.

But no matter how thrilling his touch, no matter how amazing the feel of him, what they'd shared wasn't real. It had been a moment out of time, a magical interlude. And the last thing she needed was an excuse to start fantasizing about him. She was already perilously close to falling in love with him again.

She caught her breath, horrified at the thought. *No*

way. She absolutely could not fall in love with Cole. So what if he embodied her dreams? So what if she admired the man he'd become? They had no future together. And she'd spent enough time grieving his loss the first time. She refused to go through that torture again—no matter who'd been at fault.

Cole pulled Gunner to a stop. She straggled to a halt beside him, struggling to harness her traitorous thoughts. But then she dragged her gaze to where he was looking. Dark-red splashes dotted the snow.

Blood.

Her breath stopped. She pulled her rifle from her scabbard, her senses suddenly alert.

"Stay behind me," Cole said, urging his horse forward.

Her heart beating fast, she fell in behind him as he threaded his way through the trees. The trail of blood continued. The bitter wind thrashed the pines. They rode for dozens of yards, the bloodstains growing bigger. Then, by the edge of a tiny clearing, tufts of fur stood out in the snow—the remains of a Black Angus calf.

Her stomach tumbled. Cole leaped down, his horse shying from the scent of blood. Bethany leaned over and grabbed Gunner's reins while Cole inspected the calf.

"What do you think? Coyotes?" she asked, a heavy feeling settling inside her at the thought of the helpless calf.

He walked around the carcass, pausing to study the tracks. "Wolves, judging by the claw marks."

"Wolves?" She frowned at that. There were a couple known wolf packs in the area, but they normally left the livestock alone.

"Either way, they haven't gone far," Cole said. "The kill is fresh."

His eyes troubled, he came back and took Gunner's reins. Then he swung himself into the saddle and rode off, following the churned-up snow.

Her own misgivings growing, she clucked Red into motion and trailed him up the slope. Poor Cole. He definitely didn't need more trouble. That secret society had shot his cattle. They'd killed a man, burned his barn, and tried to murder him. And if that weren't enough to deal with, he now had to contend with wolves.

And this was partly her fault. She'd contributed to this mess indirectly, allowing those men to get close. Which meant she had to help fix it. But how?

The sound of lowing cattle reached her ears. Cole nudged Gunner into a trot, and Bethany followed, the freezing wind lashing her face. She crested a rise, then spotted the herd below them in a meadow ringed with towering pines. The cattle were huddled together, indicating that the predators weren't far off.

"You think they're all here?" she asked Cole.

"I hope so. I'll try to get a count. Wait here and make sure they don't take off." He reined Gunner around and rode up the side of the herd.

Bethany sipped some water from her canteen, the half-frozen liquid making her molars ache, then scanned the rugged terrain. Dense stands of timber covered the mountains below the tree line. At higher elevations, granite outcrops jutted from the mounting snow. Gunmetal clouds inched across the range, their wispy edges obscuring the highest peaks.

The wolves were their immediate problem, along with the deadly cold. But assuming they survived those issues, they still had to deal with those killers, who'd be lying in wait below. And there wasn't another route down the mountain.

Unless they went over the pass…

Her pulse quickened. She peered through the blowing snow, wracking her memory for details of the terrain. From what she remembered, it wouldn't be easy. The slope was steep, treacherous, especially in the snow. They'd have to cross various streams, making it hard to manage the herd. But if they succeeded, they could escape those men.

And just maybe, she could make up for the harm she'd done.

But first she had to convince Cole.

He rode back a minute later, snowflakes covering his wide shoulders, his face swarthy from the cold. Her traitorous heart faltered when his gaze landed on hers. She wondered wildly if she could ever react normally to this man.

"They're all here," he said. "It looks like we only lost that one calf."

"That's a relief." Although she still felt bad for the calf.

"Yeah." He angled his stubble-roughened jaw toward the trail. "We'd better start down while we've still got light. We'll set up camp when it gets dark."

"I have a better idea. Let's go across the divide." He opened his mouth to argue, and she forged on. "It's a risk, I know. But it would shorten the distance a lot. And once we get near the highway we can pick up a signal on our cell phones and call for help."

"It's not just risky, it's suicidal."

"So is riding into an ambush. You know those men are going to come back."

"But at least this way we have a chance." He shook his head. "We're tired. The horses are nearly done in. We can't keep pushing them all night. And that storm's about to pick up. It could dump a couple of feet of snow before daylight, closing off that pass."

"All the more reason to try it. You know those men won't expect it. They'll be waiting for us to go back the way we came."

"Because it's the only way we *can* go."

"No, it's not. We can make it across that pass."

His mouth flattened. "I'm not willing to take the chance."

"But why not?" He had to know it made sense. And he wasn't the type to quail before a challenge, especially if it would save his herd.

She frowned at him in frustration. They would run into an ambush down the trail. He knew that as well as she did.

Unless he planned to sacrifice his cattle to get her through.

Horror rippled through her. She stared at him, aghast. But she knew instantly that she was right. He'd protected the father who'd treated him badly. He planned to fire Tony for insulting her, even though it hurt his ranch. And now he was willing to risk himself—and the future of his beloved ranch—to make sure she survived.

And suddenly, she realized she wasn't close to falling in love with Cole, she'd already taken the plunge.

He exhaled. "Look, Bethany. You're exhausted. We both are. Let's head down the trail a ways and make camp. We'll deal with the danger in the morning."

Badly shaken by the revelation, she looked away. She was tempted to agree. Her body ached. She could hardly feel her frozen toes. And the thought of going over that pass in the darkness, the cold wind howling around them, didn't appeal to her in the least. They could get frostbitten or attacked by predators, lose their footing and stumble over a cliff. And she needed time to compose herself, to sort through her emotions and gather her defenses against Cole.

But she'd damaged him enough. She'd hurt him badly when she'd left after high school, reinforcing his lack of trust. Maybe she could never repair that. She couldn't undo the past. But she could save the one thing he cared about—his ranch.

She stuffed her rifle back into the scabbard and tightened her grip on Red's reins. And a deep feeling of certainty settled inside her. *This was right.*

She wheeled her horse around, then glanced back and met Cole's eyes. "Suicidal or not, I'm taking the cattle over that pass."

Then, with the snow whipping against her, she started to ride.

Cole didn't know which he wanted to do more—strangle Bethany or hole up in a cave somewhere and make love to her for days.

He picked his way down the icy hill in the predawn darkness, riding ahead of the exhausted herd. He still couldn't believe she'd insisted on taking this treacherous route, risking her life to save his cows. He'd never been more in awe of her courage and determination.

Or more scared.

The wind gusted sideways, pelting Cole with ice. His back ached; his face was frozen stiff. His stomach had gone beyond empty the day before. Even his horse could barely stay upright, plodding wearily through the snow.

He brought his worn-out horse to a halt and glanced back at the lowing herd. Incredibly, they'd navigated the slippery slopes without a mishap—thanks to Bethany's skill. And he couldn't believe her stamina. They'd spent twenty hours straight in the saddle, and she still kept slogging on.

But at long last they'd nearly reached the road. As soon as he could get a signal bar on his cell phone, he'd call for trucks to pick up the cattle and get the sheriff to deal with those men.

And then he'd get as far from Bethany as he could. He desperately needed space to regain his equilibrium and get his mind off the torrid sex. Because if he didn't come to his senses soon he'd do something he'd regret.

Like beg her to stay.

Without warning, Gunner balked. Snapping his attention back to his horse, Cole reined him hard to the right. But Gunner only pranced sideways, trying to distance himself from the trees.

Alert now, Cole scanned the forest for signs of danger. Gunner tossed up his head and snorted, sensing something Cole couldn't see. The cows continued plodding past him, funneling into a valley flanked by the timbered hills.

Bethany rode up a minute later, her eyes exhausted, the wool scarf she'd wrapped around her face crusted with snow. "What's wrong?" she asked, her voice muffled.

"Nothing yet, but Gunner's acting spooked."

"You think the wolves are still nearby?"

"Something is." He returned his gaze to the timber, and uneasiness crawled through his nerves. "Take the lead. I'll bring up the rear." Wolves would be more likely to attack a faltering cow. "Turn the herd when the valley levels out. If you go straight you'll go over a cliff."

"All right." She nudged Red forward.

"And Bethany?" She halted Red and looked back. "Be careful."

Their eyes held. Emotions swirled inside him, a jumble of feelings he didn't care to name. She nodded, then rode up the line.

Still beating back his tumultuous feelings, Cole waited for the rest of the herd to pass by, his eyes on a trio of dawdling cows. Reining in Gunner with effort, he circled behind the stragglers to hurry them back into the herd.

But Gunner ignored his command and spun around. Cole hauled on the reins, battling to control his panicked horse. "Whoa," he said. "What the…"

And then he saw them, their eyes glowing, creeping silently from the woods.

Wolves.

His heart stopped. Still fighting his spinning horse, he grabbed his rifle from the scabbard and racked a round. The wolves began to spread out, acting on some hidden signal, forming a semicircle around the frightened cows.

Using all his strength, Cole forced his spooked horse backward, trying to stay between the wolves and the vulnerable cows. But a huge black wolf stalked forward. He paced back and forth, steadily coming closer, then stopped and began to howl.

The others joined in. The eerie sound sent a chill

jolting down Cole's spine. Gunner rolled his eyes and tried to run, but Cole managed to hold him in place. He couldn't abandon his cows.

The lead wolf yipped. The wolves began to move. Cole continued riding backward, praying Bethany stayed away. He didn't want her trying something heroic that could get her killed.

The leader growled, his hackles rising, his wild eyes fixed on Cole. Cole's fingers twitched, but he held his fire. He couldn't legally shoot the endangered wolves unless they attacked him first.

Suddenly Bethany came racing toward him, and his stomach coiled with dread. "Get back," he shouted. "For God's sake, get away."

Ignoring him, she pressed forward. She pulled to a stop beside him, then fired a warning shot in the air.

The wolves turned toward her, their attention snagged.

And then the lead wolf charged.

Chapter 13

Cole didn't hesitate. He fired at the wolf just as Bethany's gun barked out. The animal stumbled, then dropped in its tracks.

The other wolves paused. Behind him, the panicked cows scattered, racing down the valley toward the herd. His heart galloping, Cole hauled on the reins, battling to keep Gunner from bolting after the cows. A flight response would trigger another attack.

He kept his gaze on the ring of wolves. Their savage eyes gleamed back. "Don't move," he warned Bethany.

"I'm trying not to," she gritted out, struggling to control her frantic horse.

He rose in the stirrups and waved his gun at the wolves. "Go on. Get out of here!" Several turned tail and slunk back into the woods.

Encouraged, he fired a shot in the air. "Get out. Go!" he shouted again, and the last few wolves disappeared.

His eyes still locked on the forest, Cole hissed his breath through his teeth. That had been too damned close.

He waited several heartbeats to make sure they wouldn't come back. Then he reined Gunner around, giving vent to his gut-wrenching fear. "What the hell were you thinking? I told you to stay away. Those wolves could have—"

A deep drumming sound snagged his attention. He snapped his gaze to the valley and peered through the shadowy snow. Bethany shoved her rifle into the scabbard and urged Red forward just as he registered what was wrong.

Stampede.

His heart stumbled hard. Fierce dread shot through his veins. The cows were running through a valley. At the end was a cliff. If the herd didn't turn in time…

And Bethany had just leaped into the melée.

He kicked Gunner into action, then charged down the snowy slope after Bethany, pushing his horse to a breakneck pace. He had to get Bethany out of there before they reached that cliff.

"Bethany!" he shouted, but the bellowing of the herd, the thundering of hoofbeats drowned him out.

Fueled by abject panic, he dug his heels into Gunner, accelerating to a reckless speed. The bitter wind whipped past. The horse skidded, but regained his feet. Cole squinted, riding like a fury, trying to see Bethany in the blinding snow.

"Come on. Come on," he urged Gunner. He hurtled down the icy valley, leaping over rocks and deadfall, terror lodged tight in his throat. Then he drove his exhausted horse even harder. He knew he was risking a deadly crash but didn't have a choice.

After a moment he saw her, riding near the edge of the panicked herd. He knew what she intended. She'd try to outrun the cows and turn them, curving them inward to end the stampede.

But if she failed…

His heart congealed. A wild feeling of dread seized his gut. Forcing Gunner to the absolute limit, he raced alongside the herd, slowly gaining ground on Bethany as they neared the cliff. But they would never make it. They were running out of time.

She miraculously gained the lead. The valley leveled out—and his heart stopped dead. Only a few more yards to the cliff.

But she pulled out her rifle and fired into the air. The lead cows balked and turned away. She held her ground, still shooting above their heads, and the column began to curve. Cole reached her side a second later, and added his shouts and shots to hers.

The startled cows slowed. They gradually began to mill around, their frenzied flight finally subdued. Cole let out an incredulous breath, amazed that Bethany had pulled it off.

But she had nearly died.

He pulled his blowing horse to a stop. He leaped down and stormed through the snow, then pulled her off her horse.

Her full mouth wobbled. Her eyes were huge in her pale face. Her courage and fragility slammed through him, a sucker punch to his heart.

Overwhelmed by a barrage of emotions, he hauled

her into his arms. He closed his eyes, buried his face in her silky hair, and then just held her, his heart beating violently, relief shuddering through him, his feelings a disordered mess. She'd risked her life to save his stampeding cattle. She'd endangered herself to fight those wolves.

He'd never met anyone so brave or reckless or amazing in his life.

He lifted his head, raised his hands to her delicate jaw, framing her ashen face with his hands. He gazed into her glimmering eyes, still unable to form a word. Then he bent and fitted his mouth to hers, glorying in the soft, living feel of her, giving vent to his terror, his awe.

His love.

His heart tumbled hard. He pressed her tighter against him, buffeted by his raging emotions, pouring everything into the kiss—everything he couldn't say. Revealing his fear, his yearning, his need.

He'd nearly lost her. That horrific thought kept ricocheting through his mind, threatening to drive him insane. He plundered her lips, her mouth, needing to convince himself she was alive.

With effort, he ended the kiss and tucked her head against his neck. For an eternity he continued to hold her, stunned by the feelings churning inside him, absorbing the wonder of her safe in his arms.

Words bubbled up, but he steeled his jaw to keep them from breaking free. No matter how desperately he wanted this woman, he couldn't go through this again. She was going to leave. He had no right to ask her to stay. He couldn't put his heart on the line.

Still badly shaken, he filled his lungs with the frosty

air, then forced himself to pull back. "Are you all right?" he asked, his voice rough.

"I'm fine. Now." She managed a crooked smile, but he saw how shaken she was. "Just exhausted and anxious to get home," she added.

Home. Chicago. The place where she belonged.

He took another step back. "We're almost to the road. We might be able to get a signal on our cell phones now." Still struggling to control his emotions, he turned away and mounted his weary horse. She'd exposed feelings he'd stifled for years, longings he shouldn't have—no matter how right she felt in his arms.

Tossed thoroughly off balance, he waited until she'd mounted Red, then started herding the weary cattle toward the road. But as they plodded along, he had to face the truth.

He loved her. He always would.

And there wasn't a damned thing he could do about it, except to protect himself the only way he knew how—by shutting down.

Bethany awoke from an exhausted slumber hours later. She opened her eyes, disoriented, and blinked at the fresh patches of snow dotting the gravel road. She glanced out the window, recognized the old stagecoach stop on a distant hill. They'd nearly reached Cole's ranch.

She turned her attention to "Rocky" Rockwell, the deputy sheriff driving the SUV, and the past few hours rushed back. They'd loaded up the horses and cattle. They'd reported the wolf attack to the feds. Cole had hustled her into the deputy's SUV, turning the heater on full blast, then talked to the sheriff about the men. She'd fallen asleep the minute she hit the seat.

She spotted Cole's truck ahead and sighed, missing him already, but knew the separation would do her good. She'd been far too tempted to blurt out that she loved him—which wouldn't have been fair to him. They had no chance for a future until she revealed the truth.

And maybe not even then. Assuming he forgave her deception, even if he wanted to share her future, where would they live? He'd never leave his ranch and move to Chicago, and she still couldn't stay here.

But first things first. As soon as they arrived at the ranch she had to tell him about the attack in Bozeman and apologize for endangering his life. She also had to get answers from her father, confess that she'd suspected him all along—and hope Cole understood.

They hit a section of washboard, and the SUV rattled as hard as her jittering nerves. Then they crested a rise outside the ranch. Dozens of trucks and cars crowded the gravel road, taking her by surprise.

"What's going on?" People congregated in the neighbor's field. A television van recorded the scene. More people toting cameras surrounded the wooden gate.

The deputy grimaced. "Word of Lana's kidnapping leaked out and the media is going nuts."

"Oh, no." The blitz surrounding the senator's infidelities had been bad enough. This would feed the media frenzy and fuel the tabloids for weeks—causing headaches Cole didn't need.

The deputy slowed as they neared the crowd, catching up to Cole. Journalists swarmed both vehicles, flashing cameras and hurling questions their way. "Idiots," Rocky muttered. "Trying to get run over." He honked and inched toward the gate.

Minutes later, they made it through. The reporters hung back, unable to trespass on private land. Bethany exhaled, relieved to finally escape the frantic crowd.

But now she had an even bigger hurdle to face.

The deputy parked beside the machinery shed, alongside Cole. Bethany climbed out, her muscles stiff, her head still dizzy with fatigue. But she'd sleep more later. She had to make a confession first.

Her heart beating triple-time, she went in search of Cole. She found him beside the machinery shed, talking to Earl. "Can I help?" she asked, glancing around.

His eyes met hers, triggering the usual sensual jolt. "No. Earl's taking care of the horses. Go grab something to eat. We need to give the sheriff a statement as soon as he shows up."

"All right." She hesitated, her belly fluttering. "But if you have a minute, I need to talk to you…alone."

"Sure."

She waited while Cole wrapped things up with Earl, her tension rising with every second that passed. Why had she waited so long to tell him? How could she possibly explain?

They began walking toward the ranch house. She sneaked a glance at his rough-hewn profile, experiencing another attack of nerves.

"So what did you want to say?" he asked.

She inhaled. There was no good way to say it. She had to blurt it out. "I, um… I didn't tell you, but that day I went to Bozeman to do research at the library someone tried to run me off the road."

He abruptly came to a halt. "What?"

She hugged her arms, but couldn't stem the anxiety welling inside. "On the way home that night there was a truck. I couldn't see who it was. He had his bright lights on… He hit my bumper and tried to force me off the road."

"And you didn't tell me?"

"I should have, I know. But I thought…" She dragged in another breath. "You wouldn't let me go to the mountains if you knew."

He gaped at her, incredulity in his eyes. "And that mattered?"

"Yes. I thought Tony was causing the problems on the ranch. It was my only chance to confront him. But I was wrong. I made a mistake. I let my feelings about him cloud my judgment. And as a result… I put us all at risk."

His eyes stayed on hers. Several heartbeats passed. Then he tore his gaze away and stared into the distance, as if grappling for something to say.

"You lied to me." His voice sounded dead.

Her stomach swooped. "I… Yes, I did." She searched for a way to explain. But she had betrayed his trust. How could she rationalize that?

"Cole, I…"

The sheriff's deputy sauntered over, his boots crunching on the gravel drive. "Sheriff Colton's almost here," he said. "He said to tell you he'll need a statement from you both."

Cole nodded and glanced his way. "We'll wait in the house." His eyes cut back to hers. The coldness in them froze her heart.

And the terrible realization slammed through her. He wouldn't forgive her deception.

And he hadn't even heard the worst.

* * *

Bethany huddled in an armchair a short time later, nursing a hot cup of tea. Despite a scalding shower, an afghan wrapped around her shoulders and her thickest pair of wool socks, she still couldn't seem to warm up. Cole hadn't looked at her since she'd sat down.

"How about you, Bethany?" the sheriff asked, drawing her reluctant attention to him. "Do you have anything to add to Cole's report?"

"Not that I can think of." She'd told him about the truck. She'd described the man she'd shot. "I only saw the one man."

The sheriff snapped his notebook closed. "I've put out an alert. If he goes anywhere for medical treatment, we'll pick him up." He paused, then glanced around the group. "If there's nothing else, I'll head back to town."

Her stomach like lead, Bethany looked at her father. He sat across from her on the couch, his wrinkled face pasty, his gnarled hands tightly clasped.

Why didn't he speak out?

The sheriff stood. Dread settled around her heart. And she knew she had to act. She hated to confront her father in public, but she had to reveal the truth.

"Wait," she said. The sheriff turned back. Everyone looked her way.

Swallowing hard, she met her father's eyes. "Dad?" she whispered. "You know something, don't you?"

He opened his mouth, as if to protest. "Dad, please," she pleaded. "We really need to know."

He hesitated, then seemed to deflate. He slumped back against the cushions, his face even more waxy, looking every one of his sixty-eight years.

"You're right. I… I do have something to say," he

admitted. "Something I should have said a long time ago. I know who's involved in this."

The sheriff sat back down. Bethany braved a glance at Cole, who sat with deceptive stillness, his arms crossed, his eyes riveted on her dad. Her hopes plummeted. He was furious. She should never have concealed the truth.

Her father let out a breath. "You were right that someone at the ranch was involved. It's Kenny Greene."

"Kenny?" she repeated, stunned. The mild-mannered boy she'd gone to school with? The boy Tony had bullied along with her? "But why?"

"Money. I guess he wanted to buy that fancy rig."

"You'd better start at the beginning," the sheriff said, sounding grim.

Her father nodded, but dropped his gaze to his hands. "The day I got hurt, I was riding in the pasture by the teepee ring. I saw Kenny with some men I didn't know. I went to find out what they were doing on the ranch.

"They were going to shoot me. For what it's worth, Kenny convinced them I wouldn't talk. They tied me to the stirrup, made Red drag me a ways. After my leg broke, they cut me loose."

Bethany closed her eyes, not wanting to imagine the horror, the humiliation and pain.

"They told me if I kept my mouth shut no one else would get hurt." He lifted his gaze to Cole. "I didn't know about your sister, the kidnapping. I thought they would cut some fences, maybe break another window, and you'd make the senator leave."

"And when they killed that mercenary?" Cole asked, his voice so icy it made her heart lurch. "Why the hell didn't you say something then?"

"I wanted to, but Kenny cornered me the day before. He said they'd kill Bethany if I talked."

Her mind flashed back to the day they'd brought the cows in, when she'd seen them beside the corral. She'd attributed his pallor to his injury, not fear.

"They'd already broken my leg. I knew they'd follow through with their threat. But now..." His voice dropped. "It's gone too far."

Dead silence gripped the room. Her heart wrenched for her father, even as her anger rose. The man she'd idolized all her life, the man she'd revered, had let her down.

But he'd kept silent to protect her. Hadn't she done the same for him? They'd both acted badly.

And as a result, they'd hurt Cole.

She looked at Cole. His jaw was bunched, his eyes cold. And panic spurted inside her. Somehow she had to convince him of their good intentions. Somehow she had to explain.

"Can you describe the men who hurt you?" the sheriff asked.

Her father nodded. "Yeah. I'm pretty good with faces."

"Good." The sheriff stood. "Be at the station at four. I'll call in an artist from Bozeman so we can start circulating some pictures of these guys." He turned to Cole. "I'll put out an APB for Kenny, but he's probably skipped town."

Suddenly remembering the bridle piece in her pocket, Bethany rose and fished it out. "I found this in the field. I don't know if it means anything." She handed it to him.

"I'll check it out. Maybe we'll get lucky and find a match. God knows we can use a break." The sheriff and his deputy went to the door. Cole let them out, and their footsteps slowly faded. A hush fell over the room.

Her father grabbed his crutches, then hobbled over to Cole, who still stood near the door. "Cole, I'm sorry. I thought…" He hung his head. "Hell, there's no excuse. It was a damned fool thing to do. I'll pack my bag and go."

His shoulders slumped, looking thoroughly defeated, her father limped toward his room. She watched him go, aching to console him.

But first she had to talk to Cole.

Swallowing hard, she started toward Cole. But he stalked to his study and slammed the door, the harsh finality of the sound giving rise to another swarm of nerves.

Pausing, she met Hannah's eyes. The housekeeper stood by the kitchen, a stricken expression on her face. "He just needs time. He—he's had a lot of disappointments in his life."

Bethany managed to nod. But Hannah was wrong. If she didn't reach Cole now, she never would.

Her heart pounding, she went to the study door. She raised her hand to knock, then reconsidered. She twisted the knob and went in.

Cole stood by the window, staring out at the burned barn. "Cole?" she whispered.

His back stiffened. "Go away."

"I—I'd like to explain."

"I don't want to hear it."

"I know that, but I have to tell you—"

He whipped around. His furious eyes slashed at hers. "Fine. You want to explain why you covered up for your father? Go right ahead."

Her stomach balled. "I didn't cover up exactly. I didn't know anything for sure."

"But you suspected. My cattle were dying. Men were getting killed. Hell, my sister was being held prisoner—and you didn't say a word."

"It wasn't that simple."

"The hell it wasn't.

"It wasn't. I wanted to tell you. I really did. But I didn't have anything to go on. And I couldn't accuse my dad without proof.

"You don't know what it's like," she continued. "All my life people have misjudged me. They see the color of my skin and assume all sorts of things—that I'm lazy, that I steal. Even in Chicago, where I thought my coworkers knew me, they've accused me of something I didn't do. And I couldn't do that to my father. Not without proof."

She drew in a ragged breath. "He's my father, Cole, the only family I have. I owed him at least that much."

"So you lied."

"I was wrong," she admitted. "I know that now. But you've made mistakes. You've done things that you regret."

He let out a bitter sound. "I've made mistakes, all right."

He meant her.

Her face burned. A huge ache constricted her chest. "Cole…"

"Your father's leaving," he continued, his voice hard. "I want you out of here, too."

Sudden panic gripped her. She had to reach him. *He had to understand.* "Don't do this," she pleaded. "Don't shut me out again. Can't we talk—"

"Get out, Bethany. You've done enough damage. Go back to Chicago where you belong."

Her throat closed tight. A huge wave of despair swamped her heart. He wouldn't forgive her. He wouldn't give her another chance.

And she refused to beg.

Summoning her tattered pride, she raised her chin. "Fine. I'll go. You don't need to tell me twice."

Her heart shredded, her hopes obliterated, she turned and walked away.

Chapter 14

Cole tossed down his pen, creaked his chair back, then scowled at the digital clock ticking away the hours on the corner of his desk. One in the morning. By rights he should be oblivious to the world by now. He'd worked himself into exhaustion during that ride through the mountains, fighting off wolves and gunmen, barely surviving a deadly stampede.

But damned if he could sleep.

He dragged his hand down his unshaven face, then rubbed his stinging eyes. He'd spent the past six hours doing ranch business in an attempt to numb his mind—balancing his checkbook, filing his quarterly taxes, filling out the mountain of insurance forms that had accumulated on his desk. But not even that dull work could deaden the sting of Bethany's betrayal or stop the hot, searing anger scorching through him when his traitorous mind wandered to her.

He shoved thoughts of Bethany aside. She was gone. It was over. He refused to think about her again. He'd done what he'd set out to do and had saved his ranch. That was all that mattered to him.

The clock ticked off another minute, and he shot it another scowl. There was no reason for this insomnia. He'd delivered the cattle. He'd made enough money to operate the ranch for another year. He'd lost his foreman and ranch hands, and he couldn't buy Del's land, but at least that secret society hadn't defeated him yet.

But damn... He'd known Kenny Greene since high school. They'd worked together for years. And Rusty... A hollow feeling gouged his chest. He'd never expected him to betray his trust. Or Bethany...

He shoved himself away from the desk with a growl. Determined to forget her, he strode from the study to the great room, then beelined straight to the bar.

The huge, vaulted room was draped in darkness. His father sat in an armchair by the fireplace, watching the flickering flat-screen television with the sound muted. He looked up, then lumbered to his feet as Cole took out a bottle of Scotch and poured himself a drink.

"Can't sleep?" he asked, joining him at the bar.

Cole knocked back a slug of scotch, felt the fiery burn sear his gut. "I'm not used to the quiet, I guess."

"Sorry about that. I guess I've caused a ruckus the last few weeks."

He shrugged and refilled his glass. "I'll adjust." He always did. He'd bury himself in his ranch work and concentrate on what mattered most—his land.

His father topped off his own glass with his favorite

Maker's Mark whiskey, then paused. "Listen, Cole. I know it's not my place to say anything, but about that woman, Bethany…"

Cole flinched. "There's nothing to say."

"I think there is." He paused. "I'd like to give you some advice."

"Advice? From you?" Cole snorted in disbelief. "After all those mistresses?"

His father winced. "I've been a bad example, I know. Your mother…she didn't deserve what I did."

"You got that right." He slopped more Scotch in his glass, then gulped it down with a hiss.

"I just don't want you to make my mistakes."

"I'm not making a mistake. It's over. There's nothing else to say." And he didn't need his father—the man who'd disappointed his family for decades—trying to give *him* relationship advice.

His father stared at his tumbler with a furrowed brow. "For what it's worth, I'm not proud of what I did. I took your mother for granted. All those years… I only thought about myself."

He met Cole's eyes. "The thing is, the fame, the power—none of that mattered in the end. Your mother and our marriage did. But I didn't figure that out until it was too late. And Bethany—"

"It's not the same thing."

"You're sure? It looked like it from where I stood."

"I'm sure." Cole's thoughts veered to Bethany, and his anger flared. "Look, she lied to me. She concealed evidence about the attacks. And the last thing I need is someone I can't depend on. I had enough of that crap growing up."

His father blanched. "I deserve that. I was a miserable father, I know. But I still say you're making a mistake."

"No, I'm not. And I definitely don't need your advice."

His father nodded. He drained his glass, then set it down on the bar. And in that moment he didn't look like the swaggering, bigger-than-life senator who'd wielded so much power. He looked like a tired, middle-aged man—his lined face haggard, his blue eyes filled with remorse.

"You're a lot like me," he finally said, his voice subdued. "Sometimes when I see you, it's like looking back thirty years. I used to think that was a good thing." His mouth twisted into a bitter smile. "But now I know it's a curse."

He turned, his broad shoulders slumped, his steps weary as he left the room. Cole watched him go, denials crowding his throat. His father was wrong. They were nothing alike. He felt insulted at the thought.

And his father was dead wrong about Bethany. She'd had her chance, and she'd let him down, just as she had in the past.

He started to top off his glass, then stopped. What the hell. He'd take the whole damned bottle to bed. Maybe then he could finally forget about Bethany and find the oblivion he sought.

By morning, Cole knew two things with absolute clarity. Getting drunk solved nothing, and hangovers were a bitch.

His head pounding, his stomach lurching like a fly-fishing line during a spawning run, he jerked open his blurry eyes. Sunlight stabbed his brain. The bedroom heaved and twirled, the stench of whiskey souring the air.

He rolled over, causing a thousand hammers to flay his skull. Groaning, he forced himself to a sitting position, then gripped his throbbing head to make sure it wouldn't split.

Moving as if he'd aged a hundred years, he pushed himself to his feet, staggered to the master bathroom, then grabbed a handful of painkillers and washed them down. He glanced in the mirror, his bloodshot eyes and rumpled clothes proof that he'd hit a new low.

And what was worse, even all that alcohol hadn't enabled him to avoid the truth—that Bethany had had a point.

Hell. He braced his hands on the vanity and released a breath. He'd seen the way Tony had acted. He knew why she couldn't stay. He even understood why she refused to accuse her father of any wrongdoing without proof. In her place, he would have done the same.

That thought rankling, he stripped off his reeking clothes and stepped into the shower. But while the hot water eased the ache from his muscles and helped clear the fog from his mind, it did nothing to assuage his guilt.

Not that it mattered. Whether he'd been fair to Bethany or not, she was always going to leave. There was nothing for her in Maple Cove. Their argument might have hastened her departure, but she'd never intended to stay.

He flicked off the tap, dried himself with a towel, and pulled on a clean T-shirt and jeans. Feeling marginally more human, he headed down the hallway to the kitchen, hoping a mug of strong, black coffee would jump-start his sluggish brain.

Ace padded over and whined. Still moving carefully, Cole bent to rub his ears. "What's up, buddy? Did everyone leave us alone today?"

Straightening, he glanced around the empty great room. The deep silence permeating the house indicated that he was alone. Good. He didn't feel like explaining his hangover to his father. It would only prove his point.

He started toward the kitchen, honing in on the scent of coffee like a desert survivor spotting a lake. But Ace perked up his ears and yipped, then trotted to the front door.

"Great." A visitor before he'd had a shot of caffeine. He detoured toward the door with a sigh. It was probably the sheriff, getting back to him with the latest news.

But when he was halfway there, the telephone rang. He paused, torn, but the shrill sound jackhammering his skull decided the choice. Desperate to stop the racket, he lunged for the phone. "Bar Lazy K."

"Cole? This is Caitlin. Caitlin O'Donahue. Remember me?"

"Sure." His sister's best friend was hard to forget with her fiery red hair and impressive brains—not to mention her centerfold curves. He rubbed his aching head. "How are you doing? I thought you were in South America doing the Doctors Without Borders thing."

"I was. I just got back. I heard about Lana's kidnapping on the news. I still can't believe it. It's so awful! Have you heard anything more?"

"Not really." Nothing he could reveal.

"How's your mother holding up?"

"About how you'd imagine. Not great."

"She must be devastated."

"You should call her. She'd appreciate hearing from you."

"I will." She hesitated. "If there's anything I can do, will you let me know? I mean it, Cole. I'll do anything, fly anywhere… She might…" Her voice trembled. "She might need a friendly face when this is done. I'm staying at my dad's house in California, so you can reach me here."

"Thanks, Caitlin. I'll pass that on." He hung up the phone, experiencing a sliver of warmth. At least his sister had a loyal friend. His mind instantly flashed to Bethany, but he grimly fought it down. He was not going down that futile track.

Ace pawed at the door and whined, then gave him a reproachful look. "Sorry. *Sorry,*" he said. Sending a longing glance toward the kitchen—and that desperately needed caffeine—he closed the distance to the front door. As soon as he cracked it open, Ace bolted out, stopping to sniff a small flat package by the steps.

Cole's pulse skipped. It was a cardboard mailer, the type that held CDs. He scanned the deserted yard, but whoever had delivered it was gone.

He snapped his gaze back to the mailer. An ominous feeling crept through his nerves. *Damn.* With Kenny Greene out of the picture, he'd hoped for a reprieve.

His dread rising, he scooped up the package, and returned to the house. Just as he expected, the mailer held a DVD. He crossed the room, slid it into the DVD player, and turned it on.

The screen flickered to life. A room swirled dizzily into view. He closed his eyes, cursing that bottle of

Scotch. But the unsteadiness was due to the photographer, who couldn't quite keep the camera still.

The camera swerved to a loveseat. And suddenly, his sister appeared on the screen, and he forgot to breathe. Although the camera continued to bobble, he could see her clearly enough—her mussed blond hair, the harsh pallor of her face, the exhaustion in her scared blue eyes. She perched on a white loveseat, clutching a piece of paper in her shaking hands.

His face burned. Blood thundered through his skull. And he trembled with the need to avenge her, to lash out and beat her captors, to charge through that television screen and yank her to safety fast.

But he forced himself to breathe, to take note of details instead. The white loveseat with the turquoise pillows. The thick white carpet beneath her feet. The Picasso print behind the sofa, hanging crookedly on the wall. Traffic rumbled faintly in the background. A distant siren wailed. Next to the sofa was a window, filled with autumn leaves.

Lana cleared her throat, then studied the paper, which appeared to be some sort of script. "As you can see, I'm alive," she read, her voice wavering slightly. "And I'll stay that way as long as you cooperate."

She hesitated, sending a look of desperation at someone off camera, the vulnerability in her eyes cracking his heart. Inhaling visibly, she looked at the paper again. "So please, Dad." Her voice broke. "Turn yourself in. It's the only way to…"

She stopped. She bit her lip, then lifted her chin and stared straight into the camera, a dull flush darkening her pale cheeks. And suddenly, a spark lit her eyes, the same gritty determination he'd seen when she was a kid hounding her older brothers, determined not to be left behind.

"Don't do what they say, Daddy!" she blurted out. A man lunged onscreen, his back to the camera, obscuring Cole's view of Lana, but she continued to speak. "They're going to kill me regardless—"

The man swung his arm, and the sickening sound of flesh hitting flesh cut her off. Cole surged toward the screen, his pulse thundering, the urgent need to do violence eroding what little remained of his self-control.

The man moved aside. Lana slumped against the love seat, her lips trembling, her shocked eyes glittering with tears, her dark-red jaw already beginning to swell.

Cole stared at the screen, his breath shallow and fast, every muscle poised to attack. *That man was dead.* If it was the last thing Cole did, he'd make him pay. The man moved away from the camera, and the screen went blank.

Cole had never been more scared in his life.

Two hours later, the DVD ended for the second time, and a shocked silence gripped the group clustered around the screen. Cole skipped his gaze from the grim-faced sheriff to his ashen father, to his uncle Don and Bonnie Gene. Hannah stood by the kitchen, hugging her orange cat, looking as if she wanted to cry.

His aunt finally broke the silence. "What…" She cleared her throat and tried again. "What are we going to do now?"

"Good question." Donald's voice vibrated with anger. "Maybe Hank has an idea since he got her into this mess. If he hadn't been so self-centered—"

"Lay off him," Cole cut in, surprising himself.

"What's done is done. It doesn't do any good to keep blaming him now."

Everyone turned to face him, their mouths agape. He'd never defended his father before. But what was the point of continually hurling blame?

He glanced at his father hunched on the sofa, his face chalk-white, his still-thick hair streaked with gray. He'd aged in the past few weeks, turning into a shell of his former self.

And suddenly, Cole realized he pitied his father. Hank had made mistakes, but he'd received his just due. He'd lost his job, his wife, his prestige. He was a broken, pathetic man who no longer had the power to hurt anyone.

And Cole realized something else. He'd let the bitterness he'd harbored since childhood go.

The sheriff cleared his throat. "I'll take the DVD to the FBI. They'll have a forensic team enhance the images, see if they can figure out the location."

Cole steered his mind to the DVD. "She's back in the United States. In a city." When everyone stared at him, he shrugged. "That siren you hear in the background. It's not a European type. And those leaves on the tree in the window are turning colors, so she's probably somewhere in the north or east. That room is either on the ground level or a lower floor since we can see the tree."

"By God, you're right," his father said. "Good thinking."

The sheriff nodded. "That's exactly the kind of detail that can break this case. With luck, the FBI can pinpoint her location and send in a S.W.A.T. team to get her out."

Conversation broke out around him. But Cole tuned it out, his thoughts still circling around the revelation he'd had. And he realized it was true. He'd finally freed himself from the past, giving up the bitterness that had driven him for years.

But his father's accusation still lingered. Was he really as bad as his dad?

Suddenly feeling restless, he went outside and stood on the porch. He bent to pet Mitzy and Ace, who'd instantly converged on his feet, then looked out over the yard.

Bethany had wronged him. She'd even admitted as much. But he understood why she'd done it, and he couldn't fault her for that. So why couldn't he forgive her? If he'd finally stopped resenting his father after all these years, why not her?

His arms crossed, he frowned at the distant mountains, knowing he was missing something important, something big. She'd left, just as he'd known she would—just as she had before. But had her departure really been inevitable? How would he know if he'd never asked her to stay? And why hadn't he asked? Had he been afraid that she'd say no?

Was he still reliving his childhood, expecting rejection at every turn?

He scowled, not happy with that unflattering insight, but he knew he'd discovered the truth. He'd pushed her away before she could abandon him.

But Bethany would never do that. She'd proven her loyalty time and again. She'd saved his horses from the burning barn. She'd risked her life to stop the stampede. She'd even confronted Tony—the man who'd tormented her for years—to stop the sabotage on his ranch. How much proof of her loyalty did he need?

Hell, he'd been the selfish one. He'd overlooked the

bullying. He'd ignored her medical talents, refusing to acknowledge that she'd needed opportunities she couldn't find in Maple Cove.

His chest tight, he gazed out at the ranch he'd worked so hard to attain—the wide-open plains and rolling hills, the rugged mountains covered with snow, the hawks soaring past on the wind. He loved this land. He loved the freedom, the history, the unspoiled beauty that soothed his soul.

But he couldn't ask Bethany to give up her life in Chicago, to sacrifice everything for his sake. He'd resented his father for only thinking about himself. He couldn't do the same to her.

He sighed. This land had always been here. It would be here when he was gone. And while he loved it, he'd used it as a crutch, to give purpose to his angry life.

But he no longer needed it as much as he needed her.

He went dead still. *That* was how he resembled his father. His staunch independence. His refusal to rely on anyone else. But while his father's reluctance to admit he needed help could cost his sister her life, Cole's could cost him his heart.

He strode back into the great room and headed down the hall. "Where are you going?" his father called.

Pausing, Cole glanced at the man who'd sired him, the man he was determined not to become. "I'm taking your advice and buying a plane ticket to Chicago."

To claim the woman he'd always loved.

Chapter 15

Bethany gazed out the taxi window, the bleak gray skies over Lake Shore Drive echoing her gloomy mood. She rarely splurged on a taxi, but a miserable, sleepless night and a raging headache had convinced her to skip the train. The noise from the taxi was bad enough.

They exited the busy highway, then cut across town toward Michigan Avenue, whipping in and out of traffic so fast she could barely keep her seat. An ambulance screamed past. A bus rumbled by, belching a cloud of black exhaust, then screeched to a stop and blocked the road. The taxi driver lay on his horn.

"I'll get out here," Bethany said, her head about to burst. She thrust several bills at the driver and hopped out, the cold breeze whipping her hair. Clutching her coat closer around her, she hurried past the towering high-rise buildings to the Preston-Werner Clinic. She still hadn't heard from Adam, even though she'd left him a voice mail to tell him she'd returned. She'd decided to go straight to the study supervisor instead.

A businessman strode past, and his briefcase banged her leg. "Hey!" She whirled around, but he didn't break his stride. She scowled, wondering when Chicago had changed. She used to love the energy in the city. It made her feel exuberant and alive. Now she just felt annoyed.

She walked through the automatic front doors of the clinic, her heels rapping on the shiny marble floor. Too exhausted to take the stairs, she punched the button for the elevator and stepped inside. Then she leaned back against the wall and watched the numbers of the floors flash past.

Her thoughts instantly arrowed to Cole, an unbearable ache wrenching her throat, but she pushed him out of her mind. She could not go there. Not now, not in a public place. She'd save that agony for later, when she could wallow in her misery alone.

The elevator stopped. She entered the supervisor's office, relieved that the woman had agreed to see her. In her late fifties, Marge Holbrook was a tall, thin woman with a short, no-nonsense haircut that matched her managerial style. Surely she would take Bethany's side.

"Bethany," the supervisor said when she walked in. She nodded to one of the large leather chairs in front of her gleaming desk. "Have a seat."

"Thanks." Bethany sank into the chair. "I appreciate your seeing me. I just got back into town last night. I was hoping we could talk about the information I found."

Marge quirked a well-shaped brow. "What information?"

Bethany's heart skipped. "The dissertation I discovered at Montana State. I emailed Adam a copy, and he promised to pass it on."

"He didn't give me anything."

Uneasiness trickled through her. Why hadn't Adam given her a copy? He'd had plenty of time.

Suddenly, Cole's question popped into her mind. *How well do you know the people you work with?*

Her hand unsteady, she took the flash drive from her purse and slid it across the desk. Maybe she was wrong. Maybe there was another explanation for this.

Or maybe not.

"Mrs. Bolter's death really upset me," she explained. "I *know* I didn't misjudge the dose. So I decided to investigate to see if I could find another cause."

"And did you?"

"Not at first. But I saw she'd been to rehab years ago. That surprised me because she used to bring us rum cake with a glaze that could knock your socks off. You could get drunk on the fumes alone."

Marge cracked a smile. "I had a slice once."

Bethany nodded. "So I went to the library at Montana State and used their database to do some research. Eventually, I came across a study involving a drug similar to Rheumectatan that caused reactions in patients with damaged livers. One of the reactions was sudden cardiac arrest, especially in post-menopausal women like Mrs. Bolter."

The supervisor removed her glasses and placed them on her desk. "The pharmaceutical company would have known all that before the trial began. If the side effect applied to Rheumectatan, it would have come out."

"You're right. It should have come out. But what if it didn't...for whatever reason?"

Marge leaned back in her chair, a fine line creasing her brow. She tapped a finger against her lips for several seconds, then leaned forward again. "Go on."

"I phoned Adam right away and emailed him a copy of the dissertation. He promised to make sure you got it, too. He also said you'd halt the study until you were sure the patients were safe."

Her eyes narrowed. "He didn't mention anything to me."

Bethany closed her eyes. She could no longer ignore the proof. Adam had lied. He'd set her up to take the blame for something she didn't do. *But why?*

She struggled to breathe, the terrible betrayal leaving her raw. "I know I didn't give Mrs. Bolter the wrong dose. There has to be another reason she died."

"The records show you made a mistake."

"They're wrong. Someone must have falsified them."

"The autopsy backed them up."

Bethany's head swam. The autopsy had shown the wrong dose? But how? "I don't know exactly what happened, but there must be an explanation. Adam was working that night. And if he lied about the study..."

"That's quite an accusation."

"So is blaming me for something I didn't do."

Her eyes thoughtful, Marge picked up the flash drive and turned it over in her hand. "I'll call in a forensic computer scientist to check the records. They can tell if anyone tampered with them. I'll need a copy of your plane ticket with the time of your flight. And I'll halt the study until we're sure the patients are safe."

Still reeling, Bethany managed to nod. "Thank you."

"You're still suspended until we investigate this thoroughly," Marge warned.

"I understand."

"And I don't want you mentioning this to anyone. If you're right and someone went to the trouble of falsifying records…"

She could be in terrible danger. "I won't."

She wobbled to her feet, feeling numb. She'd trusted Adam. She considered him her friend. But he'd set her up, tried to incriminate her in the patient's death. And in the process, he'd robbed her of every last illusion she'd had.

Had *her deception hurt Cole this badly?*

Unable to bear that dreadful thought, she returned to her apartment. She tossed her coat and purse on the sofa, then went to her living room window and gazed down at the busy street. Cars raced past. Skyscrapers loomed around her, blocking her view of the leaden sky. She closed her eyes and pressed her forehead against the cool glass, trying to bring sense to her suddenly shattered world.

Mrs. Bolter had died. That was a fact. She might have suffered a reaction to the drug, which Adam had covered up. But what motive could he possibly have? Did he fear a malpractice suit? But that didn't make sense. No one knew about the potential side effect or even Mrs. Bolter's stint in rehab. So why had he needed to lie?

She shook her head. One thing she *did* know—Cole's aunt Bonnie Gene was right. No one was all good or all bad. Not Adam. Not Cole's father. Not her own father, who was reduced to staying with a friend in town. Not even her.

And she'd learned something else in the past two

weeks. There was no perfect place. She'd come to Chicago to reinvent herself, thinking she could break free of stereotypes, that people would see her as herself, not just a member of her race.

But instead of finding freedom, she'd become anonymous and lost, one of millions of unknown people living in a noisy, crowded place.

She turned around and eyed the apartment that had meant so much to her only a short time ago—the Ethan Allen sofa she'd scrimped to buy, the shelves overflowing with books. She realized she could walk away right now and wouldn't miss a single thing, except the coffee table her father had made.

She walked across the carpet to the coffee table, then lowered herself to the couch. She trailed her hand along the smooth oak legs, the satiny wood her father had patiently sanded and stained. She splayed her hands across the top, her gaze lingering on the arrowhead collection arranged beneath the protective glass. And images crowded her mind, a rapid-fire barrage of memories she could no longer stem—riding her horse across the plains with Cole. Hunting for arrowheads together at the teepee ring, his blue eyes crinkling into a smile. Digging side by side beneath the buffalo jump, then rolling together in the grass, laughing and making love.

And suddenly, she understood. The truth had been here all along, literally in front of her face. Her heart wasn't in Chicago. It never had been. She belonged in Montana, just as these arrowheads did. It had just taken her a while to realize that.

Maybe she'd had to leave Montana to escape the prejudice and test her wings in a different place. But her trip home had made her realize that she liked living in Maple Cove. She liked seeing people she knew around town, even if they weren't always ideal. Chicago had great amenities—theaters, museums, amazing shopping and cafés. But she could find those things in Montana, too.

And who was she trying to fool? She could do the work she loved in Montana. There were plenty of clinics and hospitals, including one in Honey Creek. And more importantly, she loved Cole.

But did Cole love her? Did he need her? Would he want her to come back?

Her stomach jittered hard. She squeezed her arms to her chest, trying to quell the attack of nerves. She thought back to that night in the mountains and the tender way he'd made love, and the answer hit her upside the head. *Of course* he loved her. He wouldn't have reacted with such fury to her deception if he hadn't cared.

But he didn't trust her—and why should he? She'd deceived him about her father. She'd run out on him twice. If she wanted a future with him she had to prove that she'd stick around.

She nibbled her lip, suddenly uncertain—because her father was right about something else. She didn't like to reveal any weakness. Maybe it was because she'd grown up around cowboys. Or maybe it had begun with Tony, who'd thrived on inciting her fear. Whatever the cause, she never showed any vulnerability or risked her heart.

But it was time to start. If her father had sacrificed his home for her mother, she could bend her pride for the man she loved.

She jumped to her feet and rushed to the phone in the kitchen, creating lists in her mind. She had to call and resign her job. She had to arrange for a moving company to ship her coffee table and books. She could fit her clothes in a couple of suitcases and donate the rest to a charity, along with her dishes and bed.

A knock sounded at the door.

Her thoughts instantly leaped to Cole.

But that was ridiculous. He wasn't in Chicago. It was probably her neighbor dropping off the mail.

Trying to hold back her burgeoning hopes, she hurried to the door. She peeked out the peephole, but no one came into view—which was odd. Unless her neighbor had simply left the mail on the floor…

Her pulse accelerating, she put her ear to the door. Silence. She dithered, the Raven Head Society's threat springing to mind. But that was silly. They had no reason to harm her now. And the hall appeared empty from what she could see. Making a face at her imagination, she slipped off the chain and peered out.

The door flew open and slammed against her. Crying out, she stumbled back. A man muscled his way inside, knocking her to her knees. Startled, she scrambled back up.

"Adam."

He stood between her and the door, his eyes wild, his breathing ragged and loud. His face was flushed, his normally meticulous blond hair awry. He wore one of his usual tailored suits, indicating he'd just finished his morning rounds.

Her mind whirled frantically through options. He couldn't know that she'd talked to the supervisor. Marge wouldn't have let that slip. So if she could just bluff her way through…

"You startled me." Did her voice sound too high? She struggled to tone it down while her pulse went berserk.

"I'm glad you stopped by, though. Do you have time to talk? You wouldn't believe all the things I went through in Montana—even a stampede."

Afraid she was starting to ramble, she turned toward the kitchen, her gaze darting to the phone. But a click stopped her dead in her tracks.

"Not so fast."

She slowly turned to face him. A gun had appeared in his hand. And dread pooled deep in her gut. "What… What's this about?"

"As if you don't know." His hand trembled. His Adam's apple dipped, betraying his unease. So he didn't like handling a weapon. If she could keep him talking and find a way to distract him…

"You weren't supposed to survive that attack," he said.

"Attack?" She blinked, not needing to feign her confusion now. "You mean those men in the mountains? But how did you—"

"Mountains? No. In Bozeman. That idiot watched the ranch for days, waiting for a chance to get you alone, and he still didn't get it right."

The truck that tried to run her off the road. "That was you?"

"Not me. A man I hired."

"But why? Why would you want to hurt me? I thought we were friends."

A flush darkened his face. His gun wobbled, and guilt flashed through his eyes. "I didn't want to hurt you, but I had no choice. It was the only way I could get that drug approved after Mrs. Bolter died."

"The drug? But what…"

"Why do you think? I need the money. I've got medical-school loans up to my ears. Rhyne-tex promised me a bonus if I got it approved. And I invested in their stock, so I'll make a bundle there, too."

The pharmaceutical company had bribed him? "But that's illegal."

He laughed. "Oh, come on, Bethany. You can't be that naive. Everyone does it—professors, medical-school boards, doctors... Drugs are big business. There are billions of dollars involved. There's no reason I can't take a cut."

She stared at him, unable to believe she'd misjudged him so badly. How could she have considered him a friend? "So you'll sacrifice your patients for money."

"No one was supposed to die. I thought the drug was safe."

"But it's not safe. Mrs. Bolter died. How can you let them approve it after that?"

"They can pull it off the market later. I only need to get it approved. I'll get my bonus. I'll sell off my stocks and make a mint. I don't care what happens after that."

Her anger rose. "So you set me up to take the blame."

"I had to. I couldn't risk that they'd stop the study. Not when we're so close."

"But—"

"I told you. I can't let them stop that trial." His eyes turned hard, and he raised the gun. "Even if you have to die."

Chapter 16

Bethany stared down the barrel of the gun, stark fear slithering down her spine. She took in the tremor of Adam's hand, the desperation in his crazed eyes. Every cell in her body went numb.

"It won't do any good," she said. "I've talked to Marge. She already knows what you did."

His eyes flickered with uncertainty, and she forged on. "I gave her the dissertation this morning, just before you came. I told her you changed the records. She's calling in a forensic computer scientist to investigate it now."

He shook his head. Perspiration broke out on his brow. "I don't believe you. You're lying."

"I'm not lying. It's the truth. Call her and ask. I tell you, I was just there."

His gun wobbled. His face turned a sickening gray.

She transferred her weight to the balls of her feet, ready to leap his way.

But he narrowed his eyes and steadied his aim. "It's too late. I'm in too deep. If I'm going down, so are you."

Panic broke free inside her. She couldn't die. She had too much to live for. She had to stop him—but how?

Her head light, her pulse frenzied, she struggled to think through the fear. "Listen, Adam. Let's think this out. There's no need for you to—"

The doorbell buzzed. Adam's eyes flew to the door.

Bethany didn't hesitate. She lunged to his side and grabbed his wrist. He whipped up his arm, his strength catching her off-balance, and it was all she could do to hang on.

The gun went off. Ceiling plaster rained down, the sulfuric smell of gunpowder filling the air. Her ears ringing from the gunshot, she clung to his arm, struggling to wrest the weapon from his iron grip.

But desperation had lent him strength. He turned and slammed her against the wall. She cried out, trying to stay upright and gouged his arm with her nails. The door burst open, but she ignored it. Adam rammed her back even harder, bringing tears of pain to her eyes.

She kneed his groin. He let out a howl of outrage, then twisted and flung her aside. She fell to the floor, pain shooting through her knees and arms, panic pounding her brain. She whipped up her head, then froze, caught in the crosshairs of Adam's gun.

Triumph lit his eyes. A wild sound formed in her throat. And she knew in that instant that she would die.

But a man barreled out of nowhere and tackled Adam. The pistol went off again. The two men wrestled to the floor, grappling for supremacy, and Bethany leaped out of their way.

The man slammed his fist into Adam's face. Adam cried out and loosened his grip. The gun skittered across the floor, and Bethany rushed to pick it up.

Her pulse going berserk, she whirled around and aimed. The newcomer turned, and she glimpsed his face. *Cole.* But how…?

She gave her head a hard shake, forcing the distraction aside. She circled the men, trying to get a clear shot at Adam, but he was still fighting, moving too fast for her to see.

More fists flew. The men grunted and rolled, crashing against the table and scattering chairs. Adam was strong, but no match for Cole, who'd worked for years on the ranch. Cole jumped to his feet and drew back his fist, putting the power of his steel-hard body behind it, then unleashed the explosive punch. A sickening thud rent the air. Adam crumpled, unconscious, on the floor.

Her heart rioting, Bethany kept the gun trained on Adam as Cole straightened and stepped away. But there was no need. He'd knocked Adam out cold.

Cole tugged off his belt, flipped Adam over, and secured his arms. Then he lurched to his feet and turned to face her, his breath loud in the silent room. She clicked on the safety and slowly lowered the gun.

His eyes met hers. Her lips quivered, the terror finally penetrating the adrenaline surge. Cole strode over, took the gun from her hand and set it on the table, then dragged her into his arms.

Her knees went weak. She clung to his massive shoulders, unable to believe he was really here. He'd saved her. If he hadn't shown up, she would have died.

Tremors wracked her body. Hot tears sprang to her eyes. She held him close, giving herself over to his power and strength, wanting to crawl right into his skin.

"Who the hell is that?" he asked, his voice rough against her ear.

"Adam. The doctor I work with. He set me up…" Her voice broke.

"Shhh." Cole tightened his hold, burying her face against his neck. "Don't talk now. I'll hear the story later when you tell the police."

Still trembling, she wiped her eyes on her sleeve and looked up. "Oh, God, Cole…" Her voice cracked. "If you hadn't…"

"It's all right. It's over."

Thanks to him.

Bethany was still struggling to gather her composure a short time later after the police had taken their statements and hauled her coworker away. She turned to Cole, overcome with a myriad of conflicting emotions—shock, longing, relief—and dragged in a shuddering breath. As horrific as that ordeal had been, it wasn't finished yet. Cole had saved her life, rescuing her from Adam's attack. But the next few minutes would determine her future—and whether it would be with him.

Afraid to hope, but needing desperately to know the answer, she stepped closer and met his eyes. "Cole… why are you here?"

He reached out and tipped up her chin. His solemn blue eyes held hers. "I couldn't let you go. I love you. I always have. I wanted to beg you for another chance."

Beg *her?* More tears flooded her eyes. She bit down hard on her lip, fearing if she let herself cry she wouldn't stop. He loved her. He was willing to give her a chance. "You forgive me for lying to you?"

His thumb stroked her jaw, regret filling his eyes. "Forgive you? I'm the one who needs forgiveness."

"But—"

"I love you, Bethany. I always have. But I was too scared, too caught up in the past to understand—to really see what you needed to do. And I blamed you for things that weren't your fault."

Her heart wrenched. Tears tracked down her cheek. "I love you, too, Cole. In all these years, I've never stopped."

He gazed at her with an expression so loving, so filled with wonderment that her throat closed up, and her heart nearly burst from her chest.

He gently cradled her head as if she were the most precious being on earth. And then he lowered his mouth to hers and kissed her until her head swam, the shivers eased from her body, and reality faded away.

After an eternity, he ended the kiss and hugged her against his heart, exactly where she wanted to be— surrounded by his strength, his tenderness, his love.

"I'll move here," he said.

Startled, she pulled back and searched his eyes. "But your ranch…"

"I like it there," he admitted. "But I need you more than I need the land. I'll go wherever you want, as long as you'll marry me."

She couldn't breathe. "You'd sacrifice your ranch for me?"

"We can go there on vacations, maybe retire there someday. Your father can manage it while we're gone."

"My father?" Her world tilted again. "But you fired him. He lied to you about those men."

Cole let out a heavy sigh. "Yeah, he lied. He made mistakes. He got in over his head, then tried to protect you from those goons. But I haven't been perfect, either. I've already hired him back."

Stunned, she shook her head. "I don't want you to leave the ranch. I love it there, too. I want to come back to Montana to be with you. There's nothing for me in Chicago. I figured that out before you came."

"You're sure? Because I don't mind—"

"I'm sure, Cole. Maybe I had to get away at first. I had to learn that there is no perfect place, that there are good and bad people everywhere. But I'm ready to come home now. To be with you."

His eyes held hers. He pulled away slightly, then tugged a small velvet box from his pocket and held it out.

Her breath backed up. She met his eyes, more tears swimming in her eyes. "Cole…"

"Take it," he whispered.

Her hands trembling, she took the box and flipped it open. A brilliant diamond ring winked back.

"You'll marry me?" he asked, his deep voice cracking.

Her knees wobbled. Emotions crowded inside her— wonder, joy, love. She slid the ring on, then clenched her fingers, hardly able to see him through her tears. "I'll marry you."

His lips took hers, and a feeling of absolute *rightness* flooded her heart. She'd marry Cole. She'd raise their children in Montana, where her roots were, alongside the man she'd always loved.

Where she knew that she belonged.

Epilogue

Senator Hank Kelley stood in the great room at the Bar Lazy K ranch, staring out the windows at the snow-covered fields. The ranch had quieted down over the last few days, but the lull only heightened his nerves. He knew the calm gripping the ranch was deceptive. Those killers were still out there—plotting, watching, biding their time…

And if he didn't do something fast, Lana would die.

He shuddered hard. Seeing his daughter on that DVD had shaken him badly. Her terrified eyes haunted him day and night. Hell, he was so wound up he couldn't sleep, couldn't eat, could barely hold on to a thought.

His cell phone rang, and he jumped, experiencing a sickening spurt of dread. His pulse chaotic, he pulled out his phone and stared at the unknown number. The police? The kidnappers? The secret society?

Feeling light-headed, he clicked it on.

"Senator Hank Kelley?" a woman asked.

"You're talking to him."

"Hold the line, please. President Colton would like to speak to you."

The president. Hank's heart sank. The FBI must have told him about the assassination plot. Colton would be furious. He'd want Hank's resignation—or worse.

"Senator Kelley?" President Colton barked out.

"Yes, sir. It's me. I…" Excuses leaped to his tongue, but he managed to bite them back. "Are you all right?" he asked instead.

"Of course I'm all right. I'll be damned if I'll let a bunch of thugs intimidate me. My reforms are going through, no matter what."

Hank's breath came out in a rush. "I'm glad, sir. I never had anything to do with that plot. I… I hope you realize that."

"That's for the police to decide. In the meantime, I recommend you resign."

Hank's stomach nosedived. He'd lost the president's trust—and rightly so. "Yes, sir. I'll do that right away."

"See that you do." The president hung up.

Hank put away his phone, then stared blankly out the window, his mind numb, a hollow ache filling his gut. It was over. He'd screwed up too many times. His children despised him. His wife was going to divorce him. The career he'd spent his life building had finally come crashing down.

The irony of it struck him hard. President Colton worked for the good of the country. Hank had only worked for the good of himself. And where had it gotten

him? Colton was popular and respected; he had an ador-
ing wife—while Hank's marriage and career had failed.

His half brother, Donald, emerged from the kitchen
and joined him at the window. Hank stood silently beside him, unable to think of a thing to say.

"Who called?" Donald finally asked.

Hank exhaled. There was no point hiding the truth.
"The president. He asked me to resign."

Donald didn't answer. Several long minutes passed.
Hank continued looking out the window at the demolished barn, a fitting symbol of his ruined life.

Then Cole and Bethany came into view, leading their
horses past the rubble. They stopped near the porch,
laughing about something Hank couldn't hear. Then
Cole tugged her close and kissed her. He didn't stop
for a very long time.

A wistful feeling unfolded inside Hank, a sense of
loss. He'd had a love like that once, and he'd thrown it
away. But at least his son wouldn't make his mistakes.
He'd found the happiness he deserved.

He cleared his throat, then turned to face his brother.
"You know… I never thanked you. For stepping in and
taking care of Cole when you did. You did a damned
good job with him, better than I could have done."

Donald's steady gaze met his. After a moment, he
dipped his head. "Cole's a good man."

His chest thick, Hank turned his gaze back to the
window again. Donald had acknowledged his apology.
It didn't solve the problems between them, but it was
a start.

Cole leaped on his horse. Bethany did the same. Still
laughing, their faces bright with the promise of love,
they loped away.

Hank stood beside his brother and watched them go. He'd been a wretched father, no doubt about that. And he'd rightfully paid the price. But he still had a chance to do something right by saving his daughter's life.

He couldn't take action yet. The FBI wouldn't let him leave the ranch. But he would watch and wait. And then act when the time was right.

Even if he had to die.

* * * * *